Robert Williams Buchanan

A Child of Nature

A romance

Robert Williams Buchanan

A Child of Nature
A romance

ISBN/EAN: 9783337049072

Printed in Europe, USA, Canada, Australia, Japan

Cover: Foto ©Andreas Hilbeck / pixelio.de

More available books at **www.hansebooks.com**

A CHILD OF NATURE

A ROMANCE

BY

ROBERT BUCHANAN

AUTHOR OF

"GOD AND THE MAN," "THE SHADOW OF THE SWORD,"
"LADY KILPATRICK," ETC.

A NEW EDITION

LONDON
CHATTO & WINDUS, PICCADILLY
1896

Printed by BALLANTYNE, HANSON & Co.
At the Ballantyne Press

CONTENTS.

CHAPTER   PAGE

I. ONE WHITE SAIL IN A WASTE OF GREY 1

II. THE FAIR PILOT 6

III. AN OLD LETTER 10

IV. MUSIC, MOONLIGHT, AND AN INVOCATION . . . 18

V. AN INTERIOR, 'IN THE DUTCH MANNER' . . . 23

VI. DOCTOR OF SOULS AND DOCTOR OF BODIES . . . 30

VII. ANGUS OF THE DOGS 37

VIII. CANINE WAIFS AND STRAYS 41

IX. THE WANDERER FINDS QUIET QUARTERS . . . 46

X. A SPORTING EPISODE AND ITS TERMINATION . . . 52

XI. IN THE PARSONAGE 58

XII. MINA'S QUESTIONS 66

XIII. COREVEOLAN CASTLE 75

XIV. GRAHAM COMES HOME 82

XV. BY THE FIRESIDE 91

XVI. KOLL 96

XVII. THE FAIR AT STORPORT 101

XVIII. FINE FEATHERS IN THE FAIR 109

XIX. 'PETER NA CROICHE' 114

XX. LORD ARRANMORE AT LAST 119

XXI. THE MASK FALLS 128

XXII. ARRANMORE'S HOME-COMING 135

XXIII. A MYSTERIOUS MESSAGE 140

XXIV. MINA KEEPS TRYST 147

XXV. GLENHEATHER LODGE 152

XXVI. GRAHAM BECOMES ENTHRALLED 162

CHAPTER		PAGE
XXVII.	KOLL'S WITCHRAFT	168
XXVIII.	FACTOR AND LORD	171
XXIX.	A LOVE-STORM	177
XXX.	A MEETING AND A PARTING	186
XXXI.	SHADOWS IN THE MANSE	192
XXXII.	KOLL ON THE WATCH	198
XXXIII.	THE DEVIL'S BRIDGE	205
XXXIV.	GRAHAM TO THE RESCUE	215
XXXV.	KOLL'S AXE	223
XXXVI.	THE DARKENING OF THE DREAM	227
XXXVII.	MINA IS CONVALESCENT	233
XXXVIII.	GRAHAM AND ARRANMORE	240
XXXIX.	CROSS PURPOSES	245
XL.	SUNSHINE AND STORM	255
XLI.	KOLL'S TRIBUTE	262
XLII.	A HIGHLAND FEAST	272
XLIII.	ETHEL AND MINA	283
XLIV.	A LITTLE SUNSHINE	290
XLV.	A PROPOSAL	296
XLVI.	COREVEOLAN IS DESERTED	302
XLVII.	ETHEL SPEAKS THE EPILOGUE	308

A CHILD OF NATURE.

CHAPTER I.

ONE WHITE SAIL IN A WASTE OF GREY.

ON the afternoon of a summer day, a small schooner yacht, closely reefed, made her appearance off the mouth of Loch Uribol, a long and lonely sea fjord in the remote north of Scotland, and while beating to and fro in the open sea, in the midst of the southerly squalls from the neighbouring mountains, hoisted the inverted red flag to the foremast, as a signal that the parties on board were in need of assistance.

It had been a dark, dry day, with the wind blowing fresh from the south-east very steady and strong, and the yacht, a tiny thing of fifteen or sixteen tons, with a small cockpit, had beaten round Cape Wrath at early dawn, across the tossing waters which divide the dark serrated peaks of Scotland from the far-off Norwegian shores. Lightly as a bird she had bounded over the great rollers of the sea, splashing the foam over herself from stem to stern, but seldom taking on board a drop of 'green.' The wind was almost steady ahead, so that her progress eastward was slow indeed.

The time slipped by, however. The gloomy crags of the wild North Cape grew fainter and fainter, and the shores of the northern coast, which at first had been scarcely distinguishable on the horizon, gradually loomed more and more distinct—stretching in one desolate and lonely direction from the high hills of Ben Derg past the faint, low-lying flats of Roan to the dark and rocky shores which fringe the cliffs of Tongue.   Not once in the long day had the sun actually made his appearance.   The atmosphere had been full of a palpitating silver light, in which the skies seemed close to the earth and very grey, and the waves of the sea, where they did not break into white foam, unusually black and sinister-looking.

Yet it was 'good weather,' a safe, snug day for sailing, and the sombre, colourless tone of all things—sea, far-off land, and sky—was not without its charms for those who have learned to love the pathetic 'neutral tint' of the melancholy northern coast.

But as evening approached the sun looked out from a grey chasm above the outlying hills, and shed a lurid light over the dancing sea, illumining to rose-colour the white sails of the little yacht, which was now within a few miles of the dangerous coast.   Just about this time a weather-beaten West Highlander, who was steering the little vessel, cocked his eye up to the sunset, and, relinquishing the tiller to a young man who sat in the cockpit beside him, said quietly :

'She's going to give a puff out o' the east yonder, and Loch Uribol's a terrible place for squalls.   We'll take off the foresail altogether, and let her sail cannie wi' mainsail, staysail, and jib.'

Scarcely had the speaker, with the assistance of another man who had been lying listlessly in the fore-part of the vessel, carried out his precaution, and taken the foresail down, when the first squall from the land came up white as foam, and laid the vessel over to the cooming of the cockpit.

Squall after squall followed, while the light from the sun-set grew every moment of a more lurid crimson, and the wind streamed out of a great rent in the vast mountains of cloud to the south-east.   The yacht was too lightly ballasted to carry her canvas well, and more than once the wind struck her so savagely as to threaten to founder her out-right, the water passing along the lee decks in one green torrent, and drenching the helmsman to the skin.   The sea was comparatively smooth, however, owing to the shelter of the hills.

From the dark precipices and distant misty glens the gusts shot out with a force only realisable by him who has navigated these coasts in a small vessel. With the fury of hate and the strength of despair, so to speak, they plunged one by one upon the schooner, like wild beasts frantically endeavouring to tear her to pieces.

With a light laugh, the helmsman dashed the wet hair out of his eyes, and strained his gaze towards the land.

'Which is the Uribol land?' he cried to the old Celt who had first spoken. 'Can you make out the mouth of the loch?'

The old man shook his head.

'I know fine she lies somewhere in yonder,' he said; "but I've never passed the mouth. Luff, sir, luff! We'll put about directly—there's a nasty bit o' water fair ahead.'

The young man uttered an exclamation expressive of impatience.

'Here, Calum, take the helm, and let me have a look at the chart.'

So saying, he again resigned the tiller to the old man, and plunging down the 'companion' to the cabin, soon re-emerged with the Government chart of the coast in his hand. Spreading it out on the 'coach roof,' and following the marks with his finger, he studied it attentively, now and then glancing at the land, while the yacht, having put about, was dashing along through squall after squall, and coming nearer and nearer to the shore.

He was a man of eight or nine and twenty, with a rather handsome style of face—broad high brow, a nose of the so-called Grecian sort, and a proud, sarcastic mouth. His skin was dark and tanned, as if he had lived long in the sun of warmer climates. He was clean shaven, all save the upper lip, where he wore a thick, flossy moustache, very fair in colour. His eyes were blue and very large, though he had a habit of contracting them very much when he was looking at any person. In his whole person, and in every gesture, there was a certain air which bespoke the gentleman by birth. His expression, nevertheless, was marred by audacity

and superciliousness, and his laugh had not the ringing clear-
ness of youth, but sounded hollow at times, with a sort of
spasmodic gaiety his face did not share.

As he studied the mysterious lines of the chart his face
grew very black.

'Why the devil did I come here without a pilot?' he
exclaimed. 'Look here, Calum. The mouth of the loch
is full of sunken rocks in every direction. Far out to the
right hand there's Bo Scarbh, a regular reef, three feet under
water at high springs; close by—see! there's another—Bo
Something else; and then there's half-a-dozen rocks
peppered *here*, and another half-dozen *there*. To crown all,
there's only six feet at low water in the deepest part of the
channel, although we are drawing seven feet aft; and, by
George! the channel itself at the Narrows is about two
cables' length across. It would be certain shipwreck to
enter without a pilot. What are we to do?'

It was in answer to this question that Calum recom-
mended that they should signal to the shore for a pilot,
and so the little yacht was kept running to and fro on the
wind just off the shore. On coming thus close in under
the mountains, they could just distinguish, about a mile
ahead, the silvern gleam of the mouth of the loch, and,
seen from afar, it looked very narrow indeed—only a few
yards across. Just inside, as they knew, there was good
anchorage in a small snug basin nearly opposite the
'village.'

An hour of great excitement passed, and there was no
answer to their signal from the shore. Every instant the
squalls grew more terrific, till it seemed the little vessel
must be lost indeed. Worst of all, night was near; the
hills were already growing dim.

'It's an awfu' coast,' said Calum, reflectively, as he
shook the boat through a violent squall. 'I mind once
of a hooker of a hundred tons being clean foundered just
off here. And there wasna any sea; she was running for
the south with herring, and had twa or three empty barrels
on her deck; and the wind came aff yonder hill and sank
her as ye'd sink a spoon in a bowl o' milk. I wouldna'
sail na open boat here for a heap o' money.'

'No one appears to take any notice of us,' cried the young man. 'What is to be done? The boat won't stand much more of this.'

'The boat's a good boat,' said Calum, 'but the nicht's going to be bad; and nae yacht o' this size can live if it comes on a gale. If nae man comes off from the shore, we'll have to run for Loch Uish, straight down the coast. It's no a cannie run in the dark, for there's the Mackenzie Rock, and the reef where Sandie Gow lost the *Spell;* and forbye that, there's the Black Rocks; but we'll dae our best.'

'Humph! then it's only a chance that we get clear out of this confounded mess?'

'Oh ay, just a chance,' said Calum dryly. 'The folk'll be awa' at the fishing, and it's a bad nicht for a boat like this in the open.'

Something in the perfectly unmoved and phlegmatic tone of the speaker took the other's attention, for the young man stared at him for some time with a half-comic, half-sneering look of astonishment; and seeing the grim, weather-beaten features perfectly unmoved, he broke into a hard laugh.

'You take it coolly enough, at any rate,' he cried.

'And what for should I no tak' it coolly? I'm only a common man, and maun tak' the winds as they come, an' earn my bread.'

'Can you swim?'

'Not a stroke,' replied Calum, burying his face in his hands to light his black cutty pipe, while the man at the forepart of the vessel, reclining against the bitts, hummed in a low voice the doleful lively ditty of 'Ghillie Callum.'

Still finding secret amusement in the stolidity of his companions, the young man laughed again; then entering the cabin once more, he re-emerged with a fowling-piece, and fired two shots rapidly into the air. Scarcely had he done so, when an enormous black dog sprang up the companion, and, rushing to the bulwarks, gazed eagerly out on the waters.

'Down, Nero, down!' cried the young man. 'He

thinks I have shot something.   Ha! the noise seems to have attracted attention at last.   Look yonder !'

On a small eminence overlooking the entrance of the loch two or three figures were now dimly seen ; but it was already too dark to make out who and what they were.   The twilight had quite fallen, and the wind was rising with great fury.

'Hang off ten minutes longer,' the young man said, 'and then, if no one comes, we must risk the run back again along the coast.'

The helmsman nodded, 'put about' once more, and ran through the wind.   The squalls could still be seen whitening the sea to windward when they struck the water; but every minute the coast grew dimmer, so that only a very familiar eye could have made out the landmarks.

Ten minutes passed, and the order was already given to let the vessel run with a free sheet, when Calum, knocking the ashes of his pipe out into the water to leeward, said quietly :

'Wheest a minute !   I hear the sound of oars between us and the shore.'

CHAPTER II.

THE FAIR PILOT.

LISTENING intensely all could hear the splash, splash of oars coming nearer and nearer.   Immediately afterwards a small boat, rowed by a solitary figure, shot out of the shadow of the hills.

It seemed to be a rude coble, quite at the mercy of the wind, but very skilfully managed.   While Calum brought the boat up to the wind, the young man leant over the side of the vessel and regarded the small boat intently.   Presently he uttered an exclamation which bore a suspicious resemblance to an oath, and turned angrily to Calum.

'Look there !   Confound the idiots !   They've sent out a *woman.*'

Calum, who was quite as astonished, but exhibited more self-control, nodded sharply.

The boat was indeed rowed by a female, to all appearances strong and young, but her head was covered by a dark hood, and they could not see her face.

Angrily enough Calum addressed the stranger in Gaelic. He was answered in clear ringing tones in the same tongue; and almost before he could say another word the coble was alongside the yacht, and a light girlish figure with a speed and agility perfectly marvellous to the Southerner, had sprung on board.

It was too dark to distinguish her features plainly, but she seemed fair-complexioned and very young. Her hood had fallen back, and her face and hair were damp with spray. Perfectly lost in amazement at so strange an apparition, the young man stood staring open-mouthed, while the stranger and Calum spoke to each other rapidly in Gaelic.

'What does the girl say?' he at last inquired impatiently. 'Is any one coming off to pilot us into the anchorage?'

Calum replied in the methodical way peculiar to him and to his class:

'The lassie says there's no a man in the village this night that can pull an oar or draw a net. The whole village is awa' after the herring at Loch Uish, and there's naething left but wives, bairns, and old bed-ridden men.'

A furious squall struck the yacht as the fisherman spoke, and almost capsized her, for she had entirely lost way through being brought up to the wind. Again addressing Calum rapidly in Gaelic, the girl pushed him aside and seized the tiller.

'Hullo! what are you doing?' cried the young man. 'You're never going to trust the boat to a girl like that?'

The girl seemed either to understand what was said, or guessed at the meaning, for she laughed. By this time the yacht was again running rapidly through the water, steered by the stranger.

'The lassie says,' observed Calum phlegmatically, 'that there's no better pilot in the place than hersel'; and if we leave the boat to her, she'll take us in all snug. The tide's

at the flood, she says, and we'll hae plenty o' water at the
Narrows.'

'But it's nearly pitch-dark, and this is a mere child.'

'Never you fear, sir. See that! She kens how to steer
a boat; and take my word for it, she'll take us safe. I've
had worse pilots than this before now. She's a bold lass,
and a cannie, and better than many men.'

A loud cry from the girl interrupted him. She seemed
giving instructions in her own tongue. In a moment he
ran forward to assist the other hand with the sheets, while
the girl brought the vessel round just a few feet from a large
black mass projecting out of the sea.

"That's close work," cried the gentleman nervously.
"I'm afraid we'll come to grief."

The girl spoke again to Calum, and he interpreted.

'That's Dhu Squr, she says. But there's three fathom
water to the very edge of the reef. We're coming up to the
Narrows now, and need every inch o' room.'

Another cry from the girl, and the vessel was round again
on another tack. They were now quite in the shadow of
the hills, and all seemed darkness and confusion, especially
to the unaccustomed senses of the young man. To him the
land seemed closing in on every side, the mountains towering straight above, the wind coming in all directions. A
wild roar was in the air, and the water seemed swirling and
boiling below them with an angry roar.

'We're in the Narrows now,' cried Calum; 'that's the
boiling o' the tide.'

The wind was sweeping dead out of the mouth of the
loch, and again and again the vessel put about—so rapidly
indeed that she scarcely got way upon her on one tack
before she had to come round again. Once, for this reason,
she refused altogether to answer the helm in coming round,
and seemed drifting right on the rocks of the channel; but
in a moment, urged by the girl, Callum boomed out the
staysail to windward with an oar, and the vessel slowly com-
pleted her swing out. All seemed to grow darker and
darker after this, for they had got more and more in the
shadow of the hills; but by-and-by the young man saw that
they had emerged into more open water, and that several

lights, like those of a village, were glimmering from the darkness of the shore. The wind still shrieking loudly.

'All's safe now, sir,' said Calum. 'We're close to the anchorage, oot o' a' danger.'

So saying he ran forward and assisted his fellow-seaman to haul up the chain on deck, that it might run free, and to hoist the anchor over the bows. A minute afterwards the vessel was brought up to the wind, and glided steadily along through smooth water for about a hundred yards, when the girl cried out to the men forward, and released her hold of the tiller.

The yacht was quite stationary. Down went the anchor, with that delicious sound which only the weary cruiser knows and loves. For some minutes there was confusion in the darkness. The young man went forward to see all snug, and to take a look about him. So far as he could make out in the night, they were in a nice natural harbour, surrounded on every side by hills, and sheltered almost, entirely from the wind then blowing.

'Five fathom water,' said Calum, hauling in the lead-line; 'and a fine soft mud for the bottom. We couldn't be in a snugger berth.'

The young man, who had been plunged in deep reflection, touched him on the shoulder.

'Come aft with me, and speak to the girl. In all probability she has saved our lives.'

But when they went in search of her she had disappeared, and the old coble in which she had rowed out to their assistance had disappeared also. They strained their eyes into the surrounding darkness, and listened for the sound of oars; but all was quite still, and they could not see a glimpse of the stranger.

CHAPTER III.

AN OLD LETTER.

'You will perceive from the superscription and postmark of this letter that I have at last arrived at Ultima Thule. I bought a clipping little yacht, bran-new, for three hundred and fifty pounds, fitted her up snugly in the Clyde, and worked my way slowly up here with a crew of two—one of them an old fisherman, who knows this coast as well as the lines of his mother's face. On the way we put in at Iona, and were nearly blown to bits in Loch Scavaig, Skye. From the last-named place we sailed round Cape Wrath, and arrived off Uribol on the afternoon of the 5th. The whole journey was great fun, though I missed the comforts of the dinner-table. What I had in the way of food had to be cooked by myself, for I could not have trusted either of the men to cook for me; so I contented myself with boiled eggs, hard biscuits, a little fish occasionally, tea and coffee made over the spirit-lamp, and any number of cigars! I took a couple of dozen of claret aboard in the Clyde, but it vanished in no time, and since then I've been sticking to the national liquor, and really find it agrees with me exceedingly. The *modus bibendi* is to throw back your head, and pour a glass of plain whiskey down at one draught, and then, with watering eyes and burning throat, to chuck approval in a certain indescribable way, by sticking the tongue against the roof of the mouth.

'The climate is detestable, and tries even my temper. Since I began to sail on this coast I have scarcely seen my old friend the sun; all is grey, melancholy, dark, and though there has not been a great deal of actually heavy rain, the Scotch mist—which means an insidious dew-fall, turning your clothes into a wet blanket—has been perpetual. One scarcely wonders that the population is so small, when the cheerlessness of all things is taken into consideration. For my part, I can't understand how people can exist for a

lifetime in so cool a temperature. Although I am a Scotchman by birth, my blood runs freer in southern latitudes
than here. If I stopped here long, I should become as reserved, as phlegmatic, and as superstitious as the natives.

'And yet, for all that, don't run away with the impression
that I am disappointed. These weird, grey solitudes and
lonely seas impressed me more than you can conceive, just
as some old engravings, with their one sombre hue, haunt
the imagination even more than the finest pictures. I have
washed in two or three sketches in Indian ink—one of Loch
Scavaig, another of the heads of Sutherland, etc., and really
they seem strangely to reproduce this landscape without a
tint of colour. Still, when you look closely into the tints
of hill, lake, and sea, there is colour of the most subtle sort.
I never knew how many different greys there were till I made
this journey; their combinations are most extraordinary, and
(in the artistic sense) most pathetic.

'I have travelled far, as you know, but never, either on
the American prairie, or in the Canadian backwoods, on
the old continent, or on the new, did I find more perfect
loveliness than surrounds me here. Few vessels navigate
the seas, the inhabitants of the north are few and far between, and the whole prospect seems ages back in time.
A letter from the remotest capital of Europe would reach
you sooner than this will, though I am only about five
hundred miles away as the crow flies, and this will be
carried over waters as dangerous to the frail craft which
navigates them as the Pacific waters are to the great mail
steamers. In fact, Livingstone in Africa is not farther
removed from civilisation than I am at this moment! Yes,
I am wandering like a lonely traveller indeed. My object
you know; I need not allude to it here. All around me is
strange—landscape, manners and customs, language. My
old pilot is the only man who can speak a word of English.

'I fancy I can see you shrugging your shoulders with
pity as you think of my forlorn condition, and hasten to
flirt away the afternoon in roseate delight at the feet of a
certain dark-haired and elegantly-attired young lady with
luxurious eyes. "Poor devil!" I hear you cry, "not even
a pretty woman to talk to." Not so fast, however; don't

B

talk to me of your languid drawing-room beauties, your
dainty dreamers over the last new poem, your conventional
dolls that melt like wax in the sun of life, and only smile in
the gaslight.   Give me rather the mild beauty of the
American plains, adorable, refusing nothing, and demand-
ing nothing ; or the antelope-like maiden, so to speak, of
southern latitudes.   Give me rather some humble fisher-
maiden, light, fresh, unsophisticated, graceful as a fawn,
and blooming as a rose !

'Here I seem to hear your cynic laugh.   "Yes," you say,
"the conventional creature of third-rate poems and novels ;
but I, who am acquainted pretty well with the lower orders,
have never stumbled across the sylph-like being.   Fisher
maidens, even at Newhaven, where they bloom the best,
have ugly feet, hard hands, shapely bodies, coarse features,
and unclean tongues."   And, speaking generally, I believe
you are right.   Beauty does not improve with rough labour
or with utter idleness, any more than the mind brightens
with the ordinary conventional cramming at college.
Beauty, modesty, and grace are rare in low life—about as
rare, you know, as virtue in some walks of high life—still,
they do exist.   Here and there in my short pilgrimage I
have come across some flower of wondrous loveliness, some
perfect specimen of uncultivated nature, all the more
dazzling from the low and seemingly barren soil in which it
grew.

'I know you are pricking up your ears now.   You are
right.   I have discovered a phœnix, or something of the
sort.   It began in the most romantic way, as you shall
hear.

'On the afternoon of the 5th, as I mentioned above, we
arrived off this coast—wind, very stiff—squalls, dreadful—
night coming fast on us, and the sea all round us sown
with sunken rocks.   The mouth of Loch Uribol is very
dangerous, and I had relied on getting a pilot from the
shore to take me to the anchorage.   We signalled again and
again in the midst of the peppering wind, but not a soul
came to our assistance.   Twilight fell, and we were about
to run for it when Providence intervened, and sent us a
deliverer in the shape of a young native.

'Guess my astonishment when a girl, still in her teens, rowed up to the yacht's side, jumped on board without so much as "by your leave," and actually took command of the vessel under my very nose, giving her orders in a strange tongue, and being obeyed by my mutinous crew as if she were some spirit from another sphere. I was simply fossilised, with my eyes on the apparition. It would be quite in vain to explain what followed, unless you had a chart of Loch Uribol before you, and knew all the dangers of the passage. Enough to say, that the young girl of whom I speak, with a nautical skill that elicited my warmest admiration, took us through every danger in safety, and deposited the whole vessel, cargo, and crew at the proper anchorage inside the loch.

'So far, so good; but I know the question on the tip of your tongue is the old one, "Was the girl good-looking?" and should I answer in the negative, I see all your interest in this narrative vanish like smoke. So superficial are men, so credulous of the impression which is only skin deep. Let me tell you, however, for your satisfaction, that this young creature seemed not only good-looking, but positively pretty; and not only brave as an eagle, but elegant as a wild swan. I am speaking now merely from a first impression, and possibly she would appear very different in broad-day. In the dusk of the hills that night she seemed of almost unearthly loveliness.

'Conceive the situation! A stormy night—a vessel in distress—dangers on every side—and the apparition of a spirit, such as might have come to Ulysses in the old days, when there were fair spirits in the sea. The whole thing seemed unreal—a picture remembered out of Byron, or one of the "Sturm und Drang" German novelists. All I could do was smoke like—like blazes, and, standing upright in the cockpit, stare like a great goose at our angel of deliverance.

'Of course, if I had been able to talk Gaelic, I might have opened a conversation. I never in my life so regretted my ignorance. I rather fancy, however, she understood my English to a certain extent, for she laughed at some of my remarks to the pilot. On the whole, however, she seemed to treat me as a person of very small account indeed, addressing herself entirely to old Calum, and taking command of my vessel as if I were a person of no importance whatever.

'I mean to paint a picture of the whole thing some day, when I get more skill in colour.

'With the wind blowing in her face and slightly dishevelling her hair, her neck arched forward like a swan's to point the eager head, while her eyes peered forward into the darkness, she stood in the boat's cockpit, clenching the tiller with one hand, and slightly pressing it with her side. The whole look and gesture was magnificent, and I could not help enjoying it, though I expected every moment we should go to smash. Then her quick bird-like cries to the the man, making the air ring! I thought the Gaelic language very ugly before I heard this girl talk; but she speaks it softly though very clearly, without the offensive guttural tones of the ordinary natives.

'At one moment she put me in mind of some beautiful sea-bird darting its head this way and that, and uttering its weird cry; at another moment, when she was just about to put down the helm, and bring the boat off some critical corner, the creature looked like marble, so fixed and moveless did the whole figure become till the danger was over; and sometimes, especially when she was offering some explanation to Calum, she resembled one of the sea-nymphs of old, sparkling and trembling with the foam.

'Such, I say, was my impression. Against the romance of my description you have to set the particular facts—that my imagination was greatly excited by the lonely coast and the special danger, and that it was not light enough for anything like a thorough criticism. So uncertain am I as to details that I would not even swear an oath to the colour of her hair or eyes, nor to her attire. As well as I can remember she wore, in addition to a dark hood hastily thrown on, only a gown of blue serge or wool, and a short white jacket reaching to the waist, such as you have seen in pictures of Scottish milkmaids.

'You will wonder that I have not since taken care to solve all doubts as to the fair creature's personal appearance

Well, the fact is, my adventure ended as mysteriously as it began. Scarcely had we arrived in safety at the anchorage when we missed the stranger. She had taken advantage of the darkness and confusion, and rowed away before I could thank her for having preserved us, or offer her, as of course I was bound to offer her (for the girl is obviously poor), any reward or remuneration. The most extraordinary part of the whole affair is the girl's indifference in the last respect. In this country no one does you a special service without expecting to be paid for it.

'Confess at least that the whole adventure was very singular.

'With my head in a whirl I returned to my cabin, smoked any number of cigars, and saw the face of the girl before me in the smoke, while the wind ever and anon whistled in the rigging to remind me of the peril we had passed. At last, worn out with fatigue, I dropped to sleep, and had all sorts of wild dreams in which my deliverer figured. In company with her I went through innumerable dangers. Sometimes she was an Indian, naked to the waist, paddling to my rescue as I kicked on some wild American lake. At others she was seated before me on a fleet mustang, and we were galloping away for life pursued by a murderous crowd. I mingled her up with all the scenes of my past life and all the nonsense of my past reading. Of course, in my dreams, I was rapturously in love with her, having no earthly consideration but the pleasure of my own passion.

'When I went on deck in the morning I seemed to be in fairyland altogether. It was a dead-calm summer's morning, and every feature of the hills was mirrored in the glassy water. Our yacht was in a small bay, floating with her sails hoisted up to dry, and her image trembling in the mirror below her. Land stretched on every side, very green and undulating, rising into crags of ashened grey stone and purple heather, and far above the yacht towered Ben Eval, a wild, serrated peak, over which an eagle poised, dwarfed by distance to a speck.

'A couple of hundred yards from our anchorage was a pretty beach of white sand, and just above clustered the " village," if I may dignify it by that title. Picture to your self a great mass of gigantic boulders, deep heather and greensward, broken here and there by a whiff of blue smoke, issuing apparently from holes in the earth or fires kindled among the crags. As the eye became more accustomed to the colour of the scene, I perceived that certain brown and green excrescences, not unlike beavers' houses, were the huts of the population; but they were very low on the ground, and heather, grass, and wild leek grew on the roofs, while here and there a goat was browsing close to the hole whence the smoke issued, so that an inexperienced person might well be excused for not being able to pick them out at first sight. There were two or three dozen in number, each one built of rough stones or turfs, and roofed with straw, and not one less earth-looking and smoke-begrimed than its neighbour. Such habitations are worthy of troglodyte savages in the African wilds.

'The skiffs had come in from the fishing and were drawn up on the white sands, while the nets were drying on the beach. A group of wild-looking barbarians stood clustering on the beach staring at the yacht, and I almost felt I must be among the Pacific Islands, and regretted I had not brought a stock of beads and brass rings to barter with the population.

'After breakfast I went ashore, taking Calum with me as my interpreter. The spectacle of a visitor seemed to awaken the utmost astonishment, such another event scarcely having taken place within the memory of man. The savages were friendly enough, but clustered round me rather impertinently, scrutinising my face, hands, and attire, from my wide-awake hat to my boots, with every symptom of astonishment and interest. From the general indications around me, I should infer that their wonder arose chiefly from seeing for the first time a man who washed himself; for I am given to understand that soap is unknown, and that the only towel in the island has been used to patch the mainsail of the fishing-smack which carries the herring to the Kyle of Tongue.

'The more barbaric the population seemed the more ethereal grew the vision of the previous night—the one was a dark background to set off the beauty of the other. In answer to my questions, put through Calum, the men

shook their heads and gave me little information. I gathered, however, that the young girl was not a native of the
village, but resided some distance up the interior, whither
she had indeed taken her departure the night before.

'"From what the puir silly bodies tell me," said Calum,
"the lassie seems a bit wrong in the head, and to be not
quite cannie. They call her in Gaelic, Mina nan Oran,
which means in English, Fair-Haired Mina o' the Songs;
but why they gave her any such outlandish title it beats me
to tell. Anyhow, she's a clever lassie, and a quick—worth
a dozen o' these lazy lumps of Highlandmen around her."

'I ought to tell you, by the way, that Calum Coll, though
a Highlander himself, combines with a Lowland accent a
great contempt for his northern countrymen and the scenery
amidst which they dwell. "The men won't stir themselves,"
he says, "and the land won't yield." He belongs to the
southern isles, where things are brighter and pleasanter,
crops more plentiful, and life altogether more prosperous.
Calum is, indeed, a man without a bit of poetry in his
composition; a most practical and uninteresting person,
whose opinion on any social or æsthetic question I should
be slow to accept, unbacked by any more enlightened
authority. In some matters, soap and water for instance,
he is not much further advanced than the people he despises
so greatly.

'Little as was the information I could get, it piqued my
curiosity. "Fair-haired Mina of the Songs!" The very
name was poetry itself. I determined, at any expenditure
of time and trouble, to know more of the girl. So far I
have not succeeded in meeting her again, but as I am in
no hurry to depart from a spot where there is such good
sport to be had, I do not despair of being ultimately successful.

'My position here is very peculiar and very delightful.
Of course I am *incog.*—not a soul in the place knowing who
I am. To Calum Coll even I am Mr. Edward Lawrance,
of Oxford and London, student and tourist, who has got
Lord Arranmore's permission to blaze away over the Uribol
heather as long as he pleases this autumn. To-morrow
week is the 12th of August, and then I shall begin, with one

of the savages for a gillie, and Nero to "run up" the game
in his wild way.   I have not seen a grouse yet, but they tell
me there are a few fine broods farther inland.   The whole
island, however, swarms with vermin : you can't go a dozen
yards without seeing a weasel or a foumart ; and as for
otters, the only decent river (if river it can be called) is full
of them.   Nevertheless, I am no greedy sportsman, and
purpose to enjoy myself thoroughly.   I have, as you know,
a more serious object in visiting this locality.   It was a
study which devolved upon me sooner or later, and, though
I shrank from it for a long time, I am now very glad it came.
As the Scotch poet says—

> ' " There are flowers about the peasant's path
>   That kings might stoop to pu'."'

Not that I am so vain as to imagine myself a king in any
sense, or that there are any flowers in the Hebrides !   What
I mean is simply this : my visit here has begun with a romance,
and I look forward to more pleasure and excitement of the
same sort by and by.'

CHAPTER IV.

MUSIC, MOONLIGHT, AND AN INVOCATION.

It behoves us now to turn aside from the occupations and
lucubrations of Mr. Edward Lawrance, and to follow for a
brief space the fortunes of his unknown deliverer.

Quietly slipping over the vessel's side and unloosening
the rope of the coble, the young girl had stolen away into
the darkness, not making for the shore, but rowing rapidly
away in the opposite direction.   When she had gone some
distance she rested upon her oars and listened, and could
distinctly hear Lawrance's eager voice from the yacht, expressing wonder at her departure.   After a moment's hesitation she rowed on.

Every nook and cranny of the coast seemed familiar to
her.   Scarcely glancing before her to notice whither she

was going, she went rapidly on. The coble was ill-shapen, but small and easy to row, and the oars, though rudely made, were very light. The girl rowed with an indescribable grace and ease, and without the slightest sign that rowing was a task. Now and then she stopped, warm and breathing quickly, but the cessation seemed due more to abstraction of thought than to fatigue of body.

Presently she began to croon to herself, in a low sort of undertone, a weird Highland melody—one of those exquisitely beautiful tunes which are half a recitative and half a melody—oratory set to cadence and sparkling into music, just as a fountain tips itself with spray. As she sang, keeping time with her oars to the melancholy burthen, the summer moon began to cast a ghostly gleam behind the mountains, and suddenly it arose above the fjord—yellow, round, and bright, suffusing the surface of the water with its rays. Through the ambient darkness glided the boat. All was still as death, save for the sound of the oar, the wild scream of the curlew flitting from one ghostly bay to another, and the faint far-off chirp of the sea-pies feeding on the black shores of the fjord.

Loch Uribol, whose lonely waters she was navigating, is one of the wildest of the strange sea-fjords which enter Scotland on the northern side—vast narrow arms of the sea, bearing in their innumerable ramifications this way and that a certain resemblance to an outspread piece of sea-tangle, the main stalk representing the main fjord, and the numberless twisted stalks and leaves spreading to left and right representing the numberless bays, creeks, and minor fjords which spread on either side.

A boatman rowing straight to Loch Uribol, and perfectly familiar with the water, would reach the head after rowing about ten miles; but a stranger, attempting to perform the same feat, would wander from left to right, this way and that, ever mistaking some false opening for the real passage, until he would abandon the navigation in despair.

Seen from the heights of Ben Ruadh, or the Red Hill, which rises above the fjord on the north, Loch Uribol seems a wandering arm of water, broken by innumerable points, coves, green islets, and savage rocks, and so creep-

ing in and out of the land that its course is very difficult
to distinguish from those of the many fresh-water lakes
and lakelets which surround it on every side.

Beginning on the northern coast, where it is fed by the
wild waters of the north, it flows in and in, and round and
round, till it comes into the very heart of the land, where
it pauses, fed by a wild stream, which is fed in its turn by a
deep and sullen lake of brackish water. This last lake,
Loch Monadh by name, stretches on inland, then is linked
by a river to a series of splendid lakes, the river winding
beneath the mountains of Sutherland.

It is difficult to convey to a stranger's mind the utter
loneliness and desolation of the whole landscape of which
Loch Uribol forms a part. Wild weltering arms of sea-
water, with deep red stains and blotches of outlying weed;
flat, green, unwholesome islands strewed with sickly grey-
stone; vast stretches of low moorland, broken by white
gleams of fresh-water lochans, whence the wild sea-ducks
arise with a startled cry; larger fresh-water lochs, very
shallow and black, with gigantic boulders and crags rising
out of them like jagged teeth; the higher hills, purple
with heather at the base and middle, but rising abruptly
into peaks of lurid granite—such are some of the features
which strike the eye where nothing is seen save in detail,
where there is no general effect save that of a map, or of
the sea in storm as seen from a mountain. The prevailing
tone of all is a dreamy grey—the grey of the rain-cloud,
which, floating hither over the North Sea, breaks here
into dark vapour and wreaths of wool-white mist.

All is still, solemn, colourless, save where the sun trans-
forms all into wondrous brightness; save where the thunder-
storm bursts, with its bright purple voids and forked
crimson lights; save where the rainbow, here glittering
with all the hues of the prism, starts out of the sea like a
spirit, while, as if in answer to a spell, rainbows innumerable issue out of the low-lying vapours and spread themselves glittering over the lakes. On every side stretches
the ocean, with its restless voices; to the north the North
Sea; to the far west the Atlantic Ocean, thundering on
open sands as ghastly in tint as a dead man's face. The

habitations of man are few, and scattered in the most lonely and unexpected recesses. At a first approach there is scarcely a sign of humanity, unless, indeed, the red-sailed fishing-skiff be crawling out to the lobster-bed in the sea, or the smoke of the heather fire be rising from the sides of the solitary hill.

Night, which beautifies and spiritualises all earthly things and scenes, is lovely on Loch Uribol, and the wild mingled outlines of land and water grow terribly pathetic in the silvern light of the moon and the fluttering phosphorescence of the aurora. As the girl crept along up the fjord in her boat, singing her solitary song, the prospect changed around her as in some fairy-tale. Round dusky points where the cormorants flutter their wings and preen their plumage in the moon; through shallow bays, with sandy shores, whereon the heron stalks like a ghost, knee-deep, with his black shadow in the silvern pool; where the mirrored stars were like gleams of pearls in the shimmering tide; through narrow black passages, where the sea-pigs were floundering with unearthly noises, uncertain whether to go this way or that; she went dreaming along, exhibiting no surprise at sounds and sights which would have filled any but an islander with consternation.

The dark scene around her was full of life. A thousand sounds, hushed by day, broke the midnight stillness. The place could scarcely be called lonely, unless life itself be loneliness.

The girl rowed on, singing like one in a dream. Suddenly she paused, conscious of something dark floating behind her in the moonlight—a small black object, which oscillated like a leather bottle, and now and then disappeared with a splash. As she leant on her oars, still intoning, it came nearer and showed the head of some animal swimming in the water.

'Earach! Earach!' cried the girl.

The animal came nearer, within a few feet of the boat, and showed the head of a large seal, with eyes which attentively regarded the speaker.

'Earach! Earach!' repeated the girl, in a low coaxing voice, leaning over the side of the boat, and stretching her hand towards the animal. Strange to say, it swam closer, uttering a low cry, and, rubbing against the side of the boat, suffered her to pass her hand again and again over its slippery head.

It was, indeed, a weird situation, and one which a stranger might readily have misinterpreted. The sight of that strange young figure in the lonely moonlight, caressing a monster of the deep, would have brought up startling memories of the wild shapes and scenes of fairy-tales. As they hovered there together they seemed two creatures of the elements : she, a fair spirit of the air, haunting the melancholy night ; it, a spirit of the deep, listening to the voice and obedient to the ministries of a superior. Seemed! nay, they were! This wondrous world of fact is, after all, the most mystic fable of all, and two beautiful spirits *were* haunting that moonlight, call them by what names we will.

'My poor Earach !' said the maiden, in Gaelic, with indescribable softness and tenderness, 'where have you been wandering, and who have been your comrades in the sea this night? Have you been chasing the herring syle round Crag Bahn, or waiting for the salmon trout at the foot of the green burn of the fall? It's far from home that you wander now, Earach, and we fear some ill may come to you when you roam so long.'

Uttering a low, scarcely audible sound, expressive of plea-sure, Earach, as the animal seemed to be called, looked up into Mina's face with large, glittering, plaintive eyes, and pressed his head closer and closer against her hand as a dog does when caressed. Then suddenly, as if seized with a frolicsome spirit, he splashed the water with his tail, swam round and round, and tried to clamber into the boat, sticking again and again with his slippery fins against the gunwale.

'Down, Earach, down ! The night is cold, and you are wetting me to the skin. You are getting an old man now to be playing these pranks at dead of night. Wheesht ! and I'll sing to you, if you will follow quietly and in peace.'

Finding all its efforts to enter the boat in vain, Earach desisted, and Mina, again plying her oars, sang aloud, raising her voice now and filling the air with strange melody.

Still and quiet as a lamb, Earach swam along by the boat's side, raising his head high out of the water, and rocking it from side to side as he listened. It was obvious that the music afforded the animal the most intense enjoyment. No less pleasure seemed to animate the singer. As she sang, with her eyes on her strange auditor, the soul of music possessed her, and her heart swelled with deep rapture and love towards all the gentle dumb creatures of the earth, and through those to all her kind. She could not phrase this emotion in words, perhaps, but it filled her none the less. The night, the moonlight, the tender solitary sound —all these mysteries blended into the strangest mystery of all, a conscious human soul. Dare we affirm that they did not mingle also into the being of the dumb creature, finding there sources of spirituality it is beyond our power to reach or guess? Nay, for the seal loved the sound, and drank it in joy. When the last notes died away, Earach floated a few moments dreamily on the water, as if waiting for the song to be renewed, and then, finding all still, sank like a stone beneath the surface and reappeared no more.

CHAPTER V.

AN INTERIOR, 'IN THE DUTCH MANNER.'

THE girl now pursued her way silently and more rapidly. After proceeding about a mile farther along the shores of the loch, she turned off into a narrow creek and ran the boat ashore by the side of a rude stone pier. Springing out, and fastening the rope of the boat to an iron ring, she walked rapidly off in the moonlight.

Her path lay among crags and boulders, through mossy hollows, and over the stepping-stones of a noisy burn. At last she stood before the lighted window of a house, a two-storied edifice of stone, very superior to the usual kind of dwellings in those wilds. There was no blind to this window, and, approaching noiselessly, she looked in.

Within a large ante-room or kitchen, lit with a peat-fire burning brightly on the flagstone hearth of an enormous ingle, were gathered several figures. In a rudely carved arm-chair sat, with his back to the window, a man with hair as white as snow, and clad in a suit of black cloth of clerical cut. Close to him, on a large wooden peg, hung a broad, weather-worn wideawake hat, in shape not unlike a Mexican sombrero, and with it, on the same peg, an enormous walking-stick, with a head in the shape of a shepherd's crook.

In the centre of the chamber a middle-aged woman sat spinning, her face brightly lit up by the fire and by the light of an old cruise-lamp. Burning very dimly indeed, the latter swung to the rafters overhead, which age and the heat of the chamber had burnished as black as ebony. The woman's face was turned, with a sad, careworn smile, to the third member of the party, who, smoking a very black pipe, and sipping grog out of a tumbler, sat talking in the corner of the ingle.

This was a very old man indeed, if one could judge by the deeply wrinkled face and stooping form ; but his eyes were so bright and black, and his mouth so lively, that he seemed the youngest member of the party. He sat in the full gleam of the light, with his face to the window, speaking rapidly, and obviously telling some story, to which the others listened in the deepest attention.

The colouring of the whole scene would have gladdened a shadow-loving painter, such as Rembrandt, or the artists of 'Dutch interiors.' Dimly, in the fine darkness, the eye picked up one object after another. The first thing noticed was the gleam of the fire, and its reflection on the human faces ; then the great black kettle swinging over the fire, and the spinning-wheel, and the polished dishes ranged here and there on the walls ; then the black polished rafters ; and lastly, back again to the human faces, which were giving to the little *genre* picture its whole interest and meaning.

The old man spoke very rapidly, with a peculiar Highland accent, only now and then pausing to give a wheezing cough.

'The fever in every knuckle of his bones, and the dance of St. Vitus in all his limbs ; that's what I weesh for him ;

and when that day comes, may I be near to mix his pheesic and tell him of his sins. Kirsty, woman, weel may you shake your heid, for the tale's true! Aal their beasts are seized, no to speak of their cocks and hens, and the big skeef with the new set of sails; and them only one half-year's rent past due. Mark my words, Peter na Croiche wants the bit of land for his ain grazing, and that's why he's so hard on the M'Kinnons.'

'Peter Dougall is a hard man,' said the clergyman, who sat with his back to the window; 'a hard man, and a curse to the poor; but the fault is less with him than with those who make him what he is and put the mischief in his power. If the lairds came now and then to look after their own land, instead of leaving it in the hands of ignorant men, whose only object it is to feather their own nests and keep their own lamps in oil, the Highlands would be better off.'

He spoke in a deep mellow voice, with a certain refinement of speech and old-fashioned dignity of manner.

'That will ne'er tak' place in oor day,' returned the other; 'it's the sheep and their masters, and tools of the deil like Peter na Croiche, that are turning the North into a wilderness, and shipping every brave Hieland heart to the land of the stranger. Where I saw a hundred families forty years syne, I noo see but twa or three, and those pinched with hunger and lonesome as mountain deer; and if God grants me anither ten years, and I can see oot of my een, there won't be a babe to bring into the world, for no a man will be left in Uribol to father ane. Think of what I was lang syne, and look at me noo! I began wi' doctoring the bodies o' men and women, wi' bringing people into the world, and helping them easily oot o' it; and I rode from door to door on my ain horse, and had baith my hands fu' of pleesant work. And when the cholera passed this way in '30, had I any rest night or day attending the sick and pulling them through? Well, here I am, seeventy years auld, and as steady at an operation as when I was twenty; and I see the waste around me, and hear the beasts howling, and if I was too prood to doctor sheep and cattle I should be starving this day. Once I could scarce rest in my bed without being knocked oot o' my first sleep. Noo I can sleep soond as long's I please. It seemed like auld times when I was knockit up the other night by Red John the. herd, from Callum's fairm in the hollow; and I hurried on my claise and went alang wi' him, but it was only the brindled coo taken in labour and like to dee if I couldna help her through her trouble.'

Without pausing to listen any more, the girl tapped on the pane, and gliding round to the back door, rapidly lifted the latch and entered in.

'You're late, Miss Mina,' said the woman, looking up quietly as the girl entered. 'The master was wondering what kept you.'

The young girl only smiled, and after shaking hands with the doctor, ran over to the white-haired clergyman in the arm-chair, leant over him, and kissed him. He looked up with a paternal nod, and put his hand on her head.

'Why, how's this, my bairn?' he said quickly; 'your hair is dripping wet, and your gown seems splashed as well. What has kept you so late, and where have you been?'

The girl did not answer, but standing before the fire quietly undid her hair and allowed it to fall over her shoulders. As she stood there with her arms raised to gather the fallen braids, and the flush of exercise on her cheek, her full and perfect loveliness was apparent.

She was a blonde of that faultlessly fair Scandinavian type found so seldom in the North, and by no means to be confounded with the so-called 'auburn' or red-haired type, which is so common. Her face was somewhat pale for a rustic maiden, though the warm lips and clear eyes bespoke perfect health. Although her hair was almost golden-yellow and waved in wild curls, her eyebrows were quite dark and her large eyes of lustrous hazel. These eyes might fairly be called the soul of her face; without them she would have been pleasant and pretty; with them she was spiritual and lovely. They were steady eyes, not wild, though bright as possible, and rather passive and dreamy than dazzling and keen. The figure of the girl was slight and tall, and gave little indication of the lissome strength she undoubtedly possessed.

The old doctor looked at her with an admiration worthy of seven-and-twenty instead of seventy.

'If the place was brighter than a bog, and as fu' o' life as it used to be,' he remarked in English, 'it's later than this she would be coming hame frae a walk in the green places wi' a lad o' her ain; but we've fallen on bad times, Mina, my doo. I doot I'll hae to mak' an offer for you mysel', auld as I am, and the ghost o' what I was.'

Here the white-haired minister broke in quickly :

'There are more ways of serving God than by marrying and giving in marriage, though to so many folk it's the end of life—more shame to them! Come, Mina, you have not answered my questions. You have been up to Uribol?'

Mina nodded.

'And you saw Allan na Hogh, and took him the flannel?'

'Yes.'

'How is he?'

'Worse, uncle; his mother thinks it is the dropsy, and is looking every hour for Dr. John.'

'I have told the doctor about him,' said the minister; 'and he will see him to-morrow. It seems a hard case, but he may come round.'

'There's strumous disease in the faimily,' cried the doctor, sharply; 'back to the third or fourth generation. It comes through the mither, though it never touches a hair of a woman's heid. But I'll do my best for the lad, and try to pu' him through.'

After this there was a dead silence, during which the minister glanced again and again at Mina, while the old woman, who was spinning, with a very grave expression kept her eyes furtively fixed on the girl's face. Thus silently urged, Mina told her tale—how, being in the village by accident, she saw the strange yacht making signals of distress; how there was not a man in the village at the time fit to be of the slightest assistance; and how, after a great deal of hesitation, she had herself rowed out in her boat, rather than let the vessel rush into further danger.

Her narrative was received with little expression of surprise, save from the old doctor, who clapped his hands and applauded uproariously.

c

' By the saul of my faither, but that was weel done ! ' cried
the latter. 'And you took her through the Nairrows safe
and sound ? Oh that was goot ! And you had the helm
your ain sel', and she never got so muckle as a scraitch, and
ne'er smelt the groond ? Oh that was brave ! And a
pleesure yacht, with a gentleman on boord ! And you
never spoke a word but in Gaelic to the men, and they did
aal you told them, withoot so muckle as a keek at the
maister ? Oh that was droll ! Did your reverence ever
hear the like ? '

The minister looked thoughtful.

'A strange yacht in Loch Uribol is a wonder indeed,' he
said. 'It is but few boats come this way on business, and
none on pleasure. What sort of a person was the gentleman
on board ? '

'A young man,' replied Mina, 'and an Englishman, 1
think ; for I am sure he did not ken what I was saying, and
he looked at me as if I was a wraith ; never speaking one
word to me while I was on board.'

'Did you not hear his name ? ' inquired the minister.

'No,' replied Mina ; 'but I am sure he is quite a
stranger.'

The doctor was still looking at the maiden in admiration.

'And who taught you to steer a boat, Mina bawn ? ' he
cried. 'Those bits o' fingers look fitter for sewing fine
threed than gripping the tiller or pu'ing a sheet.'

Mina laughed and looked earnestly at her uncle.

'I should be a poor fisherman's foster-daughter if I
couldna guide a boat on the wind ; though running before
it my heart is in my mouth ever since I put Koll Nicholson
into the water when he was at the mast-head and I jibed
the smack off the Moruig Dhu. It doesn't take strength
to steer a boat, but a quick eye and a little practice. Koll
first taught me in the skiff, holding the sheet in his hand,
and running among the squalls below Ben Eval, and since
that I've ne'er been afraid in good weather.'

Here the minister broke in with decision :

'If I had my will,' he observed, 'every woman on these
coasts should learn three things—to steer, to row, and to
swim. What are they fit for now, when danger comes, save

to make a noise and trouble the men; yet there's nothing in handling a boat a woman can't understand as well as a man, if she tries. Look at old Jean M'Kinnon. Though she's sixty years of age, she'll steer a boat and handle an oar with the best man in the parish, and she used to go every year with her man to the fishing till he was drowned at Stornoway. Not that I would have the women folk do the labour of the men folk, and desert the house, and wear the breeks altogether; but I would have them much wiser than they are in a hundred different ways.'

'True for you,' said the doctor; 'they want training; but it's the same everywhere in the warld, and if a lass or wife can wash and cook, that's all to be expectit o' her, unless she's a fine leddy, and has to sit in a drawing-room and droom awa' on the piano.'

'And there's Mina here,' continued the minister warmly. 'Do you mean to tell me she'll make any the worse wife because she can steer if need be, and keep herself afloat in the water if she's thrown into it—as people in those parts may expect to be any day of the year? Just think yourself, doctor, and remember what sort of a child she was.'

'I ought to ken,' cried the old leech; 'for I saw her before her mither or father, and a mite she was, not much bigger than my thoomb, and as red as a lobster newly boiled. We never thought you would have leeved, Mina, my doo. You were so wee, and you kept on whining—whining day and night—as if some secret trouble was wearing you awa', and save you had the seerup you wouldna sleep a wink.'

'She was a sickly infant,' said the minister; 'sickly and peevish, as you say; and she grew up into a poor frail bairn. When the time of deep trouble came, and father and mother were dead and buried, and I took her under this roof, I little thought that she would last long, though I loved her like my own. She would sit here, crouched up, looking at the fire all day long, and we had often to carry her to bed. She never seemed to care for play. Kirsty there thought there was a spell put upon her, and blamed poor old Elspeth of the Ru na Thouadh—though the Calliach was nearly dead of the palsy.'

'Aye, aye!' nodded the doctor, 'I mind.'

'Well, one day Koll Nicholson came in and saw her sitting here on the stool, poking the ashes with her crutch—for she was so weak she could scarcely walk without support. "Isn't it a pity, now, to see her sitting there so dull?" said Koll; "would she not take a sail with me in the skiff?" Mina looked round at me, and her face was quite bright. It was a fine day, and I saw that she was keen to go. So, what did we do but carry her down, with a blanket wrapt round her, and a piece of bread and butter in her hand, and put her in Koll's skiff. Koll rowed her about for two long hours, and then he brought her back, and her eyes were as bright as they are now, and there was a spot of red on her cheek, like the press of a finger. She needed no soothing that night, but slept sound. Next day there was rain, and she sat all day looking at the fire, quite bright and pleased, and when she talked it was about the things she had seen—the big sea, the fish, the birds, all the wonders He made in the beginning. Ah, doctor, His ways are strange indeed! After that Koll came every fine day and took her with him on the water; and the sea was good to her—better than any medicine—and every day she got stronger and better with the fresh air. And look at her now!'

'Weel may you say sae,' exclaimed the doctor. 'She's worth looking at! Mina, my bairn, I'll trouble you for a light till my pipe.'

CHAPTER VI.

DOCTOR OF SOULS AND DOCTOR OF BODIES.

'SHE's had one doctor,' continued the minister thoughtfully; 'one doctor only, and that's the sea, with Koll Nicholson to give the medicine! Glory be to God! His sea saved her! Was I right, or was I wrong, then, when she grew stronger and bigger, to let the sea teach her all it could, to let her spend her long days on the water, to pull herself about in the punt, to go with Koll to the fishing, to just give her the whole of the salt water's teaching, and trust to God for the rest? This is a lonely place, and she's had only one playmate—Koll Nicholson; and he has taught her some rough games—to row a boat, to steer a skiff, to reef a sail, to set a long line, to bait a lobster-pot, and to mend a net; and Koll says she knows the loch better than he does himself. Just see the ways of the Almighty God! He sends Koll to save the child's life, and to make her strong with the breath of the sea; and the signs of His grace are manifold, for after she has trusted all to Him, and been saved, she is made this night the instrument of saving others maybe from a watery grave. And look at her, as I told you! Is she any the uglier, or the coarser, because she knows these things? Does she love learning any the less, such poor learning as I can give her?'

'Deil the bit o' it,' cried the doctor. 'She reads both Latin and Gaelic at sight, and she sings like a mavis. Long life to her! She has the whole "Birlinn"* by heart, besides some sangs of my ain that I taught her when I came last this way. Mina, have you forgotten the "Gilli Dubh" yet, or Dunacha Ban's† sang about "Mairi Bhan Og?"

Mina did not reply, for, loath to listen any longer to her own incidental praises, she had stolen from the room, accompanied by the woman who had been spinning. The two old men thus left alone looked at each other for some time in silence, the doctor puffing vigorously at his pipe, and the minister looking dreamily into the fire.

There was silence once more, and the minister watched the old doctor somewhat impatiently yawning once or twice as if it was time to be in bed. While they were sitting still in the light of the peat-fire they were a curious contrast, each showing in his peculiar way the cunning handiwork of time.

Norman Macdonald, the minister of the Established Church at Uribol, was an old man of seventy, tall almost to ungainliness, thin, gaunt, with a grave, clean-shaven face, and large melancholy eyes. He had once stood nearly seven feet

---

* A well-known Gaelic ballad-poem.
† Duncan Ban Macintyre.

high in his shoes, and though his shoulders were now bent
with age, he still seemed of gigantic height when standing
erect. He was one of those men who are only to be found
in the Highlands of Scotland and some parts of Ireland—a
man of the people, and yet a scholar—a clergyman, and yet
no bigot—a man of the world who never penetrated beyond
a barren solitude. Forty long years had he dwelt in Uribol
—wifeless, almost friendless, a solitary student among a wild
untutored race. In all seasons and in all weathers, across
wild waters and over almost impassable mountains, he had
carried the Word of God in faith and humility. He knew
every face in the isles as a shepherd knows his sheep. He
had sat for days by sick-beds prescribing both for the body
and for the soul, and he had been at every death-bed like a
spirit of hope and promise. He was a busy husbandman,
and cultivated a small glebe with his own hands, and there was
no better judge of sheep or cattle in the whole district. Unlike
most of his brethren, he was a man of dreamy temperament,
a great lover of nature, and a diligent observer of natural
phenomena. He was a great upholder of the authenticity
of Ossian, and he had contributed to the learned societies of
Edinburgh, of which he was a member, many papers of
strange interest on the antiquities of Sutherlandshire.

In his own conversation with the doctor, given above, the
good pastor had said something of the fair girl who, although
not his own child, was nevertheless a member—and the most
precious member—of his little household. Mina nan Oran,
as the fishermen called her on account of her singing gifts,
or more properly Mina Macdonald, was the child of an only
brother who had been widowed during her infancy, and had
shortly afterwards died, leaving two children—Mina and a
little brother just one year her senior. There seemed little
prospect that Mina would live when the minister, from
motives of affection, had taken the orphans into his house,
and handed them over to the care of Kirsty Campbell, a
widow and his maid-of-all-work, to be dealt with according
to her sage experience. On first undertaking the responsibility, he did not expect that it would long continue; but he
speedily began, with the extreme tenderness of his nature, to
conceive a strong affection for both his charges, and to regard

the little girl—especially her—as veritably the sunshine of
his dwelling Never before, since his early boyhood, when
one unhappy passion had touched and darkly stained his
spirit for all the coming years, had he seen any object near
him which he could cherish as his own. Although his was
precisely the nature for which celibacy was unfitted, he had
never married ; and this, perhaps, had somewhat clouded his
originally gentle nature. What wonder, then, that he learned
to cherish the little Mina as something sent specially by God
to comfort his lonely years? As she grew up into a fair and
healthy maiden, his soul yearned to her as to the child of
his own loins. It was his constant care to tend her mind
and open her heart ; and he wisely saw that, if sometimes
gently guided and warned, she would gain more from nature
in mind as well as body than from all the mere routine of
study. He had no false pride. He encouraged her to seek
strength constantly in the open air and to excel in outdoor
sports. He never allowed her to forget that she was a poor
man's child, and that her place was by the side of the poor.
He allowed all the wild superstition and mystery of the
place to pass unimpeded into her soul, and to blend with
her thoughts. He might smile at fairy-tale, but he well
knew its gentle uses. He suffered her to learn from old
men and women all the traditionary poetry and romance of
the isles ; for he saw that these things brightened her eye
and sweetened her speech, rendering her as one that talks
with spirits. His own formal instruction to her was limited
to teaching her to read and write in both Gaelic and English (the former a very unusual accomplishment in the
Highlands), to read a little Latin, to sing a little, and to be
familiar with the Holy Book. It is to be noted that the
minister troubled her little with points of doctrine, or that
strangest of all mythologies concerning the lives of mediæval
saints. His religious teaching was very simple, and would
scarcely have been objected to by any of the many Christian sects.
   Nowhere, perhaps, save in the Highlands of Scotland
could a young girl so lovely and so innocent as Mina
Macdonald have lived so free and irregular a life, and con-
sorted so indifferently with all sorts of human creatures,

without being warned of danger by some open insult or
secret contamination.   But the poor Celts of Uribol were
as pure in this respect as the most perfect knights of Arthur's
court.   No rude thoughts, no lewd hint or secret rudeness,
either by word or by look, ever caused her to shrink within
herself and long for protection.   This man might drink away
his substance, that man might in ordinary life be villanous
in the extreme, but the wildest and most brutal reverenced
the young maiden, and would have protected her with their
lives.   Day and night were alike to her; she walked about
under a charm.   It may be added, furthermore, that there
was little crime of any kind in Uribol, and the worst crime
known was petty theft.   They were, for the most part, a
conscientious and a gentle people, never, even in their
worst specimens, immoral or unclean-minded.

Turning back from this digression to the two figures
seated before the fire, let us take the present opportunity to
say a few words about the doctor.

Although now so old and feeble, this curious old man
lived still in his quaint, wandering style.   He could not
walk far, however, and never visited the interior unless a
pony was specially sent for him.   However, most of his
places of call were close to the sea-shore, and he was able
to perform his duties tolerably, although he could drink
more whisky than any man in the Highlands.   Nor was
his practice confined to the poor.   He had a good practice
among the rich lairds of the West and their ladies, and he
had brought into the world many of the most distinguished
people of those parts.   It was usual, when a birth seemed
imminent, to send for Doctor John, to lodge him in the
house in readiness, and to keep him in drink and meat till
the hour came; and on occasions like these he had been
known to be retained in a state of semi-intoxication for
weeks together, till the event came, when he would thrust
his hot head under the pump or into a basin, drink a draught
of cold water, and be himself in a moment.   Many were his
droll anecdotes connected with this part of his vocation, nor
did he spare his own faults in his narrations.

He was a shrewd man, full of animal spirits, and not too
delicate-minded, content to take the world as he found it,

and not over-much given to compassion for its griefs. Herein may be noted the special difference between him and the clergyman. The latter was by far the most intelligent man, the brighter-minded, the more emotional, yet his bright thoughts and love of nature scarcely ever found vent in words. The doctor, on the other hand, who had little real imagination and no subtlety of feeling, was a poet, and actually a very successful one, his Gaelic compositions being in high repute among the islanders, and sung at many a feast and wedding, to the great delight of young and old. He excelled, too, in a species of composition very popular in the Highlands—a rude species of satiric chant, wherein the peculiarities and peccadilloes of a particular people were hit off with what seemed to the natives terrific humour. Woe to the man or woman who offended him, and earned the sharp lash of his satire! One poor girl who had loved not wisely but too well, and had for some reasons awakened the doctor's special displeasure, had been so wounded by a brief composition of the bard, that she fled ignominiously from the parish. It was also said that the use of the terrible scourge was to be purchased for money. Again and again was the doctor requested to 'compose a song' expressive of private contempt or hostility, and again and again he got payment in money or goods. We ought to add that his satire was neither very brilliant nor very delicate, though smartly expressed enough. Strange to say he made very few enemies, and his compositions were often taken in good part by the very victims themselves.

We cannot say that his influence was altogether salutary. Somehow or other, wherever he went he left a droll trail of drunkenness and disturbance. The people who sheltered him, the boatmen who ferried him, the very sick he attended, felt the wild fascination of his presence long after he had departed; and it was not at all an uncommon explanation, when this or that person was found in drink, to say quietly, 'Oh, ay! he began last week, when Doctor Shon was here, and he'll no stop noo!'

Despite all this, and despite his great age, the doctor was skilful, and the islanders believed in his skill. He was a physician of the 'old school,' and did not excite suspicion by any alarming experiments; and leaving a great deal of his cures to nature, he was in the majority of cases very successful.

Seated in the minister's kitchen, invariably used as a smoking room and place of homely festivity, he smoked his pipe and blinked with his old wrinkled, weather-beaten face at his host, until the latter, with a great yawn, rose out of his arm-chair and stood erect, his snow-white head nearly reaching to the black rafters.

'It is past midnight,' he said, 'and I must be up soon after daybreak.'

If there was one thing the doctor hated more than another, it was retiring to bed at a rational hour. Give him a drop to drink and some one to talk with—or, what was the same thing, to be talked to—and he would remain up any night till daybreak. How his constitution endured the trials he gave it—infinite alcohol and little or no sleep—is a question not to be answered by any mere mortal. Nature sometimes makes men like him to show what she can do when she has a mind to put out her strength—veritable men of iron, on whose mighty frames disease, pain, fatigue, dissipation, make no perceptible impression.

Doctor John looked at the minister and nodded.

'I'll turn in when I hae smoked this pipe oot,' he observed; 'but let me tell you—and it's mysel' that speaks as a meedical man — you hae injured your health by going to bed owre early and taking too little to drink. Owre muckle sleep is doonright ruin to the human corporation; it relaxes the humours, it spoils the circulation, and it plays the deil with the leever.'

The minister laughed.

'And too much whisky?'

'There your very speech is a contradiction, your reverence. You canna tak' too much whisky in this climate, and it's for lack o' whisky that the population is eaten up wi' ague, rheumatism, scurvy, and every disease that grows in a wet air and on a damp soil. Gie a poor man a glass o' whisky and you gie him meat, drink, claise, and pheesic aal in ane. I wish I could afford it, and I'd prescribe naething but Talisker and Long John; but it's a dear meedicine, and owre scarce among my patients, that's the truth.'

And he looked at the minister with a droll twinkle in his eye, holding out his glass to be replenished from a black bottle in the corner. At that moment a loud sound, as of singing, was heard without, and immediately afterwards a figure passed the window, singing aloud in a thin, sharp voice in Gaelic.

'Wha's that?' cried the doctor.

'Unless I'm very much mistaken, it's Angus nan Choan.'

As he spoke the latch was lifted and the door opened.

'Peace be to aal this hoose!' So saying the speaker entered, closing the door behind him, and reverently saluting the old clergyman

CHAPTER VII.

ANGUS OF THE DOGS.

THE newcomer was a man of middle age, whose large, wandering eyes and unnaturally large forehead suggested weakness of intellect, and whose straight-cut fierce mouth just as surely indicated strength of will. He was almost bald, and what hair remained to him hung in shock tangles down to his shoulders, while his long, careworn face was rendered doubly long and haggard by a pair of bushy grey whiskers. He spoke in a thin, piping voice, almost a lisp. His attitude, as he stood before the clergyman waiting for his blessing, was reverent in the extreme.

If his face was strange and wild, his dress was stranger and wilder. He wore an enormous great-coat made of fustian, very loose, and reaching almost to his heels, girt around the middle by a hempen rope very frayed and black with long use. The ends of his trousers, where they peeped under the tails of his coat, were torn and ragged, and his large feet were scantily covered by a pair of blucher-boots, so worn that they hardly held together. His coat, very tight round the waist fell open about the breast, showing that he wore neither shirt nor waistcoat, although his bosom was so covered with long matted hair as to stand in no particular need of either.

This was Angus nan Choan; in English, Angus with the dogs.

The significance of this title became apparent at a glance. Out of his breast were staring three little heads—those of very young Skye-terrier puppies; and at his feet another Skye-terrier, obviously the mother of the brood, was sitting in attendance, watching him with a wistful countenance.

'Peace be to aal in this hoose,' he exclaimed, taking off a torn Highland bonnet, and holding it in his hand.

'And the blessing of God be upon you, Angus nan Choan,' said the minister gently; 'you are a late guest.'

Angus abandoned his reverent attitude, and answered volubly in the thin piping tones of a professional mendicant:

'Better late than never, Mr. Macdonald, as folk say in the Sooth; and, glory be to God, I see you stoot and strong as ever, and weel may we praise Him, for health's a blessing There's Doctor Shon, tae, long life to him, and a grand man every inch o' him, though sair on the whisky. By the saul of my faither, it's a comfort to talk again to him and you, for it's but a poor language the English, and doesna fit in right with a Hieland tongue like mine. I've wandered east and west since I last stood under this roof—may the God in heaven protect it and its owner!—and I've sairly missed the pleesure of three things—the shake o' a Hielandman's fist, a bowl o' good oatmeal parritch, and the taste o' a good dram of Hieland whisky.'

He spoke with great rapidity, with a vacant face and wandering eye, yet with a certain indescribable air of cunning and lying in wait.

'Try that, Angus,' said the minister, offering him a glass of raw spirits.

'Long life and the love o' God!' said Angus, draining off the liquor. 'Och, but that's a goot dram!'

'Take a seat by the fire and warm yourself. Have you been far this time?'

'The warld's wide, and I've wandered far,' answered Angus, seating himself on a stool by the fire 'Through

the island of Skye to Portree, where there's muckle thieving
and little feeshing, and over the ferry at Kyle Akin, and
awa' on the road to Inverness; and a fine toon it is, wi'
plenty o' fine gentry, and kirks and hooses by the score.
Then I cam' doon the great canal to Fort William, and
there I gat a passage to Oban; and at Oban I lost the
pride o' my heart, Donacha Dhu, for he was tossed by a
bull on the quay, and cam' doon on the water as deid as a
stane. You mind Duncan, doctor !—him withoot a tail,—a
collie, and mair sense in ane of his paws than in most men's
brains. It was a sair grief to me, but I just bore up, for we
must aal dee. Then I took the road to Ardrishaig, and
had eneuch to dae wi' thieves and tinker folk wha were
travelling the same gait, and were no fit company for a
decent man. You would weary greatly, and sae I tell you,
if I spoke of a' my adventures in the Sooth country. It's
a thriving country, but a' covered owre with the deil's reek
frae a thousand lums; and the people there are mean,
fashless dirt, and the gentry meanest of all. But it would
dae your heart goot to see the big river Clyde, and the great
steamers, for all the warld like the beasts in the Revelations;
the ships sailing aboot with their white wings, and the air
sae fu' of the noise of hammers, and the making of a
thousand ships. It's an awfu' place—jest like the bad
place itsel'. And I walked awa' up the country by night,
and I saw a hundred fires flaming in the mirk on every
side of me, and I heard the foof-foofing of the crimson
flames, and I saw the black shapes walking about in the
heart of the reek, and, begging grace of your reverence,
and nae offence to Doctor John, I thought I was in hell !'

'Faith,' said the doctor, 'you're no the first man that the
same sight has led to the same conclusion. Did you see
Glasgow ?'

Without directly replying to the question, Angus kept his
eyes fixed on the fire, and continued his narrative in a
monotone as if it were something he had learned by heart.
Allied to his air of mingled simplicity and cunning, he
evinced a simpering sort of self-esteem, especially as to his
own intellectual shrewdness—a peculiarity common enough
among people of his class.

'I saw the big ceety of Glasgow, and it's a wonderfu' place, but fu' of rogues as an egg is of meat. The hooses are that big that they reach up into the cloods, and the sky above is jest reek, and the faces of aal the folk are black and grey wi' breathing o' reek and fire. I saw more horses and cairts in ae day than I ever saw in my life before, and the folk going to and fro were like waves of the sea; and the streets were fu' of painted shops for the sale of drink, and at ilka street corner there's a blackguard in black ready to take up any decent man that asks help for the love o' God. I fell in wi' bad company there—more shame to me—and the curse o' God seemed to have come upon me when I found mysel' consorting wi' thieves and bad women, and when I spoke to these same on the shamefulness of their ways, they fell upon me and the dogs, and left the whole of us in the streets for dead. Then they lockit me in a black hole o' stane, and all nicht lang I heard the dogs howling ootside in the street because they werena allooed to come to me; and when day came, and they let me oot, I shook the dust off the soles of my feet and cam' awa', for deil a ane would gie a crust or a drap to a decent man, and none would ludge me for the love o' God.'

'Well, well,' observed the doctor, 'you'll no be taking *that* road in a hurry. It's no for poor men, and you were wandering awa' from your meat.'

Angus looked at the speaker dreamily.

'I dinna ken but what you're right, Doctor John, for you're a clever man and a scholar; but, begging your pardon, and long life to you, I think it's a goot thing for a lad to see the world he lives in, and study the wonderfu' works o' Nature to the best of his pooer; and knowledge doesna come to a man withoot trouble, and mony a time it's bocht dear. It's a great city, Glasgow, just a weelderness whaur nae man can find his way, and though it's fu' of meat and drink, and iron ships, and silver and gold, and though they're telling me the rich folk sleep on crimson velvet beds stuffed wi' the down o' the wild swan, it made my heart sair to see the mony helpless duggies—some of them no much older than these pups I hae in my breist—wandering about the naked streets wi' ne'er a saul to own or feed them. It's a true proverb, "Bad

dug, bad maister," and the dugs of the big city have ways
ony decent man's dugs would be ashamed to own. They
cheat and steal, they curse and swear, they waylay and
maltreat the stranger, and do you wonder at that when they
ken nae better, and they're following the wicked ways of
man ? They're a' breeds but the best, and mostly vaga-
bonds : no but what I saw many decent-like dugs at the
West End, playing on the doorsteps and in the parks,
though some of these sought to drive me frae the doors.
But, as I was saying, my heart grieved for the creatures
with neither hoose nor hame, and many a crust I gied them,
when I had a hungry belly myself, when I saw them standing in the street, maybe sniffing the steam o' the cook-
shop, and licking their chops, wi' their een fu' of grief and
longing.'

Here the speaker's eye fell upon Mina, who had re-entered
the kitchen, and was listening attentively to his monologue.

'And praise be to God, there's the bonnie face I was
thinking of—mair bloom to it, and a brave gentleman to
kiss it aal in goot time. I'm talking, miss, of the poor
wandering outcasts of the earth. I was wondering whether
you would take a preesent from a puir man like myself,
that has more children than he can manage, and more
mooths than he can feed.'

CHAPTER VIII.

CANINE WAIFS AND STRAYS.

WHILE he spoke Angus had shuffled over to the door;
opening it now, he gave a low whistle. The signal was
immediately responded to by no less than four different
animals of the canine species. First there ran in, wagging
his tail very rapidly, a wretched-looking cur of no particular
breed, which Angus addressed as Shemus or James, and
bade him lie down in a corner; next stalked in a doleful
looking white dog, not unlike a French poodle, but very
dirty and disreputable indeed; thirdly, a collie pup, very

long in the legs and soft in the head; lastly, with his tail
between his legs and his whole air expressive of disgust,
a small black and white terrier, very small and prettily
formed.

'That's Shemus, and you aal ken him weel,' said Angus,
as they entered one by one; 'and this is Phemus Ban, and
wha doesna ken Phemus between this and Stornoway?
And the next is wee Duncan, Donacha Dhu's son and heir.
And the last—see till him, Miss Mina, hoo he leuks at ance
to yoursel'—is the dog I was speaking aboot. He's a clever
chiel', though his troobles have preyed heavily upon his
mind; and if you'll tak' him, I'll gie him till you wi' my
blessing. He'll mak' a brave beast to run after a bonnie
young leddy like yoursel'.'

One might have almost fancied that the wretched object
in question knew every word that Angus was saying, for,
crouched upon the ground, he looked with a curious eye at
the girl. Wet with rain, worn with fatigue, and possibly
very hungry, he looked by no means a desirable acquisition;
but there was something in his forlorn face which appealed
to pity, and Mina took him at once on her lap and began
to caress him. He received her advances without enthusiasm, sullenly awaiting the issue of the conversation.

'Poor wee man,' said Mina. 'Is he hungry?'

'I'll ask him,' said Angus, quietly. 'Are you hungry,
Billie?'

The dog, as if he understood the question, thrust out his
tongue to lick his wet jaws, and slightly wagged his tail.

'He says he's ready for his supper,' cried Angus, inter-
preting, 'though he's had many a scrap by the road. It's
low speerits, darling, not hunger, that's the matter wi' *him.*'

'What's he low-spirited aboot?' asked the doctor.

'Ask your ain heart, Doctor John,' returned Angus, 'what
you would be low-spirited aboot, if you had gane athegither
wrang and were wandering amang strangers. Dogs are like
men—they can be sorry as weel as hungry, lonely as weel
as feared, dull in the spirits as well as cold in the wame.
I found him up a dark entry in the ceety of Glasgow, sleeping his lane, oot of the cold, in a place where I meant to
sleep mysel', for ne'er a saul would gie a decent man a bed;

and he was stairving, and I gied him meat; and he was cauld, and I warmed him here on my ain naked flesh. Then I thought I'd bring him back wi' me to Uribol, as a present to the colleen with the bird's voice; for, look you, my braw leddy' (here he addressed himsel to Mina), 'the dog is a good dog, wi' real blood intil him, though he had fallen on evil ways. It's no me that would come here asking your acceptance o' a beast o' nae quality, after aal you've done and said to me and mine.'

Thereupon, better to illustrate the game qualities of the animal, Angus proceeded to lift him by various parts of his person successively,—by the tip of the ear, by the mouth, by the skin of the neck, by the tip of the tail—all which indignities the unfortunate stranger bore without a murmur, though his eye was fixed, as if in sullen protest, on the face of the mendicant.

'There!' said Angus, in a tone of approbation; 'you'll ne'er regret his keep. It'll dae your heart goot to see him on rats, and the weasel doesna walk he willna face. You'll find him a constant soorce of deevairsion, and muckle sport he'll bring you.'

Although this last recommendation could scarcely be said to have much weight, seeing that Mina's favourite diversions were certainly not those of rat-killing and vermin-hunting, Angus obviously thought that he had triumphantly shown the preciousness of the prize. Meanwhile Mina was feeding the little outcast with scraps of meat.

One word as to Angus's peculiar taste, from which he received his popular name. It must not be imagined for a moment that he was a dog-fancier or dealer in dogs— nothing of the sort; he kept dogs about him simply because he loved them, and one animal of the species was generally to him as good as another. He knew a first-rate breed when he saw it, and often turned a good penny by selling a fine specimen to this or that gentleman; for his knowledge and good faith were both trusted. Any houseless dog, however, was sure of his protection till he could get an owner for it; the wretcheder and uglier it was, the more it seemed to move his compassion. He was a severe but a just master, with a singular power of eliciting the best

D

qualities of a dog. Many an utterly stupid animal was handed over to Angus as a last resource, and given back to the owner, after a month or two, thoroughly reclaimed and enlightened.

Speaking generally, however, Angus had no regular profession, not even that of a mendicant. He belonged to that almost extinct class of persons, the Fools, who were regarded in the Highlands as under the special protection of the Almighty, and entitled to 'bite and sup' wherever they chose to pause and rest in their pilgrimages.

Many of those fools were utter idiots; others, again, like Angus, were incomprehensible persons, so shrewd and clever in a thousand ordinary matters, and so wild and eccentric in one or two particulars—notably as to dress and personal bearing. In either case they were generally strong, able-bodied men, capable of enduring infinite privation and fatigue. They came and went as they listed—as if blown by a divine breath, and under the divine care. No man molested them; few or none denied them their crust, their drop of milk, and their night's shelter.

All his life Angus had wandered about the north, and especially about Uribol; and that life had, on the whole, been a happy one. He was not lonely, for he had his dogs —his 'bairns,' as he called them—for company, and there was always some new member of his family to train and instruct. He never suffered them to steal even so much as a bone, but educated them virtuously with the greatest care and tenderness. He was, indeed, after his own dim lights, a creature of unblemished honour, ever priding himself, as we have seen, on his character of 'decent man,' though never forgetting that he possessed a certain divine privilege to receive alms, if he demanded it, 'for the love of God.' Through cold and wet, through storm and snow, by land and water, in all weathers, he wandered with his little family. At night the dogs nestled round his body, giving and taking warmth. Most of his meals were docked for their sake, and often he would sit by hungry and see them eat, showing in his treatment of these dumb things the nicest honour, the most fatherly care, and the tenderest affection.

Of late years he had taken to wandering far from the land of his birth, and had assumed more of the habits and ways of professional beggars. His desire, as he said, was 'to see the world.' In the course of this laudable pursuit, he received, as most men do when they first wander out world-seeing, a good deal of rough treatment and sorry dishallucination. He was not daunted, although he speedily discovered that he was denied abroad the privileges which he had enjoyed from time immemorial at home. He attributed this fact to the ignorance and inferiority of strangers, and merely compassionated their unhappy condition. To his poor wandering wits the world was wonderful and beautiful. Roaming in the lowland districts of Ayrshire or on the banks of the Clyde, he felt as far from home and kindred, as mighty a traveller over the earth, as others do who explore the American prairie or wander along the great wall of China. He was among a strange people, in a far land, speaking with difficulty a foreign tongue. In the course of his happy pilgrimages—happy with all their privations, because he thoroughly enjoyed them—he had, as we have seen, gone as far south as Glasgow, and the sight of the great city had been a wonder and a portent great enough to last the poor wanderer all the rest of his life.

Angus would have talked on by the hour, but the minister now interposed, and insisted that the whole party should retire for the night.

A bed in the house had been prepared for the doctor. As for Angus with the dogs, he was lighted out to his usual sleeping-place, the byre, where, on a deep warm bed of fresh straw, surrounded by his children, he slept such sleep and dreamed such dreams as Solomon in all his glory never enjoyed, and as are granted only to a clear conscience, an innocent mind, and a gentle heart.

CHAPTER IX.

THE WANDERER FINDS QUIET QUARTERS.

ABOUT a mile from the manse, and nearer to the cluster of mud huts known as the clachan, stood a one-storied white-washed building, surrounded on every side by open heather and tracts of soft marsh. This was the abode during a small portion of every summer of Mr. Peter Dougall, resident factor to Lord Arranmore.

Some days after the entry of the little yacht into Loch Uribol, Peter Dougall sat alone in the best chamber of the cottage, which he called his 'office,' but which was furnished very plainly as a parlour. He was a grim-looking, elderly man, clad in a rudely-cut suit of the kind known as pepper-and-salt, and bearing in every lineament of his hard counte-nance the signs of low intelligence, cunning, and tenacity of purpose.

He was busily engaged in looking over certain papers, docketing them, and arranging them upon his table, when a barefooted Highland woman, who did for this grim bachelor the duties of maid-of-all-work, announced a visitor.

She spoke in Gaelic, and Dougall was questioning sharply in the same tongue, when with little or no ceremony, a tall athletic figure entered the room.

'Excuse me for intruding upon you,' said a clear, sharp voice; 'but you are Mr. Dougall?'

'Yes, sir,' said the factor, staring in some surprise at the intruder.

'My name is Lawrance, and I have just come from the South. I have a letter for you; will you be kind enough to read it?'

So saying, the speaker opened a pocket-book and took from it a note, which he quietly handed over. Dougall started slightly and knitted his heavy brows as he looked at the handwriting on the envelope. Then opening the letter he read as follows:

'My Dear Sir,—This note will be given you by my friend Mr. Lawrance, who is on a tour in Scotland this summer. I have advised him to visit Uribol, and promised that you will put him in the way of some wild sport, of which he is very fond. Consider him as my representative, and let him do whatever he pleases with whatever is mine.

'Take no steps whatever in matters of business till you hear from me again; I have not yet decided on the changes you were good enough to suggest. When you write next, address Messrs. Thompson and Threadneedle, my agents, as before. I leave London to-morrow, and shall be absent for some months. Yours, etc., ARRANMORE.

'To Mr. Peter Dougall, Factor, Uribol. N.B.'

The factor glanced from the letter to the bearer, from the bearer to the letter, in momentary embarrassment; then, forcing his face to a smile, he welcomed Lawrance, with great respect and a certain cordiality, to the Highlands.

'And you will be the shentleman,' he said, 'who came ower in the small pleesure yacht?'

'Yes; she is now lying at the mouth of the loch.'

'A ponnie vessel! I saw her fine frae the hill. I'm concerned that I didna see you pefore, sir, when you arrived. Weel, you hafe come to a poor country for pleesure. It is seldom I am in Uribol, unless I hafe beesiness here; and my ain hoose is at Storport, fifteen miles down the coast. Did you leave my lord weel, sir, may I ask?'

'Never better.'

'Ah! he is a grand man, Lord Arranmore; and he has gone again aproad?'

'I dare say,' said Lawrance carelessly; 'he hates the English climate.'

'It is a pad climate for shentry,' said the factor; then, moved by hospitable intentions, he went to a cupboard in the room, and, unlocking it, produced bottles and wine-glasses.

'What will you tak', sir? Whisky or sherry wine?'

'Neither, thank you.'

'It is goot whisky, and the wine is goot. Let me give

you a glass of the sherry wine ;' and he added thoughtfully, while Lawrance took the proffered glass, 'I am glad, fera glad, that my lord is weel.'

In a few minutes Lawrance and Dougall were seated face to face, talking without restraint of general matters, but chiefly about Loch Uribol, its sports and its population. The old factor had obviously been a sportsman in his youth, and he soon afforded his guest much valuable information on the amusements to be had in the locality. He knew the best streams for fishing, the lochs most frequented by the wild geese, and the portions of the moor where grouse were likely to be most plentiful. On the whole, he impressed Lawrance as a shrewd, serviceable old fellow, with a good deal of common sense.

Despite his pleasantness of manner, however, he was clearly a little suspicious that his visitor might have been sent over by Lord Arranmore to report secretly on the state of the estates—a course of proceedings which he would have been strongly inclined to resent had he been certain of the fact.

'And his lordship is weel,' he repeated for the third or fourth time. 'May I ask, sir, does he never think of vceesiting his Hieland estates?'

'I have heard him talk of doing so a dozen times, but he is fond of great cities, and rather dislikes his native country. Doubtless, though, he'll soon take a run over.'

'May it pe soon!' said the factor, with some fervour. 'A shentleman should see his ain groond, and find oot if it is goot groond, and if the rents are goot.'

Lawrance shrugged his shoulders.

'It strikes me that Lord Arranmore would not be much wiser if he came. He is no farmer, and scarcely knows a harrow from a plough.'

The factor took a pinch of snuff, drew down his brows, and looked keenly at the stranger.

'That may be, sir, but he's a poorer man this day than he need be if he would do as I weesh him, or if he would come for himsel' and see. There's no an acre of his estate, from the Point of Raw to the Sound of Cule, but should be down in sheep.'

'Indeed.'

'And what is mair,' continued Dougall excitedly (for he was on his hobby), 'he should be getting rent for every armful of kelp that is burnt on his ain foreshores. The land is goot land, but it is covered with the scum of the earth, sir—lazy peasts of men and women that should be shippit across the sea.'

Lawrance looked at the speaker with some curiosity.

'Ah, yes,' he said, after a moment's reflection. 'Lord Arranmore told me something of this. You think the place over-populated.'

Dougall's face flushed, and he struck the table with his open hand.

'If I had my will I would tooble the rent in five years. I would have nane upon the land but the shepherds, and I would pring hands from the sooth to make kelp in the season, and I would tak' it to my ain market, for my ain price.'

'A policy of extermination,' remarked Lawrance, with a yawn, real or assumed. 'It seems rather sharp practice, doesn't it?'

'I told my lord's faither, again and again, to clear the land; and through my advice, sir, he pulled toon mony a hoose that was a disgrace to ceevilisation, and shipped awa' mony a lazy loon that cumbered the goot land. He would have done mair but for meeschief-makers and meddlers, sir; and if he had done mair he never would have died in debt. I would give my right hand, sir, if the young laird would come and see the place for himsel'.'

'And he will come, of course, some day.'

'And if he does come,' exclaimed the factor irritably, for on this subject he was hard to please, 'what do the shentry ken apoot the land? There would be meeschief-makers and meddlers, sir, to mak' oot I was wrang. There is in this clachan, sir, a meenister of the Kirk, and that meenister should be trooned in the sea, like all the rest of his kind. Would you pelieve, sir, that once when the old laird was alive, but pad wi' the gout, I wrote a letter adveesing him to turn the folk from Plabba Island and gife it to my ain son for sheep for tooble the rent; and the tamned meenister made oot a peteetion, and made every man, woman, and child put his mark to the peteetion, and sent it to the laird by the post; and sure enough the old laird wrote back that I was to let the people of Plabba pe, whether they paid their rent or no!'

Lawrance, who had been listening throughout with a curious expression, half severe, half cynical, here said quietly:

'After all, it is rather a serious responsibility to turn people wholesale out of house and home. Don't you think so?'

'That is true, sir,' returned the factor; adding triumphantly, 'but if it was for their ain goot, sir? They ruin the goot land, and they're eaten up wi' hunger and disease, when oot yonder in America there's meelions o' miles o' airable land to be had for the asking. The land here was made for sheep. It'll no grow a crop, and it canna feed a man. It's my opinion, sir, that it's pad for Hielandmen to remain at hame. There's nae competeetion here, and there's nae industry. It would pe far petter if the whole Hielands were doon in sheep—petter for the lairds, petter for the people, petter for the cattle, and petter for the markets of the sooth.'

This seemed to settle the matter, so far as the factor was concerned, and Lawrance seemed far too indifferent to pursue it further. Chiefly to change the subject, but with a practical object in view, the latter now consulted Dougall about a lodging. His vessel, he explained, was too small to be a comfortable home when at anchor, and as he intended to stay in the neighbourhood for some ·weeks, he would, if possible, live ashore.

With some little hesitation, the factor offered the use of the cottage in which they then stood, adding that he himself would be pleased to return after he had transacted some little business in Storport, and be the stranger's guide over the whole district.

To the latter part of the proposal Lawrance strongly demurred.

'I will accept the cottage with pleasure,' he said; 'but I insist that you shall not put yourself to any personal inconvenience on my account. Indeed, I infinitely prefer to be left alone, and to acquaint myself with a locality in my own way. Even so invaluable a guide as yourself would be superfluous and irksome, though I thank you all the same.'

'As you please, sir,' said Dougall, rather grimly. 'But if I could be of any service it would be a pleesure.'

'When do you go?' asked Lawrance brusquely.

'It was my intention to gang to-day; but I will stay on till to-morrow, and see you made comfortable.'

'Don't delay an hour on my account,' said Lawrance. 'To a citizen of the world, and to one who has roughed it in the bush, and camped out on the prairie, this is as good as a palace. Calum shall bring my lumber ashore, and his services, with those of the woman already in your employ, shall be more than sufficient.'

'But you will need a guide upon the hills, sir. They are goot for game, but you must be weel acquaint wi' the ground to find it. Now, I mysel'——'

'Don't think of it, I pray,' said Lawrance. 'Trust an old sportsman for discovering whatever he wants. I like to potter about in my own way, and acquire my own information without assistance.'

So it was settled, not without a certain curious misgiving, felt but not expressed, on the factor's part. That afternoon Dougall departed on the back of a rough Hebridean pony, purposing to ride down the road to Tongue, crossing the numerous narrow estuaries by finding them at low water. He had scarcely disappeared when Calum, assisted by a couple of bare-legged lads from the clachan, brought ashore Lawrance's goods and chattels—a couple of portmanteaus, gun-cases, fishing-rods, fishing materials, a few books, some boxes of cigars, and divers odds and ends for the cruise.

Late that evening Lawrance sat alone in the little parlour, surrounded by his portable property, and waited upon by Dougall's Highland servant, with whom he vainly tried to conduct a conversation by signs and interjections; while here and there in the clachan gathered excited groups discussing with many wild words and gestures an extraordinary and unprecedented phenomenon—the arrival of an entire stranger, and that stranger an English gentleman, among the solitudes of Loch Uribol.

CHAPTER X.

A SPORTING EPISODE AND ITS TERMINATION.

A DARK sky, a land mist, and a stiff breeze from the sou'-east
—we might have known before we started, Calum, that these
vould not make a good sporting day, even in Sutherlandshire.'

It was Lawrance who spoke, and as he did so he lay
ndolently back in the stern of the boat, and glanced at the
cold grey prospect of sea and sky.

It was one of those dark summer days so common in the
Highlands.　The sky was one great pall of shifting vapour,
through which the sun's rays struggled faintly, touching here
and there to dim silver the edges of the black waters of the
och.　On the peaks of the hills stirred a white steam of
cloud, while the waters of the loch were rippled into heavy
wavelets by the sea-breeze, which every moment seemed to
be waxing stronger.

Two hours before, the boat, a small light thing of some
twelve feet in length, had glided away from the side of the
Tenny, and passed right into the mouth of the fjord; and
though before starting Lawrance had anticipated a good
day's sport, nothing much had been done.　True, he had
bagged a few sea-birds — among which was a remarkably
fine specimen of the eider-duck—but, on the other hand,
several of his shots, through the continual tossing of the
boat, had whizzed harmlessly through the air, and he had
been left to stand and watch, with straining eyes, the fading
of his coveted prize.

'Suppose we give up?' said Lawrance at last; 'it's a
detestable day.'

Calum, who was at the oars, glanced phlegmatically
round.

'The day is nae sae bad,' he said; 'and up till this the
sport hasna been sae bad.　You'll shoot better when you
come to the seals.'

At this Lawrance seemed somewhat appeased, and as

the boat glided gently on, he took up his glass and carefully scanned the water and the shore. Suddenly he rose excitedly to his feet, almost upsetting the boat as he did so.

'By Jove!' he exclaimed; 'Hamish, look through the glass at that black rock yonder, and tell me if it isn't covered with something living?'

'Maybe,' said Hamish quietly; and having by a look through the glass satisfied himself that it was a fact, he advised Lawrance to make ready while he rowed on. So Lawrance, rifle in hand, crouched down in the stern of the boat, which, with muffled oars, crept stealthily along the shore. The seals were distinctly visible by this time—they clung like seaweed to the rock, their silken coats shining in the light. But all at once the liquid eyes of one of the beasts rolled round and perceived the oncoming boat, which was by this time within a distance of ninety yards of the rock itself. Instantly the creatures, as if from one impulse, rolled rapidly off the rock, and sank with wild splashes beneath the surface of the water.

The boat stood still; Lawrance shouldered his rifle.

'Steady, sir, steady!' cried Calum.

One moment more and the water all around the boat was clothed with floating heads. Lawrance aimed at the one nearest to him and fired; as he did so the boat gave a lurch, the bullet sped harmlessly through the air, and every head disappeared.

'Like my ill luck,' cried Lawrance. 'It is this confounded coble which does it all! Pull for the shore, Calum; I'll perhaps get a shot from the beach.'

Without a word Calum obeyed. Almost immediately the boat was run upon the shingle, and Lawrance leapt ashore. But the seals did not reappear, and Lawrance was at a loss what to do. Presently, however, at Hamish's suggestion, he walked quietly along the shingle, and kept a sharp look-out over the water, leaving Calum himself to stay by the half-stranded boat and keep watch too.

Suddenly, and before he had gone many yards, his eyes were attracted to a black mass which lay dead-still on the beach, close to the edge of the water—a big, black, shapeless lump, which might be a weed-covered rock, it was so still. Lawrance strained his eyes, but could make nothing of it—he used his glass with the same result. He walked rapidly on, keeping his eyes fixed upon it. All at once the black mass stirred, and slightly shifted its position. Yes, there was no doubt of it—it was a seal !

Rapidly he surveyed the ground, and came to the conclusion that the animal might be stalked. Fortunately for his purpose the wind was blowing from the water, and about thirty yards above high-water mark, or sixty from the unconscious seal, there was a large boulder, from behind which it would be easy to fire the fatal shot at close range. Taking the necessary marks, and making a long detour, Lawrance gradually approached the shelter of the boulder.

Hamish remained seated in the distance, and watched his master with no little excitement.

All went well, and Lawrance, having reached the boulder, peeped over and saw the animal still in the same position. The sunlight glimmered upon its moist skin, so that it shone again, and its head turned seaward, while its nostrils sniffed the breeze. The tide was running past with great rapidity, and half-a-dozen cormorants, diving repeatedly, were drifting swiftly down the fjord.

Stooping softly, he took his rifle and noiselessly prepared to take aim. At that very moment he heard a sound in the distance like the sound of a voice singing—the seal pricked up its head listening—then suddenly, and before Lawrance could fire, slipped into the water and disappeared.

With an angry exclamation Lawrance started out from his shelter and began moving towards the water, in the hope of getting a shot swimming. He was disappointed. The seal rose several hundred yards away, and then, after drifting rapidly along with the tide for a moment, dived again.

Lawrance stood baffled, knowing well that it was useless to follow. Suddenly, however, he was startled by certain wild manœuvres on the part of Calum, who was frantically waving his hat and pointing towards the sea. Full of impatience, and irritated, Lawrance strode over and rejoined him.

'Well, what is it?'

Calum answered by putting his fingers on his lips, stooping

low, and jerking his thumb towards the water. So Lawrance crept cautiously forward, and, peering over the rocks, saw a sight which filled him with amazement. Two hundred yards below him lay the boat where they had left it, with its stern just in the water, and sitting on the stern seat, having obviously just climbed thither from the sea, was the seal !

Such supreme impudence in so cautious an animal—one which habitually shrinks from anything handled by human touch—almost took away his breath, but not for a moment did he suspect the truth. Rifle in hand, he began creeping over the rocks to a spot which would afford him another excellent chance. This time he felt tolerably certain of his victim. Reaching a rock about a hundred yards from the boat, he prepared to fire. The gun was lifted to his shoulder, he was about to take aim, when suddenly, to his intense astonishment, a figure stept from among the rocks and rose between him and the water !

The figure of a young girl, with neither hat nor bonnet on her head. She did not seem conscious of his presence, but was looking towards the sea.

In a moment he had crept forward, and had silently reached her side. She turned at the sound, and looked at him in some surprise. He, for his part, was not a little amazed, for the face he saw was pretty and young, and he dimly remembered having seen it before. His excitement as a sportsman, however, so carried him away that, scarcely looking at her, he made her a sign to be silent and pointed to the water ; then, before she could interfere, knelt down to take aim.

A wild cry interrupted him, and just as his finger was on the trigger, the rifle was nearly knocked from his hand. The bullet sped harmlessly through the air, while the seal, obviously astonished, slipt again into the water and began swimming to and fro, his uplifted head turned in the direction whence the sound had come.

He looked up. Over against him stood the young girl, pale with excitement, her lips quivering, her eyes flashing. At that moment Calum ran over, and attacked her fiercely in Gaelic. She answered in the same tongue, pointing now to the rifle, again to the swimming seal.

'What does it mean?' cried Lawrance; 'what does she say?'

Calum scratched his head and grinned.

'She's saying that she daurs ye to touch yon creature, and that we desairve to be shotted oursels for molesting it. Speak till her, sir. She beats me a'thegither.'

'Can you speak English?' cried Lawrance sharply.

To his surprise the girl answered him in his own tongue.

'I can speak English,' she said, steadfastly fixing her eyes on his; 'what then, sir?'

Lawrance forced a laugh.

'You have spoiled my shot, that's all. But for you, I should have bagged my first seal. Why did you inter-fere?'

The girl, in the Scottish fashion, answered the question with another. It was clear that she was much agitated, but she managed to preserve her outward composure.

'Why should you take the poor seal's life? It's not like a gentleman, let alone a brave man, to kill a poor creature that never did him any harm.'

Lawrance gazed at the speaker in still greater astonish-ment. He now recognised her perfectly as the girl who had piloted his vessel into Loch Uribol, and recovering his self-control, he smilingly raised his hat.

'I am a brute for my pains,' he said. 'Why, now I know you? You got us out of our scrape, the other day, entering the loch, and I have never yet thanked you.'

'I'm asking no thanks,' said Mina; 'only let Earach be.' Then, moving quickly away, she leapt up on a rock, and cried, in a clear voice, 'Earach! Earach!'

The seal heard, raised his head eagerly, and looked towards her. So far from flying from her, the seal swam swiftly to the shore, and floundering out on the tangled weeds, awaited her coming.

Not a little excited by what he saw, Lawrance followed and watched the meeting. Mina stood on the water's edge, and the seal crawled to her feet and looked up in her face.

Lawrance gave a low whistle.

'Why, it's *tame!*' he cried. 'What a fool I've been!'

Mina made no reply, but laid her hand caressingly on the

animal's glistening head. Its dim, gentle eyes looked softly into hers, with perfect confidence and affection.

'It does not seem the least frightened,' continued Lawrance.

Mina answered him without raising her eyes, which were .ixed on those of the animal.

'Why should it be afraid? No man hereabouts would harm Earach. See how he speaks to me, sir! See how he slips his cheek into my hand! He's as wise as a human creature, and twice as kindly.'

For a time Lawrance did not reply. He felt his position a foolish one. Not only had he been caught in the extremely ignominious pursuit of shooting at a tame seal, but he seemed in a fair way of being lectured on cruelty to animals by— well, by a peasant girl.

Calum helped him very neatly out of his dilemma.

'You're a braw leddy and a brave,' he said, gazing admiringly at the girl's graceful slim figure and lovely face. 'And hoo is it that ye ken sae weel how to handle a boat?'

At that moment Earach rolled lazily on to his side, and falling heavily into the water, splashed the girl liberally with spray. She laughed as she shook her dress, and stepping lightly from rock to rock, leapt on to the shingle. Then, after speaking a word or two to Calum in Gaelic, she seemed about to depart.

But Lawrance stepped forward.

'Pardon me,' he said, with a courtesy which was scarcely habitual with him, 'I do not even know your name.'

The girl paused and looked at him.

'My name is Mina Macdonald,' she said.

Lawrance bowed.

'I shall remember it as long as I keep the life which you gave me!'

At this the girl flushed and dropped her eyes.

'Please, dinna speak of that again, sir. I was because there was no other soul in the village that I came out!'

Lawrance was puzzled. He had already discovered by intuition that she could be no common peasant girl, and so had banished from his mind all thoughts of remuneration. It now remained to find out who she could be. He must say something, and quickly—the girl seemed impatient to be gone.

'You live in the village?' he asked.

It seemed a superfluous question, but he could think of no more direct mode of obtaining what information he desired.

'Yes,' she replied.

'Then perhaps, some day before I leave, I may call—we may meet.'

He was jerking out his sentences in a confused, uneasy way, when the girl interrupted him.

'If you care to come to our house, sir,' she said gravely, 'you will be welcome; every stranger is. I live in the clachan with my uncle, Mr. Macdonald, the minister of the parish.'

And without more ado she bowed to Lawrance, nodded smilingly to Calum, and walked off.

'You're a bonnie lassie,' said Calum; and turning to Lawrance, he added, 'There's no her like to be found in Uribol!'

Lawrance said nothing, but as he watched the girl's fairy-like form passing silently away, he secretly resolved that he would not be too proud to accept the off-hand invitation which she had given him.

CHAPTER XI.

IN THE PARSONAGE.

LATE that night, when most of the inhabitants of the clachan were at rest, when all about the manse was very quiet, and the old minister himself—always the last to seek his room—lay quietly asleep, Mina sat by her open window looking out upon the moonlit sea, and thinking over the scene which she had passed through that day. She had not had time to think over it before. After she had bowed to Lawrance and smiled her good-day to Calum, she had hastened home with

eager steps, and finding her uncle there, had dutifully re-
counted to him all that had passed.

Mr. Macdonald listened quietly. When the story was
done, he said:

'And so, Mina, your were unmaidenly enough to ask the
gentleman to call?'

'No, I did not do that,' returned the girl quietly. 'He
asked me if he might come, and I said to him that at this
house any stranger would be made welcome.'

'An exemplary speech, my bairn, and one that was quite
worthy of you. I am glad you did not discourage the young
man. I should not find it unpleasant, I think, to have half-
an-hour's chat with an educated stranger.'

After that nothing more was said on the subject. Mina
went through her evening lessons with as much care, and
perhaps rather more thoughtfulness, than usual, and when
they were over she took a book and sat down to read. It
seemed she had not even been thinking of the stranger, for
when, on wishing her good-night, the minister again casually
mentioned his name, she gave a start of surprise.

'I forgot to ask you, Mina, and I think you forgot to tell
me, what the strange gentleman is like?'

'What he is like?' she repeated, feeling the tell-tale
colour suddenly suffuse her face.

'Yes; I have settled in my mind, and I don't know why,
that, if he is not old, he must at least be middle-aged.
Young men are not generally in the habit of seeking solitudes such as these.'

'No,' said Mina thoughtfully; 'indeed they are not;
and when I saw the strange gentleman to-day I was
surprised.'

'Then I suppose he is young.'

'Yes, uncle, quite young?'

Mina looked down as she made the admission; she
therefore felt rather than saw the minister was disappointed.
The two stood silent for a moment, then Mina raised her
eyes.

'I'm thinking the gentleman will not trouble *us* much
while he is in Uribol,' she said.

'Maybe not, my bairn; nevertheless, if he does come he

E

must be made welcome !' Then he kissed her, and she
went away to her room.

She went to her room, but she did not prepare for rest.
Long after her uncle had retired she sat at her open window,
thinking partly of his words and partly of the scene which
she had enacted on the seashore.

Her conduct during that scene had been very proper
indeed, she said to herself with pride—quite as proper as
the conversation which she had just had with her uncle
downstairs ; but though she had felt it right to cloak her
feelings before both of these men, she could at least unveil
them when alone. Therefore as she sat at the window
listening to the soft murmuring of the sea, she allowed herself to conjure up a vision of the stranger's face, the outline
of his slim figure ; to recall the pleasant tone of his voice
when he courteously addressed her ; the light which shone
in his eyes as he had looked into hers. Perhaps it was
wrong of her, she thought, but she had certainly been unable
to share her uncle's feeling of disappointment on finding
that the stranger was young—indeed, she thought it was
pleasant to have seen so young and fair a face among the
wilds of Uribol—pleasanter to know that she was likely to
look upon it soon again.

Soon ?—would he be likely to come soon ?—or was it
probable that her formal coldness would have the effect of
keeping him away ? She had certainly given him so little
encouragement that she would have no right to blame him
if he chose to take no further notice of her at all.

This idea was so painful to her that it troubled her continually during her sleep that night, and the next morning
it was so strong in her mind that she mentioned it to her
uncle at breakfast.

The minister looked very grave.

'You seem to be very anxious that this young man should
come to us, Mina,' he said.

'No, not that, uncle. I'm only feared I may have been
rude !'

'Then set your mind at rest, Mina ; you behaved with
great courtesy and discretion. If the young man wishes
to come, depend upon it he will deem the invitation strong

enough ; if he does not, perhaps it will be for the best ! '

' For the best ! '

' Even so, my bairn. A wealthy young Englishman is hardly the sort of companion I should choose for either of us two ! '

But Mina thought differently.

She felt that it would be pleasant to feel the young stranger's presence in her uncle's lonely dwelling, even though it should come like a ray of sunlight to brighten and fade. But she spoke of him no more.

Meanwhile Lawrance, strolling about the heather before his door, was thinking over the invitation which Mina had given him, and wondering how soon it would be polite for him to take her at her word.

' I confess,' he said to himself, ' I should like to see my mysterious heroine at home—and had she infused anything like warmth into the invitation I should have thought nothing of strolling over to-day; but she gave it so coldly —and had I not almost asked for it I don't believe she would have given it at all. Well, after all, it does not matter. These sort of people don't stand upon ceremony. And they would not be very much surprised if I did stroll over. Calum,' he added, as the old seaman suddenly appeared, ' which is the clergyman's house ? '

' I dinna ken the exact road till it, sir ; but it lies in that direction, somewhere among the trees. Will you be going out in the boat to-day, sir ? '

' No—yes. Go into the kitchen ; I'll let you know in a few minutes' time.'

With a respectful pull at his forelock Calum walked off, and Lawrance recommenced his meditative stroll. The result of his meditations was that he did go for a boating excursion, but so little interested was he that by three o'clock in the afternoon his boat lay upon the beach, and he himself was striding rapidly over the hills towards the manse.

Seen by daylight it was a small two-storied house with a slated roof and white-washed walls. Its face was turned seaward, while beside it arose a few straggling trees. It was surrounded by the rough heather-clad hill—indeed wild grass and heather grew up to the very threshold; its size and its slated roof only distinguished it outwardly from the huts of the people who lived in the clachan. But inside it was comfortable enough.

Lawrance having searched the door in vain for a knocker, rapped smartly with his knuckles, and was thereupon admitted by an old woman, dressed with studied neatness and cleanliness, who evidently spoke nothing but the Gaelic tongue. She soon understood the stranger's errand, however, and, having courteously admitted him, conducted him along a narrow passage, and ushered him into what was evidently the only sitting-room, except the great cosy kitchen, which the house contained.

A square, lofty room, which afforded a striking contrast to the outside aspect of the building. Its floor was covered with a carpet which, if worn here and there into threadbare patches, was warm and comfortable to the tread, its walls adorned with row upon row of quaintly-bound volumes, curious old maps, treasured manuscripts, brown and yellow with age, while over the chimney-piece hung portraits of the master's literary gods. In one corner stood a curiously carved ebony writing-desk, which was covered with manuscripts and books of reference of every kind; and presiding over this was a statuette of Sir Walter Scott caressing his favourite hound.

Having in one quick glance around the room noted all this, Lawrance stood for a moment completely amazed. Had the old servant conducted him to a room which smelt of tarpaulin, and was littered with rope-ends, he would not have been surprised. The picture would have been all in keeping with the girl who steered his yacht through half a gale of wind, and afterwards appeared upon the sea-shore to protect the life of a seal; but that he should find her buried deep in the dusty recesses of learning seemed strange indeed.

A still greater surprise was in store for him. His eyes having swept the room, returned to the hearth, and remained fixed upon two figures who were seated there. The first, the clergyman himself, habited in clerical clothes, which were quite rusty with age ; the second, a young girl, who, standing gravely before the priest, was reading aloud some easy Latin prose. It was Mina, but how changed ! No longer the child of the elements, but a tall, grave, thoughtful student, habited in a plain, tightly-fitting home-spun dress, and with neatly braided hair. She read in a low, sweetly-modulated voice, glancing now and again into the grave face of her pastor as if for his approbation.

It was during one of these glances that her eyes met the wandering gaze of the stranger, who having approached noiselessly, now stood in hesitation at the door, and she lowered her book and blushed.

The minister, whose back was towards the door, had not perceived the visitor, but he noticed the hesitation of the girl.

'Go on, Mina,' he said quietly. 'You make slow progress in the Latin, my bairn, and must devote more time to the grammar.'

But instead of proceeding with her work, the girl reso-lutely closed her book, and holding forth her hand to the still hesitating figure on the threshold, bade him welcome.

'This, uncle, is the gentleman who came up to Uribol in the little yacht,' she said quietly, as he stepped into the room.

The colour which at first suffused her face had by this time completely died away, and left her very pale, yet she looked very grave and completely at her ease.

Not so Lawrance. One surprise had followed so closely upon another, that when the courteous old clergyman arose to his full height, and fixed upon him his calm, thoughtful gaze, he stood completely dumb-stricken. He recovered himself quickly, however, and tried to speak with his usual easy grace.

'Pray do not let me disturb you,' he said ; 'with your permission I will retire, seeing that I have called at so very inopportune a time.'

The clergyman having by this time descended from his airy castle, stretched forth his hand.

'Sir,' he said, 'in Loch Uribol we can always find time to pursue our studies ; but we cannot always have the pleasure of welcoming a stranger. Mina, my bairn, we will put away our books if the gentleman will do us the honour to stay.'

Neither of the young people needed a warmer invitation. Mina was ready enough, at her uncle's words, to collect her books and lay them aside ; while Lawrance gladly took the chair which was offered him.

But very soon he began to observe that the visit was not exactly going on as he had planned. He soon recovered his presence of mind perfectly, and was able to rattle on with his usual off-handed gaiety ; but it was rather hard, he thought, to extract answers from no one but Mr. Macdonald. Nevertheless, Macdonald had strong convictions on certain subjects, and Lawrance, discovering his hobby, had been quite willing to display his stock of learning by discussion. He was glad to see the old man warm to his subject—glad to see him assume a more friendly tone towards himself when he was told that the 'wealthy' English stranger was nothing more than a simple student of the law, who had come to the Highlands for quietness and sport, and to learn something of the Ossianic tongue.

'I must confess that my affection for the language dates from the time when I heard it spoken by your niece. Her lips and voice infused into it a music which it always lacks, to my ear at least, when it is spoken by the peasantry. But, then, sir, I suppose she has learnt it from you ?'

'Yes ; Mina has had no other schoolmaster, except perhaps, Koll Nicholson—an old fisherman, who taught her how to sail a boat.'

At this direct allusion to herself, Mina, who hitherto had sat silently apart, raised her eyes and smiled.

'And Koll always says *he* was the best schoolmaster of the two !' she said.

Lawrance laughed.

'Perhaps,' he said, 'I ought to endorse the fisherman's words, since through your skill in seamanship you saved my life. And that reminds me,' he continued, slipping his hand into the side-pocket of his coat and drawing forth a small packet, 'I have never yet thanked you properly for bringing in the *Jenny*, and so getting us out of a dreadful scrape that

night; but as thanks at best are useless things, may I beg
of you to accept this?'

As he spoke he undid the paper roll after roll, and held
forth the contents to Mina.

A little drinking cup of solid silver, quaintly moulded
and worked inside with gold.

Mina looked at it, blushed, and hesitated, and Lawrance
continued:

'If you will be good enough to accept it, Miss Macdonald,
you will do me a favour, I assure you. It is a little prize
cup which was won by the *Jenny* last year; not of much
value, it is true, but the most suitable present I have to
offer you.'

And without giving her time to refuse he put the cup in
her hands.

Nevertheless, although she held it and admired it, she
could not at first be brought to look upon it as her own.
The fear of offending Lawrance ultimately won her into submission, so the cup was placed upon the ebony cabinet above
the musty manuscripts and before the statuette of Scott.

When Lawrance said good-bye, he added:

'I hope, Miss Macdonald, you will allow me one day to
show you the creature which you saved from a watery
grave!'

'Thank you,' returned Mina quietly.

'And I trust, sir,' he continued, turning to the clergyman,
'that we shall not remain strangers to one another. At
present I am staying in the Lodge which belongs to Mr.
Dougall, the agent on Arranmore.'

Mr. Macdonald bowed.

'As I disagree entirely with the factor on many subjects,
I would rather not visit at his house, but I shall be pleased
at any time to see you here.'

And with that they shook hands and parted.

When Lawrance was gone the clergyman returned to his
studies, but Mina, after watching his figure fade away, stood
looking thoughtfully for a long time at the present which he
had left.

CHAPTER XII.

MINA'S QUESTIONS.

'A WEALTHY young Englishman,' the minister had said, 'was certainly no fit companion for himself or for Mina.' Nevertheless, when the wealthy Englishman was metamorphosed into a poor student, the complexion of matters became somewhat changed. It was quite a relief for the clergyman, and he deemed it a very pleasant relief, too, to find a young man sufficiently interested in literature as to be willing to listen to long dissertations from the divine without showing impatience or unconcern.

Whenever, therefore, Lawrance chose to present himself at the manse, he was always sure of receiving a welcome— of getting a hearty handshake from the minister and a bright smile from Mina.

After the first few days Mina herself grew quite at her ease while in the company of the young Englishman. Had he been, as she at first had suspected, an aristocrat, she might have continued to regard him as a being completely outside her sphere of life; as it was, she deemed him an equal—one whom she could assist her uncle to welcome to their house and to the Highlands.

Her nervousness, therefore, completely wore away, and ere a week had passed from the day of their first meeting, she began to treat him quite like a friend.

It seemed only natural that he should drop into the parsonage of an evening, and listen quietly while she went through her lessons, conjugated Latin verbs, and read interminable Ossianic poems.

Sometimes he joined her when she was reading the Gaelic; and when there were no lessons to do, he would take her and the old man for a sail in the *Jenny*. Or sometimes Mina herself would take a walk with him up the stream to show him a pool where fish were likely to be found.

Since the unfortunate episode with Earach he had given up all thought of shooting seals.

To Lawrance this chance friendship was quite as interesting as it was to the Macdonalds, and he did not attempt to conceal from himself the fact that his pleasantest hours were spent in their company. Indeed, so lightly did the days go by, and so friendly did he become with the inmates of the manse, that he seemed to forget altogether that he was only a visitor. He was reminded of the fact by Mina.

'How long are you going to stay in Uribol?' she asked of him one evening, as the two sat alone in the old clergyman's study. After his dinner Lawrance had strolled over to the manse, and on learning that Mr. Macdonald had gone up the mountain to answer a sick call, had expressed his willingness to stay for a chat with Mina. With her usual candour Mina had consented, and had asked him into the sanctum of learning. She had seated herself at the open window to watch the hazy mist of light which was thickening about the mountain tops, and Lawrance had adopted his usual plan of walking restlessly about the room, pausing sometimes to lift and examine some well-thumbed book, or to glance carelessly at the maps upon the wall.

It was during one of these pauses, while he stood with his face raised, his hands clasped behind his back, that Mina asked the question. He turned when she did so, and smiled curiously.

'Suppose I said until I have a thorough knowledge of the Gaelic tongue? How long would you give me, Miss Macdonald?'

'Oh, a very long time. You would not be very quick at learning a language, I'm thinking.'

'I could not hope to be so quick as you, but then perhaps I have not had your advantages. It is not vouchsafed to every one to be able to steer a boat in a gale of wind, and read a page of Latin or Gaelic. Miss Macdonald, what possessed your uncle when he conceived the idea of making you such a bookworm?'

'Of educating me himself, do you mean?' answered the girl simply. 'One reason was, because he could not afford to pay folk to do it for him, and save him the trouble. The minister of Uribol has not a large income, Mr. Lawrance, and all the siller we can spare has to go to Graham.'

'To Graham?'

'Graham is my brother,'

'And he does not live here?'

'Yes, of course; this is his home.   For a long time my
uncle used to teach the two of us together, but since then
Graham has lived in the south to pass through college.   I
think he is going into the kirk.'

'Indeed!'

'I was thinking of Graham when I speired at you how
long you were likely to stay.   He has written to say that
he intends to come home before the hairst sets in, and I
was thinking it would be much pleasanter for you when he
came!'

'I know you too well, Miss Macdonald, to accuse you
of fishing for compliments,' said the young man, with a
careless laugh.   'Nevertheless, I must speak the truth,
and say that—under no circumstances whatever could my
time be more pleasantly passed!'

She laughed.

'You say that because you do not ken Graham.   Once he
came, you and he would be great friends, I am sure!'

'Is he a sportsman?'

'He used to be fond of shooting wild-fowl—he had not
permission to shoot on Arranmore.'

'Permission?   I am sure he need not wait for permission.'

She smiled and asked—

'Ah, but would Lord Arranmore say that?'

The young man flushed now, almost as deeply as she did
herself.   Turning carelessly to one of the maps, he began
to examine it carefully.

'Arranmore?' he said.   'Why, yes, of course he would.
He isn't a bad sort of fellow, I believe, in matters of that
kind!'

She was silent for a few moments; then she again turned
to her companion.

'You ken his lordship, maybe?' she asked.

'I know him a little,' he answered with a peculiar
smile.   'Well, yes, I do know him.'

'Well, sir?'

He shrugged his shoulders and again became interested in the map.

'As well,' he replied, 'as an out-at-elbow student can know a member of the aristocracy.'

'Do you like him?'

He laughed very awkwardly this time as he replied:

'My dear Miss Macdonald, if you were often to subject me to such a severe cross-examination, I should think you were practising for the bar.'

'I am interested in Lord Arranmore.'

'I thank you in his name.'

'You need not do that, Mr. Lawrance. It is not because I like him, for I do *not.*'

'But you don't know him?'

'No—there is no one in Uribol who does. He became Lord Arranmore and inherited all this land when he was twelve years old, now he is about twenty-four, and he has never once been up to see his home!'

'He may have had powerful reasons for staying away.'

'Then if he has no interest in the land he should have sold it to somebody who had. I am sure if you or any good man possessed an estate like this, you would not leave it to the care of a wicked factor like Mr. Dougall.'

The young man laughed again.

'Of course you know the saying about old maids' children and bachelors' wives, Miss Macdonald?' he said. 'Although I am fond, as you see, of visiting solitudes such as these, I might not in the character of landlord prove to be one whit better than Lord Arranmore. I suppose,' he continued, after a moment's silence, 'it would be better for you if Lord Arranmore were to come here for at least a part of every year?'

'It would be better for the poor folk,' returned Mina quietly. 'It would make no difference to us. Lord Arranmore belongs neither to our religion nor our sphere in life, therefore he could never be our friend.'

'Morally he is not one whit your superior; surely the difference of religion (if there is any, which I doubt) would not be an insuperable barrier.'

'Maybe not—still, little good ever comes from such friendship as that.'

'Then if he came he would have to shut himself up in Coreveolan Castle and lead the life of a hermit during his stay !'

She smiled brightly.

'Indeed he would not.   My uncle and I are not the only folk with whom he could forgather.   If he came to Coreveolan Castle he would have heaps of friends of his own.'

'And if he happened to see you, it would either be sailing on the sea or roaming on the sea-shore, as I first saw you. You could guide his yacht to anchor as you did mine, but you would never accord to him the happy privilege of knowing you as you are—yet you accorded that privilege to me.'

'Mr. Lawrance,' said Mina, 'you and Lord Arranmore are two different folk.   Were it not so, you would not be sitting here the now.   Do you know what my uncle said when he first heard you were going to call here ?   " For once we will bid him welcome, but remember, Mina, that a wealthy Englishman is no fit companion for you or for me." '

'He said that ?'

'Indeed, then, he did !'

'Then I am glad —very glad that——'

'That—what, sir?' she asked, as he paused in embarrassment.

'Why, that I told him so frankly that I could not boast of worldly possessions at least.   Poverty is sometimes a blessing, you see.'

Mina did not answer him.   She was gazing steadfastly at a long range of hills which, with the fading light, was fast fading away.   While her companion had been speaking she had not seen his face, but the tone of his voice had sent the hot blood mounting to her cheeks and made her heart beat quickly.   Very often while sitting at the window thus, watching the young man's slight figure pass rapidly over the hill, her unspoken thoughts had made the very admission which her companion had now put into words.   If the friendship had become a great boon to the stranger—

so great a boon as to make him thank the God who had made him poor—what had it become to Mina, she whose whole life had been spent among the fishermen of Uribol? She remembered now what a strange feeling of disappointment had filled her breast when her uncle had said, 'Remember, my bairn, a wealthy young Englishman is no fit companion for you or for me.' She remembered the revulsion which came when she learned that the stranger was comparatively poor—so poor as to throw down at once the barrier which Mina had feared would keep him from their house. But although she had felt all this, and admitted it all to herself over and over again, she had never once permitted herself the gratification of believing that her thoughts and feelings had been shared even in the remotest degree by their new acquaintance. Indeed, up till that moment her reason had told her that this friendship was to him only a means of passing away a few hours which, under ordinary circumstances, would have hung very heavy on his hands.

She had reasoned all this out again and again after she had bid her uncle good-night, and had retired to her room to sit by her window and dreamily watch the moonlight on the hills—to picture his face, recall every tone of his voice, but never once had she said to herself, 'Perhaps he is thinking of *me*—perhaps it is to see me and to talk to me that he comes so often to the manse, and not to discuss Ossianic literature with my uncle.'

We fancy that if such a thought had ever been inclined to spring up within her she had resolutely forced it away, thinking—'that is only my stupidity—it is not likely that a fine gentleman like Mr. Lawrance, who has travelled over much of the world, and seen many people, would find it a pleasure to spend evening after evening with *me*. He likes my uncle because he is learned, and a student like himself.'

But she could shut her eyes no longer; whether she would or not, the conviction suddenly forced itself upon her that hitherto she had been totally wrong. Her companion had spoken no words of love to her—he had simply said, 'Poverty is sometimes a blessing, you see;' but while saying this he had managed by the tone of his voice to imply—'because, through poverty, I have been brought near to *you.*'

Mina was not well versed in love-making—indeed, this was her first experience of anything like the tender passion at all ; nevertheless, she was not so great a novice as to betray herself altogether. Although she felt that the young man's words sent through her heart a thrill of happiness which she had never felt there before, although she felt as if an invisible hand was suddenly drawing her to his side—she commanded herself sufficiently to turn from the window and speak to him again. ·

'I am very glad,' she said, with rather more coldness than usual in her tone, 'and I am sure my uncle will be glad, to ken that we have helped to make your visit here pass pleasantly. We should not like you to carry away unpleasant thoughts of Uribol !'

Mina began the speech bravely, but ere she had ended she dwelt sadly on the words, and the corners of her mouth began to tremble. Lawrance could not see her very distinctly—only the lovely outline of her face—the rounded chin, long curved lashes, and glittering golden hair, but he heard the sweet tones of her voice tremble as she spoke. Bending his head he was about to answer her, when the two were suddenly startled by a voice replying from without :

'And who is this that is going away, Mina ?'

It was the clergyman who spoke. As he uttered the words his tall form emerged from the protecting shades of the twilight, wrapped in his long priestly coat, and with the broad-brimmed hat to shade his eyes. His trousers were rolled up above his ankles, and his thick-soled, laced boots were black with mud.

'You have had an unpleasant walk, I fear,' said Lawrance, after he had been warmly shaken by the hand, while Mina asked, as she took his hat and stick and unwound the muffler from his throat :

'How did you find old Donald, uncle ?'

'Badly, Mina, badly,' returned the minister, 'and as much in need of the butcher as the doctor, my bairn. For weeks he has been kept alive on the drops of milk they get from the cow, but last week that scoundrel of a factor went to the hut with two of his men and seized the cow because they couldn't pay the rent—said his lordship advised him to give short shrift, since indulgence did not pay—that he himself was in want of money for his travels, and must get the rents of Uribol.'

'He said that?' interposed Lawrance hotly; 'then the man must be a scoundrelly liar!'

The clergyman looked quietly into the young man's flushed face.

'I am afraid,' he said, 'that the factor knows Lord Arranmore better than we do. He would not dare to act as he does, in opposition to his lordship's will. At any rate, if Lord Arranmore is kept in ignorance of individual acts such as this, he is greatly to blame for remaining absent for so many years, and leaving the entire management of his estate in the hands of such a man as Mr. Dougall.'

'He may not know the man's character.'

'Then it is clearly his duty to become acquainted with it —to see for himself the kind of thing which takes place on his land, to stop this wholesale murder!'

'Murder!' exclaimed Lawrance.

'What else do you call it, sir, when the only drop of sustenance is taken from the lips of a dying man?'

'But I will see that the factor restores the cow. I will not permit such things to be!'

The clergyman smiled.

'If you were Lord Arranmore you would, of course, succeed in your mission—as you are not, you will assuredly fail.'

Lawrance bit his lips.

'You think so,' he said. 'Then perhaps I had better not try. At any rate, no man can hinder me from giving the poor creature some assistance from my own pocket. I have a dislike to visiting such cases myself,' he added, 'but if you would use this for the poor creature's benefit, you would do me a great favour.'

He held forth a couple of sovereigns, which, after a while, the clergyman was persuaded to accept.

'If there are any other cases which I could assist I hope

you will not be reluctant in telling me of them,' said Law-rance. 'Of course,' he added quickly, noting perhaps a look of surprise on the clergyman's grave face, 'I am not a rich man, but I have managed to save a little, and to what better purpose could my savings be applied than in assisting the unfortunate?'

Then in order to avoid being thanked for his generosity, he quickly turned the conversation into other channels.

Presently he rose to go.

As he shook hands with Mina at the door, he said—

'You will not forget, Miss Macdonald, our engagement for to-morrow?'

'Our engagement?'

'Yes; is it possible you have forgotten? To-morrow is the day on which you were good enough to say you would show me over Coreveolan Castle.'

'Oh yes, I did say so.'

The admission was made so coolly, it induced Lawrance to say, with very much the air of a man who had received an injury:

'If you would rather not carry out the compact, you know, perhaps I had better go alone.'

Mina's cheek flushed, and a half-reproachful look forced itself into her eyes as she looked up into the young man's face.

'Indeed, I shall be very glad to go, if you still care about it. Koll Nicholson will take us in the lug-sail boat as far as Bara Point, and it will be quite easy to walk from there.'

'Very well, then; if the day is fine I will come over as soon after breakfast as I can.'

As he spoke he took her hand, and Mina felt, or thought she felt, that he gave it a warm pressure. At any rate, the handshake sent the blood rushing again to her cheeks and made her droop her eyes as she wished him 'Good-night.'

As soon as she was in her room that night Mina sat down to wonder if she had done right. Of course she had never once forgotten about the engagement; but ever since he had spoken so softly to her she had been wondering whether or not it would be right for her to go. His tone of dis-appointment decided her, and she wondered now whether or not her decision had been a wise one. She could arrive at no satisfactory conclusion that night, so she lay down to rest in a very perturbed state of mind.

In the study below the clergyman was pondering over the same theme. While the little scene was being enacted he had sat apart keenly watching the two. He had seen the light on Mina's cheek, the half-admiring, half-loving look in the young man's eyes, and as he had watched he had wondered if it was incumbent on him to interfere. But he had said nothing—and on reflection he thought that he had done well.

'Young folk are best left to themselves,' he thought; 'he's a fine young fellow, but after all he's not one whit better than Mina.'

CHAPTER XIII.

COREVEOLAN CASTLE.

AT seven o'clock the next morning Mina drew aside her window-curtain, and looked anxiously forth. What kind of weather she wanted to see she did not exactly know. She was in a mood to be piqued at anything. When, therefore, she saw that the day was fine, that the hills were bathed in sunlight, the sky was of azure blue, with no sign of clouds anywhere, she drooped the edges of her mouth in real or feigned disappointment. But the cloud was only transitory, and as it passed away it left her face as bright as the sunlit hills.

She proceeded to dress herself with unusual care. With her the process of dressing was usually a simple one. The means of self-adornment at her command were not large, and as she turned over her small stock of dresses she could find nothing more suitable for the day than the tight-fitting grey tweed which Graham had sent her from the south, and which up to that day she had carefully preserved for evening wear only. Neatly clad in this, she finally descended the stairs and found her uncle awaiting her at the breakfast-table.

F

A message had been sent to Koll Nicholson that the lug-sail boat would be required ; and when, shortly after break-fast, Mina ran down to the beach, she found it there awaiting her. Koll had been unable to come, but he had sent two stout young fishermen to do the rowing. The thought of sailing was utterly impracticable—there was not a breath of wind anywhere.

Having satisfied herself that the boating arrangement was complete, Mina was about to return to the house, when she suddenly descried the slight figure of Lawrance coming over the hill. He had evidently been to the manse, for Mina saw that he carried her cloak over his arm. He smiled and nodded when he saw Mina, and pulled off his hat.

'Who loaded you with all those things for me?' she asked, for want of something to say.

'No one; I saw them in the hall, and I appropriated them, and I have no doubt you'll bless me before the day is over. You see I don't let my experience of Highland weather count for nothing.'

Mina laughed, and said she wouldn't have given him credit for such thoughtfulness; then as the boat was ready he handed her in. It was quite a new experience for Mina to be guarded with such care. In the old times she had been accustomed to place her foot on the gunwale of the boat and spring unassisted to her seat. She prepared to do so on this occasion, but before she knew she found her hands imprisoned in those of Lawrance—his warm pressure continued until she reached her seat ; then, when all wants had been carefully attended to, Lawrance took his place by her side, and the boat pushed off.

On the night before, Mina had half-longed, half-dreaded to be with Lawrance again, but she did not find the trial after all a very hard one. The boatmen could not speak a word of English, and as Lawrance could not understand a word of Gaelic, Mina had all the conversation to herself; and long before the boat had left the manse half a mile behind, Mina had forgotten all about her nervous foreboding concerning the events of the day.

But no sooner did the keel of the boat grate upon the

shingle at Barron Point than Mina began to feel nervous again. There, close to the bow of the boat, stood Mr. Lawrance with outstretched arms, and although she protested, and asserted her ability to help herself, she had in the end to remain very submissive while he lifted her tenderly to the shore.

' It is the only thing you will allow me to do for you,' he said, ' and a very poor return it is for all that you have done for me.'

In her confusion Mina had forgotten to speak to the boatmen ; Lawrance reminded her of the fact.

' Owing to my ignorance, Miss Macdonald, I must trouble you to tell these men that, as we shall not want them again, they had better hasten home.'

' But if they do, how shall we get back?' she asked in amazement.

' If you will only leave it to me,' he returned quietly, ' I will undertake to deposit you at the manse in very good time. But we will not return by water. Although it is fine now, I am enough of a weather prophet to know that we shall have a strong breeze of wind before night, and I don't mean to run the risk of giving *you* a wetting.'

The slight emphasis on the pronoun made Mina blush again, but Lawrance did not see it. She turned to give the necessary orders to the boatmen, then when the boat pushed off she turned and walked away by Lawrance's side.

Since they left Uribol the weather had not changed. There was still no breeze blowing, and the sun still poured its warm rays upon the earth, but the sky was gradually being covered with a white, feathery film. As Lawrance looked around he felt more than ever glad that they were not going to return by sea. They had a walk of quite half an hour along a narrow footpath which was cut through luxuriant heather and curling ferns, then through a gloomy mountain-gorge, emerging from which they came into full view of Coreveolan Castle, a structure consisting of two dilapidated, round, empty towers, and one tolerably comfortable modern wing.

Lawrance paused.

' It looks passable from here,' he said, ' but I suppose the

outside of it must be the best.   For many years now the
moths and the damp must have had it all their own way.'

'You must judge it when you have seen it,' said Mina,
and she turned from her companion and led the way to the
door.

Although the Laird of Arranmore was a regular absentee
the castle had not been left to utter ruin.   Certain apartments in it had been placed at the disposal of a widow and
her daughter, who, in return for being allowed to live rent
free, readily undertook the task of seeing that every other
portion of the building, save the two towers, was kept habitable.   The castle was never open for public inspection, but,
as Mina was very well known to the people who lived in it,
she was sure of gaining admittance.

Not only did she gain admittance, but a hearty welcome,
and before she was allowed to go over the castle she and
her companion were literally forced to partake of a plain
lunch, which they were doubtless very much in need of.
So, while they ate, Mina was plied with and answered
question after question about her uncle, her home, Graham,
who was still in the south, but who was every day eagerly
longed for.   While she answered these questions, put to
her garrulously by the old dame, her companion sat quietly
eating and looking on.   When they were finished the dame
put a bunch of keys in Mina's hand.

'Ye ken the way yersel', my bairn, so gang yer gait.   I
canna spare the time to come wi' ye mysel', and Maggie
must rin ower to Storport.'

In truth, the old woman had nothing whatever to do;
but, imagining as she did that Lawrance and Mina were
'courting,' she deemed it only right to leave the young folk
alone.

Quite unconscious of this, Mina took the keys and led
the way along the gloomy hall into the castle.

The rooms were numerous, but there were few good
chambers among them.   Many were unfurnished, and
appeared never to have been used at all.   The walls, moreover, showed grievous signs of damp.   But to Mina's simple
eyes the drawing-room, and another saloon adjoining, were
magnificent beyond measure.   The carpets were rolled up,

and the furniture was higgledy-piggledy; but there were gold cornices round the ceiling, and numberless mirrors on the walls to reflect her face wherever she went. In the dining-hall, an oak-panelled and fairly comfortable room, hung a number of paintings in oil, representing deceased members of the Arronmore family.

Mina thought it was this gloomy grandeur which had depressed and awed her companion. He walked from room to room with a sad, thoughtful look upon his face, though he did not seem so overwhelmed as she thought he would be by the magnificence of all he saw. When he came to the family portraits he positively laughed.

'How they frown,' he said; 'it seems to me they resent being shut up amidst all this cobwebby gloom. Well, no wonder; it would make *me* melancholy mad. Which is young Arranmore, Miss Macdonald?'

'He is not here,' returned Mina, 'but they're saying he is very like *that!*' she added, pointing to the portrait of an ill-favoured youth in uniform of the Hanoverian period, with a face and head like yellow ochre.

'Flattering to his lordship, I should say!'

'Not at all,' returned Mina simply. 'Lord Arranmore is a very braw-looking man!'

'Indeed!' returned the young man with a strange smile. 'I thought you had never seen him?'

'Neither I have, but I have heard about him,' she added quickly. '*You* ken him, sir, and you can tell me if I am right.'

'If you are right?'

'Yes. Is he bonnie—handsome, I mean?'

'Well, really, Miss Macdonald, I don't think I'm a judge of masculine beauty, but I think I can safely say he is not like *that!*'

As he spoke he strode over to a dingy grand piano, opened the lid, and ran his fingers carelessly along the rusty keys.

'It is being ruined for want of some one to play it,' he said. 'You ought to have it over at the manse.'

Mina laughed as she replied:

'And suppose we had it there, who would play it?'

' You of course ! '

' I ? I don't ken a note of music, and cannot even play by ear.'

' Then it shall remain where it is,' he said, as he dropped the lid and moved away.

In the next room Mina admired a pair of handsome fire-screens which were fastened to the chimney-piece. Lawrance immediately said :

' Take them, Miss Macdonald ; they are just what you want for your study at the manse.' Then seeing Mina looked shocked, he added : ' I'll write to Arranmore, and say *I* took them.'

As he turned it into a joke Mina laughed, and Lawrance did not again attempt to make free with the chattels of his friend.

By two o'clock their inspection of the castle was over, and Mina was beginning to wonder how they were to get back to the manse, when, to her amazement, an open dog-cart and pair came clattering up to the castle door. Law-rance had sent to Storport and ordered the vehicle, in order that they might enjoy the drive home. Mina said nothing to all this, but when he handed her in, and wrapped the rugs about her before taking his seat too, he noticed that her face was pale and rather grave.

' Is anything the matter, Miss Macdonald ? ' he asked, when the carriage was rolling on its way home.

' No. I have heard that the young laird is expected ; that is all.'

' Indeed ! And who told you that, if I may be so rude as to ask ? '

' The housekeeper at the castle. She has orders to get every room ready for use, as he will certainly be here in hairst, if not before.'

After this there was silence for a time. Lawrance's prophecy about the weather was being fulfilled : a strong breeze blew from the west, and rain was beginning to fall. Presently Lawrance spoke again :

' I thought you were anxious for Lord Arranmore to visit his home ? '

' So I was.'

'And you are not now?'

'Well, maybe I ought to be, for it will be better for all the poor folk here; but there is so much dissatisfaction in the place now that I am afraid the laird will not find his visit a pleasant one; and my uncle is on the side of the tenants.'

'He will act according to his convictions.'

'Of course, sir; but his convictions might force him to oppose the laird, and it would be very hard for us to live in Uribol if Lord Arranmore became our enemy.'

'If that is what troubles you, then set your mind at rest.'

Mina raised her eyes to his. She was astonished at the grave look in his face. She opened her lips to answer him, when he spoke again.

'So long as I have life and influence,' he said, 'believe me, Lord Arranmore shall never bring harm to you or yours.'

'Mr. Lawrance,' she answered quietly, 'you cannot know what you are saying, sir.'

'Yes, I know what I am saying—I do not speak rashly, Mina. *May* I call you Mina?'

'Oh yes.'

'Well, since that day when I first met you I have found in this lonely place such happiness as I had formerly searched the world for. You saved my life once. I only ask you now to serve me a little more.'

'What can I do for you?' she asked, with trembling lips.

'*Trust* me, Mina! Put your hand in mine, and say, "I will have implicit faith—I will"'——

Mina heard no more; her heart was throbbing wildly—her cheeks were crimson. She could not answer him, but she timidly reached forth her hands and put them into his own. Lawrance raised them to his lips, and imprinted upon the fingers one long kiss.

When the carriage drew up at the door of the manse there was a half gale blowing, and the rain had ceased to fall. Lawrance alighted and lifted out Mina. As she stood inside the doorway she saw him lift his hat to her as the carriage bore him away.

Throwing off her hat in the hall, and running to the

study, she threw her arms around her uncle's neck and kissed him. At this sudden exhibition of feeling the old clergyman looked up astonished.

'Why, Mina, my bairn, what ails you?' he asked.

'Nothing, uncle—nothing at all—only I have had such a happy day.'

CHAPTER XIV.

GRAHAM COMES HOME.

SIX weeks after the scene described in our last chapter, the members of a shooting-party were taking their noonday rest among the mountains immediately surrounding Coreveolan Castle.

'Gott bless my soul, Miss Sedley, you hafe come like an angel from de skies!' said Baron Bromsen, a little black-eyed, white-haired sportsman, as he sank with an exhausted sigh in the long heather, and gazed up with a feeble smile. 'Tamnation to these Scotch hills, say I; we hafe been scrambling up them, and scrambling down them, until I hafe no scramble left!'

His shooting companion, a swarthy gentleman, also advanced in years, laughed as he took his seat on the heather close to the cloth which a dark-eyed young lady, elegantly attired, was spreading out for lunch.

'You look pretty well played out, baron,' he said. 'It strikes me we were both on the point of giving way when we saw the baskets appear. It was a deuced good idea of Ethel's to bring us a little lunch during our first day on the moor.'

'Goot!' echoed the baron, who had by this time somewhat recovered his breath and his colour—'it was superb —it was sublime!—but she is always so. As I say, she is like an angel which drops from de skies!'

The other sportsman, who, possibly because the young lady was his daughter, seemed less inclined for rhapsodies than his friend, merely nodded his head and said:

'Yes, baron, you're right; Ethel's a good little girl when she likes.'

Meanwhile the subject of these compliments continued her work as if she did not hear a word. She deftly spread the white cloth upon the heather, emptied the baskets which had been brought with her, poured out the wine for her father and his friend, and when they were both busily employed with their knives and forks, she too sat down amongst the heather, opened her parasol, and indolently looked on.

'You need not be so free with your compliments, baron,' she now said. 'I brought you some luncheon to-day, because—well, because I felt so dreadfully bored, and I couldn't think of anything else to do!'

Then, turning to her father, she added:

'I can't imagine what induced you to come to this outlandish place!'

'To shoot de grouse, to be sure; and a very good shooting it is,' said the baron, with a grin. He had imbibed a couple of glasses of champagne, and disposed of a goodly portion of game-pie, and he began to think that to make one of a shooting-party, even on the remote Highlands, was not a bad way of amusing one's self after all.

'Ay, yes, of course,' returned Ethel with a smile, 'you have the shooting, but what have I?'

'De scenery,' said the baron, with a majestic wave of his hand, 'and a very good scenery too—look and say if it is not so?'

The girl smiled again, and throwing herself back, with the palm of her right hand pressed on the ground and supporting her, she gave an indolent glance at the wild prospect which surrounded them.

'Yes,' she said drily, 'I have the scenery, and I suppose that ought to satisfy me, but somehow it doesn't. At first I amused myself by visiting the peculiar-looking huts and studying the natives, but in two days I have exhausted all the amusements of that kind, and now I've nothing left. Heigh-ho! I wish we had gone on the Continent, or re-visited some of those pretty little German towns.'

'Don't be a fool, Ethel,' returned her father, leaning

affectionately towards her, and speaking so low that the attendants who were squatting around on the heather could not hear. 'We went on the Continent last year and found it a bore. You must be patient. In another week or two his lordship will be here, and then I suppose you will be contented.'

'Yees,' put in the baron with a grin, 'and if it comes to dat, Miss Sedley might take to some sort of shooting too.'

Ethel frowned.

'But in the meantime,' she said, 'I must content myself with superintending the removal of the empty plates—not a very entertaining occupation, I should have thought a month ago, but really quite a blessing up here in the Highlands.'

As she ceased speaking another sound struck upon the ears of the little party, causing them to start in wonder. The sound was a shriek of mingled fierceness, horror, and fear, and, looking up, they saw that it came from a figure which stood upon the brow of a hill just behind them—the figure of a man, who, to their unaccustomed eyes, looked as if he had just escaped from Bedlam. His dirty brown kilt exposed a pair of huge horny knees, which were tanned like a cow-hide; a mass of fiery red hair shot up from his head like the bristles on a hedgehog's back. He had a game-bag slung across his shoulders, and his long, thin arms flourished about, like the arms of a windmill, waving a Highland cap.

He uttered the shriek; then, before the party had time to recover from their surprise, came racing wildly down the hill, then, having reached the party so comfortably encamped at the foot, he began gibbering, shrieking, panting, and capering about. In fact, he imitated very well the mad antics of an angry sheep-dog baying at a flock of sheep.

But it must not be supposed that he was long allowed to remain in sole possession of the field. No sooner did he make his appearance at the foot of the hill than the two Highland gillies, who had been in attendance on the gentlemen that morning, and the sturdy Highlander who had escorted Miss Sedley over the hills, jumped nimbly to their feet, and attacked him with such a ferocious volley of words as almost took away his breath. Little Baron Bromsen, who could never keep cool when a dispute was going on, joined heartily in, heaping upon each one indiscriminately such a medley of broken English and German as would have staggered any cooler men.

Meanwhile Sir Charles Sedley and his daughter, the sole rational beings of the party, had remained coolly looking on, the former from indolence, the latter from amusement; the fiercer grew the tones of the combatants, the wilder their gestures, the more Ethel laughed, but Sir Charles Sedley at length thought it prudent to interfere.

'Baron,' he said, seizing the little man by the shoulder, 'why the deuce can't you keep cool?' Then turning to the fierce invader, he added, 'It seems to me, my man, you're either a madman or a fool, and the sooner you make off the better.'

Then he addressed his own servants and asked, 'What the devil is the idiot raving about?'

'He was asking,' returned one of the gillies quietly, 'if we didna ken that we had crossed the mearn.'

'Well, it seems to me,' returned the baronet, with an indolent smile, 'that he needn't have wasted so much exercise in asking that.' Then, turning again to the frantic Highlander, he asked, 'Suppose we *have* crossed the boundaries, what's that got to do with you?'

'What is that to *me!*' returned the man, speaking for the first time in English. 'Is not this the land of the Macpherson of Pherson?—am I not the gamekeeper of the Macpherson of Pherson?—and is it right that the land of Macpherson of Pherson should be trespassed upon at all, at all?'

'Bosh,' said Sir Charles coolly. 'What harm have we done the moor by having our lunch beside the brook? Ethel,' he continued, turning to his daughter, 'you're the culprit, remember—you found out the shady nook, so you'll have to make our apologies to the Macpherson; but it strikes me,' he added, with a laugh, 'that if the Macpherson, whoever he is, were here, he wouldn't turn out to be such a fool as his keeper.'

'You are right, sir,' returned a voice, and every member

of the little party knew that another individual had joined in the discussion.

At the sound of the voice all eyes were instantly turned upon the new-comer, who for the last minute or two had commanded the undivided attention of Miss Sedley alone. He was a tall, muscular young man of about five-and-twenty, who wore the English costume, and carried a thick shepherd's stick in his hand. Behind him stood a fisher lad, carrying a small portmanteau and leading a rough deerhound.

The moment the young man spoke, the Highlander, who had described himself as one of the Macpherson's keepers, uttered a yell of delight, and seizing him by the hand, wrung it wildly, and burst into a torrent of Gaelic, evidently a sort of Highland welcome. The young man laughed good-humouredly, and clapped him on the shoulder; then said a word or two in Gaelic, upon which the keeper drew back.

Turning again, the young man regarded the shooting-party with a gloomy smile; his eyes suddenly meeting those of Miss Sedley, he courteously removed his hat; then turning towards her father, he said:

'Pray do not disturb yourself.' As no one seemed inclined to answer him he continued, 'If you find this spot more pleasant than elsewhere, I am sure you would be welcome to stay. Donald here is a little over-zealous, and forgets the respect due to strangers.'

'May I ask your name, sir, and whether you are a native of these parts?'

'My name is Macdonald,' answered the young man quietly; 'and I have just come from the south. The steamer's small boat landed me off the headland yonder, and I was making my way across the hills.'

Here the gamekeeper broke in eagerly in English.

'O Master Graham! it is wild Miss Mina will be to see you come hame! and it is wild all the folk in Uribol will be this night!'

And again he wrung the young man's hand, and burst into Gaelic. Just then Sir Charles Sedley rose to his feet and took up his gun.

'Now we've finished our luncheon, I think we had better be on the move again. We were just thinking about going when your countryman here came down like a maniac and attacked us.'

'I am very sorry,' returned the young man gravely.

'Oh, not at all—no need to apologise for him; it's my daughter who ought to apologise to the Macpherson. She brought up the luncheon, and found out the place, and made us camp here, and deuced pleasant it's been,' continued the baronet, looking at his watch, 'for the time has flown. Good afternoon, sir. Come along, baron. Ethel, my dear, you'll have to find your way back to the castle as you came.'

Before the young lady could protest, the baronet had walked off, dragging the somewhat unwilling baron in his wake, and nodding to the gillies to follow.

Being thus so unceremoniously left to themselves, the young people did not know very well what to do. Macdonald, undecided whether to walk off or remain, adopted the latter course from sheer embarrassment. Accordingly he stood looking confusedly, and somewhat sullenly, at Miss Sedley; while she, with all the *sang froid* in the world, gravely ordered her attendant to pack up the empty plates and glasses, and carry them quickly home.

When this was done, and she was about to depart, she suddenly seemed to remember that she was not alone. For the first time she looked full in the young man's face and smiled.

'Are you waiting for me to cross the boundaries, sir?' she asked; then she added quickly, noting the grave look on the young man's face : 'Perhaps the best reparation I can make is to leave the forbidden spot at once. Good-day.'

She bowed her head, and was about to pass on, when Macdonald stopped her.

'I beg your pardon; I have no more to do with the land than yourself. The fact is, I was rude, and was wondering to see strange folk on these hills.'

'Indeed?'

'It is not often we see strange faces here. May I ask your name, madam?'

'Mine? Oh, my name is Miss Sedley; that gentleman

who spoke to you is my father; the other is his friend,
Baron Bromsen; and we live in the castle over yonder on
the hill-side.'

'Then I think we have met before,' said Graham.   'Do
you know Lady Murray?'

'Of Edinburgh?   Oh yes—the queer old Highland lady
who takes "sneesh," as she calls it, and talks as broad as a
spade.   Perhaps I saw you at her house?'

'I think so.   I—I have a good memory for faces.   Lady
Murray is a distant kinswoman of my own.'

'Indeed?' murmured Ethel with a shrug.

'Yes,' said the young man.   'But I see you are in haste,
and I will not detain you.   Good-day.'

And before she could say another word he lifted his hat
and strode away.

The fisher boy, as if catching the reflection of his mood,
walked behind him with hanging head, while beside him
strolled the keeper, still casting reproachful glances back at
the figures who had thus openly dared to trespass on his
master's ground.   For some time the young man walked
on, silent and thoughtful; at length he paused upon the
brow of a hill, sank down among the heather, and gazed at
the prospect which opened up around him.   Not critically
or with surprise, for he knew every varying look of the
landscape by heart.

It was a scene, nevertheless, which it would be difficult
to match even in Scotland for combined splendour and
terror of natural effect.   Far below him, creeping in in one
long, glimmering arm through the heart of the hills, now hidden by heathery promontories, now stretching out into broad
and glistening bays, lay Loch Siloart, and in one of its most
sheltered creeks, on the very edge of the strand, lay a white
shooting-lodge.   Far away at the mouth of the loch, beyond
the lodge, a red-sailed fishing-smack was becalmed on a patch
of perfect blue.   On either side of the fjord the hills were
low, and covered with heather from base to summit.   But
as the arm of the sea crept inland the hills grew wilder and
steeper, till, above its furthest extremity, there rose a range
of livid mountains stretching in jagged lines against the
faint pink sky.   These mountains dominated the entire

scene. The purple heather clung around their base, but from centre to peak they were sheer scalps of naked volcanic stone. In the calm light of the autumn afternoon they looked almost soft and still, and on the horn of the highest, Ben Glamaig, one bright silvern star was beginning to glimmer: but their general aspect, and the tone they gave to the entire scene, was one of utter silence and desolation.

For some time Macdonald remained moveless, with his eyes on the sea far beneath him. Presently his attention was attracted to the shooting-party, which was slowly and laboriously ranging the heathery slopes below; now pausing, as a dog stood stiff and silent in advance of the party; now firing, with a sharp sound soon swallowed up in the mountain silence, and leaving a tiny wreath of smoke to ascend and join the faint white wreaths which circled round the hill-tops.

A somewhat contemptuous smile passed over the young Highlander's face as he beckoned his wild acquaintance to him.

'Do you ken those folk, Donald?' he said in Gaelic. 'How long have they been at the castle?'

'They will have been at the castle since a week,' answered the keeper; and he continued garrulously, 'They will be saying he is vera rich, and that his companions are vera rich, and that the leddy is a great leddy; but for all that they had no right to cross the mearns. And with my own een I saw them find a pack on the Macpherson's ground, and when they fired only one bird fell, and it was a grey hen, and the Macpherson doesna shoot the grey hens; and a snipe got up under the wee fat man's nose, and when he missed it he began to sweer.'

'Have they rented Sloachan Forest as well as Muir o' Lairg?' asked Macdonald impatiently. 'I never heard that it was let.'

'Na, it isna set, for these English will only shoot the grouse, and indeed it would be a peety to let them disturb the deer.'

And with a sort of sovereign contempt the keeper gazed down on the party, who were now making the welkin ring

with shouts.   One of the dogs was in wild pursuit of a hare,
and the baron, with his hat off, was yelling and gesticulating
wildly.   The deerhound pricked up his ears, and seemed
about to spring away, when a sharp word from his master
restrained him.

The same supercilious smile, expressive of much the same
contempt as that felt by his attendant, passed across the
young man's face.

'If you are going down to the clachan,' he said, 'see if
Rone, the smith, has finished the lock of my rifle; I left it
with him when I went away: if so, bring it with you.   Take
Shon with you; I shall cross the hill.'

A minute later the keeper took a path down the hill-side,
followed by the fisher-boy and the dog; Macdonald passed
slowly upward.

His face was languid, and his appearance was that of
a man in a brown study.   At every step he took the
heather grew more and more scanty, the hill more stony
and bare.

'What has come o'er me, I wonder?   Is it that English
lassie's face?'

His own fair face took a heightened colour as he uttered
the surmise.   As if impatient with himself he strode on.
But his thoughts still flowed in the same current.

'Curious folk, not unlike many of these sporting English;
but the lassie is something different.   What eyes she has!
great black piercing eyes, such as one does not often see in
the north.   And her shape—as lithe and graceful as a red
deer's—a proud little devil, I should say!   She looked me
from top to toe as if I were of no more account than
Donald, or one of their own gillies!'

Thus thinking, and sometimes muttering to himself, he
reached the hill-top, and passing rapidly along the summit,
soon found himself upon another and wilder mountain,
rising precipitously as if into the very sky.   It seemed a
terrible ascent, but following a track evidently well known
to him, he mastered it with careless ease.   Nothing but
rocks and boulders stretched on every side.   The heat was
intense, though every crag and peak was now crimson with
the setting sun.   And now at last he saw far below the

waters of Loch Uribol, and in one green spot the clachan, with its white lodge—the house of the village pastor.

For a few moments he rested upon the brow of the mountain, gazing at the clachan below, then he rapidly descended.

The sun was setting as he entered the village, and walked with long, swift strides towards the lodge. As he drew near he saw that the door was open, and that a figure sat on a stool close beside it.

The figure was that of a young man, no other indeed than Mr. Lawrance, who, dressed in his loose shooting-suit, was lazily sorting some fishing-tackle which he held in his hand. Macdonald paused in wonder; as he did so, Lawrance raised his head, and the young men regarded each other with a steadfast stare.

Neither spoke. The sullen look—half of wonder, half of resentment—deepened on Macdonald's face, while Lawrance's animated features soon broke into an amused smile.

'Who is this?' he seemed to say: 'and by what right does he seem to question my presence here?'

Suddenly, and before either could say a word, there was an unlooked-for interruption. Lawrance was startled by a glad cry which came from the window of the house. The next moment he was amazed to see Mina rush eagerly forth and throw her arms around the neck of her brother.

CHAPTER XV.

BY THE FIRESIDE.

SEVERAL hours later, when the village lay enshrouded in darkness, a happy party gathered in the great kitchen at the manse. Mr. Macdonald sat in the ingle quietly smoking his pipe, Lawrance had ensconced himself close by, while near them sat Mina, her face turned towards her brother Graham, her lips questioning him minutely as to his doings since he went away.

During the last few hours Graham had gone through so

much exertion, both mental and physical, that he seemed now utterly disinclined for intercourse of any kind. The news of his arrival had spread like lightning, and very soon the cottage had been besieged by wild figures innumerable who had come to give him a welcome home. Under this benign influence the sullen expression which had at first darkened his face gradually wore away. He had cheerfully complimented Angus, who was still in the village, on the good looks of his canine family; he had run down to the beach to see Shamus Beg's new fishing skiff; he had explained to some of the croft-holders the kind of machines which were used for tilling the land in the south; and last, though not least, he had made old Koll Nicholson happy by promising to go with him on the following day to fish some of the best pools in the broad burn which runs through Coreveolan.

But when at length the cottage was still again, when darkness had driven the people to their homes, and Graham found himself seated quietly in the great kitchen with Mina by his side, the sullen look began to cloud his features again, and as he glanced from time to time at the young man who sat so coolly in the shadow, it deepened more and more. He evidently looked upon him as an unwelcome intruder—a sort of cloud on the happiness of the family circle—and though Mina had hurriedly explained that Lawrance was a stranger—a student like himself, who had been made welcome by her uncle, and who had Lord Arranmore's permission to do as he chose in the place— the explanation did not break down the barrier which had at first kept them apart.

So Graham sat grimly tolerant, answering Mina's questions in monosyllables, and glancing from time to time across at the stranger.

'How long do you intend to stay, Graham?' asked Mr. Macdonald at length, and Graham answered quietly:

'Till hairst only. Then I must go south for a month.'

'And when you come home again,' interposed Mina quickly, 'you must let us ken some time before. Then we will have a welcome for you. We will have a fire lit on the topmost peak of Benveolan, and Koll Nicholson's smack will go to Storport to bring you in, and Shamus Beg will bring out his pipes to play you a welcome.'

'Or, if *I* am here,' put in Lawrance, 'I shall be most happy to put the *Jenny* at your service. She is not a first-rate yacht, as you know, Miss Macdonald, but she would be more suitable for your brother to return in than old Nicholson's smack.'

Graham laughed uneasily, then his cheek flushed as he glanced towards Lawrance's shrouded face.

'Thanks, Mina,' he said ; 'but if it is all the same to you, I would rather not be made to look like a gowk. Such exhibitions might have suited the days when there were Highland chieftains to welcome home ; they are out of date now. A pretty figure I should have looked to-day stalking over the hills with a ragged army of croft-holders behind me, and a ragged piper before, especially in the eyes of the fine party who were bivouacking on the hills !'

'Who were *they*, Graham ?' asked Mr. Macdonald.

The young man shrugged his shoulders.

'I cannot tell ; strangers, I should fancy ; at least they were strangers to me, but you may know of them. Donald attacked them as if they had been pickpockets, for the gentlemen were shooting on Lord Arranmore's land, and had trespassed on the ground of the Macpherson.'

Up to this point Lawrance, as we have said, had sat apart, content for once to be dropped out of the family circle, to loll in his easy chair, smoke his cigar, and listen indolently, but with little interest, to the conversation which was being carried on, but suddenly he raised himself, and, looking at Graham, asked quietly :

'Strange gentlemen, did you say, shooting on my land ?'

'I beg your pardon,' returned Graham quietly ; 'I said they were on Lord Arranmore's.'

Lawrance laughed lightly, and leaving his chair, took up his position on the hearthstone, with his back to the fire. His face was still in shadow, but the faces of the others were in bright light.

'Thank you,' he returned. 'I should have said Lord Arranmore's land ; but you see I have an easy way of assuming proprietorship of my friend's goods. The fact is,

I have had such unlimited sway since I came here, that I
sometimes feel as if the land were my own.'

'What like were the strangers, Graham?' asked Mina.

She was more interested in them than in the fact that
Lawrance had by a slip of the tongue laid claim to the
Arranmore estates.

'Don't you know?' said Graham astonished. 'Indeed,
Mina, I took small heed of them. The lady told me their
names, but I forget them ; but I know there was an old
gentleman who had a gun, two gillies, several dogs, and a
foreigner, who was making noise enough to disturb all the
game lying between this and Benveolan!'

'It is very strange we have never seem them!' continued
Mina. 'I'm wondering who they can be!' Then, turning
to Lawrance with a smile, she added : 'Maybe, sir, now
you have set the fashion, we shall have plenty of visitors to
Uribol.'

At this prophecy Lawrance did not look over well
pleased.

'When I came here,' he said, sweeping his eyes carelessly
over each of the three faces before him, 'I was under the
impression that Loch Uribol did not see a strange countenance more than about once in a quarter of a century.'

'And in a measure you were right,' returned Mr. Macdonald. 'It is not a place affording much attraction to
tourists, and those who would have cared to visit it could
find no accommodation. These strangers, whoever they are,
cannot be residents here, unless, indeed, they are the shooting tenants of Castle Coreveolan.'

'That is probable,' said Lawrance quietly.

'Perhaps,' continued Mr. Macdonald, 'they are the
people who have bought the Coreveolan estates. I know
they changed hands several months ago, and what is more
likely than that the new purchaser should wish to visit his
property in person? I am thankful to say that all Highland
lairds are not as careless over their property as the young
Lord of Arranmore.'

As the minister finished speaking, Lawrance shot one
swift, keen glance into his face, then with a yawn he threw
himself into his chair again.

'Well, whoever they are, I hope they won't interfere with my amusements,' he said, 'and then good luck attend them, say I. Mr. Macdonald, may I offer you the "pipe of peace" before I take my leave?'

As he spoke he drew forth a cigar-case, opened it, and held it towards Graham. The movement was so sudden and unexpected that for the moment Graham was taken aback. He hesitated, then after an appealing look from Mina he stretched forth his hand and took a cigar.

'Thanks,' he said sullenly, 'but as I'm o'er tired to smoke to-night, I'll keep it till another day.'

And he put it on the table behind him.

As Lawrance handed a cigar to the minister, and took one for himself, he shrugged his shoulders and smiled.

'All right,' he returned carelessly; 'please yourself and you will please me. I hope we shall continue to be good friends, for I perceive with pleasure that our tastes harmonise tolerably well. You will be beating the hills yourself, I presume. I am sure,' he added quickly, 'my friend Arranmore, who is not a bad fellow at heart, would not in the least object if *you* were to make a little free with his game.'

'But I should prefer before I did so to ask his lordship's permission!'

'Not in the least necessary, I assure you,' returned Lawrance. 'I will make my permission do duty for both!'

As this speech called for no actual reply, Graham gave none, and Lawrance, perhaps feeling the silence which followed a little irksome, politely took his leave.

'The sullen young cub,' he said to himself as soon as he was alone; 'if I had my will, I would have him whipped into good behaviour!'

For several hours after he had gone, the little party sat in the kitchen talking over old times. After the minister had retired, Mina sat for a while with her brother alone.

Presently she asked, glancing half timidly in his face:

'Well, Graham, what do you think of him?'

'Of whom, Mina?'

'Of Mr. Lawrance—the gentleman who was here to-night.'

In a moment all the brightness faded from Graham's countenance. He answered her question by another.

'How long have you kenned him, Mina?'

'For several weeks. He is a college friend of the young laird, and he is allowed to do whatever he wishes on the land!'

Graham said no more, but as he was leaving the room his eye fell upon the cigar which Lawrance had handed him. He threw it into the fire.

CHAPTER XVI.

KOLL.

By six o'clock the next morning most of the members of the minister's little household were astir. Graham was the last to appear. During his sojourn in the south he had cast off, with many other of his Highland accomplishments, the habit of early rising, so when the breakfast was quite cold he came down looking only half refreshed.

'You have been studying o'er hard, Graham!' said Mina, looking affectionately at his pale cheeks. 'The fresh air of Uribol will do you good; it was well for you that you came home.'

'Yes,' said the clergyman quietly, 'it is not good for a young fellow like Graham to dwell so long in the smoky south!'

Graham only laughed; and taking his seat with them at the table, soon turned the conversation into other channels.

The meal was hurried over, for the minister had to attend a sick call, and Graham proposed that he and Mina should run down the coast to Koll Nicholson's hut, and pay the old man a visit. To this Mina readily consented, and as soon as their uncle had departed Graham and his sister set off. Mina had not seen her brother for more than three years, and the little shyness of her first meeting with him having by this time completely worn away, she found that she had a hundred things to say. So, as they walked over the hill in the glorious sunshine, she held his hand and chattered away freely; and when they were on the sea he made her sit in the stern of the boat and let him row her—while he in his turn told her of the wonderful things which he had seen in the south. But neither of them mentioned Lawrance. Mina often thought of him, but somehow she felt instinctively that the mention of the name was not calculated to bring the brightness into her brother's face.

After about half-an-hour's swift rowing Graham suddenly turned the boat and ran it ashore, and on Mina springing lightly out, he fastened the painter around a huge boulder which lay half-embedded in the sand. Then the two turned their steps towards a hut which stood upon the beach in the shadow of an overhanging crag. The oval roof of this strangely situated dwelling was formed of the upturned hull of an old fishing smack, while the walls were fashioned of loose pieces of rock and stones which had evidently been collected from the shore. About it, in time of storm, the salt sea-spray was wafted; around it the sea-weed clung; on the rocks near it the cormorants swarmed and the sea-gulls screamed; here and there about the weed-covered crags the sea-pie flashed, while far away to sea the gannet shot like a stone upon his prey. But now, save for the low, monotonous sighing of the waves upon the shore, all was still as death. The sun-rays beat fiercely upon the glittering sea, the purple hills, the jagged cliffs; and all the living things in the water and on the land lifted their eyes to the bright smiling of the summer sky.

A hundred yards from the shore a great fishing smack lay at anchor, with her red sails outspread upon the deck, her shadow dancing in the water below her, while on the shore, right opposite the hut, a rough punt lay secured by a strong rope to the grapnel which lay embedded in the sand.

With a gentle motion of her hand, and one finger laid upon her lips in token of silence, Mina motioned her brother to keep back, while she advanced with swift and silent tread, until she stood before the half-open door of the cabin. The room which this half-open door revealed was of moderate dimensions, and in every way harmonised with the external appearance of the hut. The floor was paved with small round stones, which were carefully placed and brightly polished; dried fish, coils of rope, and fishing-lines hung from the rafters, which were black as ebony. In one corner stood a pair of rudely-made oars, and in another, carefully folded, was a red canvas lug-sail. At the upper end of the floor a small square space was left unpaved, and on this smouldered away two or three clods of peat.

The only occupant of the room was a very old man, who sat on a small stool close beside the smouldering fire, busily at work repairing great rents in an old fishing-net which was spread on the floor before him. His face, despite constant exposure to sun and wind, was of that ashen-grey hue which is usually found only on the faces of the dead. His hair, which was as white as snow, was carefully smoothed off his forehead. His eyes were sunken, and around them was a jet-black ring, which gave to his face a ghastly look. His brows were contracted into an habitual frown, and the general expression of his face was wild and sad.

His figure was big, angular, and bony. He wore a blue guernsey, which was dim with age and full of darns, and a pair of trousers made of some rough blue stuff, which looked as if it was saturated with the salt sea-spray.

Although he was seventy years of age his back was straight as an arrow, as he sat upon his stool grimly pursuing his work, and glancing up occasionally to look at the sunshine which was creeping in at his half-open door.

A shadow was flung across the floor, and quickly raising his eyes, he saw Mina standing upon the threshold of the hut. All at once the pinched face seemed to brighten, the features to expand. It was as if one waft of an invisible hand had brought a new brightness to the dim, sad eyes, a glow of colour to the faded, withered cheeks.

Then in a moment it all faded, and the old man turned his face, now greyer than ever, towards his work.

'Come in, my bairn,' he said, and as he spoke there was a querulous ring in his voice. 'Dinna stand there to keep oot the sunlight frae her; 'tis aal the brightness she has left.'

Mina ran across the floor, passed her arm round the old man's neck, and pressed her warm, red lips to his cheek.

'Don't say that, Koll,' she whispered; 'you've got *me.*'

Again that indescribable look of brightness flashed across the old man's face, and faded. When he answered her it was in the usual querulous tones.

"You!' he said; 'and what for should she count *you* ¿ Is it because you come sae often to see her?'

At this a sudden pang shot through Mina's heart.

'Indeed, I have not been often to see you lately, Koll,' she said; 'because we have had company, and I've been needed at home.' She added, smiling slyly : 'Since you do not want me now that I have come, why, I can just go home again.'

She began gently to withdraw her hand from his neck, but Koll clutched it in his, and said softly—

'Mina, ma bairn, dinna heed ta old man; sit ye down and tell her the news. She's jest a peevish old man, that should be whippit for flyting ye at aal, at aal.'

So Mina laughed and kissed the old man's cheek, then she went to the door and waved in her brother.

Koll threw aside his nets, and extended his hard horny hand to give him welcome.

'You will hae grown a praw lad,' he said, surveying him carefully from head to foot—'a praw lad indeed, but your hands are o'er white, and your cheeks is o'er white, and ye'l no ken how to sail a boat like Mina. But 'tis nae fault o yours, laddie—'tis the fault o' them wha sent you awa sooth to learn book learnin' and forget the land o' your forebears.'

Feeling rather small under all this solemn censure Graham began to tell of some of the wonders which he had seen in the south. To all this the old man listened grimly with a smile of incredulity upon his face.

Presently Graham put his hand in his pocket and pulled out a neat leathern case. Springing this open, he disco vered a prettily-carved meerschaum pipe lying upon a bed of purple velvet.

'See here, Koll,' he said, 'I brought this for *you!* 'Ti

The old man took the case, lifted the pipe carefully, and examined it.

'Twas like ye to remember auld Koll Nicholson,' he said; 'you're a goot lad and a kind lad, put dinna ask her to pelieve that this braw toy was made oot o' the flashes o' foam upon the sea!'

Graham laughed.

'You don't believe it?'

The old man gravely shook his head.

'Tis like fleeing in the face o' Got Almighty to say sic-like things!'

Mina, being afraid of an unpleasant discussion, here broke in quickly—

'Koll, are you going to Storport fair on Monday?'

'Why is it you ask, ma bairn?'

'Because I want to go, and so does Graham, and uncle'——

'And the strange shentleman,' asked Koll quietly.

Mina blushed, and turned away her head.

'If he wishes to go he has his yacht,' she returned; 'but *we* mean to go in the smack.'

As she spoke she walked towards the door. The quiet mention of Lawrance's name had made her feel rather uncomfortable, and she seemed all at once eager to bring the interview to a close. So she stood there with her face turned to the sunlit sea, and talked for a few minutes over the plan of running the smack to Storport; then with her brother she took her leave.

For a time the old man stood at the door, shading his eyes with his withered hand from the dazzling sunlight, and watched the boat as it bore the two figures away. There it went, gliding softly along the smooth surface of the fjord, but growing ever dimmer and dimmer in the dazzling sheen of light. Presently Mina waved her handkerchief, Graham waved his hat, then the boat turned a corner quickly and disappeared.

CHAPTER XVII.

THE FAIR AT STORPORT.

FIFTEEN miles from Uribol, as you sail southward along the coast, opens Loch Storport, and at the head of the loch stands the town, or village, or clachan of Storport, consisting of a public-house, a shed for dried fish, and some hundred white-washed cottages clustering round a white-washed school. Several miles in the interior are churches of various denominations—Protestant and Roman Catholic—desolate-looking edifices in the midst of a desolate country. Indeed, a more cheerless prospect than Storport, and the country surrounding it, can scarcely be conceived—a flat, green, marshy district, broken up with innumerable lakes and tarns, and rising only occasionally into small hills.

The broken-down-looking inn of Storport—a one-story edifice without 'sign' of any sort—stands at the head of a large pier or wharf, and for nine months out of ten stares with two glazed and fishy-looking eyes at the cheerless waters broken with damp green islands, projecting reefs, and floating weed. The landlord wanders away wherever business or pleasure leads him, and a dirty servant roams to and fro through rooms innocent of the taste of whisky or the smell of smoke. But suddenly in the spring of the year the fishy eyes of the inn begin to sparkle, and to blaze later on into the evening with a red and festive glare. The herring-fishers, like a swarm of locusts, have descended upon Loch Storport, and the whole district is alive with the signs of life.

The day following Graham Macdonald's return to Uribol two men sat in the dark, dusky, desolate-looking parlour of the Storport inn, sharing the contents of a gill measure of whisky, and looking out of the dingy window.

One was a little red-haired, red-faced irascible-looking person, who, though of very vulgar cut, sported a sealskin waistcoat and a massive gold chain. The other was Peter Dougall, better known as Peter-na-Croiche, or 'gallows'

Peter, the humble representative of Lord Arranmore on the estate of Uribol.

'There'll pe a heap o' folk at the fair, Mister Tougall,' observed the red-faced man, speaking English through his nose with a strong Gaelic accent, 'and a heap o' fine peasts. Will you pe for puying yoursel', Mister Tougall?'

'No a heid, no a horn, Mr. Macraw; but I'll be for *selling.* I've some yews to sell for a fair price. You shall see the peasts for yoursel'—fine cattle! praw cattle! and worth tooble the money I ask for them, if you tak' them to the sooth.'

'Hoo muckle will ye pe asking for the yews, Mister Tougall?' cried Mr. Macraw eagerly.

'How muckle? Just seeventeen sheelings, Mr. Macraw.'

'Seeventeen sheelings! That's a pig price for a yew!'

'Praw cattle!'

'Hoo mony may there pe o' them, Mister Tougall?'

'Just twa score, Mr. Macraw. You shall see them for yoursel'.'

'Mister Tougall, you're a tecent man—will you tak' fifteen sheelings and a crown over the whole twa score?'

The old man shook his head. Then ensued a fresh dialogue, very energetically sustained by the red-faced man, who at last concluded a bargain to his satisfaction, and bought the ewes at what he considered a fair price.

'And hoo's aal wi' ye at Uribol, Mr. Tougall?' he observed, drinking in a more benignant frame of mind. 'Have you had a veesit yet from the young laird?'

'No, Mr. Macraw.'

'Is it no strange that the young shentleman has never thoucht of veesiting this part of his dominions?'

'Strange! And why is it strange, Mr. Macraw?'

'Becase, sir, a shentleman would naturally tesire to look at his ain ground, and to see if it was goot ground—and if the rents was goot.'

'What do shentry ken o' these things, Mr. Macraw? Lord Arranmore is put a lad, and for all that I ken he couldna tell a pleugh frae a harrow, or a tup frae a yew.'

'That's true, Mister Tougall. Hoo old is the young laird, did you say?'

'Three or four-and-twenty, Mr. Macraw, or there-aboots.'

'Three-and-twenty, and the owner of aal that land! He's a lucky shentleman, Mr. Tougall.'

'I don't ken what you mean by lucky, Mr. Macraw, but he's a *puir* man.'

'Puir, Mr. Tougall?'

The factor nodded.

'Hoo can that pe, sir?' demanded Mr. Macraw sharply. ''Tis goot land.'

'The land's goot enough—goot enough for the Hie-lands.'

'And the rents are goot?'

'So they are, Mr. Macraw.'

'Then, what way are you telling me that the laird is poor, Mr. Tougall?'

'Because, Mr. Macraw, there's no a yaird of it, from the Point of Raw to the Sound of Coil, put should be doon in sheep; because, sir, the laird should be getting rent for every airmful of kelp that's burnt on the foreshores of the estate; because it's covered with the scum o' the earth, Mr. Macraw—lazy peasts of men and women that should pe shippit across the sea.'

'Pless me, Mr. Tougall, would ye clean awa' the popula-tion aaltogether?'

'If I had my will I would treble the rent in five years. I would have none upon the estate but the shepherds, and I wad hire hands from the sooth to make kelp in the season, and I would tak' it to my ain market, for my ain price.'

'Tear me!' ejaculated the red-faced man, who, although of insolent, irascible manners, was quite staggered by this proof of unscrupulousness far beyond his darkest conception. 'Tear me!' he repeated. 'You're an awfu' man, Mr. Tou-gall. Hae ye spoken of this to the laird?'

'The auld laird knew nae mair o' the land than this gill-stoup, Mr. Macraw, and the young laird is no muckle better. Did I no tell the auld laird again and again to clear the land?'

'Maybe, maybe; but he refused, Mr. Tougall?'

'He did little, Mr. Macraw, but through my advice he pu'ed doon mony a hoose that was a disgrace to ceevilisation, and shippit awa' mony a lazy loon that encumbered the good land. He would ha' done mair, and if he had done mair the estate wouldna pe in its present shameful condeetion, and he himself would never hae died in debt. Put if I had my will I would clear every clachan on the land, and turn oot the clergy.'

'The clergy, Mr. Tougall! What have the clergy done?'

'They're the curse of the Hielands, Mr. Macraw.'

'Be careful, Mr. Tougall. I'm a goot Chreestian, and a brither of my ain is in the Kirk.'

'I care neither for you nor your brither, Mr. Macraw,' cried the factor, warm with his theme, not to speak of the whisky. 'The clergy are the ruin of the soil, and the makers of the poor; they steer up discord and dissension, Mr. Macraw, and they persuade the servant to rise against his laird.'

'Why are you sae sair on the clergy, Mr. Tougall?' cried the red-faced man, awed by what seemed to him this tremendous language bordering on blasphemy.

'I will tell you, Mr. Macraw. You are acquaint with Macdonald, the minister of Uribol?'

'Oh, I am, Mr. Tougall.'

'If I had my will that man should be drooned in the loch at his ain door. What does the likes of him do writing letters by the post to the laird in London, and making oot that it would pe a sin to clear the land, and that the laird should come and judge the case wi' his ain e'en.'

'Was that pad advice, Mr. Tougall?'

'Was it good advice, Mr. Macraw? What do the likes of shentry know aboot the land? Fast as I tried to work for the goot of the land, the tammed meenister interfered and frichted the laird oot of doing as I bade him. Would you believe, Mr. Macraw, once when the laird was pad, vera pad wi' the gout, and I had written a letter, advising him to turn out the folk from Plabba Island, and give it to my ain son for sheep at tooble the rent, wad ye believe that Macdonald made oot a petition wi' his ain hands, and made every man, woman, and child put their mark to the petition, and sent it to the laird by the post with a long letter beside, Mr. Macraw, sae full o' the threat o' hell-fire and tamnation that the old man was nearly driven oot o' his wits, and wrote off to me at once to let the people pe, whether they paid their rent or no! Think of that, Mr. Macraw, and don't ask me again why I caal the clergy the curse o' the land.'

'It's an awfu' thing to turn poor folk oot o' hoose and hame, Mr. Tougall! It's a dreadful responsibeelity.'

'Sae it is, Mr. Macraw; but if it's for their ain goot? They ruin the goot land, and they're eaten up wi' hunger and disease, when oot yonder in America there's millions o' miles o' arable land to be had for the asking. The land here was made for sheep. It'll no' grow a crop, and it canna feed a man. It is my opinion, Mr. Macraw, that it's not goot for Highlandmen to remain at hame. See them here, and it'll make your heart pleed for their idleness and their miserable ways; see them in America, and they're praw men, earning goot wages and working weel.'

Peter Dougall, who gave his opinion thus freely on the state of the islands, was really quite sincere in every word he said. He believed that the population merely encumbered the land, and that it was benefiting both them and his employers to transfer them bodily to the United States. He had no tender scruples, however, as to the execution of his desires, and he had again and again urged upon the owner of the estate that he should give him power to adopt far more stringent measures with the population.

Unfortunately for all parties concerned, the hereditary owners of Uribol had never for several generations visited this part of their possessions. In the first place, because it was very inconvenient to reach, and very uncomfortable when reached; in the second place, because they spent almost all their time abroad, and only came to London a few weeks during the season; and in the third place, because the Uribol property, although it embraced altogether a very large area of land, was in reality so barren and so badly cultivated as to represent only a very insignificant rent-roll compared with other property of the family in England and the Lowlands of Scotland, which altogether did not embrace the tenth part of the amount of the Highland property. Uribol was simply a barren waste, worthy to be abandoned at once to the fog and to the ever-encroaching sea. The money it yielded was to be counted by hundreds, whereas a few hundred fat acres in England brought in the revenue of thousands. What wonder that the Lords of Arranmore had from time immemorial busied their great brains with affairs of far more importance?

During the last years of the late lord's life, however, the southern estates had been dreadfully encumbered and mortgaged; and when my lord died, about a year before the opening of our story, the inheritor of the lands and title, an erratic nephew of the deceased, discovered that the Highland estate, though yielding so scanty an income, was really the only part of his inheritance which represented hard cash. Summoned hastily from Syria, where he had for some time been leading a vagabond life, the young laird went to London and saw his uncle's affairs administered. Almost immediately he received through his solicitors several urgent communications from Peter Dougall, the factor, entreating him to adopt very different measures to those favoured by the deceased lord; but his only reply to these communications had been, 'My Lord would inquire into the matter.'

Shortly afterwards a terrible outcry had been raised in the newspapers about certain extensive clearances in the district, and the country had rung from north to south with the sufferings of the exiles.

So much for the factor's relations with his employers. One word as to the nickname commonly applied to him behind his back, that of Peter-na-Croiche, or Peter of the Gallows. The story went that he had been, when a young man, a very great drunkard, and that one day, in a fit of *delirium tremens*, he had actually hung himself to a beam in his own byre, only being discovered by the merest chance, cut down, and with difficulty restored to life. The close acquaintance with death appeared to have done him good. He became a sober man, a strict attender to business, and as hard as iron. Only those who desired to provoke his wildest rage and deadliest animosity dared to refer to the great event of his life, and he had more than once hauled up before the Justice of the Peace, and had imprisoned, some daring spirits who, to provoke him, had addressed him publicly as 'Peter-na-Croiche.'

Mr. Macraw, the cattle-dealer, his companion in the inn parlour, was a man whose ideas worked slowly, and no hand at an argument, so he only stared at the factor with his inflamed eyes, with an expression which, to a stranger, would have seemed expressive of fiery rage, but in reality only indicated intellectual stupefaction.

'Weel, weel, Mr. Tougall, you ken pest maybe. Shall we pe having another glass ? '

'No for me, Mr. Macraw. It's o'er early in the day. See there, sir,' he continued, standing at the window and looking forth, 'there's the vera man I was speaking apout coming up the quay.'

It was not at first that Mr. Macraw, whose vision was none of the clearest, detected the person indicated—no other than Mr. Macdonald, who, shaking hands with all and sundry, was making his way up the crowded pier. Not far behind him lingered Mina, with her little hand laid gently on the arm of Koll Nicholson, who was listening to her, bareheaded, and in his shirt-sleeves.

'That's Meester Macdonald, indeed. He is a braw figure of a man. What will he pe doing at the fair ? '

So spake Mr. Macraw in disconnected sentences. Dougall growled a reply.

'I will tell you what he wil pe doing, Mr. Macraw. He will pe setting man against man, and interfering all day with honest people's business. He has come round in that thief-of-the-world Koll Nicholson's smack, and I wish him and Koll Nicholson, and the smack and aal, were at the bottom of the sea together. Good-morning, Mr. Macraw.'

With these words, spoken with an amount of choler unusual in so self-possessed a man, the factor stalked from the house, leaving Mr. Macraw to pay for the liquor already consumed, and to order another supply for himself. At the head of the quay he passed the minister. They exchanged glances, but gave no other sign of recognition. The sight of the good man who had interfered with so many of his

plans affected the factor as a red rag is supposed to affect a
bull, and he was driven doubly wild because he had no
possible opportunity of revenging himself on an individual
quite above the sphere of his machinations.

Who that has duly visited Storport in the dull season
would have known it on the day we are describing! A
quarter of a mile from the pier stretched a green flat island,
and the space between island and pier was full of fishing-
boats of all descriptions, anchored so closely together that
they seemed roosting like birds on a bough. Everywhere
the blue smoke of peat-fires; from the shores of the loch,
from the tiny islands, from the heights above the tower;
everywhere mud huts, tents, inverted boats, used by the
myriad fishermen for dwellings. The air was full of the
smell of fish, the bones of boiled fish were ·scattered everywhere on the ground, fish were drying on the beach and on
the stones above the village, the boats at the quay were full
of fish newly caught—fish everywhere and the smell of fish,
tempted by which a crowd of gulls, hundreds upon hundreds,
were hovering and darting above Storport with discordant
screams. Everywhere also were fishermen and fisherwomen
in all costumes, and from all parts of the British Isles. From
the cheery Isle of Man fisher, with his oilskin suit and sou'-
wester, to the dull and dowie Hercules of the East Coast,
wrapped in wool and flannel enough to suffocate an ox;
from the quick, shrewd girl attached to the East-country
boat, and cooking for the men and mending their clothes,
to the strapping women of all ages who earn their living by
herring-gutting, and live in all sorts of strange nooks ashore.

Everywhere close to the water's edge, and in the water,
fish, fishermen, fishing-boats, wild women, nets, ropes, and
oars—a confused, moving patchwork, which fatigued the
eye and bewildered the brain.

Passing hastily among the crowd of human beings, one
saw more magnificent specimens of male strength and
symmetry, coupled with more picturesque variety of costume,
than would readily be seen elsewhere under the circumstances.
The women were not so handsome, but there were glorious
creatures among them, 'weeds of glorious feature,' scarcely
less attractive because they could put out almost masculine

strength, if need be, and give and take these sort of jokes which are more pointed in their language than delicate in their meaning

Through the crowd which besieged the quay walked Mr. Macdonald, his white head towering over all, and his face looking at once grave, benignant, and kind. Mingled up with the crowds of strange fishermen and fisherwomen were drovers and their dogs, mendicants, shepherds out for a holiday, farm-servants in gaudy finery, cattle-dealers with their pockets stuffed full of one-pound notes, and ragged cottars of the isles. Hand after hand was thrust out to grasp that of the clergyman; greeting after greeting was showered upon him; and many a kind word and respectful salutation was addressed to his adopted daughter, when she followed and took his arm, leaving Koll Nicholson to look after her with eyes full of tenderness and admiration.

CHAPTER XVIII.

FINE FEATHERS IN THE FAIR.

IN the bright grey light of the fine morning Mina Macdonald looked very pretty indeed. She was very simply attired, with little to distinguish her from ordinary well-to-do peasant women. Her hair was bound up in simple braids under a pretty straw hat, trimmed with bright ribbons. This was her only piece of finery. Her dress, her cloak, her stockings, were all home-woven, but the hat and its adornments had come from the south, and were a birthday gift. Her boots, too, were dainty, though strong and fitting well on the shapely foot.

A pretty woman is like a sunbeam, and should set warmth and light wherever she goes. Certainly Mina did so as she walked on through the crowd by the clergyman's side.

She had left the wharf behind, and was ascending the road behind the inn, still greeted on every side with nods and smiles and 'good-days,' when suddenly she came face to face with Lawrance. He was dressed to-day like a seaman, in pilot-jacket and trousers, wearing a wide-awake hat, and smoking a cigar.

She had certainly no cause to look embarrassed, yet she started, blushed, and turned her eyes away. The next moment Lawrance was close up to her, shaking hands with her and with her uncle. After a few moments' talk, they walked on merrily together.

They were now on the declivity above Storport, on a road crowded with country people on foot and on horseback. It was obviously a gala-day, though there were no signs or booths or shows. The small, heathery knolls on every side of them were covered with black cattle, sheep, shepherds, drovers, and barking dogs—a perfect sea of bustle and commotion. On one stormy height a lantern-jawed, foxy-whiskered itinerant was preaching to the obvious bewilderment of half-a-dozen urchins and a semi-tipsy shepherd. Along the winding country road, as far as eye can see, the people were coming in a thin stream; troops of cattle driven by shouting dogs, and ever breaking from the track; poor women leading their solitary cows to the market by straw ropes; fat, red-cloaked peasant women seated sideways on horses in a wooden framework, with their fat legs cased in coloured stockings, and thickly-booted, resting on a species of wooden tray; herd girls, red-complexioned, shock-haired, white-toothed, grinning from their straw-stuffed trusses on the backs of cows or oxen; tacksmen mounted on their sturdy ponies, and crofters toiling barefoot; groups of men, women, and children, gaily dressed, jolting in rude, spring-less carts behind old horses that creep along at the pace of snails. Across the flat country inland, as far as eye can see, nothing is to be observed but low, green land and small hillocks, broken up with innumerable lakes and stagnant lagoons. In the far distance peeps a spire, and still further, far as eye can see, a great rain-cloud is hanging over the Northern Sea.

It was scarcely a scene which a person used to the great world could enjoy save as a patronising spectator, but it made the cheek of Mina go and come with unconcealed delight, and her eye wandered from group to group and from face to face, finding fresh objects of interest at every step.

Lawrance strode on by her side, and glanced hither and thither carelessly enough.

'This is really a very interesting scene,' he observed, looking, however, very indifferent; 'a most real and striking sort of picture. How I regret, Miss Mina, that I do not speak the Highland language; one misses so much when ignorant of the dialect of the country in which one travels. By the way,' he added, addressing the minister, 'is it true that the Gaelic speech is dying out?'

This was a question which appealed to Mr. Macdonald's most passionate convictions or prejudices. He gave an emphatic negative.

'As the language of mere commerce,' he observed, with some contempt, 'it may be obsolete in some quarters, for the Highlanders have to trade with men who do not understand the grand tongue, and we are bound to use an inferior form of speech. But in the ordinary conversation of life Gaelic is and will continue to be the language of the people; it is more simple, more noble, more expressive, and it is, moreover, a language hallowed by immortal tradition and a glorious literature. In my own parish I do not encourage the natives to learn English. It is not expedient. I will even go so far as to say that I have found the knowledge of the Lowland language only the prelude to the practice of Lowland vices. Simplicity, honesty, hospitality, all go with the Gaelic; all vanish when man forgets his mother tongue.'

This was the language of exaggeration, but Macdonald spoke with the strongest feeling.

'And you, Miss Mina,' inquired Lawrance with a smile, 'do you prefer the language of Ossian to that of Shakespeare?'

'I ought to do so,' Mina replied quietly, 'since it is my native tongue;' and she turned her head away, as if she did not care to be cross-questioned.

Lawrance now stopped short, and, holding out his hand, said—

'I must leave you now; I have some purchases to make, and must look after Calum, who is by this time busy at the tavern.'

'Do you remain here during the day?' asked the minister.

'I do. I ran round in the *Jenny* to have a look at the fun, and I shall return to-night or to-morrow morning.'

'Then, perhaps we may meet again in the course of the day.'

'Yes,' said Lawrance, 'and if we do, I trust your niece will go on board the *Jenny* and take another look at the creature she once saved from a watery grave. She's not much of a ladies' boat, but I'm sure she'll try to look her best under the circumstances.'

So saying, and raising his hat cavalier-fashion, Lawrance turned away, and strolled back among the crowd towards the pier. Ere long he had lit a cigar, and was strolling along with his hands in his pockets, appearing to look at the people, but in reality plunged in deep meditation.

From group to group he lounged listlessly with an easy, good-humoured, patronising air. People, however, were far too much engaged with their own affairs to notice him, save now and then, when a pretty girl was attracted by his good-looking face and dashing bearing. On the knolls above the quay, where the cattle were legion, groups of cattle-dealers and farmers were wrangling together, and bargaining at the height of their voices. The dirty inn was now crowded with drunkards, and the excitement was increasing.

Listlessly enough Lawrance made his way towards the inn. As he approached the foreshore on which it stood he saw in the distance a group of three—two gentlemen and one lady—who seemed strangely out of place in that wild scene. The men wore light tweed costumes, one of them a white Indian hat with a *puggaree*, the lady who was tall and young, flirted a parasol.

They had just alighted from a dog-cart, and were looking at the dingy inn in some hesitation and disgust.

'Tourists, by jove!' thought Lawrance. '*Here* of all places in the world.'

So, giving them a still wider berth, he passed on to the shore, off which his boat was lying.

Had he been less absorbed in himself, or had he been a little nearer, he would have been astonished to see Miss

Sedley (for it was she) gazing after him in utter astonishment.

'Papa!' she suddenly cried to her father, who was in eager conversation with the little baron.

'Well, Ethel?'

'Look at that gentleman—quick, or he will be gone!'

'Well, what about him?'

'I cannot be mistaken. It is'——

Here she paused and laughed merrily.

'Who is he, Ethel?'

Ethel blushed and laughed again, then she leant forward and whispered in her father's ear.

'You don't mean it!' he exclaimed. 'Lord, what a place to meet in! And he didn't know us!'

'He scarcely observed us, but I should recognise him anywhere. See! he is signalling to that little vessel in the bay.'

At this moment Calum, the pilot, issued somewhat unsteadily from the inn and passed the group. Miss Sedley called to him *en passant.*

'Can you tell me who owns that small schooner?' she said, with her sweetest smile. 'Perhaps you belong to her?'

Calum, who, though well-seasoned with drink, was awe-struck at the presence of so fine a lady, took off his cap.

'That'll be the *Jenny,* my leddy,' he replied, 'and I'm her pilot.'

'And that gentleman?—see, he is turning and waving to you!'

'That's jest Mr. Lawrance, her owner. A fine gentleman he is, my leddy, and a gran' sailor.'

'Mr. Lawrance?—are you sure that is his name?'

'Yes, my leddy.'

'Has he no other?'

'I never heard tell o' anither. He's up here to see the kintra, and he's staying yonder amang the lochs o' Uribol. We sailed the *Jenny* here the morn. But I maun rin—he's crying on me. Good-bye, my leddy.'

And with no very steady gait he hastened down to the shore. Sir Charles Sedley looked at his daughter.

'Then you've made a mistake, Miss Clever! It's
not'——

'I have made no mistake,' answered the young lady,
nodding her head. 'It's himself, papa!'

'But the man says'——

'I begin to anticipate something amusing. Don't say a
word, but leave me to arrange matters my own way. He is
here *incognito;* that is all.'

CHAPTER XIX.

'PETER NA CROICHE.'

LATER on in the day Lawrance came ashore. He was
quite unconscious of the new interest his presence had
awakened, and as he strolled up the village saw no more of
the shooting party from Castle Coreveolan.

From group to group he strolled, looking eagerly for the
Macdonalds, but they seemed to have disappeared. While
he was searching for them his attention was attracted to a
wild, ragged-looking man, who with shrill cries and seeming
imprecations was clutching the sleeve of an old man, and
fast causing a crowd to collect around them. The speaker
seemed one wasted by hunger and disease. His black,
sunken eyes had the sparkle of death, his cheeks were those
of a skeleton, his lean hand was nothing but skin and bone.
The old man whom he was addressing—no other than Peter
Dougall, the factor—was looking at him with ill-concealed
rage and contempt.

Lawrance could not understand a word that was being
said, though the looks and gestures of the speaker, and the
occasional groans and exclamations of the bystanders, indicated that the general tide of feeling was running against the
factor.

Carelessly addressing an old farmer who was looking on
from a little distance, and whom he had just heard speaking English, he inquired the meaning of the scene.

The farmer drew down the edges of his mouth and shrugged his shoulders.

'It's shust a tenant pody that has ta'en a drap, and is speaking his mind to the factor.   You've nae Gaelic?'

'No.   Who is the old man, and what has he done?'

'He's Peter Dougall, my Lord Arranmore's factor, and he's cleared awa' the man there, Neil Mackinnon, and the family, because they couldna pay the rent.'

'Oh, I see; and the man is giving him a bit of his mind?'

'Shust.   He's an awfu' man, the factor, but what can a pody do if a pody 'll no pay rent for the good land?   It's no wise to offend the factor.'

As he spoke, the factor, with a face cold as marble, and nearly as white, especially round the edges of the lips, shook off the other's hold and walked away.   The wretched being who had been abusing him, and who had obviously been taking liquor on an empty stomach, gazed vacantly after him with a look of wild despair, until a shepherd of his acquaintance staggered up with a bottle in his hand, clapped him on the shoulder, and offered him a draught of raw spirits. He drank from the bottle wildly, uttered a hysteric laugh, and disappeared in the crowd.

Meanwhile Lawrance had followed Peter Dougall, who was walking rapidly away, and touched him on the arm. The old man turned almost savagely, as if he expected to see his late antagonist; but recognising Lawrance, saluted him with great cordiality.

After a little talk they separated, arranging to meet again later in the day.

Dougall had just bidden Lawrance a respectful farewell, when a low voice cried almost in his ear—

'Peter—Peter na Croiche!'

Turning sharply, livid with rage, to ascertain who had used the odious nickname, he perceived nobody who appeared guilty; but a few yards off, among a group of people, stood Angus with the Dogs, gazing guilelessly at some distant object.

Dougall rushed up to the mendicant, shaking his thick stick in the sly, yet vacant face.

'Did you speak—you—you plackguard?' he cried in English.

Angus rolled his great eyes round, and answered with his lisp in the same tongue.

'Pless me, Mr. Tougall, is that you? Are you keeping weel, sir?'

'Caal me that name again, and I'll have you whippit through the parish, you teevil's limb!'

'What name, Mr. Tougall?' said Angus innocently. 'What name would a poor man call ye by but your ain name, Mr. Tougall?'

Speechless with indignation, the factor shook his stick again at the fool, and walked away, leaving the latter looking after him with a peculiar smile.

'You're Peter na Croiche for aal that,' reflected Angus. 'You hae been cut doon once, Peter na Croiche, but maybe you'll no be cut doon next time. It was a pad day for the Almighty God's poor when they *did* cut you doon; it was spoiling a goot rope, Peter na Croiche, and sae I tell you.'

So Angus shuffled away, followed by his canine family. He turned a good penny that day by putting the tailless dog, called Shemus, through certain of his tricks—such as dancing on his hind legs, smoking a pipe, and playing at leap-frog with the collie. The shepherds and drovers were free with their pence, and, moreover, treated Angus to many a glass; so that when night came he betook himself comfortably to the open hill, having, as he expressed it, 'better than a dozen blankets to keep him warm, and carrying them in the best place in the world—his ain stomach.'

Towards evening the crowd greatly diminished, for the enormous fleet of herring boats sailed like a flock of birds to the open sea, there to rock all night at their nets at the mercy of tide and wind. It was a calm day, however—far too calm for the taste of the fishermen. It was a fine sight to see the red-sailed boats creeping slowly out of the calm loch, some moving with full sails on the dark patch where there was a little puff of wind, others with flapping sails being rowed slowly through a glassy calm—all crawling to the mouth of Loch Storport, where the breeze caught them,

and they began to lie over and beat with some speed.
Smacks of all sizes, double and single luggers, great skiffs,
all sped to the deep sea fishing. The little bay between the
island and the pier was abandoned by all save two black
coasting vessels and several rakish-looking ' runners,' waiting
to carry the night's fishing south ; and the water all round
these was like oil, and a few white gulls seated thereon were
drinking the floating globules of fat, while their companions,
in one vast flock, had also departed to spend the night in
fishing on the open sea.

Meantime the fun of the fair waxed fast and furious.
Sellers and buyers had done their business, and all had
now abandoned themselves to merriment—that is to say, to
furious drinking. The lowing of the cattle, and crying and
singing of the men, the shrill voices of the women, made day
hideous.

On a smooth bit of green above the inn a ragged bagpiper
and a blind fiddler were playing different tunes, and shepherds, herd-girls, farm women, and drovers were dancing
like mad people, with the usual shrieks that accompany the
Highland reel.

Here a couple of men were fighting—not in the knock-
down English fashion, but tearing, screaming, and clinging
to each other's throats like wild-cats.

The dirty inn was crammed, and the sound of roaring
and singing came from the rickety door. Half-naked Highlandmen in kilts were rushing about everywhere with bottles
of whisky in their hands, beseeching their friends to drink.

Through the midst of the crowd, early in the day, passed
a funeral procession—six Highlanders in mourning, two
abreast, then the bearers and their load, then six more
men two abreast, all under the guidance of a man with a
staff, under whose direction the bearers would hand the
coffin over to the others, and themselves fall back into the
rear until their turn came again to carry.

Behind the party came two ponies carrying wicker creels,
with jars of whisky inside, and rolls of tobacco.

The whole had moved along to a military march played
by a grey-headed piper, and disappeared to the burial-place
up the country.

But towards night back rushed the mourners, free of their burden, laughing and singing, every one tipsy as Silenus, and these men became the wildest of the mirth-makers in the fair.

Night fell, and though the noise continued, the crowd grew thinner and thinner.

Every now and then the public-house door opened, and some refractory drunkard was shut out into the night, and the door barred in his face.

It was curious to note the different behaviour of the various parties so treated. One man stared around him vacantly, smiled feebly, and walked away unoffended; another made the welkin ring with his howls, battered at the door with fists and feet, uttered threats of the most bloody vengeance against all and sundry; another calmly lay where the enemy had deposited him, drowsily singing in chorus to the loud singing from within.

Again and again during the evening there was a splash and a scream, and the alarm was given that some one had tumbled over the pier in the dark; but there was no fatal accident, as the water was comparatively shallow, and help was at hand.

If any curious observer or midnight dreamer had been wandering that night among the hills and knolls surrounding Storport, he would have been startled every now and then by stumbling over a corpse-like recumbent figure, which would either grunt out a sleepy disapproval, or, springing to its feet, spar tipsily at the disturber of its slumber. Most of these figures would be armed with black bottles of whisky.

The highway, too, was sprinkled with drowsy Bacchanalians. More than one well-to-do farmer was already lying tranquilly asleep on the road, still gripping the bridle of the horse from which he had gently rolled; while the quiet beast, used to its master's eccentricity, was patiently nibbling the scanty herbage on the side of the road. And a little way off his head shepherd, perhaps quite as respectable-looking, and quite as respectably clothed as his master, was sleeping too, with his tired dog curled up close to his head.

With very few exceptions, there were no female night-birds

of the tipsy kind, though out on the lonely hill-side more than one girl was lying coiled up in her lover's plaid, far too sick and weary to take the dark road home.

Before daybreak, however, all the thirsty plants were cooled by a drenching shower; and when the sun arose, or rather, when he looked out of the clouds with a ghastly countenance—just like one who had been keeping it up overnight, and was suffering for it in the morning—when light came, and the herring-boats were again at anchor, and the pier and the shores were glittering with fresh fish, almost all the Bacchanalians had disappeared from the hills and knolls, and the inn had subsided into its chronic state of dirt, darkness, languor, and general misery.

CHAPTER XX.

LORD ARRANMORE AT LAST.

SEVERAL hours before the fair had terminated, Mina, with her uncle and Graham, embarked on Koll Nicholson's smack, and sailed back to Uribol.

Lawrance had asked them to return with him in the *Jenny*, but, partly because Graham seemed very unwilling, the offer had been refused.

After the business which had brought the Macdonalds to the fair was over, they had no desire to linger in Storport. The clergyman had no wish to remain and bear witness to the scenes of debauchery which, he knew from experience, would wind up the proceedings of the day, and now that their interview with Lawrance was over, Mina did not seem to care how soon she returned to the manse.

And yet no sooner was she on the smack, which was gliding along swiftly towards Uribol, than she looked back with a sad, disappointed gaze at the shore which she was leaving behind. For several weeks now life had been changing for Mina, but she had never felt the change so forcibly as she did that night. However much she might try, she could not show an interest in the neat sailing of the smack, or in Koll Nicholson's stories; in the general conversation connected with the fair—things which on ordinary occasions would have commanded her attention.

But as she sat in the boat that night looking at the slowly receding shores of Storport, she was picturing to herself a face which she had seen there, listening to a voice which she had heard.

It seemed strange to Mina that, after the words which had been spoken on the day the carriage was passing from Coreveolan Castle to the manse at Uribol, Lawrance should never again have spoken to her in the same strain.

Since Graham's return his visits to the manse had not been so frequent as they had been before, though, when he did come, his manner to her was just the same as it had ever been—frank and friendly, with just enough *empressement* in his tone to remind her of his special interest in her alone.

Altogether it was an enigma to Mina, and the more she thought over it, the more perplexed she became. Could it be possible, she thought, that those words, that pressure, that look had meant nothing—nothing, that is, more than the ordinary interest of a friend? If this was so, she thought with a pang, it would be better, far better for her, if he had never come, since with his words and looks of love he had drawn forth love in return.

Yes, she could no longer conceal from herself the fact that this man, coming like a gleam of sunshine in winter weather, had gradually become dearer to her than any member of her home.

He had irradiated by his very presence the days which crept drearily along at the manse—he had infused a new pleasure into her work—but alas! how quickly the pleasure went if once he kept away.

Mina remembered how happily the evenings used to pass when Lawrance occupied the arm-chair—she had gone through her lessons with proud consciousness that she was surprising and pleasing him. She had read Gaelic with a voice more musical than ever because he was there to hear, and then, after the tasks were done, she had sat listening to his conversation with her uncle, waiting for that pressure of the hand, that lingering look, half of love, half of admiration, which never failed to come.

But now how changed it all was ! The glamour had gone, for looks of approval seldom came to her now, except from her uncle or Graham.

Mina was very fond of her brother, and in her heart really glad to see him back again; but she felt that his hostile manner had driven Lawrance away, and it made her very sad.

As she sailed home that night she felt really angry with him, and somewhat vexed with her uncle too. She remembered how, on the previous evening, when Lawrance had walked over to the manse to ask the Macdonalds with his own lips if they would sail with him to Storport on the morrow, Graham, after gloomily refusing for himself, had signalled to his uncle to refuse also; and the minister had done as he was bid. Mina said nothing—so outrageous an act as to question the conduct of her uncle and brother never occurred to her—but she went up to bed that night with a sore heart. Her disappointment at not being able to sail in the *Jenny* was rendered so much the more acute by the recollection of the look which had passed over Lawrance's face as the refusal had been given.

But when he had turned to her the look had passed away. He had held forth his hand—

'Good-night, Miss Macdonald,' he said. 'I hope, at any rate, it may be my fortune to meet you in the fair.'

Then, with a polite but somewhat formal 'Good-night' to the minister, and a curt nod to Graham, he had taken his departure.

After he had gone nothing was said about him, but Mina felt it was finally fixed that she must not sail in the *Jenny*. She had quietly submitted to the plan of going over in Koll Nicholson's smack, and her journey was made brighter by the expectation which she had of meeting Lawrance at Storport.

And she had met him; she had had the satisfaction of seeing the familiar, fond, admiring look pass over his face as his eyes had rested upon her, of feeling again the warm pressure of the hand.

It was of this Mina was thinking as she sat silently watching the water which washed quietly at the boat's side; it was of this she was thinking when, on reaching home, she retired, not to rest, but to watch patiently for the light which would come like a messenger to tell her *he* was near.

It was a bright, clear, starlight night, silent save for the low murmur of the sea. Mina threw open the window and looked at the jet black line of mountains, at the dreary expanse of sea. Her uncle and Graham were already asleep, but until she knew that Lawrance was safe in Uribol she felt she could not rest. One, two, three hours dragged slowly past, and at length her patience was rewarded. By the light of dawn, which already reddened the east, she saw the *Jenny*, with all her white sails unfurled, glide slowly up the fjord. For a time she allowed her wearied gaze to rest lovingly on the little vessel; then, with a sob of joy, she kissed her hands. 'Good night, good night,' she whispered, before she closed her window to lie down to rest.

On awakening in the morning, Mina's first thought was, 'Will he come to-day?' She had quite made up her mind that he would come, for she thought, after that look which he had given her in the fair, he could not stay away; he had thrown his whole soul into his eyes, and his soul had said, 'I love you.'

It was very dull at the manse that day. Immediately after breakfast Mr. Macdonald shut himself into his study to work hard at a paper which, signed by all the tenants, was asking for the summary dismissal of the factor, whose tyranny had become too hard to bear, and which the clergyman intended to hand personally to Lord Arranmore, immediately that nobleman made his appearance upon his estate. Graham, still feeling the fatigue of the day before, remained mostly in his room. But Mina could not rest in peace. Now she was wandering aimlessly from room to room, startling her uncle from his labours, her brother from his reading, Kirsty, the old housekeeper, from her knitting in the chimney-nook; again she was looking from her bedroom window at the sea, or, standing upon the threshold, she would gaze towards the spot where Lawrance dwelt. But hour after hour passed by and he did not come, and

late that night Mina went to bed with a heart more sad-
dened than it had ever been before.

While Mina had been looking up towards the Lodge that
day, Lawrance had been gazing down towards the manse.
While he looked, he wondered whether or not it would be
wise for him to see Mina. He, like Graham, felt listless
after the fatigue of the fair, ready for an indolent stroll and
chat; both of which, had Graham Macdonald not returned
to Uribol, would have been well within his reach. Besides,
he could not now forego Mina's society without a pang—a
pang, however, which he seemed more willing to bear than
her brother's sullen stare.

'He is so insolent, too,' he said to himself; 'so cubbish,
rude, and disdainful, that I sometimes have a difficulty in
holding my peace, or keeping my hands from administering
a thrashing, and yet I think I could manage to bear even
more than this from Mina's brother.'

This was followed by a series of retrospections, in each
of which Mina was the central figure. Finally, cursing the
evil luck which had, at so critical a time, sent Graham back
to Uribol, he resolved to bear with his loneliness and not
walk down to the manse that day. But when he arose the
next morning, he fully determined that neither Graham, nor
any other human being, should keep him another day from
Mina. Through all his dreams that night her face had
shone, loving, trustful, with eyes full of tender, spiritual
light, gazing up into his. She had wound her arms about
his neck and smiled, while he, clasping her to his bosom,
had pressed, for the first time, his passionate lips to hers;
but even as he did so, she shivered as if with bitter cold, and
faded from his sight.

The mingled joy and sorrow of his dream was strong
upon him when, in the full, clear light of day, he opened
his wearied eyes. He resolved that, come what might, he
would that day see Mina. He would have preferred, all
things considered, to have seen her alone, but, as that could
not be done, he resolved to walk over to the manse and
run the risk of being coolly received by her irritating
brother.

He breakfasted late, and lingered long over the meal.

I

It was more than probable Graham might be going out, and, if so, he would have plenty of time to get clear away before the obnoxious stranger showed himself. It was close on midday when at length Lawrance left the lodge and took the road towards the manse.

He walked on quickly, and had gone more than two-thirds of the way, when suddenly he paused, thanking the good star which he felt at length prevailed. There, straight before him, though a good distance away, was Mina herself, walking away from the manse, and taking the road which led to the seashore. Lawrance left the footpath, cut across the hill, and in less than five minutes' time he had reached her side. Mina raised her eyes, but said nothing. Lawrance lifted his hat and held forth his hand.

'How are you?' he said, giving her hand such a tender pressure as made her blush from brow to chin. 'I was on my way to the manse, when, catching sight of you, I left my path and cut directly across the hill. Where are you going?'

'Nowhere in paticular. If you like, I will walk with you back to the manse.'

She turned as if to retrace her steps, but Lawrance laid a detaining hand upon her arm.

'No, don't go,' he said. 'I want you to stay a little while with me.'

Mina paused, not very well knowing what to do, and then the two walked on for a few minutes in silence. Lawrance was the first to speak again.

'I was sorry you were not on board the *Jenny* on Tuesday. She made a capital run.'

'Yes, and I was sorry.'

'Were you?' he said, looking earnestly into her face, and trying in vain to make her raise her eyes. 'Tell me honestly, were you sorry, Mina?'

She did not raise her eyes, she did not remind him that he had—inadverently, perhaps—called her again by her Christian name, but she answered quietly—

'Yes.'

At that moment Mina was angry with herself.

When she opened her lips she could only utter monosyllables ; she felt that her cheeks would blush, and, worst of all, when he took her hand and put it on his arm, it trembled in his grasp.

'You have not been like your old self lately, Mina,' he continued. 'You have shown a fatal readiness to refuse almost every request of mine. I wonder if you will refuse the one I am going to make to-day ?'

'Maybe ; until you have made it I cannot tell.'

'It is a very simple request, very easily complied with, and it rests solely with you.'

'Well, sir ?'

'I want you to give me a lock of your hair.'

Mina raised her eyes this time, and her cheeks went pale as death.

'A lock of my hair ?' she said.

'Yes, Mina, a lock of your hair. Is the request so terrible that you should turn so pale ? I want you to clip it from here—one of these locks that I have seen so often caressing your brow. Oh, you hesitate—you will not give me what I ask ?'

She answered his question with another.

'Are you going away ?'

'Going away ? Not that I know of.'

'Then why should you want my hair ?' she asked, turn-ing aside her head that he might not see the flush which now suffused her cheeks. 'In Scotland one only gives such gifts when '——

'Yes, Mina, go on.'

'Well, when folk care very much for one another. If I were to give my hair to you everybody in the clachan would gossip about it, and my uncle and Graham would blame me for doing what was wrong.'

'Do you think, then, if possessed of such a treasure, I should bring it forth for every soul to look on ? Your uncle would never hear of it, for none save myself would know.'

'Do not ask me to do what is foolish, Mr. Lawrance. Even if no one were to hear of it, I should never feel con-tented again.'

'Mina !'

'Yes, sir.'

'Have you no faith in me? Do you not know that I would sooner lose all I have in the world than ask you to do a wrong? Have you not seen, do you not know, how much I care for you?'

'You care for me?' she murmured, dwelling upon each word with lingering tones of pleasure. He took her hands in his—he drew her to him, and raised towards him her blushing face.

'Yes, Mina,' he said. 'I care for you with all my heart and soul.' Then putting his arm round her he added, 'Tell me now, my dear, if you care anything for me.'

She yielded to his passionate pressure, but she did not answer him.

'Mina, speak to me—just a few words, my darling. Only this, "Lawrance, I love you!"'

What need was there for words? Was there not love and trust written on every feature of her face? Her clinging figure and trembling hands made assurance doubly sure. Nevertheless, since he desired it, she felt that she must speak. She opened her lips, she raised her face.

Suddenly her cheek grew pale, her gaze became fixed, and she did not utter a word.

The cause of Mina's sudden agitation was an elegantly dressed lady, who stood upon the hillside only a little distance away. Just behind her was an elderly gentleman.

From the position in which they stood, it seemed as if they had come over the brow of the hill which rose directly behind them, and passing silently over the heather-clad shoulder had approached to within a few yards of the spot where the lovers stood, and had possibly overheard some of the conversation.

Astonished at the sudden change in Mina's manner, and noting the fixed look of her eyes, Lawrance turned too, and saw for the first time the cause of Mina's agitation. As he did so, his cheek grew even paler than her own. He dropped her hands, and, as if involuntarily, drew a few steps away.

'Ethel!' he exclaimed.

A look of pretty disdain on the lady's face deepened,

she curled her lip, and gave a peculiar laugh, as she came a few steps forward.

'Yes, Ethel,' she said. 'Glad to see me, Lawrance? You would be, I am sure, if you only knew the trouble we had taken to find you out. But it is perhaps unfortunate that we arrived at so critical a moment,' she continued, addressing the old gentleman, who was vainly endeavouring to speak. 'Come, papa, you see we are not wanted here. When Lawrance has quite finished his innocent rural studies, perhaps he will condescend to rejoin us on the other side of the hill !'

At this the gentleman put up an eye-glass, and surveyed Mina from head to foot.

Up to this time Mina had not uttered a word; she had stood pale as a ghost, looking first at Lawrance, then at the people who had addressed him. When the lady spoke she felt a sickening sense of fear gradually stealing about her heart; but when she found that she was being surveyed through the eye-glass with such insulting coolness, her face went crimson with indignation.

'Mr. Lawrance—sir,' she said quickly, 'who are these folk ? '

'They are friends of mine,' he said awkwardly, and at that moment he cursed himself to think that he could find no word to say more.

'Friends !' returned Mina, with quiet dignity. 'You said, sir, that you had no friends here.'

'Oh, indeed !' returned Miss Sedley, with a mocking laugh. 'So he has been passing as the friendless orphan, has he? How sentimental, to be sure ! But, you see, he has not told you exactly the truth—he *has* friends ; though, to give him his due, he did not know that they were so near him.'

'Or he wouldn't have been caught flirting with a milk-maid—eh, Ethel?' said the old gentleman.

'Uncle !' cried the young man, 'for God's sake, hold your peace. This young lady '——

'Oh, don't get on the stilts, Lawrance, for the game's up, my boy. I daresay this young lady doesn't even know who you are, or she wouldn't have made such a fool of herself

Well, my dear, in case his lordship has been deceiving you, I may as well tell you.'

'Uncle, hold your tongue!' thundered Lawrance, now fairly aroused to wrath. 'If she has to be told, I will tell her!'

'No, you won't, Lawrance,' continued Ethel, stepping forward. 'Since I have got to make a wry face and swallow the bitter, I mean to have some of the sweet to take it down. Madam,' she continued, making a mocking curtesy to Mina, 'permit me to introduce myself as Miss Sedley. This is my father, Sir Charles Sedley; and that gentleman whom you were so fondly caressing as we came over the hill is my affianced husband, Lord Arranmore.'

The words, uttered so disdainfully, fell ominously upon Mina's ears, but, amid all her sorrow and shame, she felt her dignity assert itself. She could not keep her cheeks from growing pale, but she forced back the tears from her eyes, and, when Lawrance approached her with outstretched hand, she proudly moved away.

At this moment she heard a familiar voice behind her, and, turning, she saw that her uncle and Graham were approaching side by side. She walked up to her uncle, and slipped her hand in his.

'Mina,' he said, 'is anything the matter, my bairn?'

'No, uncle, nothing much; only I have just heard that Mr. Lawrance is Lord Arranmore!'

CHAPTER XXI.

THE MASK FALLS.

THE revelation of Lawrance's true identity came like a thunderclap. Mr. Macdonald stood astonished and confused, while Graham, with a face made pale with passion, gazed angrily at the new-comers.

The young lord himself was the first to speak.

'The mask is torn away,' he said, with a nervous attempt at a smile, 'just as I was about to take it off. Mr.

Macdonald, will you pardon my innocent deception? I came here *incognito*, wishing to ascertain for myself the condition of these estates, and to discover if the people had any just ground of complaint. You will excuse my having passed under a pseudonym, now that you know the harmlessness of my intention.'

Mr. Macdonald was silent, but Graham now spoke vehemently.

'One deception leads to many!' he exclaimed. 'You had no right to enter our house under a false name!'

'Graham!' cried Mina, alarmed at the words and the tone.

Lord Arranmore looked quietly into Graham's face, and made no direct reply to his words, but his lips curled with an expression of cold contempt. Graham, not shrinking at the look, but resenting it with a determined scowl, clenched his hands as if for a blow, and looked interrogatingly at his uncle.

The old clergyman, with the courtesy and dignity habitual to him, conquered his first feeling of indignation, and bowed gravely to Arranmore.

'You will admit, my lord,' he said, 'that we have some reason to feel surprised, and perhaps a little annoyed. However, you had doubtless excellent motives for what you did, and at any rate it is not for me to judge your conduct. I welcomed you to my hearth as a friend and equal, and I am sorry'——

'We are friends still, I hope,' interposed the young lord, warmly, 'and equals always. Believe me, nothing could exceed the respect I feel for you and yours!'

During this little scene Sir Charles Sedley and his daughter had stood by in no little astonishment. As for Miss Sedley, whose sense of humour was fine, she was not a little amused that so much trouble should be taken to conciliate people so common, so far removed from the brilliant social sphere in which she herself moved. She at last advanced deliberately, and said—

'I think we had better go. It is a pity we came to interfere with your amusement. It must have been delightful to live here unnoticed and unknown, just like a shepherd in a

play. I quite envy you, Lawrance—upon my word I do—
and so, I'm sure, does papa!'

In answer to a questioning look from Mr. Macdonald,
Arranmore thought it necessary to go through some sort of
an introduction.

'This is my cousin, Miss Ethel Sedley. Ethel, let me
introduce the Rev. Mr. Macdonald: and,' he added, turning to Graham, 'this other gentleman'——

'Is a friend of mine already,' said Ethel airily, 'though
he won't notice me this time. We met before in Edinburgh, when I was staying with Lady Murray.'

'Indeed!' exclaimed Arranmore, while Graham made a
moody sign of recognition.

Without uttering a word, Sir Charles Sedley thereupon
favoured Graham with that stony stare which is the special
prerogative of the British aristocrat, and scowled suspiciously
at his daughter.

An awkward silence now ensued, which was at last broken
by the old clergyman.

'Won't you step back to the manse,' he said courteously,
'and permit me to offer you some refreshment? You must
have had a long walk across the hills.'

For a moment no one answered him. Lawrance looked
at Mina, but she, keeping close to her uncle, studiously
fixed her eyes upon the ground. Ethel looked at Graham,
and he would not return her gaze. Hardly noting the
general consternation, Sir Charles Sedley spoke:

'Allow me,' he said, 'for myself, as well as for these
young people, to thank you for your offer, sir. We cannot
accept it to-day, I am afraid, as it is already late, and we
have a long way to walk home; but some day before we
leave Uribol I shall hope to have the pleasure of calling
upon you.'

At this little speech Mina heaved a sigh of relief, and
turning without a word of adieu, walked with her brother
a few steps away. The old clergyman, noting her downcast
look and peculiar manner, attributed it to overwhelming
nervousness at being in the presence of people so distinguished; he, therefore, as if to make up for her nervousness,
infused unusual respect and dignity into his own manner.

'Madam,' he said, removing his hat with a grand sweep of his arm as he fixed his grave eyes on Ethel, 'I have the honour to wish you good-day. If during your stay in this district I can be of the slightest use to you, I am entirely at your service.'

Ethel bowed and smiled, but her eyes were fixed, not upon the clergyman, but upon the slowly retreating figure of his nephew.

Mr. Macdonald turned to Lawrance.

'My lord,' he said, 'if during the past few weeks I have used words which were not intended for the ears of the Lord of Arranmore, I must plead as my excuse the very peculiar and trying position in which you placed me. When I welcomed you to the manse I fully believed that I was welcoming a poor student.'

'It was, in fact, the man, and not the lord, whom you welcomed, Mr. Macdonald,' said Arranmore, heartily grasping the old clergyman's hand. 'Believe me, it will be one of the greatest pleasures of my life to remember that.'

Macdonald bowed gravely, and, after raising his hat to Sir Charles Sedley, politely retired to join Mina and Graham, who were already walking slowly towards the manse.

His first care was to admonish both of the young people for not having been more polite to the young laird and his friends, his next to launch forth into praises of the young gentleman whose unaccountable escapade had led to so much confusion. He could not but admit that, in assuming an *alias* at all, his lordship had committed an act which was deserving of very strong censure indeed ; that, still under cover of the *alias*, he had entered the clergyman's household on terms of equality, and thereby gained the special confidence of the family. He had exposed himself to still greater condemnation ; for the old man remembered with some trepidation that often, at those evening conferences which were held in the study at the manse, the young lord had sat and listened to some good round abuse of himself ! Still, amid all this mortification, it was a consolation to him to know that the young lord was a student both of books and men, that he loved his home and the home of his ancestors, which was set amidst the solitudes of the north, and that for very love of his home and his people he had been content to wear for a time the garb of common humanity. Since he had been content to endure privations in order that he might mete out justice, surely, thought the old clergyman, he would not be so ungenerous as to harbour in his mind any revengeful thought against one who had thought it incumbent upon him to speak out strongly on the people's behalf. Then he spoke out in commendation of Lord Arranmore and of his lordship's friends.

Presently he noticed, to his surprise, that he was getting no answer. He looked at Graham; he was walking along in moody silence. He looked at Mina; her eyes were fixed upon the ground too, and her face was still deathly pale.

'Mina, my bairn.'

'Yes, uncle?'

She answered him quietly enough, but she did not raise her face, neither did she remove her steadfast gaze from the ground.

'Did you happen to learn, my bairn, when these strangers arrived in Uribol?'

'No, indeed.'

'Nor where they are staying?'

'No.'

Graham remembered having seen them on the hills the very day that he arrived in Uribol, but as his uncle had evidently forgotten all about the episode, he did not think it worth while to remind him. So Graham was allowed to pursue his way in silence, while the cross-examination of Mina went on.

'Who first told you that Mr. Lawrance was the young lord, Mina?'

'The lady,' replied Mina, suddenly growing crimson at the recollection of that scene.

'Ah, she has a fine face, a very fine face, and her bearing is such as to stamp her at once as a member of our aristocracy. I was sorry, my dear, that during that scene you did not exhibit a little of her self-command; it is such a sign of good breeding to be able to conduct yourself with perfect dignity under any circumstances whatever.'

To this speech Mina did not reply, for at that moment they all three paused before the door of the manse. Mr. Macdonald and Graham walked straight into the study, and Mina passed at once up to her own room.

Having gained it she sat down on the side of her bed, and gazed around her with eyes full of despairing pain. It seemed to her as if she had passed out of the sunlight into the clammy moisture of a tomb. She could not think—the cold which crept over her shrinking frame dulled her senses and turned her very heart sick. For a time she sat gazing listlessly about her. Suddenly a vision of that scene on the hillside came before her mental sight, and with a shudder she covered her burning face with her hands as if for very shame.

Up to that day Mina Macdonald had had few sorrows, even if she had few pleasures. Her days had been spent in quiet contentment at home amid the quaint recesses of learning; abroad upon the wild waters of the sea she had been happy to think that she was seeing beautiful things and gaining strength. If at times she was inclined to wish for a gleam of that intenser joy which is generally allotted to womankind, the wish was only transitory—for she thought, 'I have my uncle and my brother, I ought to be content—only, if it pleases God that I shall one day win to myself such love as other women win, my happiness will be shared with them.'

So she had lived on in quiet contentment until Lawrance came. But Mina's nature was by no means of that weak headlong sort which would induce her to give her love unreservedly to the first comer with pleasant manners and a handsome face. Had she from the first known Lawrance to be what he was—of a rank far above her—she would never for a moment have allowed him to draw from her one sign of love. It was because she believed him to be an equal, because he assured her by his words, still more by his looks, that she had won his love, that she gave her fond confidence in return. Well, she had had one or two weeks of happiness, for even amidst her doubts and fears she had been made happy by the consciousness of his presence. But now what a terrible retribution had come with one blow

swift and sure! Her idol became, not shattered at her
feet, but lifted far above her head. He was no longer one
who had come like a blessing from God to make her life
complete, but a superior being whose presence from the
first had brought her nothing but degradation, insult, and
shame.

It was some comfort to Mina, amidst all her sorrow, to
think that her uncle, simple as a child in matters of the
world, remained in complete ignorance of the true issues of
what had passed. Her shame was keen enough. She did not
merit one look of reproach from the minister's grave eyes;
she only prayed that the young maiden who was destined to
become the Lady of Arranmore would not trouble herself to
describe to the minister the scene which she had witnessed
on the hillside. How well Mina remembered the pang which
had shot through her breast when the girl had described
Lawrance as her affianced husband. She had stood with
a cold hand pressing upon her quickly beating heart, her
eyes eagerly fixed upon her lover's face, her ears awaiting
the words which should give the statement the lie. But he
had not uttered them; he had turned his head away, as if
to avoid the look of shame which he knew would cross her
face.

What agony it had cost her then not to throw her arms
around her uncle's neck and ease her aching heart in tears;
but her pride had come to her aid and upheld her, just as
it must uphold her still. Yes, at that moment Mina felt her
whole nature rising in revolt at the trick that had been
played upon her. She could not undo what she had done;
she could not recall the looks and words which his endear-
ments had drawn forth; but she resolved not to play the
part of the broken-hearted damsel at whom the finger of
scandal could point, as at one who had brought ridicule
upon her uncle's house and shame upon herself—one who
for a few short weeks had been the plaything of a lord.
The trial was hard to bear, but she resolved to bear it
bravely, and to keep her sorrow hidden, even if it broke her
heart.

It was a brave resolve, but poor Mina lacked the physical
strength to keep it. Each morning when she looked in the

glass she found her face paler, her cheeks more pinched and thin. Each night she thought, why does he not send, or come to explain this mystery away?

CHAPTER XXII.

ARRANMORE'S HOME-COMING.

WHEN Mr. Macdonald had walked away to join his nephew and niece, the three people thus left together on the hill did not know very well what to do. Lawrance's first impulse was to rush after Mina, to take his place by her side and boldly assert his right to remain there; but, convinced by a moment's reflection of the folly of such an act, he very wisely refrained, so he stood like a statue upon the hillside, watching, with a sickening feeling of remorse and shame, the retreating figure of the girl, and forgetting for a moment the very existence of his relatives who stood near.

But they did not forget him. Sir Charles Sedley, after bestowing a contemptuous stare upon the whole of the retreating party, fixed his eyes keenly and somewhat angrily upon his nephew, while his daughter withdrew her gaze occasionally from the figure of the young Highlander to fix it with chill sarcasm upon the man who had promised to become her husband.

Presently the retreating party passed over the brow of the hill and disappeared. Then Miss Sedley turned to her father.

'Is it necessary for us to linger here longer, papa?' she said, turning her back upon Lawrance.

'Certainly not, my love,' returned the baronet. 'I am quite ready to start if Lawrance is.'

'Lawrance!' she said, with a little contemptuous shrug. 'If we wait for him we shall not get home till midnight. He is evidently bent on seeing the sun set amongst those hills. It seems to me we are quite well able to return as we came—without him.'

Here Lawrance shook off his apathy and came forward.

'Where are you staying?' he asked quietly.

'At Coreveolan, of course,' returned the baronet testily. 'We drove over in the dogcart; but as your lodgings are near at hand we'll go there first, and get something to eat and drink.'

Lawrance quietly acquiesced, and turning, offered his arm to Ethel; but she curtly refused it, and moving from his side, walked with her father across the hill.

During that walk to the lodge Mina's name was never once mentioned. Every attempt at conversation was strained, until at length all parties seemed to agree that silence was best. So they walked on, Ethel leaning affectionately on her father's arm, and sometimes making a remark to him; and Lawrance stalking moodily on the baronet's other side.

At length the lodge was reached, and Ethel, releasing her father's arm, walked into the parlour, threw off her hat and jacket, and proceeded to make herself comfortable.

'Really,' she said, looking around the room, 'Lawrance knows how to take care of himself. This is not at all a bad little place for the Highlands.'

'Do you think so? Well, it has been a perfect godsend to me, I can assure you.'

Ethel frowned and turned her shoulder. She thought her father had followed her into the room. Now she found that he had remained outside, in all probability to give her a chance of making it up with her lover. But she did not intend to make it up so readily; at any rate, not till he was ready to come as a humbled suppliant for her mercy. So she turned her back upon him, and looked out of the window; and Lawrance, noting the action and the frown upon her brow, said no more.

When they sat down to the lunch which the old house keeper had hastily prepared, Sir Charles saw at once that things remained much the same as they had been before; at any rate, no reconciliation had taken place. Ethel sat frowning petulantly, and Lawrance was gloomily silent as ever. The baronet was angry too, but he did not think it politic to show his anger at the time; indeed, he turned quite pleasantly to his nephew as he asked—

'How long have you been rusticating in this remote district, Lawrance?'

'Two or three weeks.'

'And you came *incog.* from mere caprice, I suppose?'

'Not at all. I had a motive in it, and wanted to see for myself the real condition of the people.'

The baronet made no reply to this. Another uncomfortable silence ensued, which was broken by Lawrance.

'When did *you* arrive here?'

He looked at Ethel, but, as she did not choose to notice the look, her father replied for her—

'We left London about a week ago, fully three weeks before the time that we arranged to meet you at Coreveolan. Ethel was getting knocked up in town, and I thought the change would do her good, so off we started. We found the castle habitable, but the place miserably dull. Little Baron Bromsen, who came with us, got a surfeit of it in less than three days, and started for the Rhine. Since then Ethel and I have had the castle to ourselves, and precious dull it's been!'

He ceased, and again there was an uncomfortable silence; then the baronet spoke again:

'Well, now we have run you to earth, we must try between us to make it a bit livelier for Ethel.'

'I suppose she finds it dull.'

'Well, I must confess I do, rather,' said Ethel, with a forced laugh. 'You see, we women cannot find so many amusements as you men can; and, besides, I have not got your passion for nature in the rough.'

At this covert taunt Lawrance flushed to the temples; the baronet frowned as he met his daughter's eye, and Ethel held her peace. But she was wearying to get away, so she bothered her father until he ordered out the trap which had brought them there. Ethel stepped in, unfurled her parasol, and prepared to give a stately bow to Lawrance; but to her amazement he stepped in too, and took his seat right behind her.

'What, are you coming over to the castle?' she said.

'Yes, of course.'

She did not know that her father had asked, nay, almost entreated, him to come, so she took it as a sign of penitence. She was glad, very glad, that he was going to make it up, for, after all, the quarrel was a very stupid one. He had simply been ignominiously caught giving a kiss to a pretty girl, and the girl had been thoroughly overwhelmed when she was told the rank of the wooer; and Ethel had chosen to sulk and show jealousy simply because she wanted him to kiss and pet her, and charm her frowns away. Unfortunately, Lawrance had sulked too, and things were threatening to become serious if this stupid child's play was not soon brought to an end.

Altogether Ethel was glad when Lord Arranmore stepped into the carriage, for it seemed to her that reconciliation was at hand. But to her amazement he sat in the same moody, discontented way as he had sat in the lodge. Indeed, during the whole of that long drive he scarcely opened his lips. He was thinking of the time when he had traversed that road before—of the two little hands which on that occasion he had taken into his—of the grave, truthful, steadfast eyes which had been raised to return his look when he had asked, in a voice full of passionate love, 'Mina, will you not trust me?' She had trusted him, and he had belied the trust.

Through the long delay in Uribol the Sedleys arrived at the castle only a quarter of an hour before dinner was to be served; consequently Lawrance, after seeing his cousin safely in, passed at once up to a bedroom.

In a very short time he re-emerged, and made his way downstairs.

It seemed to him as if the whole place had been transformed since that memorable day when last he came, for Sir Charles had brought a large number of servants in his train, and they swarmed about the building. Lawrance found a strange footman in plain dress ready to meet him at every turn, to glance with a sigh at the shooting suit which he had not changed, to open the door with the profoundest of bows.

Ethel was in the drawing-room when he entered it.

Though the time for dressing had been short enough, she had found it ample to exchange her travelling-dress for a dinner-dress of black and amber; to fasten in her hair a diamond spray, around her throat a diamond necklet, and to arrange her black hair with her usual negligent grace. She sat near the very piano which he had offered to send over to the manse for Mina; her cheek was shaded from the fire by one of the screens which he had begged Mina to take. The room was brilliantly lit, and made to look tolerably comfortable. The baronet, entering at this moment, cunningly made the young lord feel that, for the first time in his life, he was to play the part of host to his uncle and cousin. Lawrance, therefore, anxious at once to sustain his part well, threw off at once his gloomy preoccupation of manner, and made himself agreeable to his guests. More than a year had passed since he had last seen them, so when once the constraint between them had worn away he found he had much to tell. He chatted away pleasantly during the evening, but never once did he mention the family at Uribol Manse.

'It's all right, Ethel,' said the baronet that night after the young lord had retired. 'I daresay the young scamp felt ashamed at having played the peasant, and was a bit vexed at you for letting out the truth. But don't take any more notice of it, my dear.'

'Very well, papa.'

'And try to make yourself a bit agreeable to Lawrance.'

'I am quite willing, if he chooses to make himself agreeable to me.

'Bless my soul, Ethel, he has been as agreeable as he could possibly be all the evening; but he won't keep it up if you mean to go on sulking.'

'Then he can do the other thing, papa.'

Her father looked at her keenly, as he replied—

'You mean he can cause it to be said that he grew to prefer the society of a Scotch peasant girl to that of his cousin, the acknowledged belle of two London seasons.'

Miss Sedley flushed angrily.

'The girl is not a peasant; she is sister to Graham Macdonald, whom I met at Lady Murray's last year.'

K

'And who, pray, is Graham Macdonald?'

'I don't know.'

'Of course you don't, and neither does anybody else. And who is Lady Murray? Only a dowdy old Highland lady, who would be no one out of Edinburgh. Look here, Ethel: don't you run your head against those Macdonalds; you'll find Lawrance quite enough for you.'

They sat talking for fully half an hour longer. In the end Ethel kissed her father, and promised to be dutiful and obey him.

But Sir Charles soon found that his daughter was not his greatest care. After the first evening at the castle, Lawrance took to moping again, and the baronet presently discovered that the cause of his moody preoccupation was the clergyman's niece.

'The affair is more serious than I thought,' he reflected; 'and, if things are let alone, I am afraid Ethel will stand a poor chance of being Lady Arranmore. But I think I see a means of setting things right, and I'll do it, let it cost what it may.'

CHAPTER XXIII.

A MYSTERIOUS MESSAGE.

THE next morning as Mina sat on the shore of the fjord, a hundred yards away from the manse door, she was greeted in the well-known voice of Angus-of-the-Dogs, and, turning, she saw the mendicant himself standing close by her. His face wore its characteristic vacant smile, his large eyes rolled, and he shuffled uneasily with his feet, round which several of his canine followers were running silently.

'Good morning, Angus,' she said with a smile, speaking in Gaelic.

'Good morning, and the blessing of God on the girl with the golden hair!' he answered in the same tongue. 'I've been looking for you high and low.'

'For me, Angus?'

'For yourself, miss. Hush, and whisper! Don't pretend to be looking at me while I give ye something sweeter than honey, and better than a poor man's plaster for a sick heart. A line, darling, from the one you know.'

So saying, with many nods, winks, chuckles, and glances round, and a general air of sympathetic secrecy, he drew from his pouch an envelope and placed it in her hand.

It was quite blank, without any superscription whatever, and she looked at it in some perplexity.

'Open it quick, now,' exclaimed Angus; 'there's a word of comfort inside.'

Thus urged, she opened the envelope, and read, on a small piece of note-paper enclosed within, these words in a man's hand:

'*I must see you. Meet me at sunset to-morrow near the old shieling on the shore of Loch Drummdhu.*'

Her face became scarlet, and the leaflet almost fluttered from her hand. She knew only one being from whom such a message might come, and though she had never seen the handwriting before, she felt it must be his. For a moment her head swam round, and anger, wonder, distrust, and pleasure contended within her. He had not forgotten her. Great lord though he was, he still remembered her, and the tender greetings that had once passed between them. And he wished to meet her once more. That also was, as his poor messenger expressed it, a word of comfort. But if such was his wish, why did he not come and seek her? Why did he appoint a meeting in so solitary a place? She would not go to him; no, she dared not go. They were better far apart, since it was clear that they could now be nothing to each other.

While she stood startled and wondering, her brain full of burning fears and conjectures, Angus rolled his head at her in unaffected delight. At last she met his eyes.

'Who gave you this?' she asked.

'One of his own people, miss, and my blessings on the luck it brings you. I was to give it to your own self, and let never a soul beside, not even his reverence, know it was sent you. And now tell me, pulse of my heart, when's the wedding to be, and when is the girl with the golden hair to be the great lady of Arranmore?'

For a moment Mina looked at him in anger and surprise, but remembering his character and condition, she only smiled and shook her head. Without waiting for any further answer, Angus put his fingers on his lips as a token of secrecy, and shuffled away, followed by his canine pets.

He had not gone many yards before he turned and shuffled back again.

'I forgot to ask you, darling—is there any answer?'

Mina shook her head again.

'Maybe you'll take the answer yourself,' he cried with a grin; 'and may my blessing and the blessing of God be along with it;' and he shuffled away again.

Placing the paper carefully in her bosom, Mina walked slowly towards the manse. A strong impulse was upon her to go to see her uncle at once, and show him what she had received; yet an equally strong impulse, working in the intensity of her own personal passion, drew her back. It was clear that Arranmore solicited a secret meeting, and with this view had appointed a solitary time and place. Should she grant his wish? Would it be wise or maidenly to do so? She knew enough of his character to be certain that he did not intend her any harm; but what could he wish to say to her—what communication could he now desire to make, which could not be heard by all the world? From her simple point of view the social distance between them seemed now quite impassable. He was a great man, she only a poor country girl, and marriage was entirely out of the question. And yet, if he did not mean to woo her again, what could be his object in desiring a meeting. She was in a strange perplexity, and quite undecided how to act.

Love's secrecy conquered, and she did not speak to her uncle. She found him in the study flourishing a newspaper, and denouncing the ignorance and folly of a certain Lowland professor who had just had the audacity to publish, in an English magazine, an article impugning (for the thousandth time) the genuineness of the Ossianic epos.

The bulk of the article was reprinted in the columns of the *Inverness Courier*, which. journal the clergyman now flourished in his hand, and made the text of his furious invective. At such a time, when the very foundations of his simple faith were threatened, all other mundane matters —even those affecting his pet child and pupil—sank into insignificance. Boiling with polemical rage, Mr. Macdonald sat down and concocted a long letter to the *Courier*, rebutting in detail the professor's arguments, exposing his ignorance, and calling him innumerable hard names in Gaelic, Greek, and Latin—all except mother English, which would have been far too unpolite. The letter appeared the week after in all the glory of big type, interspersed with long sentences of early Gaelic, and with a foot-note expressing with how much pleasure the editor gave publicity to the opinions of 'one of our ripest Celtic scholars and profoundest believers in the genuineness of Ossian.'

On the whole Mina was glad that the occasion was inopportune, and that she could not take her uncle, that night at least, into her confidence. She carried her secret about with her all day, blushing and trembling over it, and half determining to make a clean breast of it on the morrow. She was unusually sympathetic with her uncle, listening all the evening to his ejaculations and exclamations on the subject next his heart, and once or twice taking down notes at his request; but she shrank from Graham's gaze, and fancied that it expressed annoyance and suspicion. Graham, however, was in reality too busy with a burden of his own to think very much about hers.

Half an hour before midnight she escaped to her own room, carrying her secret and the paper with her. Undressing that night was a slow process, and even when her light was extinguished, and she wore nothing but her white night-dress, she stood for a long time at the window looking up at the mountains in the direction of Loch Drummdhu. It was a moonlight night, and the peace of the silvern light was brooding upon the hills.

And if, before lying down to rest, she kissed that paper, thinking with a quick thrill of passion of one who was far away, who shall blame her? She was only a simple girl, and the divine instinct was strong within her. That night, as she brooded over her sweet secret, while

> 'Her gentle limbs she did undress,
> And lay down in her loveliness,'

she forgot altogether that he who loved her was so far above her; or, if she remembered, it was only with a proud pleasure which intensified her love.

Yes, she loved him—that night, at least—and sleep brought her many a quick and happy dream, with which his face and form were delightfully blended.

When morning came she awoke to a sharp dread. Having passed out of the fairy palace of her dreams, beautiful as the enchanted palace of Eros, in the Greek tale, she found herself standing bewildered in the sunshine.

She took out the paper again, read it, and re-read it. No, she could not show it to her uncle—that would be breaking confidence; but she would pay no attention to its request. That was her fixed determination during the whole of the forenoon.

But as the sun moved westward there arose within her bosom the tremulous thrill which draws lover to lover wherever hearts beat and love abides. Why should she not meet him once more? Just once—just for a moment —just to tell him how unkind he had been, and how they could never meet again! Why should she not show him how little she feared him, despite his great rank and name; how calmly she could sever, once and for always, the silken link which still held them together?

Oh, she could be very stern and cold, and he should see that her pride was as great as his; then he would understand her, and thenceforth leave her alone. Yes, she would go. Perhaps, after all, he only wished to ask her forgiveness, and if that were so, she could freely forgive him. As the gentle thought passed through her mind, her eyes grew dim with tears.

She looked up at the mountains. They were netted in the sheen of a golden day; every chasm, gulch, glen, and shadow distinct as on a map; every thread of a stream sparkling like silver; every dark lochan flashing like a shield.

Loch Drummdhu, though a solitary place, was not far away. She could walk there easily in less than an hour. Yes, she would go to him. She would meet him for the last time.

Late in the afternoon she stood ready at the manse door, waiting for an opportunity of escape.

'Where are you going?' asked Graham, who sat on the bench at the door, reading a book.

'Only down the clachan to see old Ailsa; she is sick again.'

'Well, I shall walk over to Koll, and see if he is going out to-night after the mackerel. I counted fifteen solan-geese off the lighthouse this morning, hunting the shoal, and the cormorants were thick as a flock of starlings.'

Mina made no answer, but wandered quietly away. She was afraid to walk rapidly, lest her brother should notice, and wonder at her haste. But the sun-rays were already reddening, and the great peaks above Loch Drummdhu were shining like molten brass. She had no time to lose if she wished to be punctual to her tryst.

Once out of sight of Graham, she hastened her footsteps, and was soon on the open heather.

The ascent to the lake was by a narrow footpath strewn with boulders, and winding by the side of a brown mountain burn.

There were no trees, except here and there a dwarf mountain ash, drooping with soft silvern leaves and crimson berries over some nut-brown pool.

Down below lay the village, scarce distinguishable from the surrounding flats, and enclosed on every side by the glimmering arms of the sea. Before her rose the low, dark mountains, so bare of herbage as scarcely to afford food even for mountain sheep; and between her and the mountains, though as yet unseen, was the lonely fresh-water lake.

As she reached the head of the ascent, where the brook emerged from the lake, a small pack of grouse flew past her at headlong speed, scattered, and fell severally into the deep heather close to her, and almost at the same moment a magnificent peregrine falcon, which was in pursuit, flashed past just over her head.

Before her lay the lake, some two miles long, one broad, hlack as pitch, but so shallow that here and there sharp, black rocks jutted up like portions of sunken reefs.

In the centre were several small, green islands, covered with innumerable gulls which had flocked there to build. Large numbers of gulls and other aquatic birds were floating everywhere on the water; and high in the air, circling round and round, with harsh croaks and cries, were a pair of ravens.

The light of the setting sun crimsoned the hills beyond the lake, but scarcely changed the solemn blackness of the lake itself.

Dark and solitary as was the scene, Mina felt perfectly at home in it; her life had been passed in such places, and to her they were neither dreary nor sad. But her heart was beating wildly, her face was flushed with fearful expectation, as she looked around her. Before her lay the lake, all round her the dark moorland and the lonely hills; but no human form was visible as yet.

She stood hesitating, and a quick impulse came upon her to return as she had come.

Now that she was there, fearful and expectant, she dreaded the meeting for which she had hitherto been so eager.

Should she go or stay? Perhaps he would not come at all? Perhaps it was only a trick to try her? Yes, she would go back home.

As she turned to retreat, a shot was fired not far away, and the next moment she saw approaching her, over a heathery knoll, the figure of a man. He advanced—she stood still to recognise him. To her surprise she perceived, not Lord Arranmore, but the elderly baronet who was then in occupation of Coreveolan Castle.

CHAPTER XXIV.

MINA KEEPS TRYST.

BEHIND Sir Charles Sedley, but a hundred yards away, loomed another figure, a man in the Highland costume, holding in leash two Gordon setters. As the baronet advanced, observing Mina, he waved his hand to his attendant, who immediately, as if at an understood signal, disappeared from view. Astonished and puzzled, Mina was about to hasten away, but, quickening his footsteps and making signals to her, Sir Charles rapidly approached. In another minute he stood before her, and saluted her politely by taking off his hat.

'Good afternoon, Miss Macdonald,' he said quickly; then taking out a gold hunting-watch and touching the spring, he added, 'I hope I am not late.'

Completely perplexed, Mina looked in his face, and trembled from head to foot. His countenance wore an expression of patronising good-nature, but his nervous manner and heightened colour showed that he was ill at ease.

She drew back almost in alarm, and at the same moment a terrible suspicion of the truth flashed upon her. Before she could utter a word he spoke again—

'Of course you got my letter?'

His letter? What could he mean? She gazed at him in renewed distrust.

'Yes,' he continued, smiling, 'my letter asking you to meet me here at sunset. By your coming I perceive you are a young lady of sense. But perhaps the bearer mystified you, and you came here in the expectation of meeting my nephew. Never mind. The bird has flown to the lure, and I am charmed.'

It was a trap, then, to shame and humiliate her! Her face turned white as death, and, panting like a wounded deer, she gazed at her tormentor. Something in her look made him feel uncomfortable, and perhaps ashamed, at least for the moment.

Without a word she turned to depart.

'Stop!' he cried.

She turned on him with flashing eyes, and panted:

'I do not know you, sir. If you have anything to say, you had better speak to my brother.'

'Your brother would not understand; my business is altogether with *you*. Do, pray, hear me out. The fact is, I come on behalf of Lord Arranmore?'

'Did *he* send you?'

'Well, not exactly, but I think I am justified in saying that I act with his approval. Now, understand me, my dear. I won't disguise from you the fact that when I discovered his lordship's acquaintance with you I was angry— very angry; for I justly considered that he had no right to trifle with your affections, knowing not only your relative positions, but also his formal engagement to my daughter.'

'Sir'——

'My dear, hear me out. I will not assume that you love Lord Arranmore—that would be an impertinence; but I believe you have a respect for him, an interest in him, which he reciprocates even more ardently. Having this interest in him, and feeling, as I am sure you must do, that your paths in life are far apart, you would desire him to be happy.'

He paused, but Mina said nothing; so presently he continued:

'Of course he knows as well as I do that his happiness can only be compassed by marriage with my daughter. He is very fond of her, she adores him; there is only one obstacle to their happiness at present, and that is—you!'

She turned towards him her flushed and angry face, but he waved his hand to keep her silent.

'Don't excite yourself, my dear; listen quietly to me, and I am sure we shall get to understand one another. Lord Arranmore is rather fond of your sex generally, and the one in whose company he happens to be is his

and a very high-spirited girl; and if, after what she saw
that day on the hill, his lordship were to continue his—
ahem—well, his acquaintance with you—she might, perhaps, in a moment of anger break off the match.'

'Silence, sir!' said Mina, now fairly beside herself with
anger and mortified pride. 'What right have you to speak
to me as you do? What is Lord Arranmore to me, or
I to him, that you *dare* talk to me so? Why have you
brought me here with a false message? Tell me what you
wish, and let me go.'

She stood gazing full into his face. The baronet returned that look with one of genuine admiration.

'Upon my word,' he thought, 'the young scamp had
good taste. She is a pretty creature—the sort of a rival no
woman could be ashamed of.'

So lost was he in admiration, that he paused for some
time before he spoke. Seeing he remained silent, Mina
believed the interview to be at an end. She turned to go,
but the baronet laid his hand upon her arm and detained her.

'My dear,' he said, 'one word more before you go. I
want you to promise '——

'Well, sir?'

'To promise to keep out of the way, if possible, of my
susceptible nephew, and, if you should meet him, to give
him no encouragement. I have explained his true character to you. I will not deny that your influence over him
might be fatal to my hopes—that in an evil moment he
might be tempted to compass your ruin!'

'*My* ruin?' replied Mina, in utter amazement.

'Well, honestly, yes.'

She looked at him still in utter amazement. What he
meant she could not for a moment imagine.

If he had spoken of his daughter's ruin she might have
understood; but what possible harm, she thought, beyond
that which was already done, could Lord Arranmore bring
to her. She looked at the baronet with eyes full of mystified
wonder. He did not return the look. His eyes fell in
embarrassment before Mina's steady gaze.

'What do you mean?' she asked quietly. 'I do not
un lerstand you, sir.'

'My dear young lady,' returned Sir Charles, in some hesitation, 'if I am compelled to speak plainly, believe me, I am actuated solely by a desire for your welfare. You have inspired me with a strange interest in you, and I could not stand coolly by and see you come to harm. I know that my nephew could not, under any circumstances whatever, think of making you *his wife;* so to what, therefore, could his attentions to you lead but to utter misery?'

He paused, but Mina said nothing. She had watched and listened to every word, and as he spoke her cheek had by turns grown pale and crimson. As he looked at her, Sir Charles for the first time felt pity—such pity as he might have felt for a poor hunted deer which lay mortally wounded at his feet and turned towards him its large pitiful eyes as if imploring mercy. But with his pity there was no remorse. Even as he would have struck the last blow for the life-blood of the deer, he turned to give the last stab to the broken-hearted girl.

'Miss Macdonald, you are a young lady of sense, and if you will only think over the past, you will perceive that what I say is true. Lord Arranmore may have spoken of love—he would never have mentioned marriage, for he knew that the future Lady Arranmore was already chosen.'

'Have you done, sir?' asked Mina, when he paused again.

'I have nothing more to say, my dear, but I want your promise.'

'My promise?'

'To keep out of his lordship's way.'

'Oh, you may set your mind at rest, sir. I shall not seek Lord Arranmore, be sure of that; indeed, my greatest wish now is never to see him or any of you again.'

'Then I will take my leave. My dear Miss Macdonald, you have behaved admirably. I thank you with all my heart.'

So saying, the baronet courteously raised his hat, and, with a stately bow, walked swiftly away. Mina did not move; when he bowed she coldly bent her head, and wearily watched him as he moved away. When he had disappeared, and she found herself entirely alone, with the solitary hills all round her and night coming on, she sat down on the thick purple heather, and, covering her face with both her hands, burst into tears.

Mina was not usually given to crying, but her heart was full to bursting that night, for she felt that her trouble was growing almost too much for her to bear. Insult after insult was being heaped upon her to make her degradation complete. She thought over the baronet's words, and each one was like a sharp sting—all the more poignant because of its truth. For they were true—that assurance at least she must take to her heart, although by so doing she felt that her whole life was blighted. The man to whom she had given all her faith, all her love, had come to her with a lie upon his lips, and brought her only shame and sorrow.

For a time the bitter tears flowed unrestrained; then, still sobbing, she raised her head and looked around her. Night had crept on apace. The ranges of mountain were blackened with shadows, and far out at sea the last grey gleams of light were dying; she could hear all around her the soft cry of the night-birds, and the faint, far-off murmur of the sea. Her heart was aching terribly, and her bosom still heaved with hysterical sobs.

'Thank God, I did not cry before that man!' she said to herself. 'I felt my heart was bursting at every word he spoke, but I would not cry—I would not show a sign—not before *him*. Oh, he has been very cruel; may God forgive him for all he has done to me! Well, I will go home. I will try to forget all this—and *him!*—all his cruelty, all his wickedness. The thought of his love was only a beautiful dream. I am waking now!'

She rose and walked slowly through the ever-thickening darkness towards her home.

CHAPTER XXV.

WELL satisfied with the result of his interview, the baronet made his way back to his keeper, who lay awaiting him in the long heather.

'Let the dogs work,' he said; 'I'll shoot my way back to the lodge.'

An hour's shooting in the direction of the mountains brought him in sight of a small house, situated right at the foot of the hills, and surrounded on every side by excellent ground for grouse. It was one of the outlying shooting-lodges belonging to Coreveolan, and was comfortably furnished for the convenience of sportsmen beating that part of the mountains. Castle Coreveolan itself lay a good five miles away, as the crow flies, over a very difficult stretch of country; and Sir Charles had walked over that morning along a bridle-path through the hills.

At the door of the lodge, as he approached it panting and perspiring, he found his daughter, coquettishly attired in a costume of heather-coloured mixture and a hat to match, trimmed with the feathers from a cormorant's breast.

'Here I am, papa,' she cried, 'first to arrive, you see, and I have already put the house in order. Welcome to Glenheather Lodge!'

'How did you come?' asked Sir Charles, sitting down on the heather before the door.

'On the back of Sheelah,' she replied, pointing to a shaggy pony which was grazing close by, attended by a ragged Highland boy. 'Malcolm Beg was my cavalier, and I find I have made quite a conquest.'

'Where's Lawrance?' asked Sir Charles sharply.

'I left him at the castle, sulking as usual.'

'Wouldn't he come?'

'I didn't ask him, and he didn't volunteer. He expects

us back to-morrow, but I shan't go. Glenheather Lodge for me! It is twice as pleasant as that dreary, damp, dilapidated old castle, and I mean to stay in it a fortnight at least.'

'Nonsense!'

'It isn't nonsense, papa; it's capital. All the furniture is made of nice, clean, new deal, and instead of boards in the kitchen, the floor is strewn with thyme and sweet-smelling heather. There's a cow to give us milk, and a little Highland girl to milk it, and an old woman to cook the mutton and the game, plenty of new-laid eggs to be had in the village, any amount of fresh air, nobody to bore us, and such a view! I think I shall turn female hermit, and live here for ever.'

So saying, she led the way into the lodge; and when the baronet had changed his clothes and boots, and entered the little dining-room as hungry as a raven, he was fain to confess that Glenheather Lodge was very pleasant quarters. A bright fire of turf was burning in the grate, the table was spread with a snowy cloth, and old Janet, who kept the lodge, while her husband watched the game, had prepared a very good highland dinner, to be washed down with champagne, which had been brought over, with other good things, on a pony's back. To crown all, there were two arm-chairs, one on either side of the fire, and each affording the sort of lounge which weary sportsmen love after a long day's shooting.

Dinner over, Sir Charles lit his cigar, and felt particularly comfortable. Ethel now expected him to doze off for the evening, in the interesting manner of Highland sportsmen; but he kept awake, and presently became conversational.

'I've just been having rather an interesting interview,' he said. 'Can you guess with whom?'

Ethel shook her head.

'I met, down yonder, Lawrance's heroine, the old clergy-man's niece. We had a long conversation.'

He thought it quite unnecessary to mention that the meeting was not accidental, but prearranged. Ethel looked interested, but affected a certain unconcern, and waited for her father to explain matters at length, which he presently proceeded to do.

'It is clear that Lawrance has put a bit of nonsense in the girl's head, and I'm afraid she doesn't quite perceive the gulf there is between them. She's not bad-looking, but a bit of a fool. I had quite to argue it out with her before she would admit the absurdity of her conduct in thinking any more about Lawrance.'

'I wonder you took the trouble,' returned Ethel petulantly. 'I'm sure she's welcome to him, for all I care.'

'Absurd !'

'The whole thing is absurd, papa, and humiliating into the bargain. I believe Lawrance prefers this wild young woman of the mountains—at any rate, his connection with her was more than a mere flirtation, and he mopes day and night about her still. I have made up my mind, and I shall release him from his engagement.'

'What!' cried Sir Charles, in unaffected astonishment.

'I am tired of running up and down the world after a lover who does not care for me, and who likes any society —even that of a dairy-maid or a scullion—better than mine. We were betrothed before either of us knew our own minds. Our betrothal was a farce which is now over, and I mean to bring down the curtain at once.'

Sir Charles rose to his feet, and stood on the hearthrug ` scowling down at his daughter.

'You're talking bosh, Ethel, and you know it. You *must* marry Lawrance; I have set my mind upon it.'

'Can't be done, papa.'

'Lawrance is very fond of you, and has no desire whatever to break his engagement, but you know his impetuosity. By some means or other this artful young woman has managed, by thrusting herself forward and making eyes at him, to flatter his vanity, and, though he does not care a pin about her, he fancies that she is enamoured of him, and that he is to blame for having given her encouragement. Leave it all to me; I'll guarantee that Lawrance does his duty by you, and in a few months you will be Lady Arranmore.'

Ethel answered with a mere shrug of the shoulders and an incredulous smile. The *tête-à-tête* lasted a little longer, but

contained nothing else worthy of remark. In her heart
Ethel had just then no intention of breaking finally with
her lover, though she was grieved at his neglect, and could
not help expressing a little indignation. Her engagement
to him had become such a settled thing, such a changeless
portion of her daily life and thought, that she clung to it as
one clings to an old dress—from habit even more than
affection. It would cost her a pang to break it finally and
to get accustomed to the change.

Next morning it was pouring wet, but it cleared up a
little after breakfast, and Sir Charles sallied forth with his
deer-stalking rifle, anxious to inspect a certain defile in the
mountains where there was a chance of a red deer.

Left to herself, Ethel tried to read, and yawned over a
novel; then tripped out to the kitchen and chatted for a
time with old Janet. Glenheather Lodge was rather tire-
some, she began to think, in wet weather.

At last a thought seemed to strike her. Donning a
waterproof cloak and a pair of thick boots, she walked
out, and, as if by instinct, took the path which led to the
village, a couple of miles away.

Her path at first lay through a splendid tract of deep
heather, on which the sun was just beginning to shine.
She looked around her with no very profound enjoyment
of the lovely scene. Larks were singing, the cock-grouse
was crowing, the mountain hare was 'running races in his
mirth,' but her thoughts were far away. In her opinion
the prospect would have been charming but for one em-
bellishment which it sadly lacked—a person of the opposite
sex with whom to flirt.

She came down along the banks of Loch Drummdhu,
past the very spot where her father and Mina Macdonald
met on the previous evening. Here, indeed, an object of
interest attracted her attention. At first she thought it was a
mossy stone hewn in likeness of a man—it kept so silent and
so still; but on a closer inspection she saw it was a man,
indeed, very old, with hair as white as snow, and face as
grave as granite, sitting on the shore of the lonely lake, and
looking silently at the dark waters, the screaming sea-gulls,
the drifting clouds.

L

As she came close, he looked up with a gaze of strange intensity, but made no sign.

'Good morning,' she was constrained to say.

His lips moved, but he did not answer. She examined him more closely. His wild white hair, his worn face, his strange eyes, his ragged gown, all filled her with curiosity.

'A strange creature,' she reflected. 'Looks like a hobgoblin of the mountain, or a fossil man fast coming back to life. How he stares! I suppose he never saw a lady before in all his life.'

'Koll!' cried a voice below them.

Koll Nicholson, for it was he, rose to his feet, towering above her like one of the heroes of Ossian. She looked round, and there, emerging from the side of the brook, was another figure, agile this time and young, carrying a single-handed trout-rod, and holding up to view a fresh-run sea-trout of about a pound, which he had just landed from a pool below.

At a glance she recognised Graham Macdonald.

As his eyes fell upon her he started, turned red as crimson, and stood hesitating what to do; but, advancing with her brightest smile, she at once greeted him by name.

Thus addressed, he strode forward, and tossed the fish to Koll, who immediately thrust it into a canvas bag made for the purpose; then, still flushing crimson, he lifted his Scotch cap.

He wore the Highland dress, which well became his youthful frame and shapely limbs; and Ethel thought as she gazed upon him that she had never looked upon any one so handsome.

'I see you are fishing,' she said. 'Pray, who is your attendant?'

'He? Oh, that is Koll Nicholson, an old boatman, and sort of foster-father to my sister and myself.'

'How interesting! Can he speak English?'

'Pretty well when he chooses, but he prefers his mother-tongue.'

'Far better, I am sure, than our insipid Saxon. What a grand old ruin of a man!—like an old castle on a promon-

tory, grim, stern, solemn, and splendid, though all tumbling
to pieces!'

As she spoke, she eyed the old man critically, as she
might inspect some inanimate stone, or picture, or old
curiosity. Koll, for his part, stood almost motionless with
his keen eyes fixed upon her. It was difficult to read the
expression on his face, but it seemed to express strong
suspicion and dislike, blended with a certain admiration.

At this point, Graham said something rapidly in Gaelic,
and Koll answered with a harsh, peculiar laugh; then,
dropping his eyes and averting his head, the old man
passed rapidly over the knoll by which Graham had
ascended.

Ethel seemed relieved at his departure, and turned
brightly to Graham.

'Are you not surprised to see me here?' she said, smiling; 'we are stopping for a few days at Glenheather Lodge.'

'Is Lord Arranmore with you?'

'No; I am alone with papa. By the way, Mr. Macdonald, how is your charming sister?'

Graham's brow darkened, and he replied carelessly enough.
His bearing towards his companion was a curious mixture
of timidity and self-assertion. Tangled in the net of her
elegance and beauty, he struggled to seem proud, easy, and
free; but his eyes, when they met hers, burned with dangerous fire. Confident in her superiority, as she conceived,
she enjoyed his passionate uneasiness, and delighted in the
admiration he struggled in vain to conceal. Just then, in
the pride of her high-born grace and beauty, she looked
witching beyond measure, while with heightened colour,
heaving bosom, and sparkling eyes, she gazed upon the
young Highlander.

He would gladly have escaped, but her charm held him
like a hand.

'When I met you at Lady Murray's,' she said, 'you were
preparing to enter the Church; are you ordained yet, or
have you changed your mind?'

As she asked the question she glanced significantly at
the young man's very unclerical costume, and smiled. His
cheek flushed as he replied:

'Yes, I have changed my mind; I'm not the right sort of stuff for a minister. I would rather any day be fishing a stream, or flying a hawk, than blethering in a pulpit. Besides, I hate all black coats, and would rather sport the red.'

'But your uncle '——

'He is one in a thousand—a good man, and not a humbug. If I were like him, half as clever or half as good, I might follow the same vocation; but, as it is, I am only fit for a roving life, like the life of a seal or a red-deer.'

He spoke impulsively, with flashing eyes and swelling nostrils, and, while recklessly depreciating himself, shone forth in the full strength of his manhood. Certainly no tone could have suited him better, or made him more attractive in the eyes of his fair companion.

'Why not enter the army?' she said, thinking as she spoke what a splendid soldier he would make.

'I've been speaking of that, but my uncle hates soldiers as much as I hate priests. I'm thinking I'll just have to emigrate, and try my fortune in Australia or New Zealand.'

'That would be hard—to have to leave your native country, I mean.'

He looked at her intently, and then said, raising his voice:

'Not harder than to be what I am—by birth and ancestry a gentleman, and yet almost a beggar, through the wickedness and stupidity of my own folk.'

'I do not understand!'

'Little more than fifty years ago all these lands for a circle of three miles round Loch Drummdhu belonged to my father's father, and they would have been ours still if the old fool had not preferred drink and devilry to decent living and fair play. He fooled away the heritage, and it passed over at last to the lords of Arranmore. Well, it was not a grand birthright, but it was better than nothing; and if I had my rights I should at least be the laird of my own soil.'

This was really interesting! Ethel's eyes opened, and saw in Graham—almost a new being—a ruined lord of the soil, proud and poor as Edgar of Ravenswood. What had previously seemed rude assurance now looked like splendid pride.

'Is Lady Murray any relation of yours?' she said.

'A distant one on the mother's side. She belonged to the Macleods of Macleod, my mothers' people.'

'And the lords of Arranmore bought your estate?'

'Bought it, or stole it, or lied for it,' said Graham quickly. 'A lie would go a long gait in these days, and it became theirs. I cannot even shoot a hare or a moorfowl on my own heather without his lordship's leave.'

'It does seem unfair,' she said very softly. 'Is Lord Arranmore aware of this?'

'Not from me, and it would disturb him little if he knew. The Arranmores have lived little on their own acres, but have preferred to dwell in foreign parts, draw the rents when due, and leave the rest to the factor. . . . But I'm speaking of your own kith and kin; I beg your pardon.'

'Not at all,' returned Ethel; 'indeed I sympathise with you, and I am sure Lord Arranmore, when I tell him, will do so to.'

This was touching on a dangerous chord, as Ethel discovered in a moment.

'I want no man's sympathy,' exclaimed Graham, with an angry gesture, 'least of all'——

Here he paused, conquering himself with an effort; then, to end the interview, he raised his cap and turned away.

But she called him back. He turned to her, not without a certain irritation.

'Will you tell your sister how much I would like to call upon her? May I do so, do you think, while I am staying at the lodge?'

'Of course, if you wish it,' answered Graham, somewhat amazed at the request.

'Then I will come.'

Graham made no further reply, but, lifting his hat again and raising his rod from the ground, stalked rapidly away in the direction taken by his foster-father. Following the windings of the stream, and leaping lightly over every impediment, he at last came to the height immediately above the manse.

Here he found Koll Nicholson waiting, seated quietly on a great stone. As he came up, flushed and panting, the old man turned his head, looked at him with a keen, hawk-like eye, but kept quite still upon his seat.

'Wha will pe yonder?' he asked, in a low, harsh voice.

'The lady?' said Graham, with a laugh. 'That is the young English lady living with her father at Castle Core-veolan.'

Koll gave a grunt, and plunged again into silence; then after a long pause, he spoke again:

'She's bonnie, but I dinna trust her; and bonnie as she is, I would thraw her neck if I thought she meant any harm to Mina.'

'Harm to Mina! What nonsense you're talking!'

'Maybe ay and maybe no; but we'll bide and see. What brings the leddy here?'

'They are staying at the lodge.'

'And the young laird—where is he?'

'How should I know? At the bottom of the salt sea, for all I care!'

So saying, the young man strode homeward, while Koll remained quietly sitting in the same place like one in a sort of dream. The old man's brow was black and his countenance troubled, and he muttered angrily to himself. At last, rising to his feet, he gazed up the hillside towards the rugged mountains which surrounded Glenheather Lodge, and, reaching out his skinny hand, which trembled with agitation, he murmured aloud in the Gaelic language:

'The land belonged to the Macdonalds, and it shall come back to the Macdonalds. Dinna think, my brave leddy, to come between my bairn and her birthright, for it canna be. Ye're bonnie, and wicked as bonnie, and ye've an eye like hers that beguiled the strong man in the Book and robbed him o' his hair; but keep awa' from my door, and from my bairn's door, my leddy, if ye're as wise as your wicked. I would put a knife into yer heart, bonnie lamb as ye are, if ye meant any harm to me or, mine!'

As he stood thus murmuring to himself, Koll looked positively baleful. His hair fell like snow around his deeply-wrinkled face, his eyes gleamed with unnatural lustre, and his form shook with the violence of some malignant passion. He remained for some time in the same attitude, as if pointing at some unseen object; then recovering himself with a harsh croak of laughter, he moved slowly down the hill.

Meantime, quite unconscious of the old man's threat or warning, which she would have found utterly irrelevant, even if it had reached and been translated to her, Ethel was gaily hastening towards Glenheather Lodge. She was quite delighted with her morning's adventure and her conversation with Graham Macdonald. The place had acquired a new interest in her eyes, now that she had discovered in Graham so many of the characteristics of the hero of romance.

'It is just "tit for tat,"' she said to herself. 'Lawrance has amused himself with the sister, and the brother will do very well to flirt with until I return to town.'

CHAPTER XXVI.

GRAHAM BECOMES ENTHRALLED.

IT was with no little difficulty that Mina Macdonald, after her interview with Sir Charles Sedley, concealed her deep trouble from her uncle and her brother. The wound of these cruel words had gone right to her heart, and the pain was almost too much to bear. All day long she tried to keep calm, forcing her tears down and speaking little : but her nights were spent in crying, and whenever she could she escaped out upon the water or up to the lonely hillside. It has been truly and beautifully said by the wisest poet of this century that—

> 'Nature never did betray
> The heart that loved her ;'

and certainly the mighty mother, on this occasion, succoured her favourite child. If she had not sometimes wandered forth and poured out her heart to the answering waves or the roaring torrent, she would have utterly broken down. She took a strange pleasure at that time in roaming to some solitary headland, and, seated on a rock, with her cheek upon her hand, crooning snatches of old songs, Celtic

and English, by the hour together.   She had always loved
to be alone ; now her love for solitude became a passion.

Her uncle, absorbed in his favourite subject, and deep
then in the throes of a ferocious newspaper controversy as
to whether Ossian himself was a warrior or only a bard,
scarcely noticed any change in her, though once or twice
he remarked that she seemed unusually pale ; but Graham,
with a keener perception and quicker suspicion, soon saw
that she was fretting, without guessing any new or unex-
plained cause.   'She is moping after the laird,' he thought
to himself, and cursed Arranmore in his heart of hearts.

With regard to his own encounter with Miss Sedley he
was quite silent for some days ; but one morning, when
Mina looked unusually ill, and was hurrying hastily away
from the manse to seek one of her favourite haunts on the
sea-shore, he hastened after her and called her back.

'Do you know there are folk up there at the lodge ?' he
asked ; adding in answer to a quick questioning look which
passed across her face, 'No, *he* is not there.   Only the young
lass and her father.'

'How do you know ?'

'I met her by accident on the hillside.   She minded me,
and was civil enough.   What do you think she means to
do ?   To call and see you one of these fine days.'

'No, no !' cried Mina, with an expression of positive
terror.

'She inquired after you quite kindly.   If she comes,
what shall you do ?'

'Keep away.   O Graham I do you think she will dare ?'

'Dare ?'

'I don't mean that, but do you think she will come ?
What does she want with me ?   I do not know her, and
she is so proud.'

Graham smiled with an air of pleasant experience.

'She's a lady, at any rate, and worthy a dozen of the
man she is engaged to marry.'

'To marry ?'

'Yes,' answered Graham, now frowning gloomily.
'Don't you know ?   They have been engaged since they
were bairns.   The villain knew that when he ran down

here with his lies and his smooth face : yet for all that he came courting to you. And *you* have not forgotten him, Mina. Do you think that I am blind? Day and night you keep grieving after him, even though you know he woos another lass, and that he is the Laird of Arranmore.'

Pale as death, Mina turned her eyes on her brother, and her voice was thick with tears.

'I'm not grieving after him, Graham. What is Lord Arranmore to me?'

'No more than yon bit of lint-white cloud on the sky ; but for all that, you pine and you pine till your cheeks are like a wraith's. Mina, my lass,' he continued, taking her hand, 'be wise. Try to forget him. Try to think he never came this way.'

Without answering, Mina drew her hand away, with a gesture so infinitely sad and pathetic that Graham was touched to the heart. Trembling with eagerness to hide her pain, she hurried away till her slight figure was hidden from sight in a turn of the lonely road. Graham watched it disappear, and then, with another exclamation not flattering to the cause of so much sorrow, stalked moodily back to the house.

That afternoon, as the family sat together over their frugal dinner, Mr. Macdonald informed Graham and Mina, who had been absent all day, that he had had a visitor.

'As winsome a one,' he said merrily, 'as even an old bachelor would care to entertain. She came into my dingy study like a glint of sunlight, and I gave her a Highland welcome. And she is as wise as winsome. I read to her my last letter in the *Courier*, translating to her the Gaelic and the Latin phrases, and she thought my arguments perfectly overwhelming. A very well-informed young lady indeed !'

'Miss Sedley, of course,' said Graham, while Mina sat silent, trembling in her chair.

'The best of these true aristocrats,' proceeded the clergyman, nodding, 'is their perfect freedom from all that constitutes vulgar pride. This young lady—*simplex munditiis*, as Horace expresses it—is a perfect example of gentle breeding. Mina, my bairn, she asked particularly after *you*, and seemed sadly chagrined when she found you not at home. You must see her !'

' I *have* seen her,' said Mina quickly.

' You have had but a glimpse of her, just as I myself had, and not under favourable circumstances. When you know more of her you will like her well. It is not often in these savage regions, this *ultima Thule*, that you have an opportunity of perceiving how a real lady looks, speaks, and acts. Well, she is coming again, and you will have an opportunity of enjoying her company. She is greatly interested in old Highland poetry, and I have promised to read aloud to her a part of my blank verse translation of Selma.'

In good truth the young lady, with the finesse habitual to her, had fooled the old clergyman completely by mounting him at once on his favourite hobby, and expressing the utmost sympathy and interest during all the pranks he made it play. No man, however old-fashioned and pedantic, is altogether proof against genuine loveliness, and Mr. Macdonald, though a clergyman, fully appreciated a pretty face, so that the conquest was complete. Graham listened to his uncle's panegyrics, and in his heart echoed every word of them, for it is needless to say that his sullen spirit had yielded completely to Ethel's subtle charm of face and manner. But Mina listened in despair. Every word was like a dagger in her heart, since she thought, ' It is *she*, this perfect creature whom he is to marry, and she is worthy of him ; while I am a poor girl, just like the dust beneath her feet.'

Graham watched his sister in silence, and hated young Arranmore tenfold. He hated him for having encouraged the simple day-dream which was breaking Mina's heart, but he hated him as much for having possession of the pretty being who seemed to exert so strange a fascination on all she met—even on himself.

Since he had, in a moment of impulse, submitted his heart to Ethel on the subject of the family misfortunes, he felt his pride increase in proportion to his sense of grievance. Then he reflected bitterly that the broad acres possessed by his grandfather had not only been squandered away, but had actually gone to swell the lands of Arran-more.

With more than one imprecation he named the young laird's name, and felt a furious impulse to be at his throat.

The next day Graham's feet were drawn, by irresistible fascination, to the spot where he had encountered Miss Scdley. He hung for hours about under pretence of fishing, but she did not appear, and he returned home in no very amiable temper.

The next day he was there again, fishing-rod in hand, and casting wistful glances up towards Glenheather Lodge ; and on this occasion she came, even more bright and radiant than before, for it was a summer day, and she seemed to share its golden splendour.

'How glad I am to have met you !' she exclaimed, holding out her little gloved hand. 'I was just on my way to visit your sister.'

He had never held her hand before since the day when he had met her in Edinburgh. He clasped it now with a strange thrill of pleasure, for the hand-shake seemed to put them on a new equality once and for ever.

'I was so charmed with your uncle,' she continued softly, as he relinquished his hold with an unconscious pressure. 'He is so learned, yet so simple and grand, and his manners have the fine stateliness of the old school. Did he tell you that I had called ?'

'He did,' answered Graham smiling; 'and sang your praises as bravely as one of the old bards.'

'He is so different to our English ministers, who think of nothing but port wine and plum-pudding. At Feltham, where we generally spend the winter, the rector has two thousand a year, and gives one hundred and fifty to his curate, who does all the work, while he himself spends his days in drinking and gormandising. It is so different here ! You Scotch are so grand, so manly and true ! One feels quite ashamed to come from our frivolous world of fashion into a place where all is natural, noble, yet utterly without pretence !'

The crowning praise made the young Highlander flush with pleasure. He had hitherto feared that the beautiful

English girl despised him in her heart, and now she showed how mistaken he had been. His heart bounded, and he answered her look of admiration with another almost as bold.

Their eyes met, and, as if abashed by his bold gaze, she drooped hers to the ground.

At that moment he could have worshipped her. Her beauty dazzled him, but her sympathy choked him with rapture.

He answered in a tone of depreciation, through which she penetrated in a moment.

'It is a wild place,' he said, 'and we are a wild people. True, my sister and myself have had some advantages not shared by the other folk of the place, but our life is a dreary one, and you would not care to share it long.'

'Do *you* find it dreary, Mr. Macdonald?' she murmured softly.

'Sometimes—not always,' he replied; then, with his face brightening to a smile, he added, 'I do not find it dreary *now.*'

They were wandering very slowly down the hillside in the direction of the clachan, she pausing every now and again to gaze around her, he following quietly by her side.

In the course of those few minutes she knew that she had mastered this fiery spirit, and that she might now do with him as she pleased.

She was used to such conquests, and, to do her justice, seldom pursued them very far.

But in the character of Graham Macdonald there was something wilder, stronger, darker, and more dangerous than in the characters to which she was accustomed, and she began to feel a peculiar zest in arousing his dormant passions.

Physically he was a giant to her—could have crushed her at a blow, taken possession of her with a finger-touch. She admired his strength, and would have delighted in stirring it to the depths; but she little guessed what kind of storm she might arouse if she went too far.

She had begun idly, with no idea that the lightness of her sympathy would awaken serious moods, but she already began to guess with what sort of man she had to deal.

She had no intention whatever of compromising herself in the slightest degree, though she longed eagerly for a few skirmishes of real flirtation. She saw at once, however, that she must proceed cautiously, or the young Highlander, with the pride and courage of his race, might encroach.

She did not greatly care, however, what gusts of passion she aroused, so long as, whatever happened, she left the way clear behind her for rapid retreat.

Graham had little experience of the world, and had not learned to discount the fine phrases and pretty compliments, helped home by winning looks, which the young lady showered upon him. He was ready on the instant and at a word to take her brightest jest for passionate earnest.

He had moved little in drawing-rooms, and had never encountered even the commonplace coquette, whose appetite for admiration counterfeits love's tender meaning on the most trivial occasions.

He did not understand how eyes may shine with witching sweetness, hands give tenderest pressure, while all the time the moving principle of intercourse is what Heine calls 'a little heart of ice.'

In short, he was at the mercy of the first woman of the world who, with good looks and grace to aid her, might choose to make a conquest of his life.

They passed down the hillside to the manse, and found Mr. Macdonald standing at the door with the county newspaper in his hand. He welcomed Ethel warmly, and led her gaily in.

'Fetch Mina,' he said to Graham. 'Tell her that Miss Sedley is here.'

Graham walked from room to room of the house, but Mina was not to be found. Then he walked out, searched the little garden, looked up and down the shore, but could not find her.

Returning to the manse, he told the result of his search.

'Where can the child have gone?' exclaimed the old minister. 'She was there but a few minutes ago.'

Graham shook his head and looked annoyed, for he was tolerably certain that his sister had crept out of the way on purpose.

Ethel said nothing, and chatting on, seemed to have for-gotten Mina's existence. But in her heart she was quite certain that Mina wished to avoid her, and it made her rather angry.

Both Graham and Miss Sedley were correct in their surmises. Mina was at that moment in the small boat, rowing rapidly away in the direction of Koll Nicholson's cottage. Having caught a glimpse of the visitor coming down the hill, she had hastened to the shore, cast the boat loose, leapt in, and rowed off without a word.

CHAPTER XXVII.

KOLL'S WITCHCRAFT.

LEAVING Graham to feast his eyes on the fair Saxon, and to listen to her with delight as she prattled to his uncle, let us follow poor Mina, as with pale cheek and heavy heart she rowed up the ever-winding fjord.

Fortunately the tide was flowing, so that it was scarcely necessary to use the oars ; here and there it boiled with furious eddies, again it shot rapidly on between narrowing shores, and yet again it broadened out into quiet, green lagoons.

The manner in which the arms of the sea wound and wound everywhere into the land was indeed wonderful to behold, and so many were the twists and turns that no one but a native of the place could have found her way.

Instead of going direct to Koll's abode, Mina suffered the boat to drift a long way up the winding creeks of the fjord. Great flocks of curlew flew screaming over the banks, at almost every promontory a heron rose and flapped away with slow waft of wing, and broods of eider-duck were swimming everywhere along the shore. Mina saw and heard nothing. Her thoughts were too full of other things.

At last, running the boat into a creek and securing it by the rope, she hastened back overland to Koll's cabin. What impulse led her there at all she could hardly have told, and indeed she did not pause to inquire. She sought her foster-father from old habit, certain of sympathy, however strange and silent, in his company.

The door stood wide open, and looking in, she saw the old man sitting, with his back to her, in the dim, Rembrandtish light of the hut.

She was about to utter his name, when something in his appearance arrested her attention, and at the same moment she heard him muttering wildly to himself. She crept nearer, and without being heard or seen, looked over his shoulder.

He was crouching over the fire, and in his hand he held what at first seemed a handful of black mud, but which was in reality a rough clay model of the human figure. Between his teeth he held several large pins, detaching which, one by one, he deliberately perforated the figure in his hand.

'Tak' *that*, and *that*, tamn you! to close your wicked een,' he said, suiting the action to the word, and sticking two pins in the figure's face. 'And tak' anither, tamn you! through the heid and through the brain, and one now right through your heart, and your liver, and your lungs, you teevil's-limb! and now I will place you in the fire, tamn you! and as the fire burns, may your soul burn in the fire of hell, and may you wither and waste away, if you meddle with me and mine!'

Nothing could exceed the suppressed fury with which the old man spoke, perforating his clay victim at every word. As he placed it on the blazing fire, Mina touched him on the arm, and he started as if stung.

'Why, Koll, what are you doing?'

He stretched out both his arms and took her hand.

'She is only charming away a witch, my bairn,' he said with a sly smile.

'I know what it is,' said Mina, 'and it is a wicked thing to do even to a person you hate. God is angry at such things, though they are only superstition.'

'Maype, maype,' answered Koll cunningly, 'it is superstetion. She is an old man, and was only trying the charm for fun. Sit toon and let me look at you, my bairn.'

She took a stool by his side, and he gazed long and eagerly into her face.

'You have been grieving sair,' he said, 'and greeting again, for the marks of saut tears are on your een. Na, na; you needna shake your heid, for she can tell weel the pain ye thole. But never fear, my bairn. The trouble will pass away. The old man has had a dream, and in her dream she saw a praw kirk and heard the wedding pells.'

As he spoke, Mina leant forward and attempted to take the clay figure from the fire. With a cry Koll interfered, and drew back her hand.

'Tinna touch her,' he exclaimed. 'Tinna free her, but let her burn! It is only a witch the old man is charming away!'

'Who is it that you hate so much?' asked Mina. 'A man or a woman?'

Koll gave his peculiar laugh.

'Maype it would pe a man, and maype it would pe a woman. It would preak the charm to tell.'

'Do you think God is pleased with such things? It is wicked even to think of them.'

'She does not work the charm to please God, but to anger the deevil.'

'But God teaches us to love our enemies—not to wish them such cruel harm.'

'She will love her own enemies, tamn them! but she canna love the enemies of her bairn,' answered Koll, again taking the girl's hand and holding it in his. 'In the old man's dream there was a tamned witch, and it is a charm to drive the tamned witch awa'.'

Mina smiled and shook her head. She little guessed at that moment that the witch of Koll's dream and the visitor who had that day frightened her from the manse were one and the same being. With an instinct peculiar to him, Koll had grasped the whole situation at a glance. He knew of his foster-child's love for Arranmore, and he knew also of Arranmore's engagement to the English girl. One glimpse of Ethel Sedley had been enough. He saw that she was too beautiful a rival to be despised, and he credited her with the fullest powers of natural and unnatural witchcraft. Hence his endeavour to defeat her ends and confuse her spells by means of the familiar old Highland charm.

CHAPTER XXVIII.

FACTOR AND LORD.

LEFT by himself in Castle Coreveolan, the young Lord of Arranmore had full time and opportunity to survey the situation in which he found himself placed. Anything more unpleasant could scarcely be conceived. While finally plighted to one woman, his equal in social position, and far more than his equal in worldly fortune, he had slowly drifted into passionate intimacy with one who was not only his social inferior, but without a penny in the world; and he had done this, moreover, under circumstances which certainly reflected little credit on his own moral character. Had he, in the first instance, appeared before Mina Macdonald without any disguise, as a nobleman and the master of the soil, she would never, it was quite certain, have opened her heart to his influence. But coming as an equal, appealing to her sympathy with all the grace of unreserved communion, admitted to the fullest and freest intercourse with herself and her guardian, he had suffered her heart to open gradually, like a blossom, to his personal influence, and at last to expand fearlessly in the warm light of virginal passion and first love. Then had come, like a thunderclap, the betrayal of his identity, and he had shrunk away with a guilty sense of shame, irresolute what to do or say.

'I am a villain!' he exclaimed to himself a thousand times; 'I am as much a villain as if I had betrayed her in act and left her to die, for I have betrayed her soul, and God knows if she will ever recover the wound I have dealt her. How am I to make amends?'

Had he been able to break at once with his cousin, there is no doubt that in some moment of impulse he would have cut the knot of his dilemma, and boldly offered marriage to

M

Mina, for he did full justice to her character, and felt that (morally and intellectually) she was worthy to become his wife. But he was doubly and trebly pledged to Ethel, and that young lady had never shown any inclination to give him his release. So far as he knew, she loved him, though her love was a very different kind of flame to that which burned in the simple heart of Mina Macdonald. He could not forsake her without exposing himself to the reproaches of his own conscience, as well as to the harsh judgment of the world.

It was a great relief to his mind when his uncle went over to spend a few days at Glenheather Lodge, taking his daughter with him. Lord Arranmore calmly excused himself, and remained in moody abstraction at the castle. He was a little astonished, however, when nearly a week passed without his uncle's return. At the end of a week a ragged messenger brought him a curt epistle from his cousin.

'DEAR LAWRANCE,—We are in love with Glenheather Lodge, and want to stay another week. Papa has killed what he calls a stag of ten, and is enraptured with his own powers. Won't you come over and join us? or do you prefer that stupid old castle? ETHEL.'

This was at least a respite, for as yet he felt he could not bear his cousin's gaze. He sent a hasty message, saying that he would come, but fixing no day; then he again gave himself up to lonely walks and self-reproaches. Had he known that Glenheather Lodge was quite so near to the manse of Uribol, he would doubtless have hastened over at once, for already he felt a wild longing to see Mina again, and to beg her forgiveness. His knowledge of the district, however, was still rather confused, and he did not suspect for a moment that the two houses were only a few miles, as the crow flies, asunder. Meantime the news had spread that the young Lord of Arranmore had returned to his ancestral acres; and one morning as he looked out he beheld a crowd of men, women, and children, for the most part in rags, thronging on the castle lawn. Directly they caught a glimpse of him they uttered a feeble cheer. Touching the bell, he summoned a servant.

'Who are these people?' he asked.

The man (who had come with the Sedleys from the south) gave a grin.

'Some of your lordship's servants, I believe.'

'What do they want here?'

'Don't exactly know, my lord. They say they want to give your lordship a welcome home.'

Looking rather foolish, Arranmore walked to the window again. Another feeble cheer went up from the crowd.

'Rag fair!' he muttered; 'they look like the sweepings of a poorhouse infirmary, Well, I suppose I must speak to them, and gladden their hearts with a little mountain dew.'

So, putting on his hat, he went out among them, and thereupon became the centre of an enthusiastic circle. Old men and women seized and kissed his hand, many sank on their knees before him, some wept, others shouted—in fact, altogether there was an ovation. The enthusiasm rose to positive madness when he informed them that whisky would be dispensed to them at once; and when the whisky came, even the little children tasted and drank his lordship's health.

But among the assembled crowd there were not a few who remained silent and gloomy, and who gazed at the young lord with a certain prophetic dread. One of them, a gaunt elderly man, in positive rags, at last approached the young lord, and, fixing on him a lack-lustre eye, said, in a hoarse, broken voice—

'Will your lordship be geeving me back the land Peter-na-Croiche took awa'?'

'Who are you?' asked Arranmore.

'I am Tonald Paterson, him they call big Tonald o' the Glen. Will your lordship be geeving me back my goot land?'

'What do you mean? Have you been evicted?'

'I have been turned off the land, and my hoose has been pulled doon, and my wife and bairns, and my father and my mother, are sleeping oot on the cold ground.'

'Is what the man says true?' asked Arranmore, turning to the figure nearest to him.

A chorus of assent answered him, and several old men,

stepping forward, entered into a long narration of the pitiful facts of the case. It appeared that the man had been behindhand with the rent, and that Peter Dougall, without ceremony, had issued judgment, levelled the house, and taken possession of the croft, to secure compensation. He had offered the man and his family an 'assisted' passage to Canada, the Government form for which the man now held in his hand.

Arranmore listened quietly while the facts of the case were explained to him.

'Very well,' he said, ' I will inquire into it, and speak to Mr. Dougall on the subject.'

At the mention of Dougall's name there was a general groan. Several other forlorn creatures then presented themselves, and told volubly of similar misfortunes.

Tired at last of their complaints, and feeling the impossibility of comprehending them properly offhand, Arranmore bade the crowd a general adieu, and walked back into the castle.

For a long time the people gathered in knots, gazing vacantly at the castle-door ; finally they dispersed in all directions, the evicted tenants disappearing last, with many a shake of the head and muttered groan.

The very next day Peter Dougall himself arrived at the castle, anxious to pay his duty to the young laird, whom he now met for the first time in his new character. Arranmore at that juncture was glad of any occupation which would distract his mind, so he at once demanded from the factor a full account of his stewardship. For several days they were busy together, both indoors and out among the mountains. At last matters were made quite clear, and Arranmore expressed himself to the factor with his usual candour.

' I am not a sentimentalist, Mr. Dougall, but it seems to me that in more than one instance you have behaved with unnecessary severity. I have my own theories as a landed proprietor, and I do not wish to depopulate the county.'

The factor's face turned livid ; for some moments he could not utter a word.

' My lord,' he exclaimed at last, ' I have been working for your lordship's goot.'

'I have no doubt of it,' said Arranmore dryly, 'and I will do you the justice to admit that no one could have squeezed so large a sum out of so wretched a tenantry. You have literally skinned the flints, Mr. Dougall, and I— well, yes, I suppose I have been the gainer.'

'The land is goot land,' cried Dougall, 'and I have slaved to get it in goot order and to raise the rents! Does your lordship blame me for working day and night for your lordship's goot?'

'Not at all,' answered Arranmore; 'only, to be quite frank, I don't think I have a right—a moral right I mean— to draw one penny from such a place.'

'Not draw a penny!' gasped Dougall. 'My life and soul!'

'Let me make myself clear. These estates, from which I derive my title, consist two-thirds of stone and sand, not to count the water, which seems tolerably abundant! It is a wilderness still, quite as much a wilderness as the back-woods of Texas or the plains of Manitoba. Here and there a few poor devils have by incessant toil managed to turn mud, and stone, and water into crofts of decent ground, where oats and potatoes manage to grow; by which means, and by pasturing their wretched sheep and cattle in the open heather, they contrive to feed and live. Just as they contrive to keep body and soul together, you and I step in, like cormorants, and demand our moiety of what they are going to eat and drink—nay, in some cases, we demand all; for what remains to the tenant when the only stack of oats and the last cow have both to be sold in order to pay the rent?'

The factor saw here a loophole for his favourite argument.

'Just so, my lord,' he said; 'the folk are no able to cultivate the land, and therefore it should be aal doon in sheep.'

'And the people all expatriated, Mr. Dougall?'

'It is for their ain goot!'

'They don't seem to think so. Well, we will talk the matter over again; but at present I feel rather ashamed of my position. If I were a rich man, I should at once refuse to draw any monies from the estates for some time, and endeavour to assist the tenants, directly and indirectly, to recover the waste. We must solve the difficulty somehow and at once. On one point I am resolved—not to evict another tenant, unless it is clear to my mind that he is evading payment and presuming on my generosity. As to the tenants already evicted, I shall go into their cases *seriatim*, and doubtless the majority will be restored.'

Words would fail to paint the righteous wrath of the factor, as the reformatory designs of his master were then made plainly manifest. His first impulse was to stand upon his dignity, and incontinently to throw up his situation. Being a cautious and far-seeing man, however, he determined to sleep on it. So he met his employer's remarks with a surly acquiescence, and with characteristic self-command kept his righteous anger to himself.

But Mr. Peter Dougall was one of those men who cannot understand the action of ordinary conscience, and who, whenever anything interferes with their designs, at once conclude that some one else has been designing against them. It was now quite clear to his mind that his lordship's mind had been poisoned against him. By whom? That question, in his opinion, was easily answered. His old arch-enemy, the minister of Uribol, was at the bottom of it all.

In his heart perhaps Lord Arranmore cared little about the tenantry. He had described himself correctly enough when he had said that he was not a sentimentalist, if by that word he simply meant a person penetrated with the enthusiasm of humanity.

He was unaccustomed to vulgar suffering, and only understood it when associated with such picturesque griefs as appealed to his æsthetic sense. But he hated injustice in any form, and he was quite ready to redress any grievance which was fairly brought under his notice. The wrong done by Peter Dougall was unmistakable, and the young lord had too restive a conscience to acquiesce in it.

It was nevertheless a serious difficulty to him. The rent-roll of Coreveolan and Uribol was terribly small already, for though the acreage was enormous, the greater part of the ground was open heather and watery bog. If he sided witn the tenants against his own factor, the rent-roll would dwindle down to little or nothing.

'A political economist would settle the question in a moment,' he said gloomily. 'A poor man, a man without sleeping capital, has no right to be a landed proprietor. I ought to have either more money or to sell the estate.'

Then came back on his mind in full force the remembrance of his engagement to his cousin Ethel.

Possessed of her fortune he might become a benefactor to his tenants and an example to all the small landed proprietors of Scotland. He had but to say the word and the marriage might be brought about almost at once; indeed, it was almost inevitable that he should take some steps in the matter, whether he wished it or not.

But the more he saw the expediency of carrying out his engagement, the more he felt the hopelessness of following the idle stream of his own personal wishes, so much the more did he cling to his passion for Mina Macdonald.

'Why was I born a beggarly lord?' he exclaimed to himself again and again. 'Why did my parents label me "Aristocrat," and give me no money to keep up the farce? If I were only the poor travelling student I once represented myself to be! If I were only her equal, though poor as a church mouse! Ah! those pleasant days, that golden time, before she found me out! When shall I be as happy again?'

CHAPTER XXIX.

A LOVE-STORM.

THE divine spark grows rapidly into full fire when it falls upon thoroughly combustible material. At the end of a week's time Graham Macdonald was passionately in love with Ethel Sedley.

They met often, and the young aristocrat, by wicked art, rendered the young Highlander quite blind to the true rela-

fanned it carefully to flame; by a thousand arts and co-
quetries she took care that it should not die out for a
single moment. And there can be no doubt that she herself shared, perhaps for the first time in her life, the excitement of the tempest she aroused.

She was like one that walks very close to the edge of a
perilous sea, and sings in safety, drinking the salt spray in
strange rapture, though the ground is rocking underneath.

It was something, at least, to feel that she was loved by
a man; not by any of the dolls of the drawing-room, not by
one of the pets of the *parterre.* It was delicious, in fairy-
like triumph, to make the strong creature whom she had
bewitched move to and fro at the bidding of her fitful
will.

Once or twice she paused and asked herself—

'Am I going too far? Shall I be able to retreat?'

And she answered herself with the sophism that she had
never, in open speech, encouraged the young man's passion.
Warm words were nothing, burning looks were nothing;
nor soft pressures of the hand, nor all the countless tender-
nesses wherewith a woman leads captive the troubled spirit
of a lover.

Yes, she could easily withdraw; she would soon, indeed,
be far away from the Macdonalds and from Uribol. There
was no harm, therefore, in amusing herself a little while she
stayed.

Had she possessed a complete insight into Graham's
nature, she would have trembled at the spirit she was invoking thence. She understood it about as little as she understood the wild scenery—the melancholy hills, the trackless
wastes, the dark lagoons—of that sea-surrounded and lonely
land. She admired Graham's glowing and emotional moods,
during which his manly beauty seemed to shine in full per-
fection, just as she admired a sudden rainbow in the glens
or a scarf of purple sunset fading over the Atlantic. She
comprehended neither—neither the sad, solemn landscape,
nor the potent spirit of the man.

And, indeed, Graham as yet scarcely comprehended himself. He seemed just coming to life under the warmth of
her rosy touch. He went to and fro like one in a dream—

dark when he was waiting for her approach or hastening to meet her, bright when she was shining at his side.

They had no set appointments—that would have been too compromising from the lady's point of view—but they were always (as the delicious Irish bull expresses it) 'meeting accidentally on purpose.' And every time they met the spell of her influence upon him became intense, till it was almost more than he could bear.

At last, as lovers will, he encroached. Mad with admiration he seized her in his arms and kissed her. She turned on him like a tigress.

'How dare you?' she cried, panting. 'I will never speak to you again.'

He stood shame-stricken, unable to defend himself, and, taking his silence for weakness, she stabbed him to the quick.

'A *gentleman* would not have done that. If we were equals '——

She paused, looking him from head to foot in scorn. He was astonished, for she had never before appeared to him in colours so unamiable. Before he could utter another word she left him, and he was too thunderstruck to follow.

He returned home to the manse, looking dark as death, and wretched as rain on the sea.

It was now Mina's turn to remonstrate with her brother. She knew of those frequent meetings, and though at first she attributed them to accident, she soon saw how the wind blew. So that night, as she sat with her brother alone in the house, their uncle being away on a sick call, she spoke out boldly.

'Graham, what is wrong with you? What makes you seem so strange?'

He did not reply, but sat looking at the fire in moody silence. She arose, bent over him, and kissed him. The kiss spoke more than words, and, looking up startled, he saw that her eyes were full of tears.

'What ails *you*, Mina?'

'I cannot bear to see you so unhappy.'

'But I am not unhappy.'

'O Graham!' she cried, sobbing outright, 'since these

people came to Uribol we have had no rest nor peace.
First *he* came here and put me to shame; now there is
more sorrow coming, for *she* is bringing trouble to *you!*'

'Whom do you mean?'

'That lady—Miss Sedley. O Graham! are you mad?
Why do you think of her—meet with her? She is a great
lady, and she is to be Lady Arranmore.'

Graham's brow darkened and his strong frame shook.

'You are talking nonsense,' he said. 'Miss Sedley is
nothing to me.'

'But you meet her nearly every day.'

'Sometimes—by chance.'

'It is more than chance, Graham. She is an idle lady,
and she is making a fool of you to fill up her time. If you
are wise you will not go near her any more. Promise me
you won't—Graham, promise! Graham, she will break
your heart, as she has tried to break mine!'

But Graham was not just then in the mood either to
invite confidence or accept a warning. His soul was full
of a wild dread that he had given mortal offence, and that
Ethel would carry out her threat and hold no further communication with him. So he left Mina sobbing by the fire,
and went out-of-doors into the darkness of the chill moon-
less night, and he paced about for hours like a wild beast
on the open fields above the shore. The fire of the kiss
which he had taken, forcibly as it were, was still burning
upon his lips; his eyes were still full of her loveliness, as
he saw it last in the full glow of a splendid scorn. The
fury—for with such men love is a fury indeed—had him by
the hair. With strange cries and wild gestures he rushed
hither and thither, till the lights in the clachan went out
one by one, and all the place lay dead-still in the black
shadow of the hills.

Two days of torture passed, and at last he encountered
the lady of his pain again. She was sitting quite alone, on
the place where he had often met her, close to the banks of
Loch Drummdhu. On her knees she held a book, and
was reading, or pretending to read, as he appeared. He
passed by at a little distance with burning cheeks and
averted head. He was nearly gone when she called to him,

quite innocently and cheerfully, as if nothing whatever had occurred—

'Mr. Graham !'

He turned and approached her hastily.

'Papa is out on the lake fishing, and I am waiting for him here. It looks very black—do you think it is going to rain ?'

There was nothing in the look or the tone to indicate that she had ever taken enough interest in him to be angry. She scarcely seemed to look up, being half occupied with her book, though all the while she was stealing furtive glances at his face.

He stood puzzled and distraught, and stammered something to the effect that the day would continue fine. Then, lifting his hat, he turned to go. But she called him back.

'Stop, please.'

He turned again, only too eager to remain, yet ashamed of his own delight.

'Mr. Graham, I have to ask your pardon.'

The tone was soft beyond measure, the voice tremulous, as if with the weight of tender emotion.

She did not look up, but kept her eyes upon her book.

'My pardon !'

'Yes ! When we last met I was rude and ill-tempered. Will you forgive me ?'

Forgive her ! Oh, how willingly would he have laid his life down that moment for one such smile as that ! His eyes were dim for a moment and he trembled ; then with a pathos of gesture that would have touched the heart of a fonder woman, he stretched out both his hands towards her, and stood so, enraptured at her presence.

'We were both foolish,' she continued, smiling still more brightly. 'I am glad that we have met again, especially as I am so soon going away.'

'Going away !' he cried, finding his voice at last. 'Back to England ?'

'First back to Castle Coreveolan, and *then* to England.'

'When do you go ?'

'To the castle ? Oh, at the end of the week.'

'I am sorry—I mean I—how long shall you stop there ?'

'That is uncertain.   Perhaps until I get married.'

Another stab, most dexterously and cruelly given.   Graham tottered under it, went white as death, and then, recovering himself, turned again to go.

'Good-bye,' he cried, and his voice was quite choked
and broken.

'Don't go yet,' she pleaded, with sudden earnestness.
'Mr. Graham, I fear you are angry with me.   I thought I
possessed a little of your—your esteem ?'

'What is past is past,' he groaned.   'Do not speak
of it !'

'But I must, because you still remember !'

'What ?'

'Oh, nothing,' she cried, as if deeply mortified.   'Go, if
you *must*.'

With the same pathetic gesture of outstretched arms he
turned to her again, and gazed at her with burning eyes.

'Do you wish me to stay ?'

'Not at all, since you are so revengeful.'

'Revengeful ?   O God !'

'Can we not meet as friends ?' she asked, with a peculiar accent on the last word.

'No ! never !'

'Then it's really a pity that we ever met at all.'

'Amen to that !' he said solemnly, so solemnly that
she was amused, and cried, with a trill of silvery laughter,
'Thank you !'   The laughter seemed to sting him into
speech ; at all events he found his voice, and coming
closer, stood looking down, in the full strength of his
manhood and the full force of his passion.

'Yes, it is a pity that we ever met !   I did not seek you—I
tried to avoid you ; but you came my way, and it was done.
You taught me to care for you, to—to love you ; and now
you laugh at me, and would throw me away like a book
you have read to the last page.   Well, go !   I may be your
match yet, and the match of the man you are going to
marry.'

Something in this tirade roused the girl's hasty spirit ;
she rose, looked up at him haughtily, and shrugged her
shoulders.

'Since you crossed my path, sir, I had to be civil to you!'

'Yet you knew we were not equals.'

'Certainly!'—this with unmistakable emphasis.

'And that you were engaged to another man.'

'Excuse me, to a gentleman—Lord Arranmore. Was that any reason to prevent my amusing myself?'

'Amusing yourself?' returned Graham with a harsh laugh, but with no laughter in his fierce, angry, determined eyes. 'So that is what you call it? If you had a drop of kindness in your heart, you would not act so. Thank God, my sister is not like you! Oh, you may smile, but she would blush to do as you have done!'

'I'm not so sure,' answered Ethel flippantly; 'you forget she tried to inveigle my intended husband.'

'No!'

'Lawrance—I mean Lord Arranmore—has good taste, and your sister is rather pretty. Still, I think he might have looked a little higher. But there! what am I saying? If we go on like this we shall quarrel again, and I should be so sorry to quarrel just as we are going to say good-bye.'

Then this was to be the end of it all. Those glowing looks, those sympathetic words, those stolen meetings, all meant nothing, and she was about to pass out of his life for ever, like a star sinking, like a summer vision fading away. And there she stood, calm and little moved, not so much stirred as if her little finger ached, or as if she were saying farewell to a stranger whom she had met in travel at some caravansary or roadside inn. He looked at her in the stupefaction of utter despair. He seemed to have known her for a long, long time, yet their intimacy dated only a few days back. He had lived a lifetime in those quick, short hours. Oh, if she would only stay! If she would only let him be her slave, her dog, anything that might look up at her, and worship her, bear her cruelty, and crave now and then for a caress. Now for the first time he realised how far apart they were from each other.

'But is it true? Tell me, for God's sake—are you going to marry Lord Arranmore?'

'Yes!'

'*You shall not!*'

It came from his lips like a cry in spite of himself. His face was livid, his hands were desperately clenched.

'I cannot bear it,' he continued; 'it will kill me—or, what is worse, I shall kill you both!'

'Do you mean that for a threat?'

'God help me! no. But I am not master of myself. See how I shake! and my brain is on fire! Do you not know I love you? Do you not know I would die for you? Ask me anything—bid me do what you please—I will do it though it costs me my life. Only do not leave me—do not go away!—at least not yet—not yet!'

He was quite unmanned now, and his eyes were blind with tears.

Touched by his sorrow, and a little startled to find that things had gone so far, she said softly—

'Mr. Graham, I am so sorry! A little while ago I was angry, but I am not angry now. You must try to forget me.'

'I shall never do that,' he answered, 'never—never!'

'I did not think—indeed I did not—you cared for me so much.'

'Now you know it,' he answered quickly, 'have pity—do not leave me!'

'But you forget—I am engaged to another person; and if I were not, it would be quite, quite hopeless.'

'Why?'

'Do not force me to pain you by further explanations,' she said. 'It is out of the question.'

He looked at her darkly beneath his brows, while his lips trembled and his voice sobbed in his throat.

'I am a gentleman by birth. My forbears were the lairds of all these isles, and there is no stain upon our name. There is not a man or woman in the land but honours our blood more than the blood of the Arranmores.'

She shook her head sadly; then, holding out her hand—
'Good-bye.'

He took her hand and held it between both of his, and as he did so she felt the strong heart-beats shaking his frame. She was grieved now that she had encouraged him:

for she saw at last how deep and terrible his love had grown. Nor was her grief unmixed with fear. There was something in his passion, in his violence and over-mastering exaltation, which almost terrified her. He took everything so seriously, with such terrible earnestness, and until she was far away out of his sight and reach there was no knowing what he might do.

As he stood clasping her hand and bending over her, the boat in which her father was fishing appeared out in the lake, rowed by two men and approaching slowly. Sir Charles was standing up in the stern, fishing-rod in hand, and casting right and left wherever the dark cat's-paw of the wind ruffled the smooth surface of the water. The fish were on the feed, and at nearly every cast he hooked a small red trout and drew it in.

'Do go away now,' she cried; 'papa will see you!'

Sir Charles, however, was too intent on his amusement to notice anything else. Graham still retained her hand in his strong hold, and looked with strange intensity into her face.

'You have made me love you,' he said; 'we cannot part like this.'

'Release my hand, sir—you hurt me!'

'Not until you promise to meet me again.'

'I will promise nothing; *perhaps* we may meet.'

'I do not wish to offend you—I would rather suffer any pain than do that again—but let me kiss your hand.'

'If you wish to,' she said with a nervous laugh, 'I have not the power to prevent you;' and so saying, with the cunning of her sex, she placed herself with her back to the lake, so that the action could not be perceived by the party in the boat.

There was a glove on the hand, but it was loose, and did not reach far up the wrist. Raising the hand, he pressed his lips, not on the glove, but on the warm skin of the wrist itself. It was a long, burning kiss, and his mouth seemed to cling to the sweet flesh. As he looked up flushing and trembling, she saw the hot tears chasing each other down his cheeks.

Softly but firmly she drew her hand away.

He did not detain it, but without another word turned to go.

'Good-bye,' she cried; and he answered 'Good-bye' in a broken voice.

Then he moved silently away.

She remained watching him until his figure disappeared far down the hillside.   Then she raised her arm and looked critically at her wrist, where his kiss had left a soft crimson mark.   She smiled, well pleased, and raising the spot to her own lips, kissed it cordially.

'He is a dear, brave fellow,' she said to herself; 'but I wish he did not like me quite so much.   Well, it is nice, after all, to be loved like that!   I'm sure I don't know what will come of it.   One thing is certain—I only meant to amuse myself with a storm in a teacup, and instead I have raised a *real* hurricane!'

CHAPTER XXX.

A MEETING AND A PARTING.

AT the very moment that the interview described in our last chapter was taking place, another scene of a not dissimilar description was being enacted a few miles distant.

On a green lawn not far away from Koll Nicholson's hut stood Lord Arranmore in close converse with Mina Macdonald.   He had come upon her almost by accident, as she was slowly returning towards the manse, and before either could avoid the other they were face to face.

Lord Arranmore's presence in the immediate neighbourhood was easily accounted for.   Instead of crossing the mountains to Glenheather Lodge, a distance of nearly ten miles, he had sailed round by water in the *Jenny*, and had cast anchor in one of the numerous safe creeks to be found in Loch Uribol.

The creek he chose was near to Koll's lonely cabin, so he had scarcely landed, with the purpose of walking leisurely up to the lodge, when he saw the familiar figure close at hand.

While far removed from her personal presence he had been able, to a certain extent, to conquer his violent passion for her, but the moment he beheld her again the old fascination returned. His heart gave a great bound, and his face became brighter than it had been for many a day, from mere joy at the meeting.

As for Mina, she went pale as death; and as her lover approached, turned her back to hasten away.

He overtook her in a moment, and called her, as before, by her Christian name.

Finding escape impossible, she turned and faced him. Never had she appeared more lovely in his eyes. Her grey eyes shone steadily beneath her golden hair, her cheek was pale as alabaster, and though sensibly agitated, she was to all outward appearance quite calm and cold.

He reached out his arms as if to detain her.

'Please do not touch me!' she said quietly.

The colour mounted to his brow before her steadfast look.

'Am I not forgiven?' he stammered.

'Forgiven what, my lord?'

'My little innocent deception. I feared that if I told you exactly who I was it might repel you. I really meant no harm.'

'I do not blame you, my lord,' she said, and prepared again to move away.

There was the very slightest emphasis in her utterance of the words 'my lord,' and she seemed to repeat them wilfully, to remind herself at every step of the barrier between them. She walked rapidly on, but he continued at her side. At last she paused again, with a certain anger in her eyes.

'Why do you follow me?' she said.

'Because I must speak to you, Mina! Why torture me so cruelly for that past fault? You do not know the world or the women in it. If you did, you would understand why I loved to linger unknown, unsuspected, with you for a companion in this lonely spot where you dwell.'

'I am not blaming you,' she replied; 'only after what has passed, it is better that we should not meet.'

'Why so?'

'We are not equals, my lord.'

'That is true,' he cried warmly, 'for you are as far my superior as a flower is superior to a stone. I can't help my title, can I? If that is to be used as a bugbear to frighten off the people I like best, I shall soon be without a friend in the world.'

The words were spoken winningly, with something of the old frank manner which at first fascinated her, and in spite of her firm resolution they thrilled her through. Scarcely conscious of their growing spell upon her, she slackened her pace, and listened, as he continued in the same tone—

'I don't think you quite understand me in this matter. I came from a society of which I was sick into these wilds, seeking for solitude and peace; all I wanted was to be let alone, to forget for a time the existence of the fashionable world; and I came *incog.* because I knew, by precious experience, how seldom even honest people show their best side to a lord. By an accident I encountered you—that is to say, you were good enough to save my life. In return I learned to love you. I forgot the world, I forgot my friends, I forgot my miserable title—how could I remember these wretched earthly things when alone with Heaven and you? Well, you know how the world found me. I woke up from my dream, and since then I have never had a single moment's peace.'

There was no need for him to forcibly detain Mina now; the fatal fascination was upon her, and she felt she could not leave him.

The first tones of his voice—so earnest, so loving, so true—restored in a moment her old faith and trust. But at that moment the memory of the words which the baronet had uttered came back to her and stung her to the quick.

'My lord,' she said quietly, 'such deeds as you have done do not lead to happiness or peace. You came to us with a falsehood on your lips—you came to me as an equal;

and I listened to you, and believed you, and thought you true.'

'What did I hide from you? Only my name.'

'Was that all? You told me that you cared for me, and all the time you knew that your heart was already given away. May God forgive you, my lord, for your unkindness to me and mine!'

'Mina, you do not understand.'

'Indeed, my lord, I understand o'er well.'

'By Heaven you do not, or you would not wrong me so cruelly by telling me that I have been false to *you!* When I said I loved you I spoke the truth; and now, Mina, my heart is still unchanged. Yes, it is *you* I love—not her who came between our lives that day.'

He paused and there was silence. Mina could not speak; her heart was bounding fitfully; her brain was on fire; for she thought, 'Oh, that he would speak like that for ever, and that I might listen! He loves me—oh yes, I am sure he loves me!'

'Mina!'

'My lord,' she answered softly.

He came to her with outstretched hands; she offered no resistance. He took her hand in his—he drew her to his side—he raised her face, and, stooping, kissed her brow.

'Mina,' he said softly, 'call me Lawrance; say that I am happy and forgiven; tell me that you trust me!'

Her face grew pale as death; she gently withdrew from his embrace.

'My lord,' she said, 'you have no right to talk like that to me, and I have no right to listen. You forget your cousin's claim.'

'No, Mina, I do not forget; it is the thought of that which has kept me from your side, when I should have been by to help and comfort you.'

'And yet, minding that, you come to me again.'

'Even so, Mina. I love you—I do not love my cousin; I will not marry where I cannot love.'

'And you would renounce your cousin—and—and'——

'And marry *you!*'

'Marry *me* !' she repeated.   'Oh, my lord, do not talk so, even in jest.'

'Before God, I am not jesting ! Mina—tell me—will you be my wife ? '

He asked the words earnestly, quickly, and as he did so Mina felt her love for him increase tenfold.   All the shame and degradation which she had felt faded away before the bright beams of love which shone upon her now.   He was not false—he had not lied to her—he had not made her a plaything to pass a few idle hours.   No ; he had given her all his love—such love as man gives but once in a lifetime —and now he was there to lay wealth, honour, title—all at her feet !   Oh, if she could but answer him—if she could only throw her arms around his neck to say, 'Lawrance, I love you !'

But Mina quietly hung her head, and said—

'No, it cannot be !'

'Mina, do you mean that you refuse to become my wife?'

'Yes, my lord, I refuse.   Even were you free, you would not do right to look so low as I.   As your lady, I should be despised by all the world.   Your folk would scorn me as they do now ; and perhaps, in the end, you would despise me too.   But as you are bound'——

'I tell you I am not bound.   Mina, do you want to drive me mad ? '

'No, my lord—neither do I want to drive you to dishonour.   You have given your faith to your cousin and you must keep it.'

'You tell me *that* ?   Then, indeed, you do not love me ! Mina,' he continued, as she silently hung her head, 'there was a time when I thought those grey eyes looked up into mine with a wealth of affection which any man might be proud of.   If that was so—if you love me still—recall what you said and give me your little hand.   *You* have no bonds to break, and before such love as I feel for you no barrier will stand.'

Again he paused and stretched forth his hands, but Mina did not stir, neither did she utter a word.   He looked into her face ; it was as white as death, but the mouth was fixed and the eyes were tearless.

'No word, no sign,' he said bitterly; 'then it would have been better—far better—if we had never met.'

He turned, and seemed about to leave her. Should she let him go—without a word, a look, a sign—believing, as he did, that she had no love for him? She knew it would be better, and she tried to let him go.

She bit her lip until bright blood began to issue from the soft skin. She clenched her hands convulsively, but she stood perfectly silent as she watched him move away, and as he went her aching eyes grew dim.

The scene all around her began to fade as his figure was fading.

Unable longer to bear the agony of her heart, she stretched forth her hands, and, sobbing, named his name.

In a moment he was beside her. Folding her in his arms, he laid her head upon his breast.

'You love me, Mina?' he whispered softly. 'You will not send me away?'

Mina gently withdrew from his embrace and put her hand in his.

'My lord,' she said quietly, 'it is because I care for you that I think it is better for us to say good-bye. It is hard enough for me to say, God knows; you should not make it harder by any words of yours; but, believe me, it will be better for us never to meet again. You must try to forget what I have said to you.' She continued quietly: 'If you have any regard for me, my lord, you will remember me only as a humble friend.'

She spoke in hesitation, mingled with strange fear. Now that the confession was made, she felt half ashamed, half frightened at what she had done.

Lawrance, too, felt shame, but only for himself. Mina had reminded him of his duty, and in thus reminding him she had shown to him in its true light the kind of act which he had longed to do.

He knew that he was bound to his cousin Ethel almost as strongly as if she were his wife; he knew also that if he were to break that bond, and bring upon himself the contempt and hatred of all honest men, he would soon grow to despise himself; and yet he felt that he would brave dishonour, run the risk of despising himself, if by that risk he won Mina.

Again he spoke to her, again with lips, and eyes, and outstretched arms he pleaded his cause.

But Mina was now firm ; she did not look at him.   His words almost broke her heart, but the thought of Ethel Sedley kept her strong.

'God knows,' she said to herself, 'it breaks my heart to leave him, knowing that I have his love ; but it would be bitterer still to see his love turn into hatred, to see him learn to despise me for leading him into wrong.'

She was not sorry that she had told him of her devotion ; she did not feel shame now : and when she left him she held up her face for him to kiss her, believing that it was for the last time.

Having once said good-bye she feared to linger, so she passed quickly across the hill, and soon regained her own home.

On the threshold of the manse she met Graham.

He had just come from Ethel Sedley's side.   His face was as pale as Mina's, his manner was agitated, but he did not seem inclined to talk, and she was only too glad to escape.

She had noted his pale face, but she did not think of the cause—her mind was too full of her own great trouble.

CHAPTER XXXI.

SHADOWS IN THE MANSE.

MINA said she had a headache that night, and could not come down to go through her usual two hours of study ; so the clergyman wandered aimlessly about until bedtime, while Kirsty, well supplied with restoratives, worried Mina for fully an hour.   The house seemed very strange that night ; it was the first time for many years that Mina had not been at her post—the first time since her childhood that illness had confined her to her room. The old clergyman was very anxious, although assured by Kirsty that the illness was nothing more than feverishness caused by over-fatigue. He tried to settle to his studies, but could not, for he seemed to be listening for the voice of his pet pupil; and after one or two ineffectual attempts to concentrate his thoughts, he threw his books aside.

And Mina, putting aside each remedy which was brought to her, begged again and again for peace.

'If you will only leave me, Kirsty,' she said, 'and look after my uncle and brother, I will try to be all well again to-morrow.' Then, seeing a pained look of reproach come into the woman's eyes, she stretched forth her arms and burst into passionate tears. 'Oh, Kirsty,' she said, 'I know I am cross and stupid, but do not be angry with me to-night!'

And the woman, in answer to that pitiful appeal, folded the sobbing girl in her arms and laid her aching head upon her bosom and cried too. For a time they remained so, Mina drawing comfort from the kindly arms which were folded around her—from the lips which were now and again pressed upon her burning forehead; and when at length the woman left her, her troubled soul seemed more at peace.

That night Mina slept; for Kirsty, imagining that the illness was the result of fatigue, had given her a sleeping-draught which Doctor John had left behind him on his last visit to the manse. The draught was so strong a one that, although Mina's brain was excited and seriously troubled, it soothed her, and kept her in a deep sleep during the weary hours of night. When she awakened in the morning, however, and unconsciously raised her hand to her forehead, she felt that it was burning feverishly; her heart was as heavy as lead. She thought it must be late, for she heard people stirring in the room below, but she did not attempt to move. Her eyes were fixed upon the curtained window, and she felt that tears were stealing slowly down her cheeks.

Presently she heard Kirsty's step coming up the stairs, and she hastily dried her eyes, and, leaving her bed, proceeded to dress herself for the day. When she stood before the glass she started back in utter amazement. How deathly-white her face was! how dark and heavy-looking her eyes! She seemed like the shadow of her former self, and yet scarcely twenty-four hours had passed since she parted with her lover.

With a rush of memory all that scene came back to her, as she sat down before the window and gazed out at the hills in sickening despair. She thought of his words and her own—she thought of that one last look which he had given her as she turned her face towards her home. He had been willing to sacrifice all for her sake—to break every tie which bound him—and endow her, despite the opinion of the world, with his own name! Yes, he had offered her happiness—such happiness as she felt it would never be her lot to meet again—and she had voluntarily cast all these gifts away; and now what remained for her? The sunlight of her life had passed away, and left her very cold and weary—lonelier than the loneliest hill which pointed to the ever-darkening sky.

How dreary it all seemed to her now—the bay which had once held the *Jenny*, the hills where she had so often walked with the stranger whom she had gradually learned to love, all these things had passed away as he had done, and left her with a dreary life before her, and a heart as cold and heavy as a stone.

She dreaded to go down lest her pale cheeks and weary eyes should reveal her secret to her brother, but her uncle had sent twice for her, and she had to go.

She was glad to find, when at length she did go down, that Graham was not at home, and that her uncle was deep in the columns of the paper which had arrived by post that morning. He put it aside, however, as soon as she appeared, and looked anxiously into her pale face and kissed her very fondly.

'Mina, my bairn,' he said, 'you have been studying o'er closely, and getting too little of the caller air. I have decided that we will lay aside our books for a few days, until you are quite strong again.'

In this Mina acquiesced readily enough, and then in

duced her uncle to return to his paper. She did not want any comments on her pale cheeks, nor any reference made to the past.

The manse seemed drearier than ever that day, and Mina felt that she could not rest at home. After breakfast she stole from the house, and hastening down to the shore, pushed out her boat and rowed herself along the coast to Koll Nicholson's hut. The old man was at home. During the night he had been out with the herring-fishers, but now his smack was at anchor, his soaking clothes were stretched upon the beach to dry, and he himself was about to sit down to a meal of some of his own fish. When Mina entered the hut he invited her to take a seat and join in the repast.

For answer Mina put her arms round the old man's neck and kissed his cheek; and he, looking up, noted for the first time the worn, weary look on her face.

'What ails her bairn?' he asked anxiously, and Mina shook her head.

'Nothing, Koll, nothing,' she said, but the tell-tale tears would come to her eyes; and seeing his worn face grow still more anxious, she said—

'I could not sleep last night, so Kirsty gave me a sleeping-potion; it has made me feel very strange to-day, Koll.'

He took her small white hand and smoothed it tenderly between his fingers; the tears stood in his own wild eyes as he murmured—

'Her bairn mustna get sick—that would break Koll's heart; she must come oot on the salt sea—that is the best doctor of aal.'

Mina took a seat near the open door, and looked out upon the sea. It stretched calm and clear before her, its surface darkened by the chill shadows from the sky, its waves breaking with a low, monotonous sound upon the shore. She rested her cheek upon her hand, and gazed wearily forth, while the old man watched her with anxious eyes. He plied her with questions, and Mina answered him for the most part in monosyllables, seldom turning to look at him, keeping her eyes fixed with strange intentness upon the water.

Presently Koll asked—

'What of the young laird, Mina? Will you be seeing him again lately, my bairn?'

As he asked the question he looked at her even more intently than before, and he saw her shiver through and through. For a moment she did not answer him—her lip was trembling; as soon as she could command her voice she answered—

'Lord Arranmore is up at Coreveolan Castle with—with his friends.'

She did not answer the latter part of his question, and although he noticed the omission, he did not press the matter. As it was, the question had done its work—it showed him only too plainly that Mina had not cast altogether from her heart the memory of the man who had come amongst them as an equal, and so disturbed the peace of her home. He saw this, and his heart turned bitterer still within him. For a time he sat silently watching her; then she turned towards him a pale, sad, thoughtful face.

'Koll,' she said, 'when I die I should like to be buried down here on the sand, close to the line where the tide comes up. I don't think I should feel so lonely if I could only hear the sea.'

'May God Almighty give her bairn long life!' said the old man, solemnly. 'What for should her bairn talk of deeing?'

The girl laughed hysterically; then suddenly her laughter ceased, and he saw that she was crying.

'What ails her bairn?' he asked again; and Mina, drying her eyes, answered petulantly—

'Nothing—nothing. Do not watch me, Koll—go on with your work, or I shall go back to the manse and leave you!'

So the old man did as he was bidden. After clearing the breakfast-table he went outside to see to his nets, and left Mina alone in the hut. And all the time he worked his mind was troubled, and he murmured—

'Tamn her!—tamn the witch! She is bringing trouble to her bairn!'

All that day Mina stayed with her foster-father, and in the evening she took her boat to row back to the manse. Koll wanted to accompany her. The strangeness of her manner caused him some apprehension, and he did not like to see her go forth alone. He pleaded earnestly for permission to go with her, but Mina was firm, and he had to let her go.

The daylight had almost faded away. The far-off hills were wrapped in black shadow, and a cold grey light played upon the sea. The tide was high, the surface of the water very calm, and nothing was heard but its low-sounding murmur upon the shore. For a time Mina rowed steadily, for she saw the tall figure of Koll Nicholson upon the shore watching her ; but when the ever-thickening mists of night enveloped him and hid him from her sight, she ceased rowing, and bending forward to rest her body upon the oars, looked wearily around.

How quiet it was ! If she could only close her eyes, she thought, and go to sleep with the sound of the sea in her ears and the breath of heaven upon her cheek, she might find peace. And would it not be better so ?—better than to live on with all her trouble and pain, with the knowledge of his love and her sacrifice to darken every day of her life. If she could only have died in his arms that day, with his lips upon hers, his eyes gazing down upon her, she thought God would have been good ; but her way had not been His way—she was still left to suffer, and say, 'Thy will be done !'

When she got home that night she tried to go through her usual routine of lessons with her uncle, but ere the task was over she fairly broke down, and on the advice of her uncle, went up to bed.

That very night, shortly after Mina had retired to rest, Doctor John called at the manse. He did not intend to stay there—he was on his way to a house two miles distant, and he had swerved a little from his road in order to inquire as to the welfare of the clergyman's household. On hearing that Mina was sick, he at once asked to be allowed to see her, and was shown up to her room. From what the clergyman had said, he had not been very apprehensive as to Mina's state, but when he saw her he became alarmed. She was much changed since he last had seen her—she was depressed and strange in her manner, and strong, feverish symptoms had begun to assert themselves. He stayed some time with her; when he came downstairs it was time for him to go.

'The poor lass is far from weel,' he said, as he shook the clergyman's hand. 'I am glad I happened to be passing by to-night. I have given her a draught—it is all I can do for her to-night; but I'll come again, please God, to-morrow morning.'

With that he mounted his pony and trotted off.

CHAPTER XXXII.

KOLL ON THE WATCH.

THERE was no rest for Koll Nicholson while his foster-child was sick. Passing out from the kitchen of the manse, he came out on the shore of the fjord. The wind was blowing a gale from the east, and as the tide was running out, the water met the wind and roared into breaking waves. The shadow of coming winter was already on the land, and there was little light of either moon or stars.

Turning his face on the troubled sea, the man gazed at the light burning all night in the room where Mina lay; then, with a wild cry, he stretched out his arms towards it, while the salt tears coursed down his wrinkled cheek.

'Star of my breast,' he said, 'bairn of the old man that had nae bairn of his own, may God, that made the mountains, and the sea, and the angels, and the teevils, keep you safe for Koll this night and for evermore! Dinna dee, my bonnie doo, dinna dee! There will be plenty of angels in heaven without ye, and the old man she will pe missing you and breaking her heart! Dinna, dinna dee!'

For a long time he stood watching the light, while it darkened ever and anon with shadows passing across the blind. At last, as if some new thought had seized him, he uttered another low cry and left the shore. All was pitch-dark around and before him, but with the rapidity of a wild beast he began ascending the hills beyond the manse. Here the wind was shrieking, and a drizzly rain was beginning to fall; but without hesitating for a moment, he kept upon his way, running rather than walking, and pausing at long intervals to utter low moans and fling up his hands.

Following the windings of the stream and guiding himself partly by its sound, he ascended rapidly to the lonely shores of Loch Drummdhu.

Dark as it was, he could see the flashing of the sharp white waves of the lake, beaten and lashed into storm by the angry wind. He paused on the shore, stretching out his arms again, like a sorcerer invoking his familiar spirits, and though his hair and beard were dripping with rain, and the wet mist was thickening all around him, he paid but little heed.

'And it is the love-sickness that is killing her bairn,' he cried, 'and it is the wicked teevil's limb of a Sassenach woman that is breaking her bairn's heart. And it was a witch, a tamned witch, and Koll's charm was nae goot, but she will try anither, and anither, and anither, till God tamns the witch and her bairn marries the laird. Ochone, ochone!'

He rushed on again, as if the wind was blowing at his back, along the sides of the loch. Presently he paused in the very shadow of the hills, and saw, far before him, a light like that of a fixed star. No sooner had he perceived it than he hastened on towards it. He knew it well. It came from the windows of the lonely shooting-lodge where Sir Charles Sedley and his daughter were still lingering, accompanied now by the young Lord of Arranmore.

The lodge lay right across the loneliest part of the mountain, full two miles away. There was no path—only a wild stretch of heather, with intervals of deep and dangerous bog. But with his eyes on the light Koll hastened on, sometimes stumbling and falling, but scarcely slackening in his eager speed. It seemed that some fierce fascination drew him that way.

Not until he was within two or three hundred yards of

the house did he pause.   A bright light was issuing from
the window of the sitting-room on the ground floor, but the
rest of the place was dark.

There was neither wall nor paling round the lodge—only
the open heather—so, stooping down very low, Koll crept
closer and closer.   He saw now that the curtains were not
drawn, and that the whole interior of the room was visible.
Throwing himself upon his hands and knees, he crawled
forward, and when he was within a few yards of the window, raised his head cautiously and looked in.

On the table, which was covered with a crimson cloth,
a bright lamp was burning, and by the light Sir Charles
Sedley and his daughter were playing chess.   In an arm-
chair, drawn close to the bright turf fire which was burning on the hearth, sat Lord Arranmore, reading a book.
There seemed to be dead silence, but the baronet looked
rather out of temper, while Ethel was regarding him with
an amused smile.   That smile would have faded quickly
had she known with what intensity of blind hatred the
wild eyes of Koll Nicholson were even then reading her
face.

Let us use our Asmodean privilege and enter the room,
hearing the words which Koll, crouching on the heather
tries in vain to catch.

'I think that is checkmate, papa.   Move if you can!'

With knitted brow, Sir Charles scanned the pieces,
made several irritated efforts to escape from his position,
and then, throwing himself back in his chair, acknowledged
himself beaten.

'And now that I have beaten you two games running, I
think I'll go to bed.'

So saying Ethel rose and stood ready to retire, but
glancing quietly at Arranmore, who remained quite intent
on his book.   With a slight shrug of the shoulders she
walked over to the window and looked out.

'What a night!' she exclaimed.   'The rain is falling in
torrents.'

'It always does rain here,' growled the baronet, 'more
or less.'

'Generally more, papa.   It's a depressing climate, and

I'm really very tired of it. What a relief London will be after so much damp weather and ill-temper !'

'Ah !' sighed Sir Charles, with a significant scowl at his nephew.

Passing quietly across the room, Ethel stooped over her father and kissed him.

'Good-night, papa !' she said; then added carelessly, reaching out her hand, 'Good-night, Lawrance !'

With a start, Arranmore rose and bent forward as if to kiss her cheek ; but she drew back quickly, and turning her head away, quietly left the room. The young lord smiled in an awkward way and again sank into his chair. There was a long silence, which was broken at last by Sir Charles.

'How long is this to go on ?' he exclaimed. 'Upon my soul, Lawrance, I wonder at you !'

'What's the matter ?'

'As a man, I am astonished at your conduct ; as a father, I am indignant. You are treating Ethel shamefully. If it were not for her great affection for you, and the perfect sweetness of her disposition, she would resent your conduct as it deserves.'

Arranmore did not seem astonished at this sudden tirade ; he had rather the manner of one who expected, and to some extent deserved it.

'My dear uncle, it's all right,' he said with a yawn.

'It's not all right,' cried the baronet, crossing over to the hearth-rug and standing astride upon it in the full strength of his parental indignation. 'It's altogether wrong, and you know it.'

'What have I done ?'

'Done? Your unkindness is breaking the poor child's heart. You do not treat her with even common cousinly affection.'

'She has never complained.'

'She is too high-spirited to do so. You might kill her by inches and she would never complain. She's a Sedley, sir, and she knows how to take her punishment ; but I'm not going to stand by and see it without a word of remonstrance. Come, let us understand each other. Do you want to break your engagement ?'

The young man was silent.

'Have you no answer? You had better be frank with me. You ought to know as well as I do that this sort of thing can't go on for ever. How is it to end?'

'God knows!' cried Arranmore, with sudden earnestness; 'I'm sure I don't.'

'What do you mean? Are you mad?'

'I shall soon become so if you torture me with these questions. I am completely wretched, and you must see it. I wish to do my duty, to act honourably, but Ethel is not the only person in the world to be considered.'

'I see!' returned the baronet with a sneer. 'You are still thinking of that Highland hussy whom you were running after when we discovered you. I daresay you have met her again. She has thrown herself in your way, and you are too weak to resist that sort of temptation.'

Leaning back in his chair, the young man now looked steadily and angrily at his companion.

'Uncle, take care! No one—not even you—shall say a word against Miss Macdonald in my presence.'

'Bah!'

'I mean what I say. For any unhappiness that has come of our meeting I alone have been to blame. I deceived her grossly, but she has behaved throughout the whole affair with a nobility which puts me utterly to shame.'

'That's right, sing her praises. Shall I call Ethel back and let her hear?'

'Certainly not. If you think that I wish to cause any pain to Ethel, you do me cruel injustice. My sole desire is to see her happy.'

'And you show that desire by hankering after a peasant woman, her social inferior and yours.'

'Miss Macdonald is not a peasant woman, sir—she is a lady.'

'Nonsense!'

'I regard her as in every way my equal. Indeed there is no person living whom I admire and honour more.'

'Lawrance, let there be an end to this rubbish. Let me speak a few words to you as a man of the world.'

'Very well.'

'The whole matter is very simple. Strip it of the veil of rose-coloured romance which you throw over it, and look at it calmly, sir, with me. This young person, of whom you seem to entertain so high an opinion, lives in a different world to yours. You are not equals, and can never be more closely united than you are now; you are therefore doing her the greatest injury a human being could do. You know, as well as I know, that she could never, under any circumstances, become your *wife*. What character, then, would you assign to any close personal connection that might take place between you? Hear me out! You are not acting like a man of honour. You are deceiving both yourself and her by a dream that will never be realised, and you are at the same time breaking a holy bond into which you have entered with one who is in every respect your equal.'

The young man listened to his speech with some impatience; then quietly rising to his feet at its conclusion, he said emphatically—

'Every word you say is founded on a misapprehension. I regard Miss Macdonald as also in every respect my equal.'

'What do you mean?'

'I mean that, were I a free man, were there not other ties which I am unwilling to break, I would offer her my hand to-morrow.'

'And make her Lady Arranmore?'

'And make her Lady Arranmore!'

Sir Charles positively gasped with astonishment and indignation. He gazed on his nephew as upon one just ripe for Bedlam. Then, as if struck by a sudden thought, he opened the room door and peeped out into the lobby. Closing the door again, he faced his nephew.

'Thank God, Ethel did not hear that!' he cried. 'Very well, my lord. Break your engagement, insult my daughter by comparing her to a common country-girl. From this moment I wash my hands of you. I trusted you—loved you, I may say, like my own son. But there is an end to human patience, and you have exhausted mine.'

'My dear uncle,' said Arranmore quietly, 'you mis-understand me.'

'No, no! I wish that were possible.'

'I have no intention of breaking my engagement with Ethel?'

'What!'

'I merely say that I regarded Miss Macdonald as my equal, and that I should feel no shame in making her my wife. I did not say that I intended to marry her. Of course, that is out of the question, as I am already plighted to Ethel; but even if I were a free man, I doubt if Miss Macdonald would accept my hand.'

The baronet breathed again. In his heart he regarded Arranmore's feeling for Mina Macdonald as mere boyish infatuation, which would rapidly pass away; and he had set his heart on a match between the cousins. Knowing his nephew's headstrong character, however, he dreaded what he might do under the impulse of the moment.

It was a relief to hear that he had no intention of break-ing his engagement.

Sir Charles Sedley was not a sentimental man, and did not solicit, on behalf of his daughter, anything more than cool, matter-of-fact affection. Distrusting all unions built on the volcano of romantic passion, he felt quite certain that Lord Arranmore and Ethel would make a thoroughly suitable pair, while their marriage would consummate a long series of plans for the union and resuscitation of both families.

Before he parted from his nephew that night he accosted him in the old semi-paternal mood, and with tears in his eyes accorded him his full forgiveness.

'Not a word of this to Ethel,' he said, squeezing the young man's hand. 'The poor child is so sensitive, and she would not understand. You know how she worships you, my boy. Thank Heaven, you are still loyal to your first love; if she thought otherwise the shock would break her heart.'

Arranmore sighed heavily as he held his uncle's hand, then lit his bed-candle and went quietly upstairs, passing on his way the chamber where Ethel lay fast asleep and dream-ing—not of him—but of Graham Macdonald.

As the lights went out in Glenheather Lodge, a tall figure stood in the wind and rain that surrounded it. Lying upon the ground, close under the partly-open window of the sitting-room, Koll Nicholson had heard a part of what had been spoken—had heard, but had understood incompletely, owing to his want of familiarity with the English tongue. But the old man was wonderfully shrewd, and a few broken sentences were quite enough. Raising his height, he shook his fist at the darkened window of the lodge.

'The teevil tamn you all,' he cried, 'that would turn the young laird's heart against her bairn! Her bairn shall live —her bairn shall na dee! If the white witch were drooned in the salt sea, the laird would marry her bairn, and she would be the leddy of Arranmore.'

Muttering wildly to himself, he wandered away down the hillside in the direction of his hut, but later on he stood again beneath the lighted window of the sick-room in the manse.

All that night his eyes never closed. His spirit was full of a wild trouble which nothing could appease, and it was well for Ethel Sedley's peace of mind that she did not know what dark thought was rising in his soul.

CHAPTER XXXIII.

THE DEVIL'S BRIDGE.

ALL night long the rain fell in torrents, but the morning broke clear and cold, with bursts of brilliant sunshine. Soon after daybreak Doctor John, who was an early bird despite his convivial habits, appeared at the manse door, where he found Graham awaiting him, and with a business-like nod, passed at once upstairs to the sick-chamber, where Janet was keeping watch. In about a quarter of an hour he re-emerged.

'How is she?' said Graham, as he entered the great kitchen.

'The draught I gave her has done weel with her,' said
Doctor John. 'The perspiration has relieved the natural
humours of the body, and with the blessing of God she has
slept sound.'

'Is she in any danger? Is it the fever, I mean?'

'It's the fever surely; and yet it's not the fever whatever.
It's her heart that's preying on her, for all the world like a
lintie thumping its life out in a cage. But leave her to
God and Doctor John, and I believe she'll come round.'

Here the old minister entered the kitchen, shook hands
with the doctor, and, putting the same questions as Graham,
received much the same answers.

'I fear it is a chill the child has taken,' he said, seating
himself by the fire; 'and besides, she has been studying
too much. I thought she was stronger.'

'She's strong enough in the body, but she's the heart of a
little fish, all flutter, and fondness, and fear. Has she had
any mental trouble?'

'Certainly not,' said Mr. Macdonald, simply; while Graham looked upon the ground and said nothing.

'Between you and me, it's very like the love-sickness!
I've seen it on men and maids, as well as cattle and pigs,
and I knew an old man of seventy once, in Bana, who had
it sae bad in his back that he thought it was the lumbago.
Ye may laugh, Mr. Graham, but I'm speaking as a medical
practeetioner.'

'Your diagnosis will not do in this case,' said Mr. Macdonald gravely. 'Mina is not in love.'

'Are you quite sure?' returned the leech slyly. 'How
could you tell the signs of it, since you never had the sick-
ness yourself?'

Mr. Macdonald smiled, but thought a reply unnecessary.
He was too well acquainted with Doctor John's eccentri-
cities to contradict or bandy words with him. Moreover, it
just then occurred to him, almost for the first time, that
there might be more truth in the doctor's surmise than he
exactly cared to admit. He remembered Mina's brief
acquaintance with Lord Arranmore, and the fascination
which the young man had exercised over her life. Could
it be possible that the discovery of his identity had left a

serious wound? Was she thinking of him still, though she knew their paths lay so far apart? The minister could not be positive in his answers to these questions, and his mind became seriously troubled.

'Keep her quiet, whatever,' said the doctor, 'and the fever will pass away. It's a distemper that all folks are subject to, for all the world like young puppies, and the strong ones are sure to pull through. But for most of these complaints there's but one cure, and it's to be found inside the kirk door.'

'What's that, Doctor John?' asked Graham carelessly.

'What would it be but a gold wedding-ring!' cried the doctor. 'Slip it on her finger, and I'll warrant the fever will leave her in a day.'

'I believe neither in your disease nor your remedy, doctor,' said the minister, shaking his head quietly. 'You're a bachelor yourself, and no authority on the subject.'

'And must a man be poisoned himsel' to ken the use ot streecknine or arsenicum? Can a pheesycian no diagnose hydrophoby unless he's been bitten himsel' by a mad dog? I've studied medicine and I've studied marriage, and I'm familiar wi' the signs o' baith. Dinna tell me I'm a bachelor! I'm an M.D. o' the great University of Aberdeen, and I havena practised thirty years in the Hielands on baith man and cattle without knowing the signs of aal diseases beneath the sun.'

To tell the truth, Doctor John was far less clever in this particular matter than he pretended to be. Always of an inquisitive turn of mind, he had not failed to hear what common gossip said of the young Lord of Arranmore, and of his relations with the family at the manse. To make suspicion certainty, he had a little confidential talk with Koll Nicholson, who confided to him the whole truth, so far as he knew it.

This was quite enough for Doctor John, and when he found Mina suffering from all the symptoms of incipient brain fever, and ascertained that there was no exciting bodily cause to account for her indisposition, he at once arrived at the truth—that Mina's illness was mental rather than

physical, and, in all probability, traceable to a disappoin
ment in love.

Doctor John breakfasted at the manse, beguiling the tim
with many a quaint story and dry jest; then he departe
promising to look in again in a couple of days. Had I
been half as shrewd as he considered himself, especially i
the diagnosis of what he called the 'love-sickness,' he ce
tainly would have had his attention attracted by Graha
Macdonald, who was moody and vacant to a degree, le
his breakfast untouched, and altogether exhibited signs
a distempered and troubled soul. All this the doct
attributed to anxiety on Mina's behalf, without suspectir
that Graham, much as he loved his sister and lamented h
illness, had a wild sorrow of his own which he could wit
difficulty conceal.

After breakfast Graham went up to his sister's roon
where Janet still kept unwearied watch. He found Mir
lying quietly upon her pillow, her eyes open, her cheel
burning with one bright, hectic spot. She knew him, an
smiled as he kissed her; but remembering the doctor
injunctions, he would not let her speak. He alone of a
the inmates of the manse knew the true extent and natu
of her trouble.

Never had his heart yearned towards her in such utt
sympathy of sorrow, for the same poison that she had taste
was even then burning in his own veins.

He spoke a few soothing words, and then, with his ey
full of tears, went on tiptoe away.

He had now a double reason for hating the very name
Arranmore.

Not only did he consider the young lord the sole respo
sible cause of his sister's illness, but he detested him beyon
measure as being the betrothed lover of Ethel Sedley.

He had always disliked him, even when he knew nothir
of his rank and title. Now he felt a furious yearning to l
at his throat.

As he stole from the silent manse his hands were clenche
and his face was fiercely set. Had he encountered his riv
at that time there might have been an ugly scene.

Something drew him up the mountains, past the scer

of his frequent trysts. There were hurry and trouble in his heart, he did not know why, but his pace was slow.

He rambled along with head bent and brows knitted, scarcely looking to right or left.

The burn, in full spate after the heavy rain, and swollen to the size of a muddy stream, roared past him on its way to the sea.

When he came to Loch Drummdhu he stood for a time gazing up its dark expanse to the silent mountains beyond.

Before he stirred again he went over, word by word, every conversation he had had with the woman he loved, and the thought of her proud beauty brought the blood to his brow, and filled his eyes with passionate light.

At last he wandered on—not homewards, but towards the hills. Following a footpath which wound along the edge of the solitary lake, he came among mountain shadows, and saw, a mile away to his left, the lonely shooting-lodge.

Was she there still? Should he see her? Should he walk nearer, in the hope of meeting her? No; he would at least preserve the secret of their intimacy, and if he did encounter her, it should be in solitude.

But not just then—another day. He felt he could scarcely bear to meet her that day—he was so wild and troubled with all that had taken place, and the face of his sick sister was following him still.

Instead of approaching the lodge, he set his face to the ascent which led to the mountains, and began, aimlessly enough, to climb upward.

His walk soon brought him to the banks of the Finnoch River, a wild mountain stream which fed Loch Drummdhu. It came from another gloomy loch high up among the mountains, and it flowed through gorges so deep that they seemed rather the fissures made by earthquake than the bed of a stream.

Scarcely a tree or shrub overhung its banks, save here and there a lovely rowan-tree swinging its red berries high above the whirling pools.

Coming on the rocky banks, he looked down and saw the river rushing past in full flood—black, terrible, and deep, flecked with white spittle of whirling foam. Here it slipped like a sheet of black glass through a pass so narrow that a mountain-deer might have leapt across; then it came to boiling falls, beneath which there spread pools which had never felt the sun, and dark, undiscovered channels tunnelling the solid rocks.

Graham knew every turn and bend of the river, for he had fished every pool, and often, dipping his single fly dexterously in the deepest and most sunless holes, had hooked a huge fish—only, however, to lose it at the first rush.

No angler, however skilful, could have killed a salmon there.

He wandered on, pausing from time to time to watch the still rising waters.

He was in the mood to enjoy the fury of the flood, and he stood on every dizzy crag, listening to the thunder far beneath his feet. At last he came to the blackest and loneliest gorge of all, and saw hanging above him, in the dim shadow of the mountains, the desolate Devil's Bridge.

Around this gorge, for several hundred yards on either side, clustered a wood of mountain firs, the only trees for miles around. All were old trees, some huge and tall, many quite withered and leafless, from the constant force of the mountain blast.

At the top of the gorge, where the crags leaned together, leaving a gap only some twelve feet broad, a rude bridge had been fashioned, partly by Nature, partly by the hand of man.

One great tree, partially uprooted, had fallen across the gap, two smaller trees had been placed by its side; then planks had been nailed on these, on either side of the passage iron staples had been fastened in the rock, from these staples were stretched two thick hand-ropes, reaching about breast high to any person passing across. Underneath the bridge was a long, deep pool, now, in the time of flood, swollen and covered with foam.

Whoever had christened the bridge had chosen its name with more fitness than originality. A gloomier structure and a gloomier place could scarcely have been conceived. The black fir overshadowed the stream on every side, and the river beneath looked like some subterranean lava-stream sent from the innermost heart of hell.

Even with nature familiarity breeds contempt, and Graham Macdonald came up to the Devil's Bridge, and stood leaning in indolent indifference over the dark river, watching the dead leaves swirl down and the great foam-balls bubble and break.

The bridge rocked beneath his weight, but he had trodden it a hundred times, and he did not care.

Lost in thought he stood looking down. All at once, as he stood, he heard a voice singing as if from the very air above his head. He started, for the tune seemed familiar, and the melody was one of those modern melodies of the Italian school which are the delight of drawing-rooms.

Yes, it was her voice, he knew it in an instant! Eager to behold her, he ran across the bridge, and passing through the archways of trees, came out on the open mountain, where she was sitting deep in heather, freshly gathered ferns by her side, and a book in her lap.

She looked up as he came, and did not seem the least surprised.

' I thought you were not far away,' she said.

' Why ? ' he exclaimed, astonished.

' Because just before I came over the bridge I saw your familiar spirit.'

His face expressed such genuine perplexity that she continued—

' Don't you know who I mean? The grim old man whom I compared to one of Fingal's giants.'

' Not Koll Nicholson ? '

' Yes, I think that's the name. Pray, Mr. Graham, why have you instructed this disagreeable person to follow me about ? '

' I ! ' gasped Graham, in still deeper wonder.

' This morning he came right up to the lodge window and stared in. I screamed and thought it was a ghost. Twice during the day he has put himself in my path—not uttering a word, but glaring at me with a blank and fish-like eye. I don't like it, he's such an ugly old creature. You said he was a fisherman. Why doesn't he go fishing and let me alone ? '

Graham laughed. Though Ethel spoke flippantly

enough, and with her usual exhibition of courage, she was obviously disconcerted and a little afraid.

'Don't be alarmed,' he said; 'he is quite harmless. I suppose he has been up here setting otter-traps by the Black Lake, and you stumbled on him by accident. But how is it I find you here in such a lonely place?'

'Oh, it is a favourite walk of mine—I like lonely places.'

'Are you not afraid?'

'Mr. Graham, only two things in the world make me afraid—a mouse and a mad bull. There are no mice on the mountains, and the Highland bulls never go mad.'

He was silent, and now for the first time she noticed that he seemed agitated and full of gloom. She rose to her feet. He stood gazing at her with so strange an expression that she began to feel uncomfortable.

'Mr. Graham, have I offended you?'

'No, no!' he answered, trembling and turning away his eyes.

She approached him softly, and touched him on the arm.

'You know I would not do so for the world. Pray let us be friends.'

'Don't speak to me!' he cried, with a hidden gesture of pain. 'Don't touch me! I can't bear it!'

'What?'

He had taken the plunge, and now his words came fast and thick. As he spoke, his hands were clenched, his face crimson, and he trembled with excitement.

'If you had a woman's heart you would know. You have poisoned my life, and my sister's life. I have come from her sick-bed. You think I can bear to stand by your side—to look in your eyes—to hear your voice—and to know you despise me and mine, as he despises my poor sister. We may not be equals—in the world's eyes we are not—but that is the more reason you should spare me the pretence of a kindness you do not feel.'

Startled by this tirade, Ethel gazed at the speaker in surprise. Pride soon came to her aid, and with an air of hauteur she looked him from head to foot.

He laughed fiercely.

'Yes, frown upon me—drive me from you—I can bear that better; the other drives me mad.'

'What have I done?' she exclaimed.

'It is pastime for you, I know, to play with a man's heart; but,' he added between his set teeth, 'don't go too far.'

She turned on her heel.

'You are impertinent, and I will leave you.'

'No, you shall stay!'

In one moment he had reached her side, and was holding her by both hands.

Her book fell to the ground. She stood trembling with surprise and anger, unable to articulate a word.

'It is your turn now,' he cried, 'to listen to me. Remember we are alone together—this is a solitary place—cry your loudest and no man will hear you. To-day I am strong and you are weak. I asked you for pity once. It is your turn to ask for pity now!'

'No!'

'Are you not afraid?'

'Of you, sir? Certainly not. You are hurting my wrist—release me.'

'Not till you have heard me out.'

'Very well, I'm all attention.'

'I told you that I loved you,' cried Graham, hoarse with passion, and trembling with the intensity of his own emotions. 'You laughed at my love. Well, I tell it you again. I love you, fine lady though you are. Will you laugh now?'

Despite his dangerous look, she murmured—

'Yes,' and actually forced a faint laugh.

Before she could utter another sound he had lifted her up in his arms, and was running with her towards the Devil's Bridge. Before he came to the brink of the crag, however, he set her down, and still retaining his hold upon her, continued—

'Do you know the thought that often took me when we were by the side of Loch Drummdhu? It was this—to clasp you in my arms, and take you down with me to drown! Your look, your voice, drive me mad, because I love you. There runs the river—a few steps and we should die together. Tell me, are you not afraid *now?*'

'No,' she faltered, pale as death.

There was a long pause. Her eyes met his with courage, and they gazed steadfastly at each other.

'You are right,' he said, releasing her with a groan. 'You knew me better than I knew myself. I could not harm you. Farewell!'

And with broken voice and misty eyes he turned away. Touched by his terrible passion and sorrow, she said softly—.

'Why are you so violent with me?'

'Because,' he answered, with averted head, 'if my spirit did not rise against you, my love would kill me. O God! God! I cannot play with my feelings and keep calm. Go away! Tell your fine friends what I have said, and share your scorn with them.'

'You are ungenerous, Mr. Graham. I have always kept your secret.'

'Have you?' he said quickly, turning his eyes upon her.

'I have.'

'Even from him?'

'To whom do you allude?'

'To him—that man—his name chokes me—the lord you are to marry?'

'He knows nothing. But why are you so bitter against him? What has he done?'

'Bonnie as you are, my sister is as bonnie; he has poisoned her soul with his lying words of love.'

'I am very sorry'——

'Your sorrow will not heal her,' he answered bitterly; 'nor will it heal me. Tell me, is it all settled, then? *Must* you marry him?'

She was about to stammer out an evasive reply, but he interrupted her—

'No need to tell me—I see it in your face. Well, God knows you were never made for *me*, though I hope the man that gets you will love you half as well. Good-bye! good-bye!'

Before she could make any reply he was out of hearing, hurrying away as if towards the mountains. She stood silent, watching his figure till it disappeared among the crags.

'Then she smiled sadly, and began to walk slowly towards the Devil's Bridge.

She paused on the brink of the river and looked down. The spate was rushing past with a thunderous sound.

'How dark and wild!' she thought; 'how like *him!* After all, I adore a man!'

She set her foot upon the bridge, holding the guiding-rope. A few steps, and she was in the centre. Just as she reached it she glanced towards the trees on the further side of the gorge, and saw—or seemed to see—a ghastly human face glaring out upon her. At that moment the bridge itself seemed yielding beneath her tread.

She uttered a wild scream and clutched the rope. Another scream! She was hanging by the hands. She screamed again, and saw, as the loose planks broke beneath her feet, the ghastly face glaring at her again.

Then, dazed, horror-stricken, she fell with another wild scream, down into the depths of the roaring flood.

CHAPTER XXXIV.

GRAHAM TO THE RESCUE.

THERE was a roar like cannon thundering in her ears—then a crash, a whirl—followed by semi-stupor. The water had reached up its wild hands and caught her, dragging her to its heart, then with fierce lips sucking her closer and closer. She could not scream now, her brain could not even realise the peril, or comprehend the situation; only she felt herself whirling along in a dream, and was conscious of nothing else but a strange sound; not thunder now, but like the ringing of bells.

The very fury of the torrent prevented her from sinking below its surface, and her garments, inflated from beneath, helped to support her. Loose as a weed torn from its hold in the ground or in the rock, her hair washing wild and

dripping, her arms outreaching—half sinking, half sup-
ported, she was driven along for nearly fifty yards.

Here the rapid river, shooting out of the riven rock, and
from out the shelter of the overhanging woods, suddenly
broadened, and ran with slower pace, but still swiftly out
into the open sunlight; and here its hold loosening, like
fingers that relax their tension from sheer exhaustion, the
girl began to sink and drown. Beating the water with convulsive hands, she sank, and touched the bottom for the
first time. Then she rose again, and though scarcely
conscious, uttered a convulsive cry.

As she did so, a man appeared upon the bank above her,
and without an instant's hesitation leapt down into the
water. Striking out with powerful arms, he reached her
just as she was about to sink for the second time.

Quite unconscious now, she did not see him, or attempt
to clutch him; while with infinite gentleness he drew her
backward, and swimming beneath her, paddled rapidly to
shore. Touching ground, he gained his feet, and then with
a sense of horrible rapture, almost of exultation, he seized
her in his strong arms and waded to the bank.

They made a subject for a painter as they paused there
on the brink, with the wild river running passed them, and
the sun shining above their heads; she, dripping and life-
less, her hair hanging loose, her delicate dress soddened,
destroyed, and half torn from her tender body; he, strong
and determined, dripping too, but careless of his condition,
with his eyes fixed passionately and fearfully on the pallid,
death-like face.

He paused only for a moment, then, with his light burden
in his arms, he leapt up the bank, and stood knee-deep in
heather. There was a heathery knoll here, and to this he
ran, and set his burden down. Then with a sickening
dread he knelt beside her, and looked into her face.

To all seeming she was dead. Her eyes were fixed, her
breath seemed no longer to go and come; she lay like
death. With a wild cry he threw his arms around her, and
in the insolence of despair pressed her to his breast. She
did not stir.

Then a thought struck him, and with tremulous fingers

he tore open the bosom of her oozy dress, and placed his hand upon her heart. To his surprise and joy he could faintly but distinctly feel it stirring beneath his touch. A heavy sigh, almost a sob, broke from his lips, and the tears rose in his eyes.

But he was a true son of the sea, and this was not the first occasion on which he had snatched life from the destructive jaws of water. So he began, deliberately and gently, to move the arms of the sleeping girl, raising them with one steady motion over her head, then bringing them down with soft and steady pressure to her side, thus, on the principle of the bellows, inflating the delicate lungs with air, and filling the tender cells with new life. It was tedious work, and the moments seemed minutes, the minutes interminable, as he repeated the motion, and watched wildly for signs of returning animation.

She still remained cold and inert, and at last he bethought him of a plan he had more than once seen tried with success. Placing her on her side, he knelt down beside her, and still repeated the rhythmic motion of the arms, and placed his mouth to her cold lips. Drawing a deep breath he suffered the strong breathing to pass into her mouth. Thus their breaths, their very lives, mingled for the time being, and now, as if in response to the burning life within his veins, her own faint life began to stir.

There was a convulsive movement of the breast, a shiver of the entire frame, then the breath began to come.

Graham Macdonald would have given the world at that moment for a few drops of brandy, or some other revivifying fluid. Failing that, he persisted in the rhythmic movement of the arms, and kept the dying body close against his own. Fortunately the sky had cleared, and it was now one of those burning days to be known only in the brief summer of the far north. The air was full of warmth and life.

The slow minutes passed, until at last she opened her eyes.

There was a film upon them, and at first she saw nothing. Graham was now stooping over her, convulsively holding her hand.

He could not utter a word, for now, to see her breathing again, fresh from the shadow of a cruel death, he was choking with tears.

She heaved a heavy sigh, closed her eyes, and after a pause opened them again. This time she recognised the form bending over her, and a look of frightened recognition came into her face.

'Help me to rise,' she said faintly.

He put his arm around her, and lifted her to her feet. She trembled and shivered, and to his delight clung to him.

'What has happened?' she said, with a frightened sob.

'You fell into the river—you were drowning; but luckily I was near.'

She gazed at him with tearful eyes, and did not seem to understand; then again, as if involuntarily, she clung to him, with a touch that made him tremble through and through.

'Take me home,' she said.

'May I carry you?' he asked quickly.

She did not answer, so, without another word, he lifted her up, and began walking with great strides in the direction of Glenheather Lodge. Exalted by the strong stress of his passionate pity, he felt her weight no more than if it had been a feather. All he felt now was a sullen rapture, a gloomy joy. It was something, at least, to hold her in his arms, to feel her wet, wild hair against his cheek, to be conscious, above all, that she owed her life to him, and that, whatever might come between them in the future, she was in a measure, and for the time being, wholly his. Yes, that triumph, temporary though it was, was worth living and dying for. It seemed as if he had never rightly lived till that moment; and as he strode along, with heart of fire and sinews of iron, he felt the moment was sublime.

He walked some distance in silence, very rapidly.

He was bareheaded, and the sun poured its rays down with violence, but he did not feel them, though his face was like fire, and the great veins of his forehead were swollen and enlarged.

Suddenly she fluttered in his arms, and cried to be set down.

He obeyed her in a moment, and setting her down, stood flushed and tremulous before her.

'I think I can walk,' she said. 'Please give me your arm.'

He moved near to her, and, leaning upon him, she stepped feebly forward; but she was shivering, and her strength seemed very small. All at once she uttered a cry, and would have fallen had he not caught her in his arms.

By this time they had gained the summit of a small hill, and could see, far away in the distance, the white walls of Glenheather Lodge.

'Let me sit down!' she cried; and shivered violently.

He placed her gently on the ground, and bent over her.

'If you will wait here,' he said, 'I will run to the lodge and get you a little brandy. You are faint and cold, and that will be the best. May I go?'

She inclined her head, and without even looking at her, he ran down the hill. Love appeared to give him wings, and he leapt from knoll to knoll as nimbly as a deer. Pausing at the foot of the hill, with the open moor before him, he saw the figure of Ethel still sitting moveless on the height. Then he ran on.

The lodge was a good mile away, but the mile was as nothing to the young mountaineer. Before many minutes had passed he stood panting before the house. A couple of Gordon setters were basking upon the threshold, and an empty garden-chair stood in the sun. The door stood wide open, and without a moment's hesitation, not pausing to knock, he entered.

In the lobby he came face to face with Sir Charles Sedley.

'Hullo!' cried that nobleman, aghast at the intrusion.

'There is not a moment to lose!' cried Graham. 'Give me some brandy.'

Sir Charles, rendered still more aghast by the extraordinary request, positively gasped with amazement.

'Brandy!' he echoed.

'Yes, at once—for your daughter.'

'For my daughter!'

'Yes, she is ill—she has met with an accident. I must have brandy at once.'

'When? how? where?' Sir Charles began categorically; but Graham, with decision, proceeded—

'It is no time for talk. Miss Sedley is still in a fainting condition. For God's sake, get me the brandy!'

Thus conjured, Sir Charles ran into the dining-room and seized a spirit bottle and a glass. He trembled very much, for he was very fond of his daughter, and looked quite pale.

'Where is she?' he cried, rejoining Graham.

'Follow me!'

Taking glass and bottle from the baronet's hand, he ran from the house and hurried rapidly back across the moor. Sir Charles, snatching a cap up to cover his head, followed slowly in his track, silent, dumb-stricken, and amazed.

When Graham reached Miss Sedley's side he found her just as he had left her, but quite conscious now, and shivering violently.

He pressed the brandy upon her, and she drank part of a glass without water—her first experience of raw spirits in her life. The effect was almost instantaneous, and by the time her father came up the dulness of her eyes and spectral pallor of her face had almost passed away.

'God bless me, Ethel, my darling, what's this?' cried the baronet, bending down and kissing her, while he seized her hands between his own.

'I scarcely know,' she said faintly. 'I—I think I fell into the water, and that gentleman pulled me out.'

'And you're dripping wet! This is horrible. You fell into the water! What water?'

'Into the river,' answered Graham, with one of his gloomy looks. 'The Devil's Bridge gave way beneath her, and she sank into the river at full flood.'

'Good God! is it possible?'

Greatly agitated, Sir Charles gazed from his daughter to Graham, and from Graham to his daughter, and perceived their forlorn appearance and their dripping attire. Inspiration came to him at last, and he exclaimed—

'Take a little more brandy, my love.'

Graham stepped forward with the bottle, but she shook her head.

'You have taken none yourself,' she said, lifting her eyes to his face. 'You must be very cold.'

Graham smiled, and pouring out a glass of the raw fluid, drank it off with perfect unconcern. Then he turned to Sir Charles.

'The young lady is soaking,' he said. 'The sooner she is taken home the better.'

'Dear me, yes!' ejaculated Sir Charles. 'Can you walk, Ethel?'

'I will try, papa,' was the answer. 'I feel stronger now.'

So saying she arose, and, leaning on her father's arm, began moving slowly in the direction of the lodge. Macdonald followed close behind, ready at any moment to spring forward and offer assistance; but already, as it seemed to him, his time of triumph was over, and she had passed out of the sphere of his passion. That time, despite all its peril for her, had been supreme for him, and holding her in his arms as he swam to the shore, or clasping her wet form to his heart in the wild hope of restoring animation, he would thankfully have died. It was all over now. Never again perhaps would he be privileged to hold her in his embrace, to drink her breath, to feel the ecstasy of adoring, yet despairing, possession. Already, too, she seemed a different being. In her face as it was turned to her father, then to him, and in her slight form, as she quietly moved along on her father's arm, the old unconscious hauteur, the easy pride which he resented so much, but which made him admire her twenty-fold, was beginning to return. As he followed, it seemed that he had lost her. She had been his for an instant, she was his no more.

Still shivering violently, yet recovering some little of her habitual self-command, she made her way across the moor, and at last she reached the door. There she paused for a moment, and, turning on the threshold, quietly reached out her hand to Graham. He took it, and on a sudden impulse was about to kiss it, when he felt the cold eye of Sir Charles fixed upon him; and so, instead of kissing it, he pressed it warmly. She did not smile, but was deathly pale, as, turning away, she entered the house, and, calling for the female attendant, went upstairs to her room.

Sir Charles turned to Graham.

'I won't ask you to come in,' he said, 'for you are dripping wet. Stop, though! Suppose you change here, and put on some dry things of mine.'

Graham laughed.

'Thank you,' he said, 'I'm warm already. It's not the first cold bath I've taken in my clothes.'

'But you'll get your death of cold.'

'Is it *me?*' returned Graham, with a shrug of contempt.

'Then take some more brandy. No. A cigar?'

The cigar Graham accepted, and lit it quietly. As he did so, the baronet looked at him keenly, and said—

'How did this happen? It seems a most extraordinary occurrence. I've passed over that bridge a dozen times, and it never gave way. What a miracle it was my child escaped!'

'Yes, it was a miracle,' returned Graham in a low voice, and the next minute he walked away.

Instead of turning homeward, Graham Macdonald walked rapidly in the direction of the Devil's Bridge.

His physical condition was entirely forgotten, and he heeded his wet garments neither more nor less than the warm air that hung about him. His brow was black, his teeth set together, in the agony of a new fear which the words of Sir Charles Sedley had conjured up.

Running rather than walking, he approached the mountains, and was soon in the close vicinity of the Devil's Bridge.

Pausing on the river's side, he saw the water still boiling and seething, the very banks seeming to shake with the force and fury of the flood.

Then he passed upward and followed the path which led to the bridge. Passing along amidst the trees, he came to the chasm where the bridge had hung, but the bridge was gone.

One of the upper ropes still hung in the air, and part of a plank jutted out from the opposite side; the rest of the frail structure had disappeared.

Stooping down, and resting on his hands and knees, he

carefully examined the side of the chasm on which he himself was standing. In another minute he sprang up, and
with a wild gesture, threw his arms into the air. His face
had turned perfectly livid and bloodless, and he uttered an
exclamation of horror.

The cause of his horror was simple, and may be at once
explained. The portion of wood jutting out from the bank
on which he stood was not jagged, broken, or worm-eaten ;
it was clean cut, as if with some keen instrument, and
showed the marks of heavy blows, like those of a sharp
axe !

It was terrible, inconceivable, in its suggestion of human
handiwork. His head swam round.

As he stood in horrible surprise and doubt, his eyes
looked down the river towards the spot near which he had
saved Miss Sedley's life, and he discerned in the distance
something moveless as a rock, but resembling the figure of
a man.

Silently, not hesitating a moment, he moved in that
direction, his hands closing and unclosing rapidly in the
fury of his thought. Pushing his way through the intervening branches of the wood, he came out on an open
space, and saw, standing with his back to him, the shape
of his foster-father.

CHAPTER XXXV.

KOLL'S AXE.

THE old man did not hear his approach, for the river was
loud, and he himself was busy with his own thoughts ; but,
striding forward white and ghastly, Graham placed his hand
upon his shoulder.

Koll turned, and saw in a moment, by the expression of
the young man's face, that his secret was discovered. His
own countenance, however, assumed a cunning expression
of surprise.

'What are you doing here?' cried Graham, in a choking voice.

'She is looking at the river,' answered Koll quietly. 'Weel, it will be a grand flood for the salmon, and there will be goot fishing when the water begins to faal!'

Before he could say another word, Graham's fingers were at his throat.

'I will strangle you,' he cried, 'if you do not tell me the truth! Who cut down the bridge? You?'

'The bridge? And wha would cut doon the bridge? Is it Koll?'

'Some one has cut the planks with an axe, and the rope was almost severed with a knife. It was *you*. You old devil! why did you do it? Tell me quickly, Koll, or I shall strike you. Yes or no? Was it your work?'

As he spoke the young man saw something in the grass at his feet. He stooped and lifted it. It was a common axe, or chopper, and sharp as a knife.

With a cry he held it in the air.

'Yes, it was *you!* Why did you do it, why? Speak, or I'll kill you!'

Koll Nicholson stood firm, and with his still lack-lustre eyes looked at Graham. Then he drew himself up quietly and replied—

'She will tell you why she did it—she will tell you, and she doesna care if you kill her. It was to droon the wicked witch.'

'To—what?'

'To droon the tamned witch wha has broken the heart of her bairn.'

'What do you mean?' cried Graham, glaring at the old man, and dropping the arm which held the axe. 'You tried to murder that lady?'

'She tried to droon the witch, and she would have drooned her if she had her will!'

Utter horror and amazement paralysed Graham's faculties for a time, while the old man continued calmly—

'Dinna blame her, Graham—it was best that the witch should dee. And what for did you jump into the river and sweem to her, and bring her back again to land? It was not goot, it was better that the witch should droon, and then the old man's wish would come aboot, and Mina would be Leddy Arranmore.'

Then in a flash all the old man's purpose dawned upon the mind of Graham, and he went aghast at the deliberate and cold-blooded malignity. Shrinking back, he gazed upon the tall form of his foster-father with the uttermost horror and repulsion, amounting in the sum to positive hate. He could not speak at first, but his face spoke for him, and Koll saw there something appalling even to his phlematic nature.

'What ails her son?' he said, beginning to tremble, and putting into his voice a certain pathetic whine. 'What for is he angry with Koll? It is goot that the witch should droon.'

'It is well for you, Koll Nicholson,' cried Graham, 'that your devilish purpose failed, and that the lady's life was saved. Mind this, too! If one hair of her head suffers I will have justice upon you; I will drag you to prison with my own hands. Even as it is, your attempt at murder shall be known; and, if it is proved upon you, you will end your days in gaol. You did not succeed, but that is no fault of yours, and you are as guilty as if you had succeeded. From this moment never speak to me again. My uncle and my sister shall know what you have done, and they will loathe you as I loathe you, curse you as I curse you, for your devilish deed.'

Unconsciously Graham had touched the right chord at last. The old man fell upon his knees, and held him with his quivering hand.

'Kill her!' he cried. 'But dinna tell Mina—dinna tell her bairn!'

'Let me go. I will tell her, and she will never forgive you.'

'She did it for her foster-bairn,' whimpered the old man. 'She tried to droon the witch for her bairn's sake—for her bairn was like to dee, and Koll saw nae other way. But dinna speak to Mina—dinna turn Mina's heart against Koll. Take the sharp axe and kill the old man with the axe, but dinna, dinna tell her foster-bairn.'

Graham looked down at Koll with intense loathing; then, struck by a new thought, he exclaimed—

'I will tell her, and she will not pity you. She is a good lass, and would hate a murderer. But mind this—I am your worst enemy from this night. Your talk is all of Mina, but what did you think about *me*, about what *I* suffer? If you were not an old devil, blind and deaf, you would have known how much I care for Miss Sedley—you would have known that I would die for her, I love her so much. She is an angel, and you are an old devil. When I think that you dared to lift your hand against her, when I think she might have died a violent death through your infernal plot, I feel ready to revenge myself upon you. I wish my curse would kill you! Let go of me; never dare to speak to me or to my sister again!'

Tears were now running down the ash-grey cheeks of Koll, the great frame trembled like a leaf, while, seizing the hand of Graham and lifting it to his lips, he covered it with kisses, moaning and whimpering all the time like a hound in disgrace.

'Graham,' he cried, 'Graham, her ain son! dinna be sae hard on Koll. She didna ken you was coorting the leddy —she didna ken you were to marry her—she thought she was to marry the Laird of Arranmore.'

'Marry her?' echoed Graham angrily. 'I tell you she is an angel, and I am not fit to tie her shoe-strings. But I love her, for all that.'

'And you are coorting the leddy—oh, why did ye no tell Koll you was coorting the leddy? She didna ken, she didna ken.'

Graham stamped upon the ground, and shook off the old man's grasp in the very fierceness of his anger.

'Fool! are you so blind that you cannot see the difference between a great lady like that, and a wretched Highlander like me? I am as much below her as you are below her—ay, as the dirt beneath her bonnie feet.'

Koll rose to his feet with a look of pride and determination.

'Her son is a Macdonald of the Isles,' he said proudly, 'and the Macdonalds of the Isles are dirt beneath nae folk's feet.'

'And what are you,' continued Graham savagely, 'to meddle with my business? How dare you pry, and watch, and plot against me, and try to injure the only creature I care for in the world? You meddling, murdering devil! And you dare to tell me it was for my sister's sake! It is a lie. You care no more for my sister than you care for me. You care only for yourself. If I had my will upon you, Koll Nicholson, I would have you hung!'

So saying, Graham shook off the old man's clutch, and, still tremulous with passion, walked away. Koll stood on the same spot, watching him go, until he disappeared across the darkening moor. Then the old man stooped and lifted the axe, which Graham had cast furiously upon the ground.

'She doesna care if they hang her,' he muttered. 'If the heart of her bairn is turned against her, she would like to dee; but whether they hang her or no, it's maybe better to fling the axe awa'.'

And walking to the bank, he dropped the axe into the deepest part of the river, where it sank at once. Then, with a deep groan of pain, which was repeated at long intervals, and seemed to come from the very depths of his heart, he made his way across the moor.

CHAPTER XXXVI.

THE DARKENING OF THE DREAM.

BEFORE returning to the village Graham Macdonald called again at Glenheather Lodge, and ascertained that Miss Sedley was warm in bed, and showed as yet no signs of serious illness. He did not see Sir Charles, who was just then sitting by his daughter's bedside, but was assured by the old female domestic that no danger was to be apprehended. Satisfied on this point, he made his way homeward, with such a fever in his heart and brain as he had scarcely ever felt before in all his life.

The more he reflected on the proceedings of the day the more he felt bewildered and distraught. That Koll Nicholson, in the cold deliberation of his antipathy and jealousy, should actually have attempted to commit a diabolical murder, and in the carrying out of his plans should have adopted means so cunning, seemed less extraordinary than that he, Graham, should have been providentially at hand, willing and able to save the lady of his love from a watery grave. Well, whatever might be the issue, he had enjoyed for the time being a kind of savage happiness. He had been brought closer to his ideal that day than he could ever hope to come again. He had breathed the very breath of his life into her mouth, and he had warmed her cold body against his heart. Then, recovering, she had clung to him as to a natural protector, temporarily forgetful of the pride of birth and worldly position which had hitherto come between them. He carried with him, tremulous in his heart, the memory of her last ghost-like gaze as she had offered him her hand. Yes, that day at least, he had lived indeed.

As he revolved the whole circumstances in his mind his wrath against his foster-father gradually lessened, and although he hated him for what he had done, he partly pardoned him, because the issue had not been fatal, and because the event had given him so terribly sweet an experience.

He rapidly determined that he would say nothing of Koll Nicholson's crime, though he would take care that it was punished by the silent repudiation of the family. To make any sort of accusation against Koll would be to lay bare his own heart, perhaps to make his own acts open to misconstruction. He resolved, therefore, that he would screen Koll, and even, until silence was impossible, say nothing whatever of the occurrence of the day.

Fortunately for his plans, he was able to reach his own room in the manse unobserved, and to change his wet attire, which he gave Janet to dry, strictly enjoining her to say nothing to any one on the subject. Then strolling carelessly downstairs, he joined his uncle at the evening meal.

He hurried to bed early, but lay all night in an ecstasy of

feverish remembrance. Whenever he dozed off to sleep he was struggling again in the flood, with his unconscious burden in his arms, and holding her locked in his despairing yet passionate embrace.

He rose at dawn, and slipping on his clothes, wandered forth. A drizzling rain was falling, but he did not heed it. He walked up across the moor, till he came in sight of the lonely lodge, which still lay partially hidden in the slowly ascending mists of morning; and he stood for an hour feasting his eyes upon it. The sun came up red and sullen, with strong streaks upon the clouded hills, and at last, with finger red as fire, touched the lodge and made it blood-red. He watched it till the red light melted into full morning, then he turned away.

His impulse led him towards the sea-shore, towards the spot where Koll Nicholson had placed his lonely hut. Approaching the door, which stood wide open, he saw the figure of the old man seated in its usual crouching position on a low stool before the fire. He entered in, and placed his hand upon Koll's shoulder. Koll looked up without the least surprise, and held out both his hands.

'Listen to me,' said Graham coldly. 'I have thought it over, and I shall say nothing about what you have done. If your guilt is discovered, it will be no fault of mine; but, if I can, I shall keep the secret.'

'And you will not tell her bairn?'

'I will tell no one. Not because I can forgive you, but because I do not wish to bring shame upon myself. You understand?'

'She kens, she kens,' said the fisherman, wearily shaking his head. 'O Graham, her ain son, dinna be angry wi' her!'

But Graham pushed back the trembling hands that were outstretched to his.

'You must promise me, too. You must swear to me that you will never plan any such devilry again. Will you swear?'

'She'll swear!'

'Never to attempt to harm that lady—always to remember that I love her, and that her life is dearer to me than my own.'

'She'll remember! she'll remember!' cried Koll, again reaching out his tremulous hands. But Graham again shook off his hold, and with one dark look of warning, and no word of farewell, strode to the door and so disappeared.

The old man sat moveless before the slowly smouldering fire of peat, his hands expanded through old habit to feel the heat, his eyes upon the faint glow of the flame upon the ground. He had sat thus all night, until Graham disturbed him, and now he relapsed again into his old position. Pale and still, grim and great as some shape of granite, he sat, with the black walls round him, and the black roof above his head. Only now and then he muttered to himself, and shook his hoary head from side to side, as if in deep trouble. Hour after hour passed and he did not stir.

Meantime the sun was well up over Uribol, and with the rising of the sun came the news of what had befallen Miss Sedley, and of how she had been rescued from death by Graham Macdonald. If Graham had fancied that an affair so extraordinary could be kept a secret he was doomed to disappointment.

How or by whom it was spread no man knew—possibly it began with some kitchen gossip at the lodge; but before now every man and woman in the clachan knew all about it. Not but that the various accounts passing from mouth to mouth were contradictory and exaggerated. One feminine rumour ran that Graham and the great lady had then and there, immediately after the immersion, made a solemn covenant to marry each other. Another story went that Miss Sedley had wilfully flung herself into the water because she was unwilling to marry the young Lord of Arranmore. In short, every possible flight of fancy was indulged in, with the news of the accident for a basis, and the affair was a godsend to every gossip for ten miles round.

When Graham walked in to breakfast he saw at once that the news had reached his uncle.

'What's this, Graham?' said the minister, after waiting in vain to see if his nephew would broach the subject, 'what's this I hear? Is it true that Miss Sedley fell into the river, and that you swam in and brought her out?'

Graham, with heightened colour, hung his head over his cup of tea.

'Yes, it's true.   It's lucky I was at hand.'

'I sincerely trust the young lady is not injured.   The shock must have been terrible to one so delicate.   How did it happen?'

'The Devil's Bridge had been loosened by the rains; when she stepped upon it, it gave way beneath her feet.'

'Horrible!' exclaimed the clergyman.   'I always said it was not safe, and I never crossed it myself without feeling dizzy.   And she fell, you say'——

'Right down into Paol na Bedach gal.   Fortunately the flood was high, and, instead of striking the rocks, she was swept down with the current.'

'And she was not dangerously hurt?—a miracle!'

Graham smiled.

'The water took her along like a feather, as if she was too delicate and bonnie to drown.'

'Thank God, you were there.'

'Ay, thank, God!'

The minister rose and took from the wall his broad-brimmed hat and shepherd's crook.

'I will go at once and call,' he said.   'Will you come with me?'

Graham shook his head.

'I'm rather tired, and will stay at home till you come back.'

'Very well,' said Mr. Macdonald; 'I shall not be long away, and I will bring you word how the young lady is this morning.'

The minister hurried away, and in less than two hours he returned, and found Graham sitting by the kitchen fire.

'Well,' said Graham, looking up nervously.

His uncle came over smiling and clapped him on the shoulder.

'Good news, Graham!   The young lady is very little the worse, though a good deal shaken by the fright.'

'Did you see her?'

'No, she is keeping in bed, but I saw Sir Charles, and he spoke in the highest terms of *you*.   He asked about your position, your prospects in life, and seemed very much interested indeed ; said he should never forget that you had been of service to him, and offered to forward your worldly interests as far as lay in his power.'

'Very kind,' anwered Graham with a scowl, 'but I don't want his assistance.'

'Don't make sure of that. He is a gentleman whose friendship is of the greatest possible value.'

'What I did I did to please myself—not him.'

'My dear Graham, you did what any Christian man would have done under the circumstances,' responded Mr. Macdonald warmly ; 'but God has enabled you to perform a deed of mercy, and we should all be grateful. It would have been horrible indeed if that bonnie young life had been lost. Even as it is, I am sorry they are leaving with such a gruesome memory of the Highlands.'

'Leaving ?' repeated Graham.

'Yes, Sir Charles has now decided to go at once. They will depart without delay ; and Lord Arranmore will accompany them,' he added. 'I believe the marriage is to take place before Christmas.'

'Whose marriage, uncle ?'

'Miss Sedley's, of course, with Lord Arranmore. Sir Charles informs me that their attachment dates from childhood. Well, Graham, you will have made another friend in his lordship. How grateful he will be to you for having preserved his bride !'

Graham said nothing, but, with his face convulsed by agony, rose and left the house. Then he lit his pipe, and, pacing on the sea-shore, had his dark hour in silence.

As he gazed out upon the grey waters of the northern sea —cold, palpitating without sunlight—he saw a sail fading far under the horizon, and it seemed like a gloomy image of his love. He had had his supreme moment, but now he was to be left in the long gloaming of a desolate despair.

The woman of his wild desire was passing from him, never to return—fading like that faint sail, where earth and heaven mixed their lights far out on the sunless sea.

CHAPTER XXXVII.

MINA IS CONVALESCENT.

ALL that day Ethel remained in bed. The next morning she breakfasted in her room, and about an hour after breakfast she walked calmly into the morning-room, and gave her father his usual morning salute.

Her face was very pale; her left hand had a fine cambric handkerchief bound round it, otherwise she looked none the worse for her fall; nevertheless, Sir Charles Sedley thought it right to expostulate with his daughter upon the folly of rising, and insisted upon treating her as if she were an invalid of some six months' standing.

When, therefore, she lifted her pale face to give him his customary kiss, he wound his arms about her and pressed her affectionately to him; then he placed her in an easy-chair, and took his seat by her side.

'Ethel, my love,' he said, 'do you feel strong enough to travel?'

'To travel, papa!' queried the girl, raising her eyes to his. 'Why, where in the world do you want to take me to now?'

'Back to town,' returned the baronet firmly. 'Lawrance and I are both agreed'——

'Lawrie,' returned Ethel quickly. 'Why, where did you see Lawrie?'

'Here, of course. On hearing of the accident he hastened here'——

'Hoping to hear of my death, I suppose. Well, I think that fall would have killed any one else—but I suppose I am destined to do more mischief before I die.'

She spoke half dreamily, utterly regardless of the expression, first of horror, then of anger, which crossed her father's face.

After a short silence the baronet spoke, as he did so

taking his daughter's right hand and pressing it between his own.

'Ethel, my love,' he said, 'it is decided that we leave for town the day after to-morrow. Lawrie and I are both agreed that to linger longer in this place would be madness. He is tired of rusticating, and, moreover, he acknowledges that after this accident the place can never have pleasant associations for any of us.'

While the baronet spoke his daughter smiled very strangely; but as he ceased her lip curled into a sarcastic sneer. She raised herself in her chair, and turned her eyes full upon his face.

'Papa,' she said scornfully, 'when is all this humbug, this contemptible double-dealing, to be at an end between us two? If you wish us to go away, why cannot you say it is because you are afraid to let my affianced husband linger any longer in the same village with the girl whom he loves better than he loves me?'

'Ethel!'

'There, do not attempt to expostulate. I mean to speak out the truth for once, at least, in my life. If you are afraid for Lawrie, I am not; if you are afraid to linger, I am not. I have never been famed for affection, but I hope I have some gratitude left in me, and before I depart I mean to experience the pleasure of thanking the man who so bravely saved my life.'

The baronet burst into a laugh.

'Upon my word, Ethel, you ought to be a melodramatic queen upon the stage, to go into such heroics over the young gamekeeper. Depend upon it when he receives my cheque for fifty pounds he'll readily dispense with your thanks.'

'Your cheque? Have you actually sent him money?'

'Of course I have! I despatched Donald with it more than an hour ago. I was obliged to make the young fellow some compensation, and it was the only thing I could do. I have no doubt he'd make an heroic rescue every day for such a reward.'

Ethel said nothing; her cheeks, lately so pale, were burning crimson; her right hand which grasped the chair was trembling and cold; her eyes were fixed upon the window, on the glittering panes of which the golden sunbeams played.

The window was partly open; she could hear the faint rustling of the heather and long grass; she could feel the perfumed breeze creeping in to cling about her nostrils and fan her cheeks, and in this dreamy warmth and scented stillness she closed her eyes.

Then her ears were filled with the noise of a rushing, roaring torrent; she seemed to be engulphed by waters, which settled around her and sucked her down; then above the boiling eddy a face appeared, an arm was clasped around her, and at the touch her paralysed faculties seemed to brighten again into life.

It was only a repetition of the dream which had been haunting her ever since the hand had plucked her, as it were, out of the very darkness of the grave.

It had been present with her through the long watches of the night, as she had lain so calmly with closed eyes and gently heaving breast; and though the cold daylight had somewhat dispelled the vision, she had but to close her eyes to bring it back again. But, this time, having recalled it, she clung to it as a young mother might cling to some dearly loved child which she knew she soon must lose.

How could she continue to cling to her vision, to dream her dream, when her hero had accepted the price of his heroism, and brought the matter to an end!

She almost hated her father for having sent the money; yet, again, she felt rather pleased that it had gone.

If he accepted it—as in all probability he would do —she felt that she could travel back to London with a great deal of the load lifted from her heart; and if he did not—why, how much more worthy to be her hero!

Here Ethel's meditations were brought to a close. The opening of a door, an exclamation from her father, caused her to open her eyes. In the middle of the room stood Sir Charles Sedley with a torn envelope in one hand—an open letter in the other.

'The insolent young puppy!' he exclaimed; then turning to his daughter, he added, 'So much for your hero, my

Q

love. He has had the impertinence to return my cheque, and to say that if I have any money to spare, I had better distribute it amongst the poor.'

'And very good advice, too, papa, I should say,' returned the girl, whose face and eyes had grown wonderfully bright again.

'Good advice! Those sort of people have no right to give advice! It is a piece of impertinence which I should resent very strongly if he had not been of some slight service to you.'

Ethel smiled to herself, and without another word left the room.

How elated she felt! How her cheek burned; her hands trembled; her heart leapt! She walked straight to her little sitting-room, and sat down by the open window, feeling again that the breeze came with refreshing coolness to touch her lips and eyes.

Her window commanded an extensive view of the country —of hill and valley, cliff and sea. She could see the clachan clustering in its sheltered nook among the hills, the dark green cluster of trees which grew around the manse.

For a time she fixed her eyes upon this; then she withdrew them, and gazed down at the hand which was enveloped in its cambric bandage.

'The only memento which I have of that eventful day,' she said. 'The only witness of the doom from which he saved me. Well, when I have seen him, and thanked him, and said "Good-bye," I will tear off the bandages, and try to keep the wound still there. Perhaps it might have been better if he had left me there to die—better for himself, for his sister, for Lawrie. Yes; I am breaking their hearts, preparing for three victims one living grave. Poor Lawrie! How nobly self-forgetful and honourable he has been! Well, who knows—perhaps I may be able to make some amends!'

Meanwhile Lord Arranmore, walking out in the sunshine, was, like his cousin, speculating over all these things. He had had a long conversation with his uncle that morning, and half an hour before Ethel walked into the breakfast-room he had strolled out into the sunshine to think over all that had been said.

To his uncle's proposition that, as soon as Ethel's health was re-established, they should quit Coreveolan, he had not objected—not because of Ethel, but because he had learned by this time to fear himself.

Again that morning the talk of the two men had turned upon the engagement between the cousins ; again Sir Charles had pointed out the overwhelming shame which would cling for ever about his daughter should the engagement be broken through, and again Lawrance had given his pledge that the engagement should never be brought to a close by him.

So when the baronet proposed that hasty removal, Lawrance, soul-sick, and seeing no end to all this trouble, had given a ready assent. For he thought, 'Where is the use of lingering ? it will only be the means of bringing more wretchedness and misery to us both. I would not care for myself; I am a man, and can bear it; besides, I have played the villain, and deserve to suffer; but for the sake of indulging my own mad feelings I will not be the means of bringing greater pain to her. Yes, I will go, and perhaps when once I am away she may learn to forget.'

Nevertheless, despite his philosophical reasoning, Lord Arranmore had never felt more utterly soul-sick. The thought of leaving Coreveolan was like turning his eyes towards the ghastly face of death.

He had wandered some two miles from Glenheather Lodge, and stood now looking down upon the manse. There it lay beneath the shoulder of the hill, bathed in sunshine, and looking as peaceful as it did that day when his feet first wandered there. How vividly all that time came back to him now ! Again he seemed to see Mina as he had seen her there, standing before the grey, old student, reading in her musical voice the dull Latin prose ; how her hands had trembled, her face had flushed, at sight of him. It would have been better for them both if he had never lived to see that day.

He arose and walked a few steps farther, gazing at the manse as one spell-bound. His eyes, wandering from point to point of the building, at length turned towards the open front door. There they remained fixed upon a figure which was seated just outside !

Mina? Yes, of course, it was Mina; he knew that by the wild rush of blood to his head—the quickened beating of his heart; but suddenly the mad heart-beats ceased— his soul sickened more than ever to see what she had become.

Mina was seated in a well-cushioned wicker-chair—her head was thrown back, her eyes were closed—her face, so pale, and pinched, and sad, turned to the full glory of the summer sky. The sunlight fell all around her in a glitter-ing shower, touching her golden hair, her wan cheeks, her wasted hands, and flashing back brightness from a little silver drinking-cup which she held in her hands.

It was the first prize cup which the *Jenny* had won, the present which he himself had brought her, when he had first come to disturb the sanctity of her home.

Lord Arranmore gazed at this picture for a moment in painful hesitation, then, obeying a mad impulse which came upon him, he began to descend the shoulder of the hill.

Mina had fallen into a doze, lulled thereto by the warmth and brightness of the air about her, and the musical hum-ming of the spinning-wheel which Kirsty, who had come out to keep her young mistress company, was working close at hand. A step upon the ground, a movement, a certain feeling of commotion, awakened her, and opening her eyes they fell upon the face and figure of young Lord Arranmore.

He stood looking wofully ill at ease, as if he were un-decided whether to come forward or go back.

Kirsty had risen, and in her excitement at seeing the young lord, had overturned her loom; while Mr. Mac-donald, disturbed in his studies, as Mina had been in her sleep, advanced from the shadow of the door.

Mina, still dazed from sleep, gazed for a time from one to another in utter bewilderment; then her pale face flushed, she cast down her eyes, and moved as if about to rise from her seat.

In a moment Lord Arranmore was beside her; he ex-tended his hand and laid it lightly on her arm.

'My dear Miss Macdonald,' he said eagerly, 'pray do not let me disturb you!' then in a lower tone he added, 'I am pained beyond measure to find you so much changed.'

Mina said nothing. Once or twice her tremulous lips had opened, but no words came. The colour had faded from her cheeks and left them ashy-grey; she pressed her bloodless lips together, and clutched her fingers as if to calm the violent trembling of her hands.

At that moment Mr. Macdonald came forward, and having courteously welcomed his guest, proceeded to speak for his child.

'Yes,' he said, 'Mina doesn't look to-day like the healthy lassie who steered your lordship's yacht into Uribol harbour; but she is a queen to what she has been, thanks again to old Koll Nicholson and Doctor John.'

'Has Miss Macdonald been ill?'

The question was a superfluous one, but Arranmore did not know what else to say. He asked it ostensibly of the clergyman, but he fixed his eyes earnestly upon Mina, as if imploring her to speak.

But still she remained silent, her eyes wandering in any direction but his, her face growing more pinched, her cheeks more ghastly white.

The clergyman, knowing nothing of the mental agony through which his child was passing, answered the question which the young lord had put, and by his answer made her trial more bitter than ever to bear.

For he told how Mina, coming home one night three weeks ago tired, sick, and dispirited, had thrown her arms around his neck and burst into a flood of tears; how the next morning she had been found in violent fever, raving and calling on God to let her die; and how for three long weary weeks she had kept her bed, and been assiduously attended by Koll Nicholson and Doctor John; of the gradual abating of the fever which had seized her, and her quiet return to life.

'This is her first day out,' he added, 'and already the breath of air is giving new life to her. But I am keeping you standing too long, my lord. Mina, darling, shall I send Kirsty back to you while I am inside the house with his lordship?'

Before Mina could reply, before Lord Arranmore could open his lips to decline the polite invitation of his host,

Graham Macdonald, emerging from the house, joined the group outside.

CHAPTER XXXVIII.

GRAHAM AND ARRANMORE.

DURING the whole of this scene Graham had been in his uncle's study watching the faces through the open window, and hearing every word that had been said. He had not intended to come forth, for he dreaded a meeting with Lord Arranmore; but since the conversation had taken such a turn, he thought it right that he should interfere, and try in a measure to relieve the pain which was so plainly written on his sister's face. On issuing from the house he bowed politely to the young lord, then, walking over to his sister's side, turned his face towards the clergyman.

'You need not send out Kirsty, uncle,' he said. 'While you are in the house with Lord Arranmore I will stay with Mina.'

But before the clergyman could answer, Lawrance spoke.

'Thank you,' he said, 'I will not trouble you to go inside. I should not have come down at all to-day, but I have decided soon to bring my Uribol visit to a close, and,' —turning to Graham—'I wanted to thank you, Mr. Macdonald, for your heroic conduct in saving my cousin's life.'

Graham bowed and flushed. The bow was a cold acknowledgment of Lord Arranmore's thanks, the flush was called up by the memory of the way in which Sir Charles Sedley had sought to discharge the debt he owed.

The clergyman, wondering at his nephew's awkward silence, expressed a hope that Miss Sedley was not much injured by the fall.

'Thanks to Mr. Macdonald,' returned the young lord quietly, 'I think my cousin has escaped without injury of any kind. But, of course, she is very much shaken and most eager to get to her physician in town.'

'Do you leave Uribol soon, my lord?'

'If Miss Sedley's health will permit it, I believe we are to start the day after to-morrow.'

'And you are likely soon to return?'

The young man shrugged his shoulders.

'That is as the fates decree,' he said. 'I have spent many happy months here, Mr. Macdonald, and should not be sorry to linger still; but to the best of us reverses come at times, and I, like others, have at last to obey other wills than my own.'

'Let me trust, my lord, if you will forgive me for speaking plainly, that when you are again in town you will not forget the folk amongst whom you have spent a pleasant time.'

'Mr. Macdonald,' returned the young man earnestly, 'if I ever see Uribol again, believe me, I shall not forget you and yours. I owe you a debt of gratitude which I know I can never pay.'

The clergyman bowed.

'I do not speak of myself, my lord, or of my children; to us you owe nothing. I was thinking of the people of Uribol.'

The young man took the clergyman's hand.

'Mr. Macdonald,' he said, 'the kindness which I have received from you and yours shall be paid back tenfold to the people of Uribol. Command me, and I will obey. I will furnish you with my address, and I promise you that with whatever request you choose to make to me I will comply. I leave you the guardian of Uribol—look to the people; with my aid right every wrong; the more requests you make of me the happier my days will become!'

'My lord, this, I fear, is a whim which will soon wear away.'

'It is no whim, and it will not fade. I tell you I owe you all a debt which I can never repay.'

All this while Lawrance, struggling with the wild rush of emotion which seemed to be consuming his very soul, had been trying to get one sight of Mina. But she was completely hidden from him by Graham, who stood before her holding one of her hands. At length, however, unable longer to keep aloof, he walked up to her, and out of common politeness Graham had to move aside. He did not move away, however. At the young lord's approach he felt the hand which lay within his own tremble and grow cold. He clasped his fingers more tightly around it, and resolutely took his stand by his sister's side.

Having gained his place, Lawrance paused in some embarrassment. Now that he stood before Mina, he did not know what to say ; he could only gaze upon her pale, pinched face with ever-increasing sorrow. At length, however, feeling that all eyes were upon him, he extended his hand.

'Miss Macdonald,' he said, 'in case I do not see you again, I should like to say "Good-bye."'

Mina's pale cheeks flushed again ; she gazed for a moment at his extended hand, and placed her own within it.

'Good-bye, my lord,' she said quietly.

It was the first time she had spoken that morning ; the first time that Lord Arranmore had heard her voice since she had bidden him 'good-bye' on the hill ; and at the low, sweet, tremulous sound, he felt his whole frame quicken. He felt impelled to cast himself on the ground before her, to press her hands and kiss her lips ; but at that moment the clergyman's touch recalled him to himself.

'My lord, before you leave Uribol, may I have the pleasure of seeing you again ? '

'Certainly, if you wish to do so.'

'I have drawn up a petition which I should like to show to you. I have one or two plans which I should like to unfold. With your permission, my lord, I will bring the papers to you to-morrow'——

'By no means,' interrupted the young man. 'If it is all the same to you, Mr. Macdonald, I would rather come to the manse. So look for me to-morrow, or at latest the following day !'

Then, as if weary of the interview, he moved away, after having shaken hands with the clergyman, and raised his hat to Mina and her brother, who still stood by her side.

For a while the group remained at the manse door watching the agile figure as it moved slowly away among the hills. The clergyman remained for a time uttering praises of the

young lord; finally, having important work to do, he re-
entered the house, and left the brother and sister alone together.

Mina still reclined in her chair, her head resting on the
cushions, her eyes following the figure of the young lord as
it moved farther and farther from her sight. Presently it
disappeared, and Mina shivered as if a chilly wind had
struck her to the heart. She turned her head, raised her
eyes, and saw that her brother was watching her intently.
As their eyes met, he pressed her hand more tenderly between his own.

'Mina, my little sister,' he said, 'you are breaking your
heart!'

His voice was so tender it brought the tears to her eyes,
but the next moment she conquered her emotion and gave
a strange smile.

'A broken heart is a complaint which folk are not fashed
with nowadays,' she said.

'For all that, my sister, you are breaking yours. They
say deep wounds are best left to heal themselves, and,
thinking that, I have said little, but I cannot stand by any
longer and allow this to go on. Ever since the day that
man crossed your path, you have ne'er been the same. I
thought at first it was a lassie's pain that would easily pass
away; but, instead of fading, your trouble grows.'

'No, no.'

'But it does. I can see the world is poisoned to you.
Mina, it's not right; it's foolish and wicked to grieve so for
what is utterly worthless.'

'Graham, dear, you do not understand.'

'Not understand! Great God! Mina, my heart has
bled as well as yours. I too have loved, and found that
love was poison!'

'Graham—you!'

'Yes, Mina, I. Some day, may be, I will tell you all
about it; now it's enough to say that there is no sorrow in
your heart which has not found sympathy in mine. But,
there, that is all o'er. We both loved wraiths—things far
beyond us and above us — we have both been cruelly
awakened from our dreams, and must try now to comfort

one another. . . . As to that man,' he continued, gazing after the retreating figure of young Lord Arranmore, 'he came to us with a lie on his lips, and he won your heart under a lie. You must try to forget him.'

'Forget him? O Graham! I can never do that!' she said.

'He is a villain, Mina.'

'No, no, no!'

'But I say he is. He began in falsehood, and he went on in wickedness and falsehood, and now he can go gleefully back to his home, knowing well of the sorrow which he has left you to thole. Mina, my wee sister, you have been good and brave. Thank Heaven you did not let him ken that any thought of him could give you so much pain!'

'No, Graham, he does not ken.'

'Try to think that his shadow has never crossed your path. Be my own happy wee sister again. Think what we should do without you, Mina. I could never walk the hills again if I were to lose you, and Uncle Macdonald would never smile again. There are other men besides Lord Arranmore to live for. Let us try to be as happy as we were before he ever came. You must go on with your reading as soon as you are strong enough, and then, when the cold, damp, dreary weather comes on, I shall take you south for a change.'

At that moment the clergyman came out to see how his children were getting on, and was much concerned to find that Mina had been crying, and asked the cause of her sorrow. Seeing that she grew very agitated and ill at ease, Graham quietly answered for her.

'This is Mina's first day out, uncle,' he said. 'I am afraid she has overtaxed her strength, and feels her weakness. We must help her in. She must not be allowed to stay out so long another day.'

CHAPTER XXXIX.

CROSS PURPOSES.

HAVING, with his uncle's help, got Mina into the house, and settled her comfortably upon the sofa in the study, Graham left her to the tender cares of Kirsty and the clergyman, and issuing from the house, walked with rapid strides in the direction which had been taken by Lord Arranmore half an hour before. His mind was in a tumult. Anger, love, jealousy, and hatred mingled in his heart like one consuming fire. The sight of his sister's pain had again steeled his heart against Lord Arranmore, and the memory of his own humiliation shamed him. Yes, the crowning insult had been put upon him that morning when, on opening Sir Charles Sedley's envelope, he had found the fifty pounds. He believed that Ethel had ordered it to be sent as a means of pointing out the distance which lay between them, and effacing the obligation which she felt she owed in return for the life he saved.

'Well,' he said to himself, 'she need not have troubled herself to point out my duty to me. I shall not fash her again ; but as sure as there is a God in heaven he shall not kill my sister.'

For some time he followed Lord Arranmore's path ; then he took a short cut across the hills, which brought him to Glenheather Lodge. No one seemed about ; most of the windows were open, and Miss Sedley's favoured Blenheim spaniel lay near the open door, basking in the sunshine. Across the threshold a leopard skin was thrown ; on this lay a lady's cambric handkerchief. Graham saw all this as he boldly walked forward and knocked at the door. He asked for Lord Arranmore, and heard that his lordship had left the lodge half an hour after breakfast and had not returned.

'He must be lingering among the hills, then,' he thought, and without another word he turned from the lodge, and again took the path which led back to the manse. He had retraced some half of his way when suddenly he came upon the object of his search. Lawrance was seated upon the brow of a hill, which commanded a distant view of the manse. He had pulled his hat down to shade his eyes from the sunlight, lit a cigar, and turned his face towards the building which he had lately left. So absorbed was he in this contemplation that he did not know of the near neighbourhood of any living soul until Graham touched him on the shoulder. At the touch he turned, and there passed over his face a look first of anger, then of surprise. He hurriedly rose to his feet, and was the first to speak.

'Ah, Macdonald!' he said, 'do you wish to speak to me?'

'I do, my lord. I wish to ask you to forego your intention of coming to the manse to-morrow. My uncle offered to bring his papers to you. He will wait upon you at any hour or place you wish.'

'He said as much to me, but I told him I would rather come to the manse.'

'Yes, you told him, and because he is unsuspicious and does not know the truth, he said "Come." If he *did* know the truth, he would be the first man to turn you from his door.'

'Did you follow me here to insult me?'

'No, I have no wish to insult you. I only came to speak the truth, and appeal to your sense of honour. Lord Arranmore, we will not rake up the past; let it rest—what is done cannot be undone—and perhaps you are no worse than others of your kind. What was pleasant parting to you nearly proved the death of my sister. She has borne up bravely and passed the ordeal. As you are a man, do not make her pass through it again.'

Graham spoke vehemently, every fibre of his frame seemed agitated. Lord Arranmore stood very calmly before him, but over his face there passed a pinched look of pain.

'What do you want of me?' he asked.

'I want you to pledge your word never again to seek the company of my sister. You are leaving Uribol in two days, you say: surely you can keep apart till then. Come, will you give me your pledge?'

'No.'

Graham started, and for a moment stared at the young man as if about to raise his hand and strike him.

'Then, my lord,' he said, 'you are a scoundrel!'

'Macdonald, do not use language of which you may afterwards repent.'

'I shall never repent of telling the truth, Lord Arranmore. However, I am glad that you have shown me your intention so plainly. My way is clear now. To-night my uncle shall know everything, and in less than three days we will be beyond the shores of Uribol.'

'Leave Uribol! Are you mad, sir?'

'No. If you are scoundrel enough still to pursue my sister, I will prove myself man enough to save her. She shall not be tortured to death through *you*, my lord; and, mind, every pang which she is made to suffer shall be most religiously avenged!'

He turned as if to go, but Lord Arranmore laid a detaining hand upon him.

'Macdonald,' he said, 'stay; this interview must not end here. I do not blame you for what you say. It is natural that, having such a sister, you should guard her with more than ordinary care. I own that in my conduct to her I have been wrong, lamentably wrong, but I am not quite so culpable as you think.'

'Then, my lord, you will give me your pledge?'

'No, I cannot do that; but rest assured that Miss Macdonald shall suffer no further harm from me. I will not force myself upon her; I will try all in my power to make amends for the past. Ask your uncle to come to-morrow with his papers to Glenheather Lodge. I will not visit the manse, and I think it will be better for us all if you will consent to say no more.'

The young man paused for a time. Graham said nothing. He wished to act for the best, and as yet he did not know exactly what would be the best for him to do. He had no particular desire to expose Lord Arranmore, but he wished to spare his sister, and he knew that to leave Loch Uribol, where over forty years of his life had been passed, would almost break the clergyman's heart. He was not like a young man who is always prepared to begin life among new scenes and new faces ; his life was almost spent, and Graham knew that the one wish of his life had been to spend his declining years among his people, to fall asleep amongst them, and afterwards to lie in peace within sound of the sea, and with the Highland breezes blowing above his grave.　It would be a heart-breaking task to take the old man away—the cause of the departure would make it more heart-breaking still.　Besides, in exposing the young lord he must necessarily lay Mina open to censure ; and although he himself knew she had not been culpable, he knew there would be many voices to blame her.　He turned to Lawrance.

'If I promise not to divulge these secrets to my uncle, my lord, I do so in the full security that you will not subject my sister to further humiliation and pain.'

'You may do so.'

'I will tell my uncle to bring his papers to you to-morrow. I will tell my sister that in two days from this you and your party leave Loch Uribol for good.'

Lord Arranmore bowed.

'You will take no message from me !'

'None, my lord.　She has already wished you good-bye.'

So with distant bows, and no hand-shakes, the two men parted.　Graham walked quickly back to the manse, and Lawrance, after taking one long look after him, strolled slowly on towards Glenheather Lodge.

Up in the lodge the hours had passed drearily.　Sir Charles Sedley, still bent on an early departure, had shut himself in his study to work like a slave, while Ethel, busy with romantic introspections, had remained hour after hour in her room.　Some few hours after she had left her father with the torn envelope and open letter in his hand, she sat by the open window of her room looking out dreamily upon the hills, when suddenly she saw the figure of Graham Macdonald walking quickly along the path which led to the lodge door.　She started, blushed, and drew back, and from the shelter of the curtain watched him.　Graham came steadily forward without once raising his eyes.　He paused at the door, which was just below her window, and knocked. Ethel by this time was standing before the glass arranging the straggling tresses of her hair. She pulled her waist-belt in half an inch or so, looked critically at her dress, then stood as if in expectation of a summons. None came. She walked carelessly to the window, and, looking out, saw the figure of Graham, dwarfed by distance, now rapidly retracing his steps homeward. Ethel stared first in wonder, then annoyance, and going to the bell gave it a sharp pull. Her maid answered the angry summons.

'Did not Mr. Macdonald, the clergyman's nephew, call at the lodge a few minutes ago?'

'Yes, miss.'

'Then why did you not bring me his message?'

'He gave me none for you, miss.'

Ethel opened her eyes.

'Did he not come to inquire for me?' she asked in sheer amazement.

'No, miss, he did not mention your name. He asked for Lord Arranmore. I told him his lordship had not been here since breakfast, and then he went away.'

'He said nothing more?'

'Not another word, miss.'

The maid retired, and Ethel, sinking into an easy-chair, began nervously to pull to pieces the flower which she wore in her breast. She sat thus for a time, then she walked over to the window again. Graham had disappeared, but far away in the distance she saw the dim outline of two figures standing upon the brow of a hill. A powerful deer-stalker's glass lay among the knicknacks on her table. She looked through it, and, to her surprise, saw that the two men were no other than Graham Macdonald and Lawrance. She put down the glass, feeling more amazed than ever. At that moment her maid came in with a small tray bearing the afternoon tea. She was shortly followed by Sir Charles Sedley.

'I am going to take a cup of tea with you this afternoon, Ethel,' said the baronet, sinking into a chair. 'Whew! how tired I am! I ought to have been out grouse shooting all day, instead of pottering over packing-cases at home.'

'Then why did you not go, papa?' said Ethel quietly.

'Why did I not go? Because I've got such an infernal

fool of a valet, I can leave nothing to him. Have you ordered your boxes to be packed ?'

'No.'

She was still sipping her tea from the tiny porcelain shell, and looking out of the window at the two figures dwarfed by distance to mere specks, but dimly visible in the hazy mist of light. At her decided negative, uttered so quietly, the baronet looked up. Something in his daughter's face made him feel uncomfortable.

'Then it's time you did give orders, my love. We leave here to-morrow for Coreveolan Castle.'

'Do you ?' returned Ethel quietly. 'I do not ; so there is no such hurry about my packing, you see.'

'What do you mean, Ethel ?'

'Only this, papa : that I do not mean to be shut up in the nasty, fusty, mildewy, uncomfortable rooms of Coreveolan Castle while I can get a nice, wholesome, sweet-smelling lodge to shelter me. I mean that I have a fancy to live for a while in a place where I have fallen down a ravine and been rescued by a Highland chieftain.'

'Ethel, you are a fool !'

The girl shrugged her shoulders and laughed with provoking good humour.

'I believe that most men think the same of their wives and daughters. It remains for their lovers to discover them to be wise women. Therefore I presume that my wisdom, if I have any, will be hunted out by somebody !'

The baronet frowned, and for a while said nothing. Ethel continued to look over the feathers of her fan at the two shadowy figures on the hill. Presently Sir Charles put down his empty cup and walked over to his daughter's side.

'Ethel,' he said, 'what do you mean to do about Lawrance ?'

'Marry him !'

'Oh, you do, do you !'

'So it is decreed ; therefore, since such a terrible fate is in store for him, I wish to be magnanimous, and allow him to enjoy the few months of liberty which still remain !'

There was such coolness in her face, such a look of insolent laughter in her eyes, that the baronet could not trust himself to speak again. He turned on his heel and left the room. As soon as the sound of his footsteps died away upon the stairs, Ethel threw down her fan and again took up the field-glass. The two figures had separated. Arranmore was walking towards the lodge, but Graham had disappeared. Ethel put down the glass, and rang for her maid to dress her for dinner.

The dinner hour at Glenheather Lodge was five o'clock; at half-past four Ethel descended the stairs. She was plainly dressed, but wore a number of gems. A diamond collarette was clasped around her throat, a diamond spray glittered in her hair. On the fingers of her right hand she wore several rings, but the left hand was still bound up in the cambric handkerchief. Her father and Lord Arranmore were evidently dressing; both the dining and drawing rooms were empty. The hall-door still stood open, the leopard-skin was still stretched across the threshold, and the spaniel walked restlessly up and down outside. Ethel took her seat upon the leopard-skin, caressingly stroked the head of the spaniel, which had walked up to kiss her, and dreamily watched the sunlight as it played upon the hills.

It had been intensely hot all day, but now the breeze had grown a little cooler. The barren peaks of the distant hills were gradually becoming enveloped in a hazy mist of light, while over the throbbing blue sky was creeping a feathery film of white. Ethel could hear the distant sound of the bagpipes played by some shepherd gathering in his sheep. It came like fairy music from some fairy scene.

'How lovely it all is,' she said, looking at the hills, the sky, the distant view of the ocean. 'I wonder if I could endure to spend my life here. I wonder if I should weary for the sickly, killing air of the ball-room, or a place among the crowded drivers in the Park? I wonder if I possess sufficient strength of mind to snap my fingers at society, and not repent of the rash act a few months after it was done? Women are weak-minded creatures at the best: oftentimes I am, otherwise I should not possess such an insane admiration of manliness and strength in man! That is just what I do admire. I should think ten times more

of Lawrie if he'd the spirit to break with me and marry Mr.
Macdonald's pretty little sister. She is quite good enough
for him—just the kind of wife he ought to have, in fact;
and I really believe that at one word from me he would
make her Lady Arranmore.

A step upon the gravel startled her. Flushed and eager
she looked up, and saw standing before her a servant boy
from the manse.

'Well, sir,' she asked, smiling brightly, 'what is it?
Have you any message for me?'

'None for ye, my leddy, but one for Lord Arranmore.'

'Give it to me, and I will deliver it. It is from Mr.
Macdonald, I suppose?'

'Yes, my leddy. Ye'll tell his lordship, if ye please, that
Mr. Macdonald will come to him here at twelve o'clock to-
morrow.'

'I will tell him. Here is something for the trouble you
have had in coming so far over the hill.'

She opened her purse, and gave the astonished boy half-
a-crown; then as he went away she rose from her low seat
and went into the drawing-room to await her father and
cousin.

They came just before the second bell was sounded, and
then they went straight in to dinner. Lawrance had complimented Ethel upon the marvellous power she seemed to
possess of throwing off illness, the young lady had replied
with a smile and a bow, and then nothing more was said.
It was a very silent meal, owing partly to the presence of
the two servants; and as soon as they left the room Ethel
rose and went into the drawing-room, leaving her father
and cousin alone. The drawing-room at Glenheather
Lodge was now a pretty little apartment, furnished utterly
unlike what drawing-rooms usually are. The polished floor
was covered with a number of lion, tiger, and leopard skins,
taken from the animals which had been shot by Lord
Arranmore when he went to India three years before. The
cabinets and walls were ornamented with shooting trophies.
Ethel walked about the room, followed closely by her
favourite spaniel, and carelessly looked first at one thing,
then at another, as if she had never seen them before. The

inspection over, she took her seat upon the fender-stool, and looked through the window at the glorious expanse of hill and sea. As she sat there, the door opened and Lawrance came in; a footman followed with coffee, which he placed on a gipsy-table close to his mistress's side. Lawrance strolled about the room while the man remained. As soon as he had gone he took a chair close to Ethel's side.

'What is the matter with your hand, Ethel?' he asked, noticing for the first time that it was bandaged.

'Truly the eyes of love are keen,' thought Ethel, and she said, 'I cut it the other day when I fell into the ravine.'

'What a mercy young Macdonald happened to be by!'

'Was it not?—for me. I call him my Highland chieftain—he was so wonderfully brave. By-the-by you have seen him to-day, have you not?'

Lawrance started, and looked up amazed, then he stammered—

'Y—e—es; I walked down to the manse to thank him for what he had done for you.'

'Oh, indeed; very kind of you, I am sure, to take so much trouble about me. Then when you were at the manse, I suppose you saw them all?'

'Yes.'

'The clergyman, Mr. Macdonald, and his sister?'

'I saw them all; Miss Macdonald was seated in an easy-chair at the door. She has been ill; confined to her bed for several weeks, and came out for the first time to-day.'

'Indeed!'

There was silence for some time; Lawrance, looking rather foolish and ill at ease, was bending forward to pull the ears of Ethel's spaniel, while she, a frown upon her brow, was busily engaged in turning the ring round and round upon her finger. A howl of pain from the animal made her look up.

'Don't hurt the dog, Lawrance!' she said sharply, and Lawrance let the dog go.

Again there was silence. Ethel reverted to the ring-turning, and Lawrance, having now nothing to occupy his hands, strolled over to the window and looked out.

'What is papa doing?' asked Ethel.

'Sleeping in his easy-chair.'

'Then, I suppose, we had better drink our coffee alone. Will you have yours?—it's getting quite cold.'

He turned to take the cup which she offered him. Having done so, he resumed his seat at her side.

'Do you think you will be well enough to travel on Thursday?' he asked at length, after searching his brain for something to say.

'Certainly I shall be well enough,' returned Ethel sharply —she seemed wonderfully sharp that night—'all the same I don't mean to do it.'

Lawrance stared at her in blank amazement now, and she uttered a petulant laugh.

'Oh yes,' she said, in answer to his astonished look; 'I know you think it is all settled : but I don't mean to be hurried out of paradise merely to satisfy a foolish whim of papa's.'

'Then we all remain?'

'_I_ do—for a few weeks, at all events. If you particularly wish to go away, you can. I do not wish to detain you. Perhaps you have had a surfeit of the place ; you were here for several months before we came.'

'I have not had a surfeit ; there is plenty here for me to do, and I shall remain.'

Again he walked over to the window, and Ethel instead of turning her ring, this time occupied herself by watching him.

'Lawrance,' she said, at last.

'Yes?'

'Mr. Macdonald called here to-day, and asked for you.'

'Did he?'

'Yes ; and this evening, just before dinner, a boy came up from the manse with a message for you.'

'What was it?'

'Only this, that Mr. Macdonald would meet you here at twelve o'clock to-morrow.'

'Oh,' he returned indifferently.

Ethel looked puzzled. The effect of this conversation upon Lawrance was very different to what she had expected. Her curiosity was aroused. She walked over to where her cousin stood, and laid her clasped hands upon his shoulder.

'Do you know, Lawrie,' she said, 'I am rather anxious to know what you and my Highland chieftain will find to talk about during your solemnly planned interview to-morrow!'

'Do you mean young Macdonald?' returned Lawrance in amazement. 'He's not coming here!'

'Not coming here? I tell you he is—at twelve o'clock to-morrow.'

'Why, Ethel, that is his uncle, the clergyman. He wants to have a talk with me about improving the condition of the people here before I go away!'

Ethel dropped her hands from her cousin's shoulder and walked away.

'It is horribly dull this evening,' she said impatiently. 'What can be making papa sleep so long?'

She went into the dining-room, woke up her father; then, pleading as her excuse fatigue and pain in the head, she wished both the gentlemen good-night, and retired alone to her room. She did not ring for her maid; she pulled off her jewels with a series of angry snatches, and threw them on the dressing-table, where they lay in a glittering burning pile. Then she took off her dress, and wrapping a white cashmere dressing-gown about her, sunk into an easy-chair.

'He thinks I am leaving on Thursday,' she said to herself. 'He is not coming to-morrow, and yet he could stand at the very door to-day and not even ask for me. After all, perhaps it is a pity I did not consent to go!'

CHAPTER XL.

SUNSHINE AND STORM.

THE next morning Miss Sedley had not changed her mind. As she lay in her bed looking at the light which crept in to her through the soft silken folds of rose-coloured curtains, she readily admitted to herself that it might be better for all if on the following day she were to follow her father's advice and quit Loch Uribol for ever. Nevertheless, she said to herself that she did not intend to go.

A splendid spell of weather seemed to have set in; this day was even finer than its predecessor. Sir Charles Sedley, relieved now of his odious task of packing, set off immediately after breakfast with his gillies, his dogs, and his gun. Lawrance, who had to await the arrival of the clergyman, went to write letters in his room. So Ethel strolled forth alone. She carried a book and camp-stool with her, and her spaniel followed close at her heels. She walked leisurely for half an hour or so, then, fixing her camp-stool in the deep heather, she sat down to read.

It was intensely hot. The sunlight fell in such scorching showers upon the earth that the dog, with quivering sides and lolling tongue, stretched himself in the heather at his mistress's feet, as if seeking for coolness and shadow. Ethel opened her book. Before beginning to read she looked round to see if there was any sign of her father. There seemed to be no one near. So after another dreamy look about her she began to read. She had read for half an hour or so when a growl, then a bark, from the dog made her look up. The sun was shining as brightly as ever, the heat seemed to have grown more intense, there was a great silence all around, but in the heather, a few hundred yards from where she sat, a figure was crouching, and a face, ghastly in its whiteness and intensity, was turned towards her. Ethel shuddered as she gazed. It was the face which had flashed before her vision on that memorable day when she fell into the ravine.

She looked around her. There was no one near. The dog, still agitated, uttering a half-growl, half-bark, kept his place by her side. She turned her head again and saw that the figure was still there.

In reality Ethel was very much frightened, but she maintained a stately calm. Taking her book beneath her arm and lifting her camp-stool, she walked quickly back to Glenheather Lodge, followed closely by her dog.

To those at home Ethel said nothing of this strange figure which seemed to haunt her—perhaps because she knew that the ghostly-looking being was a retainer of Graham Macdonald's. Nevertheless she deemed it prudent to keep the house for several days to come, and during that time she puzzled her brain to discover if possible the meaning of these strange visions. But the more she thought the more puzzled she grew. She could not solve the mystery, unless, indeed, the old man was employed by Graham to watch her, and since he was not sufficiently interested to inquire for her health, she thought he would scarcely put himself to the trouble of having her movements watched. No, it could not be that; the man was some half-witted creature doubtless who was fascinated by her face.

After three days' confinement Ethel went out again, carrying her camp-stool and book with her, and followed by her favourite dog. She was half-afraid to wander far; yet she felt she could not stay in the house. Graham had not called at the lodge, nor had any message come from the manse, and this continued silence—stubbornness, as she called it—was beginning to tell upon the young lady's temper. She had wondered once or twice whether it would be consistent with her dignity to call at the manse, or to write a little note to Graham, thanking him for all that he had done. Both these ideas she had perforce thrust from her; she could only wonder and wait.

She walked for a yard or so through the long heather, when the intensity of the heat made her turn back. It was certainly far too hot for walking, so she returned to the lodge, sent in her camp-stool, had the leopard-skin again stretched upon the threshold, and reclined upon it.

Her father was out shooting, Lord Arranmore had gone on business to Coreveolan Castle. Ethel was alone. She lay for a time upon the leopard-skin; then, feeling the sun too warm, she rose and took a stroll through the shady house. The windows were open, sun-blinds were down, and every room was redolent with the sweet scent of heather and thyme.

Ethel stood in the drawing-room, enjoying the refreshing coolness and deliberating with herself as to whether or not she should again go forth into the sunshine, when a loud rap came to the door.

She started, hesitated, then, before the footman had time

to answer the summons, she quitted the drawing-room and stood in the hall, facing the open door. At that moment the footman appeared, but Ethel, waving him back, advanced herself to welcome the new-comer.

It was Graham Macdonald.

He stood first outside the doorway, his hand still upon the knocker. At sight of Ethel the knocker was relinquished, and his hat lifted from his head.

'Good-morning, Miss Sedley.'

He spoke gravely, earnestly, never once reflecting in his face the light which shone in hers. But Ethel was less formal; she advanced in smiling confidence and held forth her hand.

'Mr. Macdonald,' she said, 'what a stranger you are! Come in.'

Courtesy compelled him to press the tips of her fingers, and he did no more.

'Thank you, Miss Sedley,' he said; 'I won't come in, I am rather in a hurry; but I should like to speak for a few moments with Lord Arranmore.'

Now, no one knew better than Ethel that at that moment Lawrance was several miles away; she knew also that he would not return to Glenheather Lodge until the next day at soonest, but she felt that as if she said this, Graham Macdonald would take off his hat again, turn upon his heel, and straightway depart. He looked so grave, so ready to go—he would not even place his foot upon the threshold, lest some magic power should hold him. Ethel felt she could not lose him; she must invent some excuse to keep him, if only for a little while.

'If you will come in for a moment,' she said, 'out of that scorching sunlight, I will see if I can find Lawrance for you.'

Still he remained stubborn.

'If you will be good enough to inquire,' he said, 'I will remain here.'

The cruel sting in these words cut Ethel to the heart. Could this be the man, she thought, who had saved her life at the imminent risk of his own? Could it be the same man who had carried her with such tender care, and soothed her in her half unconscious, hysterical state with such words of tender kindness?

His face now was so cold and stern. It filled the proud girl's eyes with tears.

'Mr. Macdonald,' she said, 'what have I done that you should treat me so rudely—that you will not even cross my threshold?'

He started as if from a dream.

'Was I rude?' he said; 'then I beg your pardon, Miss Sedley. Certainly I will come in if you wish it, though I have only a few minutes to spare.'

He stepped across the leopard-skin as he spoke, and followed Ethel into the drawing-room. Once he was inside she retired, closed the door, and left him alone. In the middle of the room Graham stood like one in an intoxicating dream. He had hesitated to cross the threshold because he dreaded his own weakness, his own love for the girl who, with eager, smiling face, was again beckoning him onward. And now that he had crossed the threshold, now that he was again breathing the enchanted air which seemed for ever to halo the places where she dwelt, he felt that the spell of his love for her was taking a greater hold upon him than it had ever done before. Why had he come there? Why, in his madness, had he relied too much upon his own strength, and cast himself bodily on the stream which had so often threatened to drown him! She had made him pass through it, and even at her bidding he stood ready to venture forth again.

As he stood in the little drawing-room where she had left him, amidst the coolness of the shadow, the intoxicating scent of flowers, he thought over all that had passed between himself and Ethel Sedley since the first day that they had met, and the more he thought the more his soul revolted; his cheek burned with shame. It was the memory of all that he had suffered which kept him strong that day.

He had only been alone a few minutes when the drawing-room door opened, and Ethel stood before him again. How pretty she looked in the cool, dim light of the room. There was no curl of the lip, no haughty turn of the head to-day; the proud, heartless lady seemed to have vanished

and given place to a loving, bashful girl. Graham saw all
this, though he did not appear to be looking at her; it
made the battle which he had to fight all the harder to him.
Ethel entered the room, closed the door behind her, and
seeing him standing in the middle of the floor, said
quietly—

'Won't you sit down?'

He answered her question by another.

'Is Lord Arranmore engaged?'

'Well, yes, I suppose he is,' returned the girl in strange
hesitation; 'they tell me he left for the castle this morning,
so it is quite uncertain when he will be back.'

Graham picked up his hat.

'Thank you, I am sorry I have given you the
trouble '——

'Pray do not mention it,' interrupted the girl, in a tone
of angry sarcasm. 'I wish you would put me to a little
more trouble in order that I might repay some of my debt
to you.'

'You did all you could,' he said, 'when you sent me
that cheque for fifty pounds.'

She stared for a moment in blank amazement, then her
cheek flushed painfully. Up to this moment she had forgotten all about the transaction which, when it occurred,
had caused her so much pain.

'I never sent you that cheque,' she said quietly, 'and
when my father did so I was totally ignorant of it all. Mr.
Macdonald, on my father's behalf I beg your pardon; and
now will you try to forget that, and allow me to thank you
with all my heart for saving my life?'

He took the hand which she extended towards him, and
held it for a moment in his, looking the while with grave
earnestness into her upturned face.

'You must not think you are under any obligation to me,'
he said; 'you are not. I am very glad, Miss Sedley, that
at the time of the accident I happened to be by, and that
you have had such a marvellous escape '——

'Through you!'

He took no notice of her last words—perhaps he did not

hear them—but, having relinquished her hand, again took his hat.

'You are going?'

'Yes. Will you tell his lordship that I called?'

'Certainly; but won't you stop and have some lunch with me? He may be back soon.'

'Thank you; I cannot spare the time. I have work to do at the manse.'

'Well, will you come back to dinner? We dine at six. Surely Lawrance will be back by that time. We will have a plain, quiet dinner, and then I will give you two conspirators the drawing-room that you may chat away all the evening by yourselves.'

Again her eager question was answered with a negative. Graham assured her that his evening would be spent in hard work at the manse. Ethel winced, but she would not show her discomfiture. Raising her eyes, she asked quietly—

'How is your sister? I was sorry to hear from Lord Arranmore that she had been ill.'

'Yes, Mina has been badly, but she is much better now, thank you.'

'Would she let me go and see her, do you think?'

'You are very kind, Miss Sedley; but just now Mina sees no one.'

Ethel was nonplussed; she could not think of anything more to say; so, after a silence of a minute or so, Graham held forth his hand.

'Good-bye, Miss Sedley,' he said; then, looking around the room, he added, 'You are right to have plenty of Highland air about you. Doctor John, our physician, says it is the best medicine in the world.'

Then he stooped to pat the spaniel, walked through the hall, and out at the door, turning on the threshold to lift his hat ere he walked away.

His heart was beating madly with mingled triumph and joy. He felt like a bird which had just escaped from the net which ensnared it. For the first time in his life an interview with Ethel Sedley had brought him contentment and joy.

Not so with Ethel. Having bowed and smiled in answer

to his parting salutation, she sat down on the threshold of the house, and brushed from her eyes one or two scalding tears.

CHAPTER XLI.

KOLL'S TRIBUTE.

AND now for the first time in her life Ethel Sedley began to experience a portion of the discomfort which she had liberally dispensed hitherto to individuals of the other sex. She had played with fire—at first for mere amusement, then from sheer coquetry and cruelty ; and now a spark had fallen in the most secret place of her heart, and was rapidly beginning to spread. She could no longer conceal from herself that Graham Macdonald was her master, and that her spirit was too weak to resist for over-long the strength of his overpowering passion.

There is one road, at least, to the heart of every woman, but that one road has sometimes to be forced. No quiet approach, no delicate and over-nice respect, would have conquered the heart of Ethel. She had been used to the curled and scented darlings of the period, to the cold orna- ments of society, to the insinuating foreigner, and to the self-sufficient lord of the land ; but each and all had awak- ened in her bosom little or no interest. Even Arranmore, an uncommon man physically, and a superior person in- tellectually, found her cold and *blasé*. But with this young Highlander it was so different ! His sullen fits, his flashes of hectic rage, his gloomy resentment, and his terrible passion, had at first impressed and amused her, and had ended by making her submissive and afraid. Now, Ethel was a girl of imperious disposition, and submission, with her, meant affection, while fear meant passion.

'I wonder if I am in love at last ?' she said to herself, after their last interview. 'It feels uncommonly like the sensation I have read of in French novels, and yet, perhaps it's only admiration. I've never before, however, admired a man to the extent of wanting to put my arms round his

neck, lay my head on his breast, and have a good cry!
That's how I feel with Graham ; and the more he scowls at
me the more I long to hug him. Perhaps it's gratitude,
with a slight tinge of hysteria. I've never been quite myself
since the accident—since he saved my life ; and sometimes
I think the water must have soaked into my system, and
made me weak, and tearful, and altogether stupid ! '

She was sitting at the window of the lodge, looking out
as she mused. Her father was off for a last day on the
moor, and she was quite alone, save for the old servant.
All at once she started, for, standing in front of the lodge,
looking in at her, was Koll Nicholson.

'That terrible old man,' she murmured, turning pale.
'What does he want? Why, he is making signs to me, and
looks as if he had been crying. Good gracious ! Why, he
is going down on his knees.'

Holding his Scotch cap in his hand, and raising the other,
as if pointing to heaven, Koll was indeed kneeling, his eyes
full of tears, his whole frame trembling. He seemed
muttering to himself, but, the window being closed, she
could not catch his words. Then he rose, and after kissing
his hands in rapid pantomime, flitted swiftly away.

The next moment there was a knock at the door, and the
old serving-woman entered with something on a dish.

'What have you got there, Janet?' asked Ethel.

'It's a present frae auld Koll Nicholson, my leddy—a
troot fresh frae the sea.'

'For papa ?'

'No, for yersel'. He bade me let ye ken it was for yersel'. I'm thinking the auld carle's gone daft. 'Twasna but
yestreen he brought up a creel o' mussels ; and when I said
nae leddy would like them, he gied a grunt and gaed awa'.'

'I hope you paid him for the fish,' said Ethel.

'I offered him siller, but he wouldna tak' a penny. He
bade me gie ye the troot wi' his blessing, and to be sure
and tell ye it was for yersel'.'

Ethel was puzzled. What could be the cause of the old
man's extraordinary change of manner? Why was he bringing her those votive offerings from the sea? Before, his
aspect had been forbidding in the extreme, and expressive

of the most malignant dislike ; now, it was characterised by
the most solemn sorrow and devotion. Then, what did he
mean to express by those wild signs, by that fervid pantomime in the sight of Heaven ?

The only legitimate explanation presenting itself to Ethel's
mind was that the old man was, or was becoming, crazy;
and that, in the manner of lunatics, he was subject to
strange moods of attraction and repulsion.

The next morning another votive offering appeared, in
the shape of a monstrous living cray-fish, left at the door
by Koll's own hand ; and at midday Koll himself reappeared
carrying on his wrist a small kestrel in full plumage.

'Did her leddyship eat the wee cray-feesh she brought
her leddyship?' he asked eagerly. 'Did you roast the cray-
feesh for her leddyship?'

Janet nodded, the fact being that she had thrown the fish
into the neighbouring river without saying a word to her
mistress on the subject.

'Would her leddyship like to have a braw hawk?' proceeded Koll, smoothing the plumage of the bird he was
carrying. 'Oh, it is a grand bird, and she foond it hersel'
this year in the nest ! Will you tak' it to her bonnie leddyship?'

At this moment Ethel herself appeared. The old man
spoke loudly, and she had recognised his voice in the distance. As she entered the kitchen, looking radiant in a
morning dress of some exquisite material, the old man uttered a loud cry, and fell kneeling before her, stretching out
his bony hands, with the hawk still clinging to one of his
wrists. Then kneeling, he rapidly gave vent to a long
speech in Gaelic.

'What does he say?' asked Ethel.

'I canna richt mak' oot,' said Janet; 'but he's calling
the blessing o' God on your leddyship, and he says he would
dee to gie you pleasure, and he begs and prays your leddyship to have the hawk as a gift frae himsel'.'

'What a beautiful bird !' said Ethel. 'It is very kind of
you to bring it to me, but I'm afraid I shan't know how to
keep it, and I have no cage large enough.'

Koll, however, rapidly explained, through Janet, that no

cage was necessary, the bird being trained like a parrot to sit on a perch anywhere, and not to fly away, while, as to food, all he needed was an occasional meal of chopped meat or a piece of raw fish. He was a beautiful little bird, in full male plumage, and when, at Koll's desire, Ethel smoothed his poll with her forefinger, he merely expanded his powerful wings, and uttered a faint scream of pleasure. So, seeing how earnestly Koll wished her to do so, Ethel accepted the gift, and the bird was forthwith installed on the back of a kitchen chair, where he sat still and grim as death, watching with his great black eyes in silence.

Then the old man seized Ethel's hand with trembling fingers, kissed it reverently, and after some muttered words in Gaelic, went away.

Ethel had accepted the gift with some readiness, because it had suddenly occurred to her that the real giver was not the old fisherman at all, but his foster-son. Yes, the hawk at least was worthy of Graham—just such a present as he might send. The cray-fish and the creel of mussels were in poor taste, but had perhaps been brought because the fisherman had been instructed to take up to the lodge whatever dainty came to his net, and had scarcely known how to discriminate when a young lady's appetite was in question.

The more she thought it over the more convinced she became that all the presents came, directly or indirectly, from Graham. This made her delighted with the kestrel. When her father came home from shooting she took the bird on her wrist, hawking fashion, and carried it to him. It did not escape her fancy that, with all its prettiness, it belonged to a fierce, indomitable species, like Graham himself.

But the very next morning another present was left in the kitchen, in the shape of a dead heron, which Koll had shot, and which already emitted a very ancient and fish-like smell. Ethel laughed, but thought the votive offerings were becoming absurd.

After breakfast she took the kestrel on her shoulder and walked out on the moor, down towards the dark lake, where she had often met Graham. The bird was not fastened in any way, but made no attempt to escape; only, when his eye caught a glimpse of passing small birds, he waved his wings wildly, and exhibited much excitement.

Standing on the hillside, she took him on her gloved hand, and threw him up into the air. He made one wide circle round her, and then alighted on a rock close by.

It was very like a rendezvous, for at that moment Graham himself appeared.

'Oh, Mr. Macdonald!' she cried gaily, 'I'm so glad you have come! Will you teach me to train your bird?'

He looked at her in surprise, then at the kestrel.

'I see you have got a young kestrel,' he said. 'It is of no use for hawking.'

'I suppose not. Well, I don't want to hawk, but I should like to see it fly.'

'They are rather stupid birds,' observed Graham, lifting it up on his hand.

Ethel looked at him with her brightest smile.

'Is that why you sent it me?' she asked.

'I?'

'It is scarcely fair of you,' she proceeded, 'to pretend ignorance, just as I want to thank you for your kindness. It is so good of you to keep sending me such nice presents. Papa says the heron is a royal bird, and we are going to try it to-day for dinner.'

As she went on the young man's countenance expressed more and more surprise, deepening into dark vexation.

'I am afraid you are laughing at me,' he said. 'I have sent you no presents.'

'Not even that lovely hawk?'

'Certainly not.'

Ethel parted her lips and flushed to the forehead.

'I thought it came from you, or I should not have accepted it. I received it from the strange old man you call your foster-father.'

Graham started, frowning fiercely.

'From Koll Nicholson?'

'Yes, from him; the old man who looks like one of Fingal's giants.'

'What!—did he—did he *dare*'——

He paused, flushing crimson, and biting his lips.

'Dare ?   I am sure it was very attentive.   To be candid, I did not think you sent me the cray-fish, or the shell-fish, or even the dead heron ; you could never have thought I had such an appetite ; but I did really fancy you had given me this charming bird.'

'Was it sent—were those things sent—in my name ? '

'Oh dear, no,' answered Ethel, with her lightest laugh. 'They were normally left, as silent offerings, on Janet's kitchen-table, but I thought '——

'Why should you think that I was such a fool at all ? '

'I thought it very nice of you.'

'You are laughing at me,' said Graham firmly, irritated by the unconscious resumption of her old tantalising manner.   'I will wring the old fool's neck for daring to come near you.   It seems as if every one was in a conspiracy to make me look ridiculous in your eyes.'

'But you don't look ridiculous.'

'I do.'

'On the contrary, Mr. Macdonald, you look most interesting.   You saved my life—shall I ever forget that ? '

'I wish we had drowned together ! '

'I don't.'

'Those few minutes were worth a lifetime.   I had you in my arms—I brought you back to life—I was never so happy before, and I shall never be so happy again '——

'Though we were so wet ! '

'Ay, you may laugh, but I don't care now.   It was *I* that saved you—it was *I* that had you all to myself for those happy minutes ; it was not the Laird of Arranmore ! '

She saw his passion rising again like a great wave, and this time she felt ready not to oppose it, but to meet it half-way, and fling her arms about his neck.   Her mood changed from lightness to the tenderest pity as she said—

'Dear Mr. Macdonald, you don't think me ungrateful. I know I am very irritating—every one finds me so ; but, believe me, I would not willingly cause you pain.   I am only sorry that you did not send me the bird, because I should have prized it as a gift from you.'

He was calmed in a moment, and like all men, being

encouraged, felt ready to encroach; but something in her very tenderness of manner subdued him, and made him keep his place. He looked at her with worshipping eyes, while, with a tear trembling on her cheek, she asked—

'How is your sister?'

'She is better; she will soon be well.'

'I am so glad. Do you think she would mind if I were to come and see her before I go away?'

'I am sure she would be very pleased.'

'Then tell her that I will come.'

At this moment Sir Charles Sedley appeared, gun in hand, to break the *tête-à-tête*. He came upon them almost before they perceived him, and when he saw them in such close conversation looked far from amiable. He nodded in a friendly way to Graham, and then turned to his daughter.

'I've been looking for you everywhere.'

'Indeed, papa!'

'You're wanted up at the lodge.'

'By whom?'

'Come and see. Mr. Macdonald will excuse you; it's a matter of business.'

Ethel turned to speak to Graham, but he had already walked away. She looked after him quietly, and then turned to her father and said—

'I think you might be a little more courteous to the man who saved my life.'

'I am civil to him, and I have shown my gratitude,' returned the baronet sharply; 'but I'm not going to encourage the man in flirting with my daughter.'

'Absurd, papa!'

'There is no doubt of it, Ethel; you keep the poor devil dangling after you, although you know you have no right to give him a moment's encouragement. I thought you had more sense. Why, even if he were a gentleman'——

'He *is* a gentleman!' cried Ethel warmly.

'Gentleman or no gentleman, he is not your equal.'

'No, he is infinitely my superior.'

Something in the tone of the voice startled the baronet, and turning sharply on his heel, he looked into his daughter's face and saw, to his amazement, that her eyes

were full of tears. Brushing the back of her hand across
her eyes, she laughed nervously, and walked over to the
kestrel, which was still seated moveless upon the rock, and
took it again upon her wrist.

'I suppose the fellow gave you that bird!' said her father.

'No; if the fellow had done so, I should prize it more
than I do.'

'You are incorrigible!'

'Indeed!'

'Yes, you are a commonplace coquette—you care for no
one, but you delight in torturing every poor fool who crosses
your path. You'd flirt with an under-keeper, or with a
groom of the stable, if no one else was handy. It's scan-
dalous, Ethel. I shall never sleep in peace till I see you
transformed into a sensible married woman.'

'I'm afraid that transformation is impossible,' returned
Ethel, with a touch of her old light manner. 'I don't care
much for being either married or sensible, and I am quite sure
I shall never be both. But who wants me at the lodge?'

'Lawrance, of course.'

'No one else?'

'No; the fact is, I couldn't see you talking so closely
with that man and not interfere. I wouldn't have had
Lawrie see you for all the world!'

'Do you think he'd care?'

'Care? of course he'd care. God bless me! Ethel,
do you think Lawrance has no feeling—no common deli-
cacy? You talk as if he were some one else, instead of your
affianced husband.'

Ethel did not reply, but only smiled coldly; then, followed
by her father, who continued to fume with irritation, she
walked slowly towards the lodge. But when she reached
it, Lord Arranmore was not there. He had walked down
to the clachan, Janet said, and had not stated when he
meant to return.

The next day Ethel walked down to the lake again, but
before starting waited to see her father well away among the
hills. The fire in her heart was rapidly spreading, and she
felt that she must see Graham again. Besides they had
parted abruptly, and before they had come to a perfect under-

standing. He might still think her unfeeling and ungrateful, and that she could not patiently bear.

What was her surprise when she stood on the lake-side to see Koll Nicholson appear before her, wild, haggard, with famine-stricken eyes! He started out from behind a great boulder, and at first she shrank back with a cry. But his purpose was gentle. Stretching out his hands to her, he fell as before upon his knees, and actually kissed the hem of her dress.

'What is the matter?' she cried. 'What do you want?'

'She wants your leddyship's blessing,' said Koll in great agitation. 'She wants you to speak to her ain son, and to her ain bairn, and tell him no to be sae hard on Koll. Speak to him, my leddy, speak to her ain son Graham. Tell him to forgie her for bringing you the braw hawk, and the heron, and the creel o' fish frae the sea. She meant nae ill to his bonnie leddy—nae ill ava. But the Lord has turned the heart of her ain foster-son against her!'

He ended with a wild cry, for over him stood Graham himself, his eyes flashing, his whole frame trembling with anger. He said something to Koll rapidly in Gaelic, and Koll replied wildly in the same tongue. Ethel looked on in wonder, while the two men faced each other; for Koll had risen to his feet, and stood gazing vacantly upon his foster-son.

'What is it all about?' she cried nervously. 'Why are you angry with the old man? Why, he seems quite heart-broken.'

Without replying to her questions, Graham pointed in the direction of the village.

'Go home!' he said between his set teeth.

'She will go! she will go!' cried Koll, wringing his hands.

'It you ever again approach this lady I will have you punished, mind that! How dare you look her in the face! Go home!'

Obedient as a deer-hound, the old giant turned and moved slowly away, not without a last appealing gesture to Ethel, who turned immediately to Graham.

'Mr. Macdonald, I am sorry to see you so violent. What has the poor old man done?'

' I cannot tell you now.'

' Is it something very dreadful? Well, but see how penitent he is. You must pardon him for my sake!'

' It is just for your sake that I cannot pardon him!'

' I don't understand.'

' No, you cannot,' said Graham sadly.

' Is it because he sent me those presents?'

' No; but he had no right to send them, or to thrust himself upon you.'

' Poor fellow!'

' He does not deserve your pity. He is both cruel and
cunning, and he is most dangerous.'

' Dangerous?'

' Yes, Miss Sedley. You see I know his character, and
you do not.'

Ethel looked at the young Highlander for some moments
in silence, then she said quietly—

' Will you do me a favour?'

' Any you please.'

' Forgive the old man; go after him and tell him that
you forgive him.'

' He does not deserve it. If you knew what he has
done '——

' But I don't want to know; only I don't like to see you
so bitter against him. Whatever his offence has been, he
is very sorry, and I think you are treating him too un-
kindly.'

' I am *not.*'

' Then you won't grant me my request?'

Graham flushed and trembled.

' I have told you that I will do what you please. You
have only to command me in anything.'

' And you'll obey?'

' Yes.'

' Then I'll try you,' said Ethel, smiling. ' Follow the
old man, and say something kind to him.'

' I will do as you wish,' returned Graham earnestly;
' and I will tell him, too, that I forgive him at your desire.'

Without another word he walked off, following the path
taken by Koll. Ethel stood looking after him with a strange

smile, well pleased to find him so obedient to her slightest word, yet wondering at his capacity for violent passion of all kinds. He was her ideal of a lover; not so much her ideal of a husband. His stern and strong nature mastered her, and she trembled before his violent strength.

Graham overtook Koll at last, and called out his name. The old man turned, trembling.

'Shake hands, Koll!'

Koll reached out his hands with a cry.

'Let us forget what has passed,' continued Graham. 'Miss Sedley has pleaded for you, and I forgive you, but she does not know of your wicked attempt upon her life. If she knew it she would despise and hate us both.'

'Graham! and you will not tell Mina, her bairn?'

'No one shall know it; only remember, from this day forward, how good that lady is, and pray to God to forgive you for having tried to do her harm.'

Turning back, he came presently to the spot where he had left Miss Sedley, and found that she had gone. With a heavy sigh he turned his face homeward towards the manse of Uribol.

CHAPTER XLII.

A HIGHLAND FEAST.

IT was now late in the autumn, and the chill, still days of calm seas and silver lights and shadows were beginning to be broken by days of blustering storm. The northern ocean was troubled, wild birds were winging southward, and a cold breath from the Pole was felt upon the sea. Sport was bad, and Sir Charles Sedley began to long for the comforts of his club.

The day after Graham's reconciliation with his foster-father, Glenheather Lodge was deserted, and the Sedleys had migrated to Coreveolan Castle. Ethel departed without a word of farewell, and the promised visit to Mina remained unpaid. When the news of her departure was carried to Graham his dark fit seized him, and he almost wept.

She was still only a few miles away, but it seemed she had gone from his gaze for ever. He walked up the moor, and for hours hovered round the lodge, then, entering it, talked to the old caretaker about its late inmates. Janet was full of praise for Miss Sedley—for her beauty and her kindly ways.

But how cold and desolate seemed the place now she had gone! The whole landscape was changed, and grown stormy, sad, and wild. Graham haunted the spots where they had met, leant over the dark pool into which she had fallen, and tried to recall the rapture of that day when he saved her life. Then his spirit rose against her because she had gone so silently. She might have sent some message or a few words. She was heartless after all, and had forgotten him perhaps already.

Two days passed, during which he suffered exquisite tortures, the more poignant because he had no one to share them with him. He had almost resolved to walk over to Coreveolan, and to ascertain if Ethel was *there*, when on the evening of the second day Angus-with-the-dogs turned up with a letter for the minister.

He had been passing the castle, he said, with his canine family, when he had been called, regaled liberally, and asked to carry a letter to Uribol.

'It's frae the laird himsel',' he said, grinning.

Mr. Macdonald opened it, and read as follows:—

'DEAR MR. MACDONALD,—' Before leaving Coreveolan for the winter, I have arranged to give a supper and ball to my poor tenants, and to all friends within driving-distance. It is fixed for next Tuesday, the 20th inst. : may I look forward to the pleasure of your company, and that of your niece and nephew, who will, I am sure, excuse a more formal invitation? I have persuaded Sir Charles and Miss Sedley to remain over that date, and, with your assistance, I think we may make the little affair a pleasant one to all concerned.

'Believe me, with kind regards to all your household, Yours most truly,   ARRANMORE.'

When Graham read this note his face lightened, and he

turned eagerly to Mina, who sat writing in the room, her uncle's study.

'Shall you go, Mina?' he asked.

Mina shook her head.

'Of course we must go,' exclaimed the minister. 'It is a great occasion, and must on no account be neglected. It was very kind of his lordship to send a special messenger over. Mina, my bairn, don't think of staying at home: the fun will do you more good than all Doctor John's prescriptions, and, besides, you are now quite recovered.'

Mina cast a piteous glance at Graham, but said no more. She was resolved in her own mind that she would not go to Coreveolan Castle, but would find, when the time came, some expedient to make her uncle go alone.

Shortly afterwards Mr. Macdonald quitted the room, and Mina and Graham were left alone together.

'Shall you go, Graham?'

'I'm not sure,' answered Graham. 'After all, what do they want with the likes of us? I think I shall stay at home.'

'And so shall I, Graham.'

'And yet, perhaps, if we *don't* go they may think we're afraid to hold up our heads with theirs. It would, perhaps, be the best to show them how little we heed them, by going with all the rest.'

'Then go *you*. *I* could not bear it.'

Graham stood on the hearth looking darkly down at his sister.

'If I were in your place,' he said, 'I would go, and I would let the laird see that your heart is light as a feather, that you heed him and his no more than the cheep of a sparrow. Don't let the grand fool know that you are grieving for him. Look him full in the face, and go by him laughing with other folk, as if he had never been more to you than a whiff of wind.'

'I have not the courage,' answered Mina. 'Besides, he is so kind, and he would be sure to come and speak to me before all the others, and I could not bear it. You shall go in my place, if you are not afraid.'

Graham started angrily.

'What should I be afraid of?'

'Of your own heart, Graham. No, don't go—it would only make you miserable afterwards.'

Graham gave a short, angry laugh.

'I'll risk it,' he said, and whistling a strathspey, walked out of the house.

In his own mind he was already resolved to go. He had planned it all. He would face her like a man, like an equal, and he would ask for her hand in the dance. He would at least have the rapture of encircling her waist again, of pressing her hand, of hearing her voice. For such a happiness, however brief, he felt that he would give his very soul. Tears of gratitude came into his eyes as he thought that she was not gone yet after all, and that he should see her at least once again.

Left alone, Mina confirmed herself in her first resolution to stay away. The more she thought it over the more she felt convinced that the invitation, though extended to all equally, was meant for her particularly, and that the young lord was only seeking a pretext to see her again. But all was over between them, and though he was very kind, she felt that it was better that they should never meet.

When the evening of the festal gathering came there was excitement indeed over at Castle Coreveolan. Flags waved from the roof, large tents were erected on the heather, all the rooms were thrown open, and even the kitchen was splendidly decorated and prepared for company. Early in the evening the people began to gather; wild fishermen of the shore, with their wilder-looking women; ragged crofters from the hills, with their still more ragged children; decently clad small farmers, overseers, and tacksmen. Mounted on his pony, Peter Dougall rode over gloomily, showing in his grim face strong disapproval of the whole proceedings.

Accompanied by Miss Sedley and her father, the young lord moved from group to group and made himself generally popular. Many a smile and blessing followed him as he moved along with his affianced bride upon his arm.

There was plenty to eat and drink, though of the simplest description, mutton in all shapes predominating; but, what was of far more consequence from the Highland point of view, there was no stint of the best whisky. As the fiery fluid mounted upward tongues began to loosen, until the babble of voices was terrible to hear. At last the great hall was cleared for dancing, and two or three pipers, a fiddler, and a fife-player were installed on a raised platform to play reels and strathspeys *ad libitum.* The floor was soon covered with dancers, and the roof rang to the strains of 'Hoolaghan' and 'Tullochgorum.'

All the evening Arranmore had looked about anxiously for the Macdonalds, and though many of the same name and clan were forthcoming, he could not discern his friends from the manse. At last, however, he discovered to his delight, towering above all others, the head of the old minister.

He at once crossed the hall, and pushed his way to the spot where the clergyman stood.

'I'm so glad you have come!' he exclaimed, shaking hands. 'I hope you are not alone?'

'Graham is with me,' replied Mr. Macdonald. 'I'm sorry to say my niece was too unwell to come.'

The young lord's face fell.

'Not seriously ill, I hope?'

'I think not; but the lassie has not been herself of late, and I'm concerned about her. She bade me say that she thanked your lordship kindly for your invitation, and that she was very sorry not to be strong enough to accept!'

'I am sorry, too,' said Lord Arranmore. 'I was looking forward to a reel with Miss Macdonald as my partner.'

The minister smiled, but made no remark, while Lord Arranmore looked round for Graham.

At first he did not see him, but casting his eyes round the room he at last discovered him in animated conversation with Miss Sedley. Ethel was looking her brightest, and gazing up into the young Highlander's face with a smile such as his cousin had never seen upon her face before; in fact she seemed transformed and prettier than ever; Graham, too, looked his best.

Plainly but neatly dressed in black, with snowy linen and carefully trimmed beard, he stood and listened earnestly, quite unconscious of anything but the presence of the woman whom he loved.

When the young lord went over and offered his hand, Graham's face darkened.

'I am sorry your sister was too ill to come,' said Arran more awkwardly.

'She is better away,' answered Graham quietly.

Their eyes met; Graham's were steady. Arranmore bit his lip in nervous irritation.

'Shall you dance?' he asked, looking at Ethel.

'Mr. Macdonald has just been asking me to dance with *him*, but I never attempted a reel in my life, and I shall break down.'

'It is very easy,' said Graham.

'So it seems,' returned Ethel, watching the dancers, 'but not with a long train. They seem to enjoy it amazingly. That disagreeable-looking old man in the kilt must be eighty if he is a day. Yet he has never sat down a single dance, nor paused a moment except to go to the tables and take liquid refreshment.'

Arranmore looked at her quietly, and seemed piqued. Her manner had entirely changed, and all the light had faded from her face, to be replaced by the cold and haughty sneer he knew so well. He glanced at Graham. The young Highlander was frowning nervously and looking on the ground.

'Ethel,' said a familiar voice, and Sir Charles Sedley, bustling up and whispering, led his daughter away.

The two young men were left standing near to each other, and almost alone. There was a pause. Both looked at the dancers, but the thoughts of each were far away.

'I am pleased to see you,' said Arranmore, breaking the silence at last, 'though I should have been better pleased to see your sister with you. It shows at least that you bear me no serious ill-will.'

Graham was silent, and the other continued—

'I should like you to consider me your friend, and the friend of your family. If I have ever, in sheer thoughtlessness, caused you annoyance, I am sincerely sorry, and I trust you will suffer me to make amends.'

'Pray don't speak of *that*, my lord; let us bury the past.

'It is not so easy,' returned Arranmore; 'and after all

why should we try to bury it? In looking back we should count the bright days as well as the dark. I have spent here in the Highlands some of the happiest hours of my life.'

'With you that is all very well,' answered Graham quietly. 'You can come and you can go; everything, even Uribol, is a change. But it is different with those who have to pass all their lives in loneliness.'

'Shall *you* remain here? Don't think me impertinent; but what are your plans for the future?'

'I have none,' answered Graham. 'I was to have entered the Church, but now I am sick of it. But I *cannot* remain here; I *hate* Uribol.'

'You hate it? Why?'

'For a hundred reasons. It is a barren wilderness, not fit for a man. I should kill myself, I think, or kill somebody else, if I was compelled to live here.'

Arranmore looked at the speaker in surprise. His face was flushed, his eyes burning, and he evidently spoke under the influence of strong emotion. Nor did Arranmore fail to notice that his gaze had followed Ethel Sedley from one part of the room to another, and was now resting upon her as she stood talking to her father at the other end of the hall.

'How different your feelings are to mine!' said the young lord earnestly. 'Do you know I think I could live and die in these wilds, which you dislike so much? I suppose it is the contrariety of human nature. Just because I belong to the busy world I hate it; while you, on the contrary, being surfeited with solitude, seek excitement. Upon my word, Macdonald, I wish we could change places —I should be quite content!'

Just then Mr. Peter Dougall came up, smiling grimly, and began talking generally over the affairs of the estate. Lord Arranmore had not altogether conquered his dislike to, and want of confidence in, the factor, but he had scarcely decided as yet to dispense with his services. He strolled away with him in careless chat, leaving Graham alone.

The hall was now uncomfortably warm, the fun was growing fast and furious, and the giver of the entertainment had wisely arranged that the tenants should amuse themselves in their own way, without any settled programme, and with little or no supervision. One or two choice spirits, tenant farmers and drovers, had constituted themselves masters of the ceremonies, prepared to keep the ball going and the liquor flowing till dawn of day. The dancing grew wilder every minute, the screams of the pipes, the babble of voices, the clatter of feet on the bare boards, and the whirl and noise of people coming and going, was rapidly passing into 'confusion worse confounded.'

Gloomy enough now, Graham passed out of the dancing-hall, through the intervening chambers, and out into the night. Various groups were gathered about the castle door, but no one took any notice of him. He moved on, and found an empty seat on the terrace before the castle.

It was a still, cold night; the sky was thick with stars, and the aurora was flashing far away to the north. From the distance rose a deep, solemn murmur—the heavy, slumberous breathing of the sea.

He lit his pipe, and sat brooding over his own dark thoughts for some minutes. He was startled by a low laugh behind him. Turning, he saw a slight figure standing close to him in the starlight.

'Is that Mr. Macdonald?' asked Ethel's voice.

'Yes!'

'Why did you run away? They are going to try a country-dance, and I want you for my partner.'

'I am ready.'

'Oh, there is no hurry—the reel is not finished yet, and it is so hot in there!'

'But a heavy dew is falling here. You will catch cold.'

'It doesn't much matter if I do,' said Ethel quietly, sitting down beside him. 'I should not be much of a loss if I caught cold and died.'

'God forbid!'

'Papa would fret a little, and I suppose Lawrance—I mean Lord Arranmore—would wear mourning for a little—then he'd cheerfully marry some one else.'

The moment was propitious, and poor Graham could not resist the temptation.

'You forget *me*,' he said softly.

'No, I don't. You, my Highland chieftain, would be rather sorry, I suppose. What a pity you did not let me drown!'

'Why?'

'Because I am what they call an incubus, annoying to myself, and of no use to anybody. Now, a romantic death by drowning would have redeemed my life from commonplace, whereas I shall live on to become a humdrum married person, to whom life is a bore.'

There was a pause. The silence was at last broken by Graham.

'I don't like to hear you talk like that,' he said in a broken voice. 'Perhaps this is the last night we shall meet on this earth, and I should like to think of you at your best, as you have appeared to me now and then. You have been a bright star above my head—something I shall always remember as the best memory of my life.'

'Please don't talk sentiment.'

'Sentiment or no sentiment, it is God's truth,' returned Graham solemnly. 'You know I have dared to love you well — treat my love gently, not by approving it, but by being just to yourself.'

'How strangely you talk!'

'I feel strangely, for I came here to-night to say "good-bye." I want you, if you ever give me a thought, to think the best also of me. Forget my sullenness, my fits of passion, my infernal insolence; only remember how I respected and admired you, and how I tried to conquer my presumptuous passion. I *have* tried to conquer it, God knows! And you—you have been very kind. Where another lady would never have forgiven me, but would have hated and despised me for my insolence and my mad ways, you have taken it all so brightly and nobly, like the high-bred lady you are. Well, you have cured me better by your kindness than I could have hoped; you have made another man of me; and I see now how mad it was to dream of loving a lady like yourself. Not that I ever thought, even for a moment, that my love was anything but presumptuous. My God, no! I knew from the beginning how hopeless it was, but for all that it was none the less sweet.'

He paused and gazed at her, his throat choked with emotion. She was listening quietly, with her face upturned to the starry sky.

'But don't think I wish the love had never come; don't think that! Take sweet and sour together, and the pleasure's more than the pain. You'll go away from this, and you'll marry another man, but I shall always have the dream of your bonnie face to comfort me. You cannot take that away, and that's enough for me. I've looked in your face, and I've heard your voice, and I've held you in my arms, and what more should I dare to wish? Ay, and I've dared to tell you what I thought of you, and that's more comfort still. I walk the heather like a new man, I feel gently towards my fellowmen, I can pray more freely to my God—all through the love I've felt for *you !*'

He had gone on speaking with a fluency he had never felt before, for the words had bubbled silently up from his heart like water trickling from a fountain in the ground: and as he proceeded, though his emotion was so deep, his speech had grown more and more calm. Now, however, he started and trembled, with a sudden thrill through the heart, for he felt, rather than saw, that she was weeping.

She did not move, but, leaning back as before, looked at the sky, while the tears flowed, and her delicate frame shook and quivered.

'Miss Sedley! for God's sake, don't cry! I am a wretch to pain you so!'

'Don't mind me!' she said with a sob; 'I think it does me good!' and she hid her face in her hands.

He leant towards her, and watched her with strange tenderness as she wept in silence; but soon the wave of grief subsided, the heart ceased to heave in tumult, and drawing forth a delicate handkerchief, she dried her tears.

'It is very stupid of me!' she murmured; 'but I could not help it. I feel as if I had used you very badly.'

'No, no!'

'How much better it would have been if we had never seen each other. I seem doomed to bring misery to every one I meet.'

'You have brought no misery to me,' he cried, though a

voice in his wounded heart all the time echoed, 'Misery, misery!'

'I have! Oh, forgive me!' she cried, stretching out her hands towards him.

The temptation was too much for him to bear. He seized her hands, and lifting them to his lips, covered them with kisses. She trembled violently, but did not draw them away at first.

Then she sprang to her feet.

'Let us go in,' she exclaimed.

'Ah, now I have made you hate me,' said Graham sadly.

'I hate myself—I hate all the world ; but not *you* !'

'What !'

'Do not say any more to me. Take pity upon me. Remember I am engaged to be married, and that I ought not to have listened to you at all.'

She moved towards the lighted door of the castle, Graham following. Rapture was again pre-eminent in his heart, for he felt now that, had fortune been kinder to him, she might have loved him. Yes, there was no mistaking her manner towards him. He had mastered her first aversion, and had made her fitful nature gentle as a lamb.

'I forgot to ask you,' she said, pausing on the threshold, 'if you return to the manse to-night ?'

'No. My uncle and I are to sleep at a shepherd's hut on the hill, and to-morrow we are going to walk across the strand to Storport. I shall not return to Uribol till to-morrow night.'

She still lingered.

'When do you leave for the south ?' he asked.

'Papa is anxious to go at once—in two or three days at the latest, I think.'

'Then I was right. I shall not see you again.'

'No.'

'Shall you return here after'——

'After !' she repeated, seeing that he paused.

'After your marriage ?'

'Don't speak of anything so disagreeable,' she said with a forced laugh. 'I suppose, however, that I shall come back to Coreveolan some day.'

'Well, I shall not see you, for I shall be gone.'

'You are going away?'

'This place will be dull to me, and I shall go abroad—very likely to Canada or the States. I have often longed to try the New World, and I shall sail there as soon as I can.'

She answered nothing, but heaved a deep sigh, and then, slipping her little hand into his arm, she moved into the house. The sense of parting was upon them, and the heart of each was deeply stirred. Never before had they seemed quite so near to each other as in the sadness of that last adieu.

Wild streams of music were still issuing from the dancing-hall, and from time to time there arose loud shouts and laughter. Ethel shrank back for a moment before she entered, then, resigning Graham's arm, and casting into his face one eager look, she passed in among the throng. Graham fell back like one dazed. He heard nothing—saw nothing. His head went round, and sinking into a chair in a corner of one of the outer apartments, he hid his face in his hands.

CHAPTER XLIII.

ETHEL AND MINA.

WHILE Graham Macdonald, in a wild fever of excitement, was lingering outside the ball-room at Coreveolan Castle, with Ethel's last look upon his soul, and Lord Arranmore, moody, silent, and ill at ease, was thinking of the one being the want of whose animating presence made that gay scene almost a blank to him, Mina was trying to steep her soul in forgetfulness and to make the weary hours pass pleasantly at the manse. She had asked her uncle for some work, and he had given her some copying to do—a philological article which he intended for some dry review—so, as soon as the two men were gone, Mina set to her task and worked as assiduously as if her very life depended upon its completion. She made some dreadful mistakes, but she was wholly unconscious of them, and toiled away proud of the manner in which she believed she was concentrating her

T

thoughts and preventing them from straying to Coreveolan
Castle.

An hour or so at the writing cramped her hand ; she put
the paper aside for a while, and walked into the kitchen
to see how Kirsty was getting on. On the previous day
one of the gillies had come over from the castle, bringing
the old woman an invitation to the ball, written in the
laird's own hand ; but since Mina had decided not to go,
Kirsty, with a very sore heart, had refused her invitation
too. She would not leave her young mistress to spend a
whole night, or part of a night, alone in the manse, yet she
chafed terribly at the sacrifice, and proved herself a very
unpleasant companion to Mina that night. But Mina,
grown very weak in spirit, bore the complaints of the old
domestic without a word. When she had done, she put
her arm around her neck and kissed her cheek.

'You should have gone, Kirsty,' she said.

The old woman was partly pacified.

"'Tis not for the likes o' me to go dancing o'er the
country,' she said, 'when a wee bairn like yoursel' will
choose to stay at hame. I'm no thinking o' mysel' or the
pleasure to mysel', but o' the insult till the laird. I'm
thinkin', my bairn, if I should just walk o'er to the castle
the morn and mak' my apologies till his lordship !'

Mina smiled. The idea of Lord Arranmore being pained
by Kirsty's absence amused her.

'You need not be unhappy about that, Kirsty,' she said.
'I told Graham to make excuses for you, in case my uncle
should forget.'

She remained a little longer in the kitchen, sometimes
walking about with her hands behind her, sometimes pausing to watch Kirsty spin ; then she returned to her writing.
Kirsty would talk of nothing but the ball, and that was the
very thing which Mina was striving to forget. So the
evening passed very wearily, and when ten o'clock struck
Mina was glad to go to bed. She felt depressed and sick
at heart, and once alone in her room, had great difficulty
in keeping back her tears. She passed a weary, restless,
feverish night ; and in the morning felt more sad at heart
than she had ever done before.

She found a nice breakfast laid for her in her uncle's study. Kirsty, overcome with remorse at her ill-humour on the previous night, seemed anxious to atone, and did so by procuring little dainties to tempt Mina to eat. The sight of Mina's face shocked her; it looked so white and thin; there were dark rings round her eyes which told of mental suffering. Mina sat at the table and sipped a cup of tea, but she could not eat—the very sight of the food was nauseating to her. Then, when Kirsty had cleared away the untouched dainties, she went over to her uncle's desk and tried to finish the work which he had given her to do. She worked steadily for some time; suddenly she threw her pen aside, let her head fall upon her hands, and burst into tears.

'God help me,' she sobbed. 'I think my heart is breaking. Oh, it's very cruel that I am bound to thole all this. He never loved me. He could not have loved me, or he would not continue to torture me so much. It is very cruel. If I could only die, and be at peace for ever up among the Uribol hills. God is not merciful, or He would let me die, since I have prayed for death so often. Well, they say people cannot live very long with a broken heart, and perhaps my troubles are almost done. Oh, I am very lonely! I did not think such sorrow was quite so hard to bear!'

'Good-morning, Miss Macdonald!'

Mina started, hurriedly wiped away her tears, and rising to her feet, found herself standing face to face with Ethel Sedley. She stared; she could not speak; while Ethel, still standing with her right hand extended, said pleasantly—

'Pray do not be angry with me. I know I have no right to intrude upon you unannounced like this. I knocked twice or thrice, and at last, receiving no answer, and finding the door open, I took the liberty of coming in.'

Still Mina stood in speechless amazement. At the best of times she would not have appreciated a visit from Miss Sedley, and the knowledge of how she had been discovered annoyed her more than all. She knew that her cheeks were flushed, her eyes swollen with crying, and she was angry that Ethel should have seen her thus. Besides, she could never forget the fact that it was this woman who, after having made her brother's life desolate, had come between her and her love, and wrought her all the pain.

So, although she saw Ethel's extended hand, she did not take it, but drawing herself up proudly, said, as soon as she could command her voice sufficiently to speak—

'Miss Sedley, neither my uncle nor my brother is at home to-day, and I '——

She paused in some hesitation, too sensitive to utter the rude speech which forced itself upon her tongue. Ethel smiled, and closing the room door, walked straight up to Mina and took her hand.

'Miss Macdonald,' she said very kindly, 'I do not want either your uncle or your brother just now. I have come here with the sole object of seeing *you*.'

'Me !'

'Of course. When I heard that you would not come to me last night, I made up my mind to come to you to-day. I have so much to tell you. Now do let us make ourselves comfortable. Will you not sit down ? I've come to talk it over.'

Mina coldly withdrew her hand.

'I do not understand you, madam,' she said. 'You are almost a stranger to me. If you wish to come here you had better do so when my uncle and brother are at home to receive you. To-day I would rather be alone.'

But Ethel was not to be daunted. Again she looked with a pleasant smile into Mina's face.

'I wish you'd trust me,' she said. 'Come, I'm not very formidable. Do sit down.'

'I will stand, if you please, until '——

'Well ?'

'Until you are gone.'

After this speech there was silence. So many rebuffs were not very encouraging, but Ethel, having an earnest purpose in view, was not easily turned. Still it was very awkward ; she had not anticipated quite so much coldness, and for the moment she hardly knew how to proceed. She had been sitting thinking, with her eyes fixed upon the ground ; suddenly she raised them to Mina's face. How wretchedly ill the girl looked ! how terribly she must have suffered! and Ethel knew that all this suffering was trace-able to her.   She rose and again took Mina's hand.

'Miss Macdonald, do you know what brought me here to-day?'

'No, madam; nor do I wish to know!'

'I have come, then, to talk about your acquaintance with my cousin, Lord Arranmore.'

Mina's face flushed painfully.   By a violent jerk she re-gained possession of her hand.

'I cannot!' she cried passionately.   'I *will* not—least of all with *you!*'

'Oh!'

'Lord Arranmore is nothing to me—I am nothing to him. We have met, but we are not likely to meet again.   Why should I be persecuted by those who call themselves his friends?   You are a great lady, and I am a poor girl; and this house is my house, and I beg you to leave it that I may have peace!'

'There, now, I have offended you.'

'No; but, as I told you before, I wish to be alone.   Pray go!'

'What, *now?*'

'Yes.'

Ethel rose, walked over to the window, and looked out.

'The rain is falling in torrents,' she said.   'If I go, in ten minutes I shall be soaked to the skin.   I promise to go as soon as the shower is over; until then *do* let me make my-self at home.   After all, I only come to give you a little advice.'

'I tell you I do not want it.'

'About Lawrance — Lord Arranmore, I mean.   He is going away.'

'Madam'——

'To the Antipodes,' continued Ethel, fixing her eyes firmly upon Mina's face.   'He has always had a hatred of monarchical government and a love for colonisation, so he means to transport himself and his opinions, for a time at least, to New Zealand.'

'To New Zealand,' said Mina, trembling.   'Why, I

understood that when he left Uribol he was going straight
to London to be married.'

'Indeed—to whom?'

'To you.'

'*Me!*'

'Yes.'

'May I ask who told you that fine tale?'

'Your father!'

Then I am much obliged to my father for his impudence.
Dismiss that notion from your mind, my dear—it's absurd.
To me Lawrie was always disagreeable in the extreme, so
you need not be jealous of me.'

'Jealous—I?'

'Why not? isn't that love's privilege?'

'You mistake me. I am not in love.'

'Don't say that again. It's blasphemy against your cause,
treason against your colours. I know you love Lawrie,
though he doesn't deserve it; and I tell you he would lay
down his life for you. Will you sit down now, or shall I
go?'

'No—do not go!'

'Ah, I thought we should be friends. And now that we
are comfortable, I am going to give you a little advice, for
I am quite an old woman—old in experience, you know,
for in our world we measure time not by years, but by
episodes. But first let me confess and crave absolution.
Lawrie is not going to the Antipodes at all!'

'Not going?'

'No—that was merely a little invention of mine to find
out whether or not you loved him, and could still forgive him
all the cruel wrong that he has done to you. But to return to
my story. Last night he was wretched because you did not
come to the ball; so after the thing was over I asked him
to come to my room and have a little private talk. He
came, and I spoke to him like a mother. "Lawrance," I
said, "this engagement of ours, which was always absurd, is
becoming tragical. We neither of us care for each other,
and we both love somebody else. I see you mean to be
honourable enough to keep your word to me, therefore I
release you. There is your engagement-ring; the best

thing you can do is to lose no time in giving one to Miss Macdonald!"'

'You said that? But what did he say?'

'Well, my dear, he said nothing at first, but stared at me as if I were a revivified corpse. Then he took the ring, shook me cordially by the hand, and paid me the compliment of saying he had never liked me so well in his life. "But, Ethel," he added, "I am afraid my freedom comes too late. I have behaved like a villain to Miss Macdonald, and I fear she will never forgive me!" Then he told me how coldly you had treated him lately, and I got frightened, and determined in my own mind to come down here this morning and ascertain if possible the real state of your feelings towards Lord Arranmore. . . . You love him, do you not, dear, and you will be his wife?'

Mina started.

'His wife? Lord Arranmore's wife. Oh no, it cannot be; he is far above me.'

'*I* thought so at one time. As a rule equal should mate with equal, and when I first met you I did not think you his; but I know now that you are worthy a better man than he! I shall be proud to call you—cousin; and I am sure it will be the happiest day of Lawrance's life when you allow him to make you Lady Arranmore.'

Mina blushed, but said nothing this time.

She had drawn so much comfort from Ethel's talk that she was only too glad to sit and hear her speak on. As yet she could hardly bring herself to believe that all this was true—that it was not all a dream, from which on the morrow —nay, perhaps in a few hours—she would awake to find the world again grown dreary. Nevertheless, it was sweet while it lasted. So she sat and listened, growing each moment brighter; and when at length Ethel rose to go, Mina tearfully kissed her hand.

'No, that will not do,' said Ethel quietly. 'Kiss me on the lips, my dear. I deserve it, I am sure. Why, I have only been here a couple of hours, and yet I have made you look at least ten years younger than you did when I came. So much for my skill in healing. Good-bye, love. Mind that you don't treat my cousin Lawrance as you wanted to treat me.'

CHAPTER XLIV.

A LITTLE SUNSHINE.

On leaving the manse Ethel walked straight down to the shore. There she found awaiting her the boat which had brought her down that morning. She entered it at once, and ordered her boatmen to row her straight back to Coreveolan Castle.

The heavy rain had ceased to fall, but the day had not brightened much. A thick mist veiled all the hill-tops, the air was clammy and rather cold, and a chill, fitful breeze was ruffling the surface of the sea. It was not a pleasant day to be out, but Ethel did not heed the weather. The chilly wind blew upon her—the water washed over the boat, saturating the thick ulster which she wore, but she took no heed; her mind was too fully occupied with other things.

In thinking over the interview which she had just had, her feeling was one of self-congratulation. In freeing Lawrance and consoling Mina she knew that she had done well. She did not fear for them; she knew that for them there were many years of happiness in store. But what of herself? She had no kind friend to intercede for her, no penitent to bring her lover to her feet. She knew that Graham Macdonald loved her; but what of that? She felt almost certain that, although he loved her—although she had shown him, as plainly as a woman can show, that she loved him—he would never again ask her to be his wife. Yes, she felt certain of that, after what had taken place last night. If he had meant to ask her he would have asked her then—when she fully expected the question to be put by him, and was ready with her reply.

The men had rowed quickly, and by this time the boat was nearing the landing-stage which lay below Coreveolan Castle. The mist which had been blown down from the hill-tops thickened the air, and fell upon the earth in thin white rain. Ethel's clothes were saturated; she felt very chilly; so, as soon as she landed, she walked very quickly up to the castle. She entered with her private key, and reached her room unperceived. Having exchanged her wet clothes for dry ones, she went downstairs, intending to find Lawrance and tell him what she had done. Her maid had told her that Lord Arranmore was somewhere in the castle, but for some time he was not to be found. She searched several rooms unsuccessfully; she was passing along one of the lobbies towards the billiard-room when her quick ear caught the sound of two voices in eager conversation. The voices were those of her father and young Lord Arranmore.

'I wonder what they're talking about?' said Ethel. 'Perhaps Lawrie wouldn't like to be disturbed. There won't be much harm done if I listen for a moment just to hear.'

She gathered up the train of her dress and walked quietly back in the direction of the sounds; they issued through the half-open door of a room which had been furbished up for her father's use, and called his study. Standing just outside, Ethel could hear the voices and see the men who were arguing together so warmly.

Sir Charles Sedley, flushed and angry-looking, paced the room with restless, irritable steps, while Lord Arranmore, leaning against the scarlet board of the chimney-piece, watched him in moody silence. They had ceased talking as Ethel stood before the door.

She was about to push it open and walk boldly in, when the conversation between the two men was begun again. Sir Charles paused before his nephew, and said—

'Once for all, Lawrance, what do you mean to do?'

'My dear uncle, if you will only calm yourself, and look at the matter like a sensible man, you will admit, I am sure, that I can do nothing. So long as Ethel wished to keep our compact, I did not say no, but I tell you she herself brought the engagement to a close.'

'Brought the engagement to a close! Stuff and nonsense! I tell you I don't believe she did any such thing. It's not like Ethel. I dare say she talked in a wild, foolish way, as girls often will do, and then, to her amazement, you took her at her word. Do you think I am a blind old fool? Do you think I can't see that this shameless, dishonourable conduct of yours is breaking my poor girl's heart?'

'I tell you, uncle, Ethel does not care for me.'

'And I tell you she is ready to adore you at a moment's notice, if you will only encourage her by a little ordinary civility. But you won't even do that. Now that you are infatuated by this Highland peasant girl, who under no circumstances could ever become your wife, poor Ethel, who has wasted all her life for you, may go to the wall. No, Lawrance, if you can't love my poor girl as much as she deserves, at least don't do her such vile injustice; don't altogether break her heart and ruin her young life. Go to her, tell her how heartily you repent of all this nonsense, and see if she doesn't gleefully throw herself into your arms.'

As Sir Charles paused, Lord Arranmore opened his lips to speak; but the door of the room was quietly thrown open, and Ethel, the object of all this discussion, stood facing the two men. They both started; Sir Charles flushed from brow to chin, then nervously grasped the back of a chair which stood near. Lord Arranmore, looking somewhat uncomfortable, but not quite so guilty as his uncle, straightened himself up from his lounging attitude, and took a few steps towards the girl.

'Ethel!' he exclaimed, 'you here! Why, they told us that you were on the hills.'

For a minute or so Ethel could say nothing. Anger, shame, and mortified pride kept her silent. Her face was white as death, her lips were quite bloodless, her hands trembling. Never in his life had Lawrance seen her so moved, and he grew really alarmed.

'Ethel,' he said, 'my dear cousin, do not excite yourself so much. What is the matter?'

'The matter? Not much,' said Ethel, forcing her white lips into a smile. Then taking her cousin's hand, and utterly ignoring the presence of her father, she said—

'Lawrance, when you and I parted last night I thought—if it is not possible for us to love, we can at least respect one another. I wonder if you will ever be able to respect me after the conversation which you have had with my father to-day.'

'Ethel!'

'Nay, do not speak. I know what your kind heart prompts you to say, Lawrance; but nothing that you could say or do will ever wipe from my memory the shame of to-day. It is unpardonable. To think that my father, who of all men should love and respect me, should take such shameful liberties with my name. To think that he of all men should hawk me about as if I were some negro slave to be put up for sale in the market-place, and knocked down to the first person who chooses to pay the price.'

Here Sir Charles Sedley, who had by this time recovered his presence of mind, came forward to where his daughter stood.

'Ethel,' he said, 'for pity's sake, don't make a fool of yourself by going on like a tragedy queen in a play. It strikes me we've had enough posing and speechifying lately; it's high time you began to talk a little common sense !'

Instead of answering her father Ethel turned again to Lord Arranmore, who, deeming his presence a superfluity, had moved towards the door.

'Lawrance,' she said, 'I have something to say to you by and by. I suppose you're not going out?'

'No, you will find me in my room until dinner-time.'

Then he went, glad of a chance to escape and leave father and daughter alone.

To tell the truth, he was half ashamed of the part which he was compelled to play in this domestic drama, and he felt he would give a good deal to bring these unpleasant scenes to a close. Every day some new phase of ill-feeling was sure to spring up somewhere, and it seemed to him that in the end this eternal playing at cross purposes would serve to alienate the friendship of every one. Ethel was right ; if people could not love one another, there was no reason whatever why respect and affection should be abandoned. Yet so it was; the breaking of his engagement seemed likely not only to put an end to all friendly affection between himself and Ethel, but now, through some ridiculous accident, threatened to imperil the kindly feelings which had always existed between Sir Charles Sedley and his child.

Lord Arranmore had reached the door of his room, when he turned and walked back to that in which he had left his uncle and cousin. They were still there. Sir Charles was seated in an easy-chair, looking repentant and miserable enough, while Ethel, who had turned her back upon him, stood looking out of the window with her forehead pressed against the cold panes of glass.

Lord Arranmore walked up to his cousin and took her hand.

'Ethel,' he said, 'I have come back to be peacemaker. Come, you must not quarrel with your father, least of all through me. I have caused misery enough during the last month or so without having that upon my conscience. What if he did speak a little warmly? It was all the result of his affection for you. Shake hands, uncle,' he added, turning to Sir Charles. 'Some day you will have a better son-in-law than I am. If Ethel and I have made up our minds not to marry, remember we are still cousins—almost brother and sister—and we must not allow ourselves to be separated for the sake of a stupid blunder which only wants a little explanation to set it right.'

For a while father and daughter remained stubborn, but at length the persuasions of the young lord won upon them, and they kissed each other and agreed to try and forget.

The baronet's greatest trouble at this time was the thought of Graham Macdonald, for in him he seemed to see the stumbling-block to his daughter's marriage with Lord Arranmore. When, therefore, the shock of the news of the broken engagement was over, the baronet calmly awaited that other blow which he believed his daughter was preparing for him —the announcement of her engagement to Graham Macdonald. But the blow did not come, and after a while the baronet began to think it was not likely to do so. Instead of wandering about the hills as she used to do, Ethel kept continually in the house, and remained hour after hour shut up in her room, under the pretext of helping her maid to prepare for her departure. She was affectionate in her manner to her father, friendly and quite unrestrained with Lawrance; but there was a dreamy look in her eyes, a strange preoccupation in her manner, which neither could understand. One night, as she and her father sat alone in the drawing-room at Coreveolan Castle, her father called her to him and kissed her.

'Are your things all ready for to-morrow, my love?'

'Quite ready, papa.'

'That is right, dear. I am rather glad we are going so soon. An overdose of this Highland air is making you look pale. I suppose you'll be glad to get away?'

'I suppose I shall.'

'You speak as if you didn't know your own mind, Ethel.'

'I sometimes fancy I do not. How stupid of me. I have set this wound bleeding again.'

'It is a long time getting well. It couldn't take much longer if you tore it open every day.'

'No, it couldn't, could it?' she said, with a laugh; then, bending down to kiss him, she said: 'Good-night, papa. I have one or two little things to do before I can go to bed, so I will retire, as we have to rise so early in the morning.'

The baronet kissed her, and she left the room. In the hall she was met by one of the footmen, who told her that the young man from Uribol manse had called to see her. He was in the dining-room. Ethel walked straight there and found Graham. He rose as she came in.

'I heard this afternoon that you leave to-morrow, Miss Sedley,' he said, 'and I called to wish you a safe journey and to say good-bye.'

'Yes, we leave to-morrow,' she said. 'It was very kind of you to call. How is your sister?'

'Much better, thanks.'

'Have you seen Lord Arranmore?'

'I left him just now at the manse.'

Oh indeed! He's gone to say good-bye, I suppose. Such a lot of leave-taking when one is going away. Well, Mr. Macdonald, if we both live long enough I suppose we shall meet again?'

'I hope so.'

'Will you come and say good-bye to papa? He is in the drawing-room.'

Graham assented, and was at once marshalled into the presence of Sir Charles Sedley.

The baronet was affable, condescending, and most polite. He desired to be very kindly remembered to all at the manse, and hoped if any of them ever happened to be in town, they would pay him a visit. As the baronet forgot to add in what quarter of London he and his daughter were ever likely to be found, Ethel handed him a card bearing their town address. Sir Charles frowned, but said nothing, and Graham at once wished him good-night. Ethel went with him to the door.

'Give my love to your uncle and Mina,' she said; 'be sure you don't forget, now. Good-night—Good-bye. You have got a very weary walk home.

He took her hand in both of his, and raised it to his lips. Then, without a word, he left her. Ethel walked wearily upstairs, and sat down alone in her room.

'It seems to me that I have played the fairy, and made everybody happy,' she said. 'Oh for some good fairy to wave her wand over *me !'*

CHAPTER XLV.

A PROPOSAL.

ETHEL SEDLEY had indeed played the part of the good fairy in the play during her last visit to Uribol manse. Later in the afternoon, when Mr. Macdonald and Graham got home, they found Mina looking brighter than she had done for months; moving about the house with her old light, fairy-like tread, and now and then humming over snatches of song.

It was wonderful how this change in the girl brightened the whole house. Mina's dog, catching the spirit of his mistress, frisked wildly about the girl, and gave little shakes at her dress whenever she went and came. Kirsty's spinning-wheel seemed to hum more blithely, and every room looked as if it had been brightened by the sudden shining of the midsummer sun.

Mina knew pretty well when her uncle and brother would be home, and she had tea ready for them; and when the meal was over she opened the windows, for the evening was quite fine, drew up two easy-chairs for the two men, and, taking her seat between them, asked them to tell her all about the ball.

Graham said little, but Mr. Macdonald, delighted at this change in the girl, told her all. Then Mina produced her copy, laughed heartily over the mistakes which she had made, and promised to do every line of it again. Her brother looked at her in puzzled silence, and as soon as they were alone, asked her what it all meant.

The clergyman, being tired, had retired early, leaving the brother and sister in the study alone. The lamps had not been lit, but a flood of bright moonlight pouring into the room illuminated with a pale, soft radiance the two figures still seated by the open window.

'Mina,' said Graham quietly, 'what has happened since yesterday?'

'Miss Sedley has been here.'

'Ethel—Miss Sedley?'

'Yes, indeed. She came over from the castle this morning, and stayed nearly two hours. Do you know, Graham, that she has broken off her engagement with Lord Arranmore?'

'She told you that?'

'Yes.'

'And said that his lordship intended to propose to you?'

'No, she did not.'

'She has done the same thing, Mina; she has made you believe so. Well, remember if he does so, that your birth is as good as his, but that under no circumstances whatever will he ever regard you as his equal.'

Mina was silent. She had not expected the conversation to take this turn. Hitherto she had been quite frank with Graham, but now she felt that she would much rather have him leave her love affairs alone. His own were complicated enough. Why not try to disentangle them? So, instead of answering his question, she bent forward to look into his face, and said quietly—

'Graham, Miss Sedley is a free woman now!'

'What of that, Mina?'

'She loves you. She almost told me as much to-day!'

'About as much as she loved me a year ago, when she treated me with such scorn.'

'She did not! she could not! If you were to ask her *now*, she would be your wife!'

'My *wife!* Ha! ha! ha!'

'Don't laugh like that, Graham. Is it so amusing?'

'Very. The idea of Miss Sedley becoming a wife. She is one of those ladies one meets occasionally in the world who is for ever craving for the impossible. The moment I show my love, she repulses me. When I cool, she encourages me again. But I'm too old to be a woman's plaything now. I can better afford to remain her friend !'

'You are too hard upon her, Graham.'

'Tit for tat, Mina. She was once too hard upon me.'

Nothing more passed between them that night, but the short conversation had had more effect upon Graham than he cared to show. For hours after Mina had gone to bed he sat by the window, pressing his heated head between his hands, and thought over what he had heard. When he had spoken so callously to Mina he had simply done so to hide from her the real state of his heart. He felt that Ethel loved him; he knew that he loved her; but he dreaded to speak lest his words should bring into her face the cold, proud look which he had seen there before.

Meanwhile active preparations were on foot for the departure of the party from the castle, and Mina was wondering each day why Lord Arranmore had not paid a visit to the manse. After what Ethel had said she fully expected him, and although she pined to see him, she seemed to dread his coming. At last, however, when Mina began to think that he had given up all thoughts of seeing her, he came. It was the evening before the day on which the party at the castle were to take their departure from Uribol. The family at the manse were seated at tea when they saw Lord Arranmore walk past the window, and a minute or so after he was ushered into the room by Kirsty.

The clergyman received him cordially, for the young man had become a great favourite with him ; Graham gave him a more than usually friendly handshake ; while Mina, who, with all her self-control, could not keep the tell-tale colour from rising to her cheeks, gave him her hand too. How kindly he took it ! how warmly he pressed it ! Then he gratefully accepted the offer of a cup of tea, and sat down amongst them as if he were one of themselves.

It seemed to Mina that the old times had come back again—the dear old times when she had walked about the world in a dim, delicious dream, from which she had been destined to have such a sorrowful awakening. There sat Lawrance, just as he had been wont to sit, sipping his cup

of tea, and gazing upon her with eyes that bespoke his admiration, and Mina felt that she was blushing and trembling
just as she had been wont to do before the intensity of that gaze.

'I am glad, Miss Macdonald, to see you more like yourself than when I was here before.'

'Thank you, my lord, I am quite recovered now.'

She spoke quietly, laying slight stress on his title, as if to
remind herself of his rank. She felt that she needed to do
so. His greatness seemed to have fallen from him that
night, and transformed him into the poor young student
who had come to them some months ago. Lawrance
winced slightly at the title thus emphatically bestowed upon
him, and turned to Mr. Macdonald.

'If you remember,' he said, 'I bade you good-bye once
before, and nothing came of it. But I am really going this
time. I leave Uribol to-morrow.'

'I hope you will soon return, my lord.'

'I hope so too. It is necessity, not inclination, which
takes me away now. As I told your nephew a few days
since, I should not mind if I had to spend my life here.'

As he spoke Lord Arranmore looked at Mina, but she
had turned to arrange some things on the table, and he
could not see her face.

Mina now dropped out of the conversation altogether, for
the clergyman and Lord Arranmore began a long discussion
about the land question. In the midst of it Kirsty came in
to say the minister was wanted in the kitchen. With many
apologies Mr. Macdonald left the room, and Lord Arranmore, glancing quickly about him, saw that he was alone
with Mina. In a moment he was by her side.

'Miss Macdonald—Mina!'

At this sudden impassioned address Mina felt her hands
begin to tremble, her cheeks to blush. She lifted her head,
and raised her eyes confidently to his.

'My lord?'

He bent towards her, and took both her hands in his.

'Do you know what has brought me here to-night, Mina?
I have come to ask you to become my wife!'

At this Mina blushed more vividly than ever, but she
could not reply, for at that moment the door of the sitting-
room opened, and the minister returned. Lord Arranmore

U

dropped her hands and frowned, but his frown soon cleared away. Mr. Macdonald came to apologise again. He had some business to attend to which would occupy him for a quarter of an hour or so—would Lord Arranmore excuse him for that time? He had hunted for Graham, thinking that he would entertain his lordship, but the lad had disappeared, and was nowhere to be found. However, Lord Arranmore, who seemed to be very accommodating that night, expressed himself perfectly willing to be left alone with Mina, and the minister retired. Then Lawrance, remembering that he had only a quarter of an hour before him, again approached her.

'You have had a visit from Ethel, have you not?'

'Yes, Miss Sedley came down to see me the morning after the ball.'

Then Mina, glad of a reprieve, launched out into such praise of Ethel that Lawrance smiled.

'I am glad you like her. You two will have to be fast friends. She will be your cousin, you know!'

'My lord!'

'There, do not call me that—say Lawrance; but I forgot, you have not answered my question. Well, Mina, which is it to be? Yes—or no?'

'No.'

Lord Arranmore started, and looked at the girl's bowed head and pale face in blank amazement.

'Mina—Miss Macdonald—do you know what you have said?'

'Perfectly, my lord!'

'You refuse to marry me?'

Mina did not answer this time; she only bowed her head.

'Is it because you do not love me? Is it because you think I have treated you like a scoundrel? Tell me, my darling, what has changed you so?'

'My lord, I am not changed.'

'But you are, I say. Nine months ago if I had asked you to marry me, you would not have hesitated for a single hour.'

'Ah, but you were different then, or I thought you different. I could have married Mr. Lawrance, the student, but I cannot marry Lord Arranmore.'

'And yet they are both the same.'

'To you, maybe, but not to me. In Mr. Lawrance I should have found my equal. Lord Arranmore, the laird of Uribol, can only remain a friend who is far above me. My lord, you are always very kind, and I hope this will not put an end to our friendship. I thank you for the honour you have done me, but, believe me, it is better for us to remain as we are.'

'And so, because you have got this idea of inequality in your head, you deny me the only thing which will make my life worth living. Mina, if you loved me you would not talk like this.'

'It is because I love you that I say it.'

There was silence for a moment, then Lawrance, taking her trembling hands in his, pleaded his cause so eloquently, that for the moment she forgot the events of the last few months, and thought that the young student who had so effectually won her heart was again before her with his honeyed words of love.

Presently she spoke.

'Do you think,' she said, 'that your love for me will last a year?'

'It will last all my life.'

'Well then, listen. If in one year from this day you feel that you would like to marry me, come back to Uribol and ask me, and maybe I will say yes.'

'One year—Mina, it will be an eternity to me!'

'You will not consent?'

'My darling, I would consent to anything which would help me to win your hand. So be it—I consent. Mina, at the end of one year I shall come back again.'

Mina smiled.

'At the end of three months, my lord, you will have forgotten Uribol and forgotten me.'

'You think that; well, you shall see.'

When the minister returned to the room he found Lord Arranmore ready to go. As he had already said good-night to Mina, he cordially shook the clergyman's hand and took his leave.

CHAPTER XLVI.

COREVEOLAN IS DESERTED.

THE day after the parting of Mina and Lord Arranmore, the Highland steamer *Quiraing* 'laid to' off Castle Coreveolan, and took on board the whole party, masters and servants, with all their bag and baggage.

Large numbers of people lined the shore, while the great northern skiffs took the luggage on board; then, as Lord Arranmore and his friends were rowed out, cheer after cheer ascended into the air.

Standing on the gangway of the dingy vessel, Ethel gazed shoreward through slowly gathering tears. She had been dreaming of Graham since their parting the day previous, and up to the last she had hoped that he would re-appear. When he did not come, and while the hours went rapidly by, and brought the time of her departure, her soul was sad indeed.

The sun was bright that day, though the weather was bleak and cold. Clad in sealskin jacket and sealskin hat to match, with dainty boots bordered round the ankle with the same material, she looked her very best; and it was lucky for her lover's peace of mind that he did not see her.

But if he did not see her beauty from close at hand, he could at least see the vessel which was bearing her away. On the top of one of the highest hills above Coreveolan, invisible to all the eyes below, Graham was standing. Gazing downward through the sunlight, he saw the calm sea wrinkling into innumerable creeks and coves; then the steamer, dwarfed to the size of a skiff, crawling along the coast till it halted off Coreveolan; then the people, small as mice, upon the shore, and the tiny boats creeping out heavily laden to the steamboat's side. Straining his ears he fancied he could hear a faint sound as of human voices, but he was not sure.

Presently he saw the water whiten behind the steamboat; her paddles were moving, and with the long string of black smoke behind her, she was crawling out to the open sea. Solitary, desolate, despairing, Graham stood on the mountain and watched her go. Smaller and smaller she grew in the distance; and at last a pale mist, which was creeping in from the ocean, obliterated her wholly from his sight. He strained his eyes in vain; only wreaths of smoke, still hovering far behind upon her track, showed where she had been.

Nevertheless he did not stir yet. He stood like a marble man, his eyes fixed upon the spot where she had disappeared.

.   .   .   .

Still standing on the gangway, Ethel saw the frowning cliffs of that stormy coast fade away, then she looked around her, and saw her father standing close by, with a face full of gloom, while Lord Arranmore, cigar in mouth, was pacing up and down.

She beckoned to the latter.

'What are your plans?' she said.

'I shall go straight to Edinburgh, where I have some business to transact with our family solicitors; then, I think, to Paris.'

'When do you think of returning to Coreveolan?' she asked quietly.

'Not until next summer.'

She was silent, looking sadly towards the shore. He glanced round towards the spot where Sir Charles was standing, and then said in a low voice—

'I have something to tell you.'

'Yes, Lawrance?'

'Now that it is all over between us, I think you will be glad to hear I have asked Mina Macdonald to become my wife.'

'You have?' she said, looking up in surprise.

'Yes; I went over yesterday. I saw her alone—she spoke much of you, of your goodness, your sympathy—then I spoke of myself, and asked her to marry me '——

He paused nervously.

'Yes?' she exclaimed, looking up in his troubled face.

'And she refused me.'

'No!'

'It is a fact, Ethel. She thanked me for what she called the honour I did her, but declined to accept it.'

With a little laugh of delight Ethel clapped her hands

together. Then looking slyly up in her cousin's face, she exclaimed—

'I admire her spirit. You have got just what you deserve. I told her when I spoke to her about you that she was far too good for you, and you see she is precisely of my opinion.'

'And she is right,' said the young man firmly.

'But has she positively refused you—point-blank, I mean?' said Ethel, with more concern than she had at first shown. 'You seem to bear it very well, if it is so.'

'I'll tell you,' replied Lawrance with a quiet smile. 'She refuses me for the present, but she has given me this much consolation—she promises that if I come again in a year, and she is still unmarried, she will think it over.'

'I see—a year's probation!'

'She told me candidly that she did not expect me to remember her ten days after I left Uribol. I am afraid she has a very low opinion of me, chiefly because I belong to the aristocracy.'

'That shows her good sense,' said Ethel, quietly taking her cousin's arm, and walking with him up and down. 'But now, tell me, Lawrance, do you seriously think of returning and marrying this person?'

'Most seriously—most solemnly.'

'And you think you will be happy—if you marry her, I mean?'

'As the ancients said, I leave *that* to the gods.'

'She is your inferior socially.'

'Of course.'

'I have heard it said by clever people that a woman can raise a man to any level, but that it is impossible for a man to raise a woman. Take a female from the gutter and the taint of the gutter will always cling to her; whereas a man, though born and bred in a ditch, may become anything he pleases, and never show a trace of his origin. Do you believe that, Lawrance?'

'I don't believe it; but even if I did'——

'It would not apply to Miss Macdonald. No, you are right.'

'The Macdonalds, you know, though fallen upon dark days, belong to the best blood in the Highlands. If things were as they ought to be. young Graham would be a chieftain in his own right.'

As he said this Lawrance watched his companion closely, and he saw the bright blood mount to her cheek.

'I dare say,' she returned carelessly; 'but in this world we have to deal with things not as they ought to be, but as they are. The Macdonalds are good people, but hardly up to your form, from the world's point of view.'

'The world?—I'm sick of it.'

But you're going back to it.'

No fault of mine, as I have explained. You see, Ethel, I am quite as frank with you as you were with me. I hope you're not offended.'

'Oh dear, no! Only look at papa—I'm afraid he is.'

Lawrance looked at Sir Charles, who was at that moment gazing at the sea with an expression very like a person in the first stage of sea-sickness. He was supremely and utterly disgusted with the failure of all his plans. The world seemed becoming topzy-turvy; all, he reflected, through that 'd——d Radicalism' which was rapidly poisoning society. He had come to the Highlands hoping to combine business with pleasure; to enjoy some very good shooting, and to complete the matrimonial scheme on which he had set his heart. Everything had gone against him. Everybody seemed to have become infected with a state of feeling to which Chartism was child's play. First, Lawrance had set common sense and decency at defiance by running after a person who was little better than a milkmaid or an upper housemaid. Under his infatuation he had practically broken his engagement. Then, to crush all, Ethel had taken his part, and deliberately broken with him. Had it entered into the worthy baronet's head that she had done so because she seriously cared for young Graham Macdonald, he would have had no hesitation in believing her fit to be incarcerated in a lunatic asylum.

Still, now that they had fairly left the wilderness of Uribol behind them, the worthy baronet did not quite despair. He saw the young people talking earnestly, and he determined to leave them as much together as possible. Future intercourse, under more conventional conditions, might re-unite them and save the honour of the family.

.   .   .   .

Meanwhile Graham Macdonald crossed the hills to Uribol, and entering the manse quietly, heard the voice of Mina singing a verse of an old Scotch song. The tone was happy, almost gay, and he listened in surprise. Entering his uncle's study, he saw his sister sitting at the window sewing, and singing as she sewed.

She looked up with a bright face as he entered, and ceased her song.

'Well, they have gone,' he said, throwing himself into a chair. 'I saw them sail away.'

He waited for some expression of pain or regret, but none came. Mina was looking quietly out at the sea, and her face was quite calm.

'I hope they will have a pleasant sail,' she said simply. 'Koll says we are to have good weather.'

He started up with an exclamation.

'I cannot make you out,' he cried. 'When the young laird was here you moped after him day and night; now that he has gone, you seem quite merry. Are you glad that he has left you?'

'Maybe he'll come back,' said Mina.

'Never! We have seen the last of them all. Why do you smile?'

Then Mina told him of what had taken place before Arranmore departed—of how he had asked her to become his wife, and how, when she held back, he had sworn fidelity, and had promised to ask her again 'in a year.'

'And you believe that he will keep his word?' said Graham.

'Maybe,' again said Mina; 'but even if he does not, I shall know that it is better for us both. I am quite content.'

'You are a strange lass. Any other in your place would have been greeting and mourning.'

'Why should I mourn? I mourned when I thought he despised me, and when I thought he had been unkind. Now that I know how good he is, and how much he has cared for me, I am proud and glad.'

Graham looked at his sister for some minutes, then rising, he bent over her chair and kissed her gently on the forehead.

'I wish I had your heart,' he said; 'I wish I could bear my cross like you. You are braver than I am, Mina. But you have something at least to console you; I have nothing.

That lady filled my life. Now that she is gone I feel like a boat adrift without an oar or a sail.'

'Did you say good-bye?'

'A last one. O God! I shall never see her again!'

And the strong man hid his face in his hands and sobbed.

After that the old life went slowly and wearily on. The iron hand of Winter was now outstretched over the north, and dreary days of rain and hail began. Storms came, with intervals of cheerless calm. With a strength born of a faithful and constant nature, Mina went back to her old ways— read and studied with her uncle, wandered by the shore, visited the sick and comforted the poor. 'The love-sickness,' as Doctor John called it, seemed to have only left her stronger and purer. To her the world was full of a new hope, and the thought of her lover comforted her as it had never comforted her before.

But the spirit of Graham fretted in passionate unrest. He took no interest in the place or in any of its outdoor occupations. Sometimes, indeed, he took his gun and wandered out in pursuit of wild-fowl, but he generally returned empty-handed, weary, and taciturn. Occasionally he would lift a book, but even as he held it in his hand his thoughts would wander far away. Mina watched him in pain, trying her utmost to console and comfort him; while the old minister, quite unconscious of the state of affairs, attributed his strange moods to the natural restlessness of an idle disposition.

At last one day he announced his intention of going south and resuming his studies in Edinburgh. The minister approved, but looked less pleased when Graham explained that he had finally abandoned all thoughts of entering the Church.

'I am not fit to be a minister,' said Graham; 'I have neither the heart nor the head. I think I shall prepare for the civil-service, and try for an appointment abroad.'

'It is a lottery,' observed Mr. Macdonald, 'and you will find it harder work than the other.'

'What else can I do? I should like to enter the army, but I cannot become a common soldier, and I am too poor to purchase a commission.'

'How much does it cost?' asked the minister thoughtfully.

'Some hundreds of pounds—I'm not quite sure how much; but of course it's out of the question.'

'Maybe not,' returned his uncle. 'I think it could be managed, if I were quite certain that you would be more faithful to this calling than the other. I have a little money put by—more than enough, I think, for the purpose; and although I am myself a man of peace, I believe the profession of a soldier, nobly followed, to be honourable and just. Your forebears were soldiers, Graham! They fought on the losing side, but they lived and died like good men and true. If you were to become like one of them I think I should be well content.'

The project, thus accidentally broached, grew in the minds of both Graham and his uncle. Inquiries were made, and the minister ascertained that the price of a commission was well within his means, and that he could annually afford a small sum—trifling, but sufficient with strict economy—to supplement a subaltern's pay. His heart bounding with gratitude to his uncle, Graham went south to make more definite inquiries, and to select a suitable regiment. Before long he wrote home in high spirits, saying that he had passed the preliminary examination with ease, and that he had arranged for the purchase of a commission in the—the regiment of Highland foot.

CHAPTER XLVII.

ETHEL SPEAKS THE EPILOGUE.

LESS than one year after Lord Arranmore and the Sedleys left Coreveolan, and sailing away southward, were watched from the lonely mountains by the desolate eyes of Graham Macdonald, Graham sat one afternoon in the coffee-room of a small inn in the outskirts of the town of Brieg, at the foot of the Simplon. He had only just arrived by diligence, and having hurried to the post-office and procured his letters, was reading them at the window of the room.

Far away in the distance were the snowy ranges of the Alps—clear and distinct against a daffodil sky; but as he read, he saw in his mind's eye other and sadder mountains in their dreary garment of northern mist and rain.

Over one letter, written in a clear and flowing hand, he

lingered eagerly and long, for it contained news which brought the eager blood to his cheek, and made his eye flash fire. At last he folded it up, and rising, gazed up darkly at the silent mountain range.

'So Mina is happy,' he said to himself; 'her dream has come true, and her faith is justified. She will be the Lady of Arranmore, and I shall be alone in all the world. Well, thank God for it! She deserves her happiness. She is a good lass; she has dree'd her weird, and it has all come right at last.'

Here the waiter of the inn, a very small but preternaturally old youth, entered, and with much effusion inquired at what hour monsieur would dine.

'At the table-d'hôte, whenever it was served,' said Graham.

'Pardon, but there was no table-d'hôte. It was so late in the year, and it had been abandoned since the summer. Monsieur was alone in the hotel with the exception of a a young countrywoman of monsieur, who had ordered dinner at six precisely. Perhaps monsieur would dine at the same hour?'

'Certainly,' said Graham. 'Meanwhile, bring me the visitors' book to pass the time.'

Thereupon the waiter fetched an unclean-looking volume and placed it on the table before the guest. Graham turned it over carelessly, amusing himself with the absurd entries made by idiotic travellers of all nations and all dispositions. Suddenly he started as if he had been shot, for on a blank page was written, in an elegant hand—

'*Miss Sedley and Monsieur Wolf—en route to Basle.*'

He sprang up and rang the bell. The very small waiter appeared, smiling.

'What is the description of the young lady who is staying here at present?— Miss Sedley—I see it written down here.'

'Yes, that is the name,' said the waiter.

'A *young* lady, I presume?'

'Young and *très gentille*, but pardon, *très excentrique*,' opined the little waiter. 'She had been staying in the inn for a week, and had occupied herself in long walks up towards the Pass and on the mountains. They were rather alarmed on her account at present, because it was past the hour for her return, and she had not taken—it was her custom never to take—a guide.'

'But she is not alone,' observed Graham. 'The gentle-man who is with her'——

The little waiter looked puzzled, until Graham pointed to the entry in the book.

'Who is Monsieur Wolf?' he inquired.

'Pardon, but monsieur was the dog? It was the custom of mademoiselle to be accompanied by a large hound of the boar-hound species, which slept at her chamber door and accompanied her in all her promenades. But it was strange,' continued the little waiter, going to the window and looking out, 'that mademoiselle had not returned. If she had lost her way upon the mountain, or if snow had fallen '——

'You think she is in danger?' cried Graham, seizing his hat from the table.

'Not exactly in danger, perhaps, but monsieur and madame were both alarmed on her account. Monsieur might see them now standing at the door and looking up towards the mountains. Mademoiselle was as a rule so punctual, and snow had fallen during the night.'

Without another word Graham hurried down to the door.

.   .   .   .

A black speck upon the snow, far up on the Simplon Road. It is moveless; but not far from it is another small speck moving. Graham sees both as he climbs the mountain.

Coming nearer, after a long and weary climb, he sees that one is a human figure, sitting as if wearied out, and that the other is a large dog.

The sunset is blood-red in the snow, and night will come suddenly, when the sun sinks quite behind the hills.

He comes closer. He shouts and waves his cap. The dog barks, and the lady, raising her head, shows the face of Ethel Sedley. She does not recognise him, but rises slowly, as if fatigued.

But when he comes close up and names her by her name, she knows him, and reaches out both her hands.

'*You!*' she cries. 'How did you come here? Have you been sent to look for me?'

Graham rapidly explains—how he has discovered her presence in the neighbourhood, and how, alarmed at the anxiety of the innkeeper, he has come up to search for her himself.

'I think I lost my way,' says Ethel; 'but Wolf is a splendid guide, and would have brought me home. I was only resting when you arrived.'

She leant upon his arm, and they descended together, the dog running races before them on the mountain-side. Presently she says, smiling up at him—

'How strange that we should meet *so!* You seem to be constituted my special preserver.'

'Ah! fortunately you were in no danger this time.'

'I think I must have been; indeed, I'll *try* to think so, for I like the idea. Are you not astonished to find me wandering about alone? Papa, who has been very disagreeable lately, has gone to Canada with Lord Belford, and I have been travelling about.'

'Alone! unprotected!'

'I have Wolf—Monsieur Wolf. Besides, who would molest an old maid like me! But what brings you to Switzerland?'

'I came over for a holiday, after many months of hard work. I have entered the army.'

'The army! Then my Highland chieftain has found his *métier* at last.'

'What's that?'

'Leading forlorn-hopes and rescuing females in distress. How is your sister? Stop! you need not tell me. I have heard all about it from Lawrance himself.'

. . . .

The little waiter is in high glee as he serves the dinner for two, and sees the English monsieur and English mademoiselle eating amicably together. He smiles upon the lady like a father, and he recommends the dishes to the gentleman with the cordiality of a brother. It is something in the dull season to see such pleasant company.

For the first time in their lives Graham and Ethel sit together as equals—as equal man and woman. She is no longer the great lady, he the somewhat sullen Highlander. They are fellow-travellers, each under the care and blessing of the little waiter.

After coffee they are left alone. Ethel is unconcerned, but Graham looks uncomfortable.

There is a long silence, broken by Ethel—

'After all,' she observes thoughtfully, 'this sort of thing can't go on for ever!'

'Unfortunately, no!' cries Graham, misunderstanding her.

'I mean, it would be quite ridiculous for you to spend your life in meeting me by accident, and rescuing me from danger.'

'I should delight in such a life.'

'But it would be highly absurd.'

'Not so, it would be Paradise.'

She smiles, and relapses again into silence. She watches him intently for a time, and her next remark, when it comes, startles him.

'Don't you smoke?'

He stammers 'Yes—but'——

'Then oblige me by lighting a cigar!'

At her entreaty he rings the bell, and orders a cigar from the little waiter. He blushes and frowns, and will not light it; but she is firm, and at last he puts it into his mouth. His confusion is perfect when she strikes a wax-light and holds it to the cigar's end. Then he laughs and lights the cigar, but smokes it reluctantly, as if fearing to pollute her presence.

'Pray enjoy your cigar,' she says, 'and remember I like it. Papa has seasoned me, and I have smoked a cigarette myself.'

It seems as if she were resolved, by one means or another, to reduce the social distance between them; but the more she advances, the more he retires into himself, for the familiarity is almost more than he can bear. He remembers the capriciousness of her moods, and how, once or twice, when he has been led to encroach, she has stabbed him with her unexpected scorn.

'Mr. Macdonald,' she says presently, 'it is Leap year.'

'Leap year?'

'Yes. Well, listen to me, and please don't scowl so, for I want you to be very amiable. Last year you told me you rather liked me.'

'Please don't speak of it.'

'I was a giddy girl, and I played with you; when you

went too far I said you were impertinent, because we were not equals.'

'I knew it, and I know it. Why open up those old wounds?'

'Because I'd like to heal them. Mr Macdonald, when I told you we were not equals, I only told you the truth'—Macdonald winced—'I did not know then how infinitely you were my superior.'

'Miss Sedley!—Ethel!'

'Hear me out. I could not help admiring you. That was the reason I annoyed you so much—if I hadn't kept you in a state of chronic irritation you would have discovered my secret. Well, you saved my life at the risk of your own, and I showed my gratitude by moving away from Scotland.'

He looked at her intently. Despite her assumed lightness of manner she was trembling, and her face was very pale.

'It is now my turn to sue,' she continued. 'I have been very miserable. Forgive me. I once humiliated you, and it is now my turn. Mr. Macdonald, I love you, and I throw myself upon your mercy unconditionally.'

'You—love—me?'

'I have loved you from the beginning.'

He rose to his feet, and threw the cigar into the grate. Still something of his old dread was upon him, and he hesitated to catch her in his arms. He stood trembling.

'No,' he said, 'it is impossible—or it is a dream. To-morrow you will mock me, and drive me from you.'

'Never!—so long as you are willing to stay.'

'O Ethel! my love! is it real?'

'Substantial fact, Graham!'

'I may kiss you?'

'Try.'

He sprang forward and caught her in his arms. Then came one of those moments which occur only once in a lifetime. She lay smiling on his breast, and he kissed her over and over again—her lips, her eyelids, her forehead, her scented hair. At last she looked up, radiant.

'Well, am I accepted?'

'O Ethel!'

'I was determined to propose, and I have proposed

Will you be mine—that is, may I be yours? And,' she added, as he beamed upon her, 'O Graham! So great, so strong, so true! You're like a big strong oak. I'm a poor little flower of a thing, only fit to look up to you, as I do and will. Are you quite happy?'

'Yes; but your friends—the world'——

'Friends? I have only papa, and he's prepared for anything. The world? You shall be—you are—my world, the only one for which I care.'

'God bless you, my darling!'

'May He bless us both!'

They sat for hours side by side, going over the past, talking of the future. To both their minds it almost seemed as if a kindly Providence had brought them again together.

Late in the evening, when the little waiter came in to fasten up the windows and put everything away for the night, he was astonished to see monsieur and mademoiselle seated on the sofa side by side, but, being a boy of vast experience, he simply smiled upon them in token of approval.

They stood talking on the hearth, Ethel holding her bedroom candlestick in her hand.

'Next month,' she murmurs; 'it is very soon.'

'*Too* soon?'

'Not if you wish it. Yes, we will be married when Lawrance is married, at dear old Uribol; and your uncle shall marry us as well as them.'

'O Ethel!'

'O Graham!'

A little more whispering, then a rosebud of a mouth is put up, quite innocently and calmly, as if as a matter of course, for Graham to kiss.

'Good-night, my darling!'

'Good-night, dear Graham!'

And so, good-night all.

Printed by BALLANTYNE, HANSON & CO.
Edinburgh and London